THE GAZA INTERCEPT

THE GAZA INTERCEPT

E. HOWARD HUNT

STEIN AND DAY/*Publishers*/New York

FIRST STEIN AND DAY PAPERBACK EDITION 1984
The Gaza Intercept was first published in hardcover
by Stein and Day/*Publishers* in 1981.
Copyright © 1981 by Howard Hunt
All rights reserved, Stein and Day, Incorporated
Designed by Louis Ditizio
Printed in the United States of America
STEIN AND DAY/*Publishers*
Scarborough House
Briarcliff Manor, N.Y. 10510
ISBN 0-8128-8066-8

This book is for Austin Dairing Hunt

THE GAZA INTERCEPT

I

"The People of Israel are to occupy themselves with matters right and proper for them, or else become wanderers."

—Piska 13
Pesikta de-Rab Kahana

ONE

Jay Black (I)

W<small>HEN</small> I got back to the embassy he was waiting for me, corpulent body stretched out on the office sofa, spidery black hair crawling out of his open collar. He looked up at me and the stony eyes glittered. "You didn't call, Jay."

"Not in Washington where embassy lines are tapped." I sat and stretched out my legs.

"Will the girl cooperate?"

"All the way. And her brother works in the same nuclear facility. They'll bring out the uranium and turn it over to me. All you have to do is get it back home."

"To Israel." His face showed a slight change of expression. "You've done well, Jacob Schwartz, very well. If you don't mind my calling you Schwartz."

"It's the name I was born with, as you well know. Now," I said gently, "I've been away from home and office for four days; at this hour there are no planes or trains to get me back to New York, and I'd like a little sleep before I begin negotiating with clients seven hours from now." I stood up. "There's a taxi waiting. Mind if I leave?"

"Are you eager to return to your *shiksa* wife?"

"Moderately." I glanced at his desk and noticed my personnel folder. "Checking through it again? Nothing better to do?"

"Your father's here."

I grunted. "Been recruiting him for Mossad?" Then I waved my hand. Fatigue had slowed my mental processes. "Why's he here? Arranging another fund raiser for Israel?"

"That's what Ambassador Blum told me."

My father is a prominent theatrical attorney and fund-raising

11

talent often came from among his clients. Israel is his ardent cause and he has always been more than willing to help.

Rosenthal picked up the nearest telephone, punched buttons and spoke in Hebrew, a language of which I had only scant familiarity.

I moved toward the door. "The day you recruited me at Kibbutz L'Grofit I was young and eager."

"And now?"

"I'm not sure anymore." I left the room.

"Jay!" My father took my arms and embraced me.

I mumbled something as the warmth of his greeting peeled away layers of fatigue. As always, he was flawlessly turned out: velvet collar; gray Homburg and gloves, double-breasted, pin-striped, gray suit. I said, "I've got a cab outside."

"To take you where?"

"The bus station. Too late for planes."

He smiled. "I've a jet waiting at National. Let's go there instead."

He motioned to the doorman, who got up from his chair and unlocked the door. I went down the steps. The cab was parked at the curb, lights out, driver slumped behind the wheel. As I opened the door I glanced back and saw my father and the doorman exchanging pleasantries as they walked toward me.

I turned to speak to the cabbie and a sound across the street stopped me. It resembled a smothered cough and behind me I heard someone gasp. As I turned around I heard a second *phutt* and saw the doorman clutch his chest and fall back, face agonized. Tires screamed as the shooter's car tore from the curb and sped, lightless, down 22d Street. My father was kneeling beside the fallen man and I yelled at him to come. He waved his hand brusquely Beyond him, Lev Rosenthal was silhouetted in the doorway.

My father was tearing off the doorman's tie, opening the collar, but I could see the dark stain on the man's shirt.

Lights flooded the first floor of the embassy, people running down the walk, but Rosenthal was not among them. I saw my father touch the doorman's neck artery, then bend forward to place his ear on the man's chest. After a moment he straightened and got up. Someone handed him his hat and gloves. He looked at me. I beckoned to him as figures screened the fallen body, and from the look on his face I realized the doorman was dead.

12

I held the door open, got into the cab after my father and was about to say something when he glanced at the driver and touched a finger to his lips. To the cabbie he said, "We'll go to National Airport. Page Aviation."

"Sure, anywhere you say." The car engine started. "Listen, shouldn' we make a report?"

"I'm sure the embassy will report promptly," my father said and gave me a thin smile. "Assuming there is anything to report."

"Jews," the cabbie said as the cab pulled away from the curb. "Troublemakers."

My father's face was grim. "A turbulent people," he said and passed the driver a folded bill. "We'd like to reach the airport without incident." He settled back beside me and said nothing more until we were airborne in the Lear.

I mixed drinks for us and brought them back to our seats. "*L'haim*," my father said and sipped. "*L'haim*," I echoed. He seemed to have forgotten the incident, but I hadn't. "You shouldn't have lingered," I said irritably. "There could have been another gun."

He shrugged. "Would you have me abandon a fallen comrade? You never did so in Vietnam."

"That's different," I said. "That was war."

"And what do you think Israel and the Arab world are engaged in, my son?"

"Whatever it is, you're on the sidelines."

He sipped again, glanced out of the window. "You're working for Rosenthal." Not a question, a statement.

"Helping out a little."

"No details, it's better I shouldn't know. But anything I can do . . . well, just tell me."

"I always have."

He gestured at the dark window. "No lights below, just thick clouds. The pilot said we might have to land at Philadelphia or Newark if the New York airports are closed."

I touched his hand. "Was the doorman the target?"

He looked away. "Teitelbaum? I've known him for years. Never heard of any enemies."

"But you have enemies."

He glanced obliquely at me. "Why do you say that?"

"Arabs like to even scores," I said and drank from my glass. "You

13

fought them once. Even today you keep working against them."

"I work against no one," he said. "I work *for* Israel."

"Same thing." I yawned again.

"You're tired," he said. "Lie down over there. Perhaps you can sleep."

I drained my glass and got up. "I think you were the intended victim. Thank God you weren't killed."

"I believe we're to have lunch today. Can you still manage it?"

"I'll be there." I lay back on the upholstered lounge and closed my eyes.

From Philadelphia we'd had to take a limousine to Manhattan, and from my father's place I continued through early traffic undecided whether to go to the Athletic Club for a shave, sauna, and massage, or home for the Jacuzzi and a change of clothing. But I hadn't seen Michael and Susan in nearly five days and I had a chance of arriving before they left for their schools. So I had the driver drop me off on Central Park South, and went up to our duplex. Unlocking the door, I went inside and heard the children at breakfast, chattering with their governess. They would be leaving shortly, and after that I had an hour and a half before the lipstick client came in for the new ad presentation.

I dropped my bag on a chair and went into the breakfast room. "'Morning, Erin," I said to the governess, then knelt and kissed my son and daughter, trying to avoid a transfer of egg yolk.

"It's nice to have you back, Mr. Black," said Erin, and I went up to the living quarters, pulling off coat and tie.

Sybil was sleeping in our king-size bed, sprawled out face down, one arm and one leg exposed. *Ma belle blonde,* I thought, leaned over and gently kissed the back of her neck. She stirred, so I backed off and tossed my clothing on a chair.

While I was still lolling in the Jacuzzi's relaxing jets Sybil came in, wrapping a robe around her nightgown, brushing back her hair. She knelt at the edge to kiss me and said, "We missed you. Trip okay?"

"Perfect. Missed you, too."

"Did you see the children?"

"Briefly. Any problems?"

"No." She stood up and glanced at the steamed, full-length mirror. "Do we have time to talk?"

14

I got out of the pool and reached for a towel. "About what?"

"Aspen. Did you put up the chalet for sale?"

"I said I'd listen to realistic offers."

"So that explains why the agent's been calling me. Apparently he's let it be known you're interested in selling."

"And you don't want to."

"You know how I feel. It's a place for the children and me—for all of us—when New York becomes unbearable."

I applied deodorant. "I bought the place in a burst of optimism, at a time when I thought I might be able to ski again, but my leg hasn't cooperated. The doctor says it never will."

"Aren't you being a bit selfish, Jay?"

"I thought we'd put the sale money into a good-sized ketch, keep it down in the British Virgins. Swimming's good for my leg—for all of us, really—and the climate is great."

"But there's no one we know."

"There's us," I said sharply. "Who needs people?"

"I do, for one. And the children need playmates."

"Which they can find only at Aspen? C'mon, Sib, you've got pals out there you can't bear to leave. Trouble is they aren't friends of mine." I tossed the towel into a hamper and opened the bathroom door. "Afraid your Nazi ski instructor might find another pretty to squire around?"

She followed me into the bedroom. "You have no right to call Horst a Nazi," she said furiously. "He's a perfectly decent Swiss-Austrian, and if you think we're having an affair why don't you say so?"

"I think you've been having an affair with him." I got into shorts and sat down to pull on a pair of socks.

She gave me her shocked, incredulous look.

I looked up winningly. "So we'll sell the chalet and dispute no more."

"Do what you want," she snapped and stormed out of the bedroom.

I got into a shirt and selected a rep tie from the rack. Kind friends had told me about Horst's attentions, so I'd decided to eliminate propinquity. Besides, I felt Aspen had changed from a tranquil mountain resort to a haven for pill-poppers, coke-snorters, wife-swappers, and oddballs.

Strapping on my watch I saw that I had just half an hour to get to the office. Before the three-million-dollar client appeared I wanted to review the presentation with the account executive, Shirley Farrell.

From Bryn Mawr, Shirley was a highly competent ad lady and perfect for the job. For me it was always a pleasure to listen to her presentations, and the aura of occult sex she exuded seemed to fascinate some of our female clients. In any case, Shirley was a dependable winner and devoted to Jay Black Associates.

I was hardly inside my office when Shirley snaked in and told me the client was already there and waiting.

That was how the week began.

My father said, "Are you going to the opening?"

"What opening?"

"Didn't Sybil tell you? I lunched with her on Saturday, left tickets for the new Hal Prince show."

"We've hardly had a chance to talk," I said, "but I appreciate the tickets. We'll go unless I'm tied up with a client."

We were seated at my father's customary window table in the downtown Lawyers Club. The luncheon crowd was there, white-jacketed waiters—old men mostly—attending. The conversational hum reminded me of an active beehive. My father lifted his glass of Evian and sipped. Then he said, "Business is good?"

"Excellent."

My father nodded. He was only twelve when his parents smuggled him out of Germany hoping to join him in America. Instead, they died at Dachau, leaving the boy to make his way in an unfamiliar land. He worked—oh, how he worked—and made it through Jefferson, CCNY, and law school. And after that he was never poor again.

My father's face is oval, with deepset, kindly eyes. What's left of his hair is silver white and close trimmed. I'm a head taller, but he's built like an All-Pro Center, and I've seen him lift a heavy chest on his back unaided. After mother died he sold our place in Islip and moved to upper Park Avenue. Barbara, his "companion," stays at his Inverrary condo except when they're traveling together, which is about four months of the year. Their last cruise took in the Balkans and China plus the obligatory stop in Israel where he manufactured enough legal business to justify tax deductions.

I said, "I want to talk about last night."

"We'll order first."

A waiter came over deferentially and took our order of two diet specials: chopped sirloin and cottage cheese with gelatin salad, Sanka and iced tea. When the waiter departed my father said, "What happened last night should remind you that you're involved in dangerous business. Isn't it more likely the gunman was trying to kill you?"

"Not unless my cover was blown."

"That is a possibility?"

"If there's an inside leak."

"Then I must ask you to be careful."

"Oh, I'm careful. You have no idea how careful I try to be. And I don't want you exposed to anything like that again."

He looked thoughtfully at his glass. "At the beginning the British and the Arabs were Israel's enemies. Now almost the entire world is hostile to Israel. Once I thought it would be otherwise, but now. . . ." He shrugged expressively.

I finished my Gibson, avoiding the speared pearl onion. "You have a fantastic ability to change the conversational direction."

He smiled. "Was there anything else to discuss?"

The waiter arrived with our plates, and as I began to eat I remembered my earlier phone conversation with Lev Rosenthal who said, "We got him inside the embassy . . . by then he was dead. Poor Teitelbaum. He was due to return to Jerusalem, but not for burial."

"Will there be services?"

"In the homeland. His body is already on the way."

"No police? No publicity?"

"We prefer to handle such things in our own way."

"I know. But it occurs to me the gunman was after my father."

"Why?"

"You know my father's record in Israel, so it's not impossible someone decided he had to be liquidated . . . vengeance for some past deed."

"That's unlikely."

"Is it? I don't want my father endangered because of what I do for you. Or if I was the intended target, there's an organizational leak you should be looking into."

"I am. Full security review. For now our presumption is that it was a random hit carried out by some adjunct of Fatah; perhaps a specialized group we've only recently known about. So until we know more of the circumstances, I'm taking you off the case."

"Fine. That takes care of me. What about my father?"

"Suggest he take precautions."

"You don't know Samuel Schwartz."

That was the extent of it, and now my father was saying, "You're overly concerned about me, Jay, that's my analysis. Now, how are things at home?"

"Compared to most marriages around me, ours is a sparkling success."

I drank more of my iced tea. "I'm going to have to run," I told him. "Another client presentation at two. This morning lipstick, this afternoon, fruit drinks. And I have to check storyboards before the client sees them."

"Variety," he said. "At least you've got variety. So, go in good health." He sighed. "I'm thinking of retiring. No, not right away, but in a year or so. Actors, actresses, producers: always the same foolish complaints, the same exaggerated demands. I should have been a *shatkin* for less trouble."

"You could have been anything you wanted."

"Except President, *nu*? Still for *goyim* only."

"Henry the K got pretty high before the fall."

My father nodded, took out a gold ballpoint pen and signed the luncheon check. I stood up and we shook hands. "Have dinner with us on Sunday," I urged.

"Thank you, but I've already made plans to go south for the weekend. Give my love to Sybil and my *ayneklach*. Our Susan, she will be a true beauty. And Michael . . . handsome as you. Does he study as hard as he should?"

"Father, he's only in fourth grade. You shouldn't expect too much."

"Wrong. We must expect everything." Smiling, he dismissed me with an affectionate wave of the hand.

As I rode uptown I reviewed my father's knowledge of events. His awareness of Lev Rosenthal's position surprised me, although I had always known him to be well connected in significant circles. Before Partition he had been active in the Jewish Legal Defense

Fund, then dropped out of sight for more than a year, a period in his life that neither he nor my mother would discuss. Slowly, over the years, it had come to me that Samuel Schwartz, attorney-at-law, spent that year in Israel fighting for the new State's survival. Thus his familiarity with such men as Rabin, Eshkol, Allon, Ezer Weizman, Bar-Lev and Begin. And his continued behind-the-scenes assistance in organizing fund-raising show-biz spectaculars.

But none of that explained last night's murderous episode, and Rosenthal had told me nothing to persuade me my father hadn't been the killer's target. If my father thought so he'd concealed it very effectively, leaving me with the same enigma: Who was supposed to have to have been killed outside the Embassy?

My father?

Or me?

TWO

Al-Karmal (I)

FROM the windows overlooking the walled garden they saw the French door open as the bodyguard came out. Over this *jellaba* were crossed cartridge bandoliers; around his waist, gathering the flowing white robe, a leather gun belt to hold the holstered Mauser. Drawing back the folds of his headcloth he looked slowly around the garden perimeter, at the shrubs and foliage along the wall, the Vietnamese gardener kneeling in the plot of rose bushes. His gaze lifted to scan the high stone wall against which clung espaliered vines whose candelabra-like branches might provide foothold for an intruder.

Satisfied, the bodyguard moved aside and the young Omani prince came after him.

Eleven o'clock. Prince Ahmad was punctual.

The other bodyguard, they knew, would remain inside the villa. Inside, also, were two maids, a footman, the chef, and a kitchen assistant. Erika, the prince's Danish mistress, would be asleep in the royal bedchamber. The armed chauffeur would be waiting outside the front entrance, behind the wheel of a silver-gray Mercedes, ready to take Prince Ahmad to his first class of the day at the Sorbonne. Normally the drive from La Muette, just west of the Seine, to the Faculté de Droit in mid-Paris took the chauffeur from twenty-eight to thirty-two minutes, depending on traffic flow.

Today, however, Hossein Bakhair's death squad was ready to prevent the trip. Today, NOW, was the culmination of weeks of surveillance and careful planning.

Prince Ahmad strolled into the garden, bodyguard at his left, a respectful pace behind. He looked around, enjoying the garden's cool fragrance, and Bakhari felt his throat begin to dry.

21

Unlike the bodyguard, the prince wore Western clothing: a beige Italian leisure suit and soft brown leather shoes with small gold buckles. His hair and scanty beard were black, seeming to darken even more as he crossed a shadowed area on his way to the rose garden.

Bakhari heard the soft rustle of slings as Fuad and Rashid gripped their AK-47s. They, too, were nervous. And why not? Bakhari thought wryly, it is their first major kill.

The gardener bowed to the prince who was among the roses bending over to inspect the progress of the spring blooms.

The three men were bunched together, as Bakhari anticipated.

"*Now*," he said hoarsely. "*Now!*"

Windows swung open, AK-47 barrels rested on the sills. Hearing the sudden scraping noise, the prince and his bodyguard turned and looked upward, so they were facing the weapons when the fusillade came.

Bakhari caught the prince with a four-shot burst that spun him around and dropped him into the rose bushes. The bodyguard was down, body bucking under the impact of Fuad's repeated firing, and Rashid had blown apart the gardener's skull.

Standing, Bakhari barked, "Grenades!", and three high-explosive grenades arced toward the moving rose bushes.

He dropped to the floor, and the combined force of the explosions shattered the window glass, shook the rented house. When he looked again, smoke was drifting lazily toward the wall and through the iron-grill gate. The gardener's clothing was burning, so was the bodyguard's *jellaba*. The prince's body lay motionless, half raised by the stump of rose bush.

"Ladders!" Bakhari shouted, and three rope ladders dropped from the windows. Weapons in hand, the squad climbed down into the garden.

His back to the villa, Bakhari knelt at the prince's body and drew out a curved dagger. Rashid and Fuad faced the rear of the house and when the other bodyguard hurtled through the garden doorway, Rashid took him with a long burst. Fuad fired at a face moving behind an upstairs window, then hurled a grenade through the open garden door.

Bakhari slit open the prince's trousers to lay bare the groin. He sliced off the prince's genitals and stuffed them into what remained of the prince's mouth. He stabbed his left hand into a blood-filled wound and lifted bloody fingers to his mouth. Fuad fired again at the villa, rasped, "*Hurry!*", but Bakhari was not to be denied. Like a gourmand he licked each finger clean, savoring the warm, salty blood, and when he had finished he murmured, "*Alhamdillah*," and said, "Go" to his men.

As they loped toward the iron gate at the garden's rear, Bakhari drew a typewritten sheet from his pocket and placed it under Prince Ahmad's hand. It proclaimed Al-Karmal's war against its enemies.

When Hossein Bakhari reached the gate, he nodded to Rashid who shot off the padlock. The three men went quickly into the narrow street where the stolen Citroën waited, Atiqa behind the wheel.

As the rear door closed, she looked hungrily at Bakhari. "*Wa-llah!*" she exclaimed. "It is done?"

"Done."

"*As-salaam 'alaikum.*" Her foot jammed down on the accelerator and the car roared away, dust rising in its wake.

From a flat in Clichy, Bakhari radioed a scornful message to Yasser Arafat in Beirut: "You waited overlong, brother. Observe and gain wisdom. Only one of us may rule."

The French radio monitoring service recorded the transmission even as it was being sent, but in that brief time they were unable to determine the transmitter's location.

Police roadblocks, interrogation of Arab informants, a sweep through the student quarter provided the French security authorities, the DST, with nothing they did not already know from the paper found in Prince Ahmad's hand. Hossein Bakhari's Al-Karmal terrorists had slain a guest of France and challenged the French nation.

Toward nightfall, police found the Clichy safehouse, but in it was nothing but a destroyed transmitter and a small cache of useless weapons. The vanished occupants, according to the *concierge*, had posed as Algerian refugees, of whom there were many in Paris.

By then Bakhari, disguised and documented as a businessman from Oran, had flown to London and entered a Heathrow washroom. From it he emerged in white *jellaba* and headcloth surmounted by a black, braided *agal*, and boarded a British Airways flight to Kennedy airport. As he came quickly through Customs and Immigration, his documents showed him to be a member of the diplomatic retinue of Iraq's delegation to the United Nations.

Bakhari was met by a chauffered limousine that drove him from Long Island into midtown Manhattan and left him at the door of an expensive apartment house off Park Avenue, in sight of the UN building.

The doorman assisted Bakhari to the foyer of his apartment and left, gratified by an unusually large tip. As Bakhari turned on the living room lights he reflected briefly on the fate of young Prince Ahmad. A dilettante, he thought, a man destined to be useless in life. So I arranged that his death would be useful.

To me.

He pulled off his false beard, the smothering traditional garb he had come to despise, and walked into the bedroom where his mistress was sleeping. She was, unfortunately, Jewish, he reminded himself; but, *Wa-llah*, here in the citadel of Zionism even that could be useful to him.

Now, with the Prince Ahmad out of the way, he could plan a strike to shake the world.

THREE

Jay Black (II)

6:12

I got off a Trade Center elevator and walked down the corridor to the sixth office on the right. The door was lettered Parlay Trade Consultants, P.A. A red-haired secretary looked up from her typing. "Yes?"

"Mr. Wellbeck should be expecting me." I hadn't seen this one before.

"Name, sir?"

"Black."

She spoke into the intercom, looked up and smiled. "He'll see you now."

Bryan D. Wellbeck was waiting behind a large antiqued desk. Behind him window shades and expensive drapes held back the setting sun, but here and there a crack of gold showed through.

Wellbeck sat forward, elbows on polished desk. He was wearing a vested flannel suit of Cambridge gray. From a link chain across his vest hung the gold talisman of his Princeton club. Red-and-white striped shirt with French cuffs and a semi-soft white collar. He could be a trade consultant, banker, or partner in a Wall Street firm. But Wellbeck was Assistant Chief of the Agency's Mid-East Division.

"Well," I said, "in case you hadn't heard, someone's played fast and loose with security, and last night I damn near got drilled. The victim was a doorman named Teitelbaum, but my father was in the line of fire. Shooting at me is one thing, I'm more or less used to it. But when my father's endangered, that's something else. Shook the hell out of me."

"How long's it been since Mossad tapped you for a job?"

"Eight months. Except for this last excursion."

"Can't imagine you in Tennessee," he said and smiled mockingly. "Gonzo ad man mingling with the moonshine crowd."

"Let's get back to Teitelbaum."

"Shall we bow our heads in momentary prayer?"

"We could . . . he took the bullet meant for my father or me."

"And I'm Johnny Carson." His arms lowered, hands opening and closing. "Where's your antenna? That was a set up from the start. I thought—hoped—you'd figure it out."

I sat back in the government's expensive chair. "Are you telling me Teitelbaum was the target, not me or my father?"

"My oath." Face bland again. "Teitelbaum had family in the wrong places. Pressure was applied to them and he began cooperating. My organization found out and told Mossad. Rosenthal found a way to let the Arabs know their man was burned. From then on it was just a question of time. Last night the threads came together."

"Rosenthal just stood by and let Teitelbaum be killed?"

"Sure. Had the Arabs do it. No Jewish blood on Mossad hands, and the moment was convenient for Rosenthal because it gave him an overt reason to take you off the uranium snatch."

"After all. . . ?" I shook my head. "Why?"

His features formed an aloof High Episcopal look, but with a trace of pity to shade the condescension. "Washington decided the Israelis have sufficient U-235 for the present."

"How much is that?"

"Enough for defense, not enough for aggression." He took out a small, antique silver box, opened it, and placed a pinch between cheek and gum, just as the ads recommend. That done, he continued. "Before you got back to Washington, plant security picked up your recruits for questioning. Delicate word was then conveyed by the Secretary to Ambassador Blum. We thought that was the way to handle it, leaving you in the clear."

"Oh, well played, dash'd well. Bully!" I shook my head. "Why not just tell me to stop fooling around with Mossad?"

He spread his hands. "You're independent, uncontrollable, no sanctions I could apply. Did Rosenthal mention Al-Karmal?"

"No."

"Bakhari? Hossein Bakhari?"

I shook my head.

"Odd, I felt he might. Bakhari runs it, you see."

"Al-Karmal?" The exchange was getting involuted and time was running short. I had to travel all the way up Park Avenue at the worst time of day. "Rosenthal said a Fatah offshoot might have made the hit."

Wellbeck sat back and fingered his vest chain. No Phi Beta key, but in his circles the gold club symbol was worth a hell of a lot more. "Clever of him, Al-Karmal's a vicious group. Bakhari pulled together dissidents and extremists from other PalLib orgs and set them to the kind of nasty work those types love."

"Such as?"

"The Cairo nursery bombing."

I felt my throat tighten. "Seventy-two kids."

"*Ach du Lieber, ja?*"

"*Ja mit* spades. Al-Karmal. Aside from killing kids do they have a program? Goals?"

"Power."

I found myself glancing at my watch. Wellbeck said, "Rosenthal planted a seed with you. I expect he'll want you to perform against Al-Karmal."

"How?"

He shifted tobacco around inside his mouth; it seemed to bother him. Canker, maybe. Maneuver completed, he said, "Almost all of what we know about Bakhari and his group comes from the Israelis: Mossad and the special anti-terrorist group that works out of the Cabinet. There have been hints Bakhari is planning something very big and very special, something of a magnitude to command total world attention and make him king of the PalLib ash pile."

"Sounds like a nut."

"Aren't they all? This one, though, Bakhari, is smarter than some. Unfortunately he's partly educated at our expense; studied politics at one of those cow colleges in Texas on an exchange." His lips moved in distaste. "So he has a smattering of English, and a rudimentary idea of how things are done over here. And he's got a heavy grudge against America."

"Routine."

"Personalized in his case. His Levantine eye fell on a Texas lass whose parents objected. Violently. Something about horsewhipping or some such. Dirty Arab, you know how it goes. So Hossein folded his rug and departed our shores, disappeared for a couple of years and surfaced at the operating end of a machine gun. Commandoing with the fadayeen, that sort of thing. Cross-border ops, hashish-running for funds, get the picture?"

"Got it. What's his plan?"

"We don't know. When the Israelis know I'm pretty sure Rosenthal will reach out for you. When he does, tell us. And while you're here you might read this cable from Paris Station." He handed me two Telex carbons and I saw that the subject was Al-Karmal.

Wellbeck said, "The *Times* will have all this tomorrow so think of this as a pre-pub peek."

According to the cable Prince Ahmad of Oman, two bodyguards, and a gardener had been slain by Hossein Bakhari's Al-Karmal terrorists. Of two servants only wounded in the assault on the Prince's villa, one was in critical condition. A female companion, unnamed, had slept through the killings until grenade explosions wakened her.

Lucky lass, I thought, and continued reading.

Three men were believed to have taken part in the assassination, but no trace of them had been found. The text summarized Al-Karmal's manifesto, which described Prince Ahmad as a decadent aristocrat, pawn of Zionists and the West, and went on to call for Arab intransigence against a false and humiliating peace with Israel, demanding Arab unity under a strong leader—Bakhari.

"That's the Al-Karmal spectacular?"

"No. Just a PR job to get Bakhari some visibility. The prince was no threat to him or anyone else. Ahmad was fourth in line of succession."

"Then why hit him?"

"Because, dear boy, he was accessible." He paused. "Bakhari is here. This morning he came through Kennedy on a flight from London. Right now he's probably less than ten blocks from your office."

"Does Mossad know?"

"They've said nothing."

"Are you going to tell them?"

"Ah, Jay, so far no decision's been made. So don't go jumping the gun."

"Hearing and obeying, *effendi*. Have you got his place bugged?"

A long pause. "That would be telling, wouldn't it?"

"So what do you want from me?"

"His target."

I got up. "Next time I survive an attempt I'll give it more thought." He was wearing his Racquet Club tie, I noticed. It was a club I was unlikely to be invited to join although my male in-laws belonged.

"Do that," he said and thrust his warm pink hand into mine. "Good of you to come."

He walked beside me to the door. "Still with Marcy?"

"Absolutely."

"Faithful type, aren't you?"

"Look," I said, "she wouldn't like you. Besides, you live in Washington and life could become very difficult, so stop lusting after my girl."

He removed a pocket handkerchief and delicately disposed of his cud.

I went through the vacant outer office and rode a bulging elevator to the street. When I reached the Sherry-Netherland bar it was seven-twenty and Marcy hadn't waited cocktails. A tall, good-looking fellow I happened to know was sitting in what was going to be my seat. I said, "My tab, Art," and he got up with a startled look. I slid next to her and she gave me a veiled gaze. "You know I *loathe* being nearly stood up."

"Nearly." I grabbed a jacketed waiter. "Double Martini, no twist," I half shouted.

Usually the S-N bar was quiet, restrained, but usually I came earlier. This late there was a noisy, near-frantic atmosphere. Bodies moved, shoved. An invisible guitarist assaulted the p.a. system. To Marcy I said, "What's going on? This is like Morey's after a game."

She took my drink from the waiter, sampled and placed it in my hand. "Kids tossing down final cups before going off to kith and kin." She looked at me.

"Well, that's New York," I said, "what young folks do."

The super-chilled drink set my teeth on edge. After the last day or two it was a reward without price. I said, "That was a perilous situation I found you in. Art's big in corporate take-overs and personal acquisitions."

"I can fend. Have a good trip?"

"So-so." I sipped again. One was not going to be enough.

"Contract negotiations going well?"

"Two locked in, three to go."

"Can't get a full sentence from you." She nuzzled my ear lobe. "You big important macho man."

Lifting her glass she drained it. I caught another waiter and reordered. Then we held hands. Marcia Cameron had mink-dark hair and translucent skin. After two years at Vassar she went into modeling and fashion photography at which she was very good. She then made the mistake of marrying a fellow photographer who took her to Tucson where she tired quickly of desert landscapes. Back in New York she was much in demand. Marcy was beautiful, talented, and knew professional people who counted. She said, "Where are you supposed to be tonight?"

"Out."

"Row with Sybil?"

I shrugged. "Where do you want to eat? Italian okay?"

"Too heavy. Staying with me tonight?"

"Couple hours. Twenty-One?"

"Perfect."

She was sleeping beside me, blue-gray light from the street faintly outlining her face, hair fanned out on the pillow. I pulled off the covers to get out of bed and glimpsed her small, youthful breasts. For now, we were for each other, I thought, but neither of us believed in long-range prospects.

Dressing, I shed a telltale "21" matchbook on her night table. As I was leving the bedroom she called sleepily, "Good night, love."

" 'Night, honey."

I let myself out. Eight minutes after midnight.

It was only half a block to Park where I flagged a taxi. Settled back on the slashed, frayed seat I began to think of Rosenthal and Wellbeck again, having blotted them from my mind since cocktails.

Something big going on, Wellbeck predicted, and I was going to be involved. Lev Rosenthal. Had he really engineered the hit on his own man, or was that a Wellbeck fabrication set before me for some devious reason? If what Bryan told me was true I could worry less about my father's safety, but was it likely I would ever know the truth?

FOUR

Jay Black (III)

THROUGH the intercom I told my secretary to call Charlie Wotkowski in Aspen. When he came on the line I said, "Any news?"

"The best. I got your price."

"Good, send me the papers."

"Will do. Closing here in thirty days."

"Pick a lawyer," I told him, "and I'll send along power-of-attorney for the sale. Good job, Charlie."

"Thanks, Mr. Black. Uh . . . your wife said you might be in the market for something in Vail. If so I've. . . ."

"Aberration," I said. "We're finished with winter sports."

"Um, well, are you interested in selling the chalet furnishings?"

"Everything," I told him. "Snowmobile and skis."

"See what I can do."

The intercom buzzed and my secretary said, "Can you go over the new layouts now? The graphics group is assembled. Ten minutes should do it."

"On my way," I said, and left for the big atelier down the hall. The work was good. Colorful, with jolly figures, it had been researched and created for the eight-to-eleven-year age group. I initialed four layouts and went back to my office. A message on my desk said a Mr. Rothstein had called and would appreciate my calling back. A local number was given.

Rothstein was an alias used by Lev Rosenthal.

The façade of the townhouse was Georgian brick. Marble steps divided at the sidewalk and led up to the doorway and down around to a service entrance. It was an expensive establishment, one likely to be occupied by someone with substantial money and a willingness to spend. Or else, like the publisher I knew who lived down the block, the townhouse was carried on corporate books and paid for by the company comptroller. But I had a feeling that this was a private place, however costly it might be to maintain.

The dark-skinned butler reinforced my thought. He took my hat and raincoat and indicated a curving staircase. "In the library, sir. Just to your right."

As I ascended I glanced briefly at paintings on the wall: Klee, Kandinsky, Grosz—at the top, Miró. The collection was breathtaking, and the casual, offhand display put the owner one-up on any other private collector in New York.

Knocking at the door I heard Rosenthal call, "Come in," and saw him seated behind a Louis XIV desk in a library that could have been one of the lesser rooms at Versailles. He rose to greet me, and as he did, another man left his chair and walked toward me.

"Jay Black," Rosenthal said. "Eli Pomerantz. I am leaving shortly for Ertz Israel, and Eli has just come from there."

We shook hands and I studied his face. He had thick, black eyebrows, deepset eyes, and the high cheekbones of the Eastern Jew.

Pomerantz was somewhat shorter than I, but he had the shoulders and grip of a weight lifter. Rosenthal said, "I deemed it important that I should introduce the two of you. No, Eli is not of Mossad. He is a military careerist seconded to the Cabinet's special anti-terrorist group."

"A junior participant," Pomerantz said casually. "Normally my rank is major but, as you see, I am in mufti."

"Eli," Rosenthal went on, "took part in the Entebbe rescue mission. I mention it because that was one of the most publicized episodes of his career. Others," he spread his hands expressively, "have received less publicity, perhaps because few of the targets lived long enough to complain."

Pomerantz's face was impassive.

Rosenthal said, "Eli is in charge of a combined operations task force whose target is the group I mentioned to you the other night. Al-Karmal is its name."

I said nothing.

Rosenthal said, "Its leader and organizer is one Hossein Bakhari."

We were all standing. I said, "Mind if I sit down?"

"Please." We seated ourselves, Pomerantz to my right, and Rosenthal said, "What took place in Paris, Jay, is Bakhari's opening gun, as it were. I believe the Paris incident is the first in which he slaughtered an armed opponent."

"That is correct," Pomerantz said, nodding, "but he did so by stealth. Ambush."

"According to the newspaper account," I said.

"I was in Paris long enough to verify it," Pomerantz said, and I sensed that he had done so meticulously.

Rosenthal saw me glance at my wristwatch. "The point of our meeting, Jay, if you will bear with me, is that Eli will be doing some business in New York. Specialized business. I have suggested that you might be willing to cooperate with him toward the success of his mission."

"Bakhari...," I began, but Rosenthal lifted one hand. "Bakhari is in New York."

Wellbeck had told me so, but I found it interesting that Mossad also knew. I said, "Do you know where?"

"We know," said Eli Pomerantz.

"Then why don't you just take him?"

Rosenthal shook his head. "Bakhari is challenging all the Arab terrorist organizations. By killing Prince Ahmad, Bakhari has lost the tolerance of the less fanatical Arab states: Saudi Arabia, Morocco, and, of course, Oman. Russian money may reach him through Libya, Iraq, or Syria, or the rejectionist states could supply him independently, their resources are sufficiently large."

Pomerantz said, "We will be interested to see whether our friend visits Cuba."

Rosenthal nodded. "I will leave you gentlemen to make such contact arrangements as you find compatible. Goodbye, Jay. Until we meet again."

He came around the desk, shook hands with us and went out. At the desk I wrote down my unlisted phone number for the Israeli major. As he took it he said, "For the present I am staying at the Hotel Claxton, do you know it?"

"Ummm, old, off Broadway?"

He smiled. "Very old. Seedy, even. But the hostelry is accustomed to strange clients. My room is eight-two-three, and the name on the register is Torres. For now I am Puerto Rican."

"If you need me after office hours, I'm in the book."

"Very well. I'm glad you are with us."

We shook hands and I went downstairs where the butler already had my hat and coat.

Outside, a drizzle, too arrhythmic to qualify as rain.

I wondered about the owner of the meeting place. Whoever he was he would be a patron of Israel . . . and Mossad. Doubtless my father would know him. I forced the address out of my mind, and crossed Park to wait for a taxi on the downtown side.

Back in the office I still had a few minutes before my next conference, so I phoned Wellbeck and summarized my meeting, leaving out the name of Eli's hotel. Whatever Pomerantz was up to I didn't want him boxed in. For the present Eli was merely going to have Bakhari watched, and if Langley raked him in I might be able to help.

I was getting a ringside view of Mossad performing in the States.

SECRET

MEMORANDUM TO: A/C   ME DIV   16 April

FROM: C Psychological Assessment & Evaluation Staff

SUBJECT: BAKHARI, Hossein; *aka* NEGEB, Mahmoud; HASAN, Suleiman Bin; LISSAN, Dhaif Mufhaddi, etc. (See CenRec for others).

1. Pursuant to your urgent request this Staff has compiled the attached detailed psychological assessment & evaluation of Subject terrorist. It is requested that it be read only by those who in your or the Director's opinion have need of the information.

2. This limitation is established in keeping with Staff policy and because certain of the information derives from such Liaison sources as SDECE, the BfV, MI-6, Special Branch, Mossad, and Egyptian Military Intelligence. Pertinent portions are source-identified in the Index which need not be transmitted to the President, SecState, the NSC or others outside the Agency who, in the Director's opinion, are valid consumers of covert biographical intelligence.

3. Anticipating media interest in Subject individual, this Staff has prepared a sterilized Bio sheet (p. 83) for use by the Press Relations

Office in meeting legitimate inquiries. Since this Staff does not determine public information policy, Bio sheet dissemination to PRO may be made only with your concurrence and that of the Executive Director, in accordance with established Agency procedures.

4. For the convenience of Senior Officials this Staff has prepared and transmits herewith a Summary of the Staff Study which, while omitting much detail, nevertheless is designed to provide the reader with an overview of Subject individual.

DIST: A/C MED (or.)   NSC
cc. The President   SecDef
    SecState
    FBI (Dir.)
    INS
    ExDir

SECRET

BIO SUMMARY & EVALUATION ——— BAKHARI,
                                       Hossein w/a/s

Believed born near Tabriz, Iran, July 1945. Father army sergeant; mother farmhand, unmarried. Mother's later protector provided son, Hossein, with religious (Koranic) schooling. On learning protector not his natural father and he illegitimate, Subject tried to kill his mother with a club. Forced out of his home, he found refuge at Church of England mission school in Khorramshahr until 15. Apprentice to gunsmith who had homosexual attachment to Subject who manipulated employer to his own advantage. Incidents of theft, womanizing, resulting in expulsion from area. Instanbul 1962. Lived in home of woman whose shopkeeper husband was impotent. 1964. Fulbright scholarship to Waco (Tex.) Southern College. Poor grades. Left 1967 under pressure from parents of girl he seduced. Aleppo. Ba'ath adherent. Mortar corporal in Six Day War, Golan Heights. Captured, repatriated after wound treatment. Received *fidayun* training at Soviet-run camp near Alexandria. Participated in cross-border ops from Lebanon PLO camps into Israel. Politically aligned with left-wing activists. Early critic of Y. Arafat. Utilitarian

Marxist, pro-Peking stance. Zurich El-Al attack (2/18/69); arrested but released by Swiss. London Zim office attack (8/25/69); escaped. Bonn bombing of Israeli Embassy (9/8/69); escaped. Athens attack on Olympia Airways plane frustrated by arrest (12/21/69); released. Munich attack on El-Al plane (2/10/70); expelled to Jordan. Istanbul bombing of El-Al office (4/24/70); escaped. Identified with Jordanian armed struggle organization Quwwat al-Ansar. Paramilitary training USSR 1970–72. Vienna seizure of OPEC Ministers resulting in four deaths (12/21/75); terrorists allowed to leave for Algeria. Cairo bombing of orphans' home (4/17/77), seventy-two deaths; escaped. Many other known or suspected incidents of terrorism. Subject has been in contact with major international terrorist organizations including Baader-Meinhof (Germany), Red Army (Japan), South Moluccan Separatists, Red Brigade (Italy), IRA (Ulster), Frolinat (Chad), ELF (Ethiopia). Subject speaks Farsi, Arabic, English, French, and Turkish with varying fluency. Evaluated as megalomaniac psychopath seeking personal power rather than cause dedication. Highly dangerous and unpredictable, will sacrifice even intimates to his own benefit (Rome 8/16/72). Highly-sexed but no stable conventional relationship with females. Regards self as professional revolutionary. Holds Islamic view of females as vassals and patronizes prostitutes. Imbued with resentment over illegitimate birth, peasant origins. Envy and hatred toward industrial world in which unable to compete. Agile dialectician, but far from True Believer. Believes self uniquely capable of unifying Arab leaders and masses (viz. Al-Karmal Manifesto, Paris). Credited with poisoning shipment of Israeli oranges to Holland where five children showed poison symptoms (2/1/78). Travels on a variety of passports and documents, some forged, some legitimate. Subject has entered JFK as Third Secretary of Iraqi Delegation to UN. Present location: New York.

Bryan Wellbeck routed the Staff Study to his deputy and dropped it in his Out box. Leaning back in his upholstered chair he gazed over the greening woods that buffered the Agency from the gorge of the Potomac. Then, as he occasionally did, Wellbeck consulted his anthropological vademecum, *Seven Pillars of Wisdom,* and turned to Lawrence's comments on the Syrians:

All of them wanted something new, for with their superficiality and lawlessness went a passion for politics, a science fatally easy for the

Syrian to smatter, but too difficult for him to master. They were discontented always with what government they had; such being their intellectual pride; but few of them honestly thought out a working alternative, and fewer still agreed upon one.

This nut was a time bomb and he hoped that Mossad would be able to find some way of preventing the terror spectacular Bakhari was planning to execute. Even if it meant losing Jay Black along the way.

He peeled back the next document's pink routing sheet and found the latest issue of the *West European Intelligence Review*. As always the *Review* was printed in violet ink on cream-colored French bond, and Wellbeck thought that for a thousand-dollar annual subscription rate it should give off a rare cachet as well. He glanced at the ostensible place of origin—a London Post Office box, S.W.1—and the name of the publisher/editor, DuVal P. L. Jerningham. The interior initials, Wellbeck had learned, stood for Phillippe Lascelles, a name as fanciful as much of the *Review*'s "intelligence."

Leafing past the sections on West Europe, America, and Africa, he stopped at the Mid-East page. Wellbeck had intended no more than a cursory scan, but a name caught his eye and fixed his attention. He read rapidly at first, slowly for detailed absorption.

Something was very wrong.

Either the story was fabricated, or Jerningham had an informant within Al-Karmal.

Dialing the division reports officer he said, "Get a quick read out on whether WEIRdy ever reported before on Al-Karmal or Prince Ahmad of Oman."

"The *late* Prince Ahmad?"

"The same." Then he told his secretary to summon the divisional security and counter-intelligence officers for an immediate meeting.

When they entered his office he gestured them into chairs. His line buzzed and the reports officer spoke. "Never until the current issue, sir."

"Thanks." To his subordinates he said, "Whaddya know, gents. The old ponce in Cope predicted the wipe on Ahmad three weeks before it took place." He tossed the *Review* at them. "Now, tell me how."

FIVE

Al-Karmal (II)

THE customary route from Manhattan to Kennedy airport is via the Queens Midtown Tunnel and over the Long Island Expressway. A mile short of Flushing Bay, Queens Boulevard intersects with the Expressway at Rego Park where Israel's Bank Hapoalim has a convenient office, subsidiary to the bank's central branch in Rockefeller Plaza.

There, at two hours after midnight the Ling armored truck had received and receipted for a large shipment of currency, gold coins, and gold bars. Three armed Ling employees rode the mobile cocoon as it sped through Queens: driver, guard on the seat beside him, another guard sealed inside the vault section of the truck. Traffic was light, mostly inbound on the parallel lane, and the truck was well ahead of schedule for the second and last pickup, at the Rego Park branch on Queens Boulevard. From there to JFK where the shipment would be forked aboard an El-Al cargo flight to Tel Aviv.

The driver picked up the transmitter mike and said, "Thirty-three crossing Greenpoint."

"Received," came back the dispatcher's voice.

"So far so good," said the guard beside the driver.

"Whattya expectin', Murray?" the driver said. "When you been in this long's I have it's all the same. Nuttin' happens, believe me. Take it easy, okay?"

"Okay Frank." Murray shifted uneasily, gripped his shotgun and peered through the bulletproof window. He didn't like being in small confined places. "What does Bork do back there, anyway?"

"You mean to pass the time? I never asked him." The driver picked up the mike again. "Thirty-three," he said.

"Go ahead, thirty-three."

"Queens Expressway." The driver replaced the mike and Murray said, "How much you s'pose we're haulin', Frank?"

"Million minimum, but could be five, ten times that much."

"I'd settle for one," Murray said longingly. "Man, would I settle for jus' *one!*"

"Million you mean," the driver chuckled. He reported the Grand Avenue crossing. A little later Murray lighted a cigarette, which was against company regulations, but the driver didn't hassle him. At Queens Boulevard Frank called in the truck's location and turned onto it.

He steered the truck to the rear of the branch bank and flashed headlights. Inside, lights went on. A bank guard came out, said, "Hi, Frank," to the driver, then helped another guard and the chief teller push a laden dolly down the ramp and around to the rear of the truck. Bork unlocked the steel doors and lowered the hydraulic lift. The men from the bank loaded the lift and Bork checked each item against the manifest. He got down long enough to stretch and breathe the moist night air, signed the shipping receipt, and rode the hydraulic lift to truck bed level. Dragging and carrying canvas sacks and bags, he stowed them toward the center for weight distribution. The men outside closed the doors and Bork locked them, sealing himself in until they got to JFK.

The armored truck backed around and drove out. When it reached the Expressway, the driver reported pickup and location, then said to Murray, "Lucky we don't have no five, six more dinky banks tonight. That's why I like night duty, mostly special shipments like this one. Jews sendin' money to the old country, you know."

"I know I never seen a Jew beggar," Murray said. "Or drunk."

"It's a fact, ain't it?"

Near Junction Boulevard there was a lighted barricade and a police cruiser. A policeman with a flashlight waved the truck to a halt. Frank braked the truck and called, "What's up, officer?"

"Hell of a wreck up ahead. Three, four cars. We got a wrecker workin' it. Ambulances. You headin' for JFK?"

"Right."

"Better go down here, catch Queens and work back up on the Grand Central. Okay?"

"Okay." Frank swore. "That'll take us another ten, fifteen minutes," he told Murray. "Goddam!" He wrenched the wheel and turned off onto Junction. Two blocks away the patrol car overtook the truck, and Frank braked. As the officer got out Frank yelled, "What now?"

"Tail light's out." He wrote out a ticket and tore it off. Frank opened the side door to receive it.

Nervously, Murray said, "That cruiser, Frank. . . ."

"Yeah? What about it?"

"No light bar on top."

The driver peered over the headlights at the cruiser and then at the policeman. Before he could slam and lock the door the policeman shot him through the chest. Murray was trying to swivel the shotgun when the policeman shot him in the neck, an upward bullet that splattered brains on the cab ceiling. Pushing aside Frank's body the policeman drove the truck around the block and into a dark alley. Another uniformed man followed in the cruiser. When truck and car stopped, two men in work clothes got out of the rear of the car. One climbed on top of the truck and pried off the ventilator guard with a crowbar. Bork fired three shots at the opening, but the man had been expecting that and stayed clear of the hole. From his pocket he took a small aluminum box shaped like a cigar carrier, opened it, and took out a glass vial. Moonlight glinted on the liquid it contained, and then the vial dropped into the opening and smashed on the steel floor. The man climbed down and stood with his companions a dozen feet from the rear door.

They could hear Bork coughing and screaming inside. Two of the men put on gas masks. The rear doors opened and Bork stumbled out. As he lay writhing in the alley one of the policemen cut his throat.

The men with gas masks climbed into the truck and began heaving out sacks and bags. They used the hydraulic lift to lower the crated gold bars. Inside the cab the dispatcher's voice kept demanding a location report from truck thirty-three.

A can of spray paint obliterated PD markings on the "cruiser" while it was being loaded with the contents of the Ling truck.

They dragged the two bodies from the cab to the rear of the truck and swung them inside. They picked up Bork's body and levered it atop the others before closing the rear doors.

The "policemen" pulled off their uniforms and walked toward the repainted car in their street clothing.

As the driver raced the engine his companion shot both of them.

He collected their weapons, stowed them in the crowded trunk and got in beside the driver. "A good night's work," he said in Arabic.

The driver eased the car into gear and smiled. "Jewish money, too," he said. "Everything as you planned, Hossein."

The car, riding low on its springs, backed out of the alley and turned onto the quiet street. Reaching the Expressway it veered away from JFK and headed back toward Manhattan. At that hour of the morning, aside from occasional trucks and buses, there was hardly any traffic at all.

At 3:23 A.M. the Ling dispatch supervisor checked with the JFK terminal, then notified police that armored vehicle thirty-three was missing. But the truck was not located until 5:18 when a delivery man who tried using the alley as a shortcut found it blocked by the truck, and noticed two bodies nearby.

At 6:42 two FBI special agents joined the throng of police and onlookers at the crime scene, and at 8:27 someone remembered to notify officials of Bank Hapoalim. Converting the stolen foreign currencies, gold, diamonds, and securities to their dollar equivalent, the Bank estimated shipment value (insured) at $9,461,000.27.

Toward noon a bank vice president routinely notified the New York office of Mossad, but it was only after two days of fingerprint identification and background checks of the slain thieves that the FBI suggested an Arab connection.

On the third day Hossein Bakhari checked into a motel in Rosslyn, across the Potomac from Georgetown, and from a pay phone called an administrative officer at the Pentagon.

SIX

Jay Black (IV)

THE yawl was a beauty, exquisitely cared for and handsomely furnished. Fifty-two foot Crimmins design, copper-sheathed hull, air-conditioned, and sleeping six with ease. Sybil and I took it out for an hour while I checked over its running gear and sailing characteristics. It handled with the precision of a Swiss watch, and before I left I gave the broker a check in down payment. Taxiing to the Ft. Lauderdale airport I calculated that I had, in effect, traded the Aspen chalet for the yawl. In time Sybil might become reconciled to the exchange, but it was a consideration that did not particularly affect me. My leg and her libido had ruined Aspen for me and the yawl represented a fresh and promising start.

The short run at sea cleared my head and when I got to Washington airport I was ready for Wellbeck.

He was already at the Admirals Club, sitting at a corner table, sipping coffee and reading a magazine. I showed my card to a receptionist, gave her my New York ticket and put my suitcase in the luggage rack. Then I went over to his table.

Wellbeck looked tired. His tie was knotted less tautly than usual and there was a noticeable shadow on his face. He waved me into the other chair and put aside the magazine. "What kept you in Houston for three days?"

"Wedding in River Oaks. Trudy Markham and Ben Thatcher. A real blast. Trudy and Sybil were at Walker's together."

"Well, I had hell's own time reaching you."

"What's the point, Bryan?"

"I'd like you in Europe for a few days," he told me. "Could you leave tonight or tomorrow?"

"Why not tell me what it's about?"

"Al-Karmal, to begin with. And Hossein Bakhari." From his pocket he took several Xeroxed pages from which the classification stamps had been sliced. "Read these en route to New York . . . as background. Where I want you to go is Denmark." He handed me an envelope. "Inside, there's a ticket to Copenhagen, an address, and a name."

I took the envelope and put it in my inside coat pocket.

Then for a while he told me about a curious old type named DuVal Jerningham, who published a fabricated intelligence review. Wellbeck's interest turned on the point that Jerningham's review had predicted Prince Ahmad's assassination well in advance of the event. He thought Jerningham might have a source inside Al-Karmal.

Wellbeck lifted his cup and drained the coffee. I looked over at the coffee warmers where transients were helping themselves.

Wellbeck said, "We'd like to know Jerningham's source."

"Lotsa luck," I said, went to the sideboard and poured a cup of coffee. Wellbeck could freshen his own. When I came back to the table he said, "That's where you come in."

I stared out at the tarmac where planes and baggage carts were moving around. After a while I said, "If Jerningham's a British subject, he's really an MI-6 target, isn't he? And why the ticket to Copenhagen?"

"That's where he lives. In Hillerod, about twenty miles away."

"Any ideas why?"

"Tax situation. In Denmark he gets to keep a good part of his subscription take. If he's only got a hundred subscribers he's grossing a hundred thousand a year, and in Scandinavia that provides a lot of comfort. But we estimate he's got as many as two hundred subscribers."

"So he could afford a good meal at Tivoli every night of the year."

Wellbeck picked up his empty cup and replaced it in the saucer. "Look in on him, Jay."

"What does he go for?"

Wellbeck's eyes rolled ceilingward. "Aside from those unspeakable indulgences that are so freely spoken of these days, DuVal Jerningham is said to adore handpainted miniatures of European royalty, and antique French furniture."

"Unfortunately I don't know anything about those hobbies. Are you sure this isn't a waste of time?"

44

"Not sure at all. But anyone I send to Jerningham would have to have an actual identity that could be checked and verified, something he's bound to do. In that regard, you qualify. Next, whoever visits DuVal will have to present a solid reason for doing so. And I'm sure you can devise one between now and your arrival." He looked at me earnestly. "Anyone now available from the Agency would have to be given a notional background and identity, quick-dipped and papered, and I'll guarantee Jerningham would see through him in an hour. That's why I'm turning to an extant individual. You."

"An unusual characterization; I never thought of myself in those terms." I fingered the side of my face. "This could run into a little dough, Bryan. I was thinking of bearing a gift, Marco Polo style; something to guarantee an audience. And above the level of missionary beads and calico."

"I might be able to scrape up a thousand or so, Jay, but I don't have an allotment for trade goods. These days we run very close to the bone."

"I'll see what I can do with a thousand," I told him and looked up at the clock on the opposite wall. "And I can't promise anything."

"That's understood." His face brightened. "One thought you might toy with over the Atlantic is the likelihood that Bakhari picked up close to ten million in an armored car robbery near Kennedy airport. No manifesto this time, but amid the five dead were two bodies that, in life, had Arab terrorist connections. Because other significant groups get their financing through oil money, we're guessing Al-Karmal found its own source."

"Heavy dough," I said. "I read about the Bank Hapoalim robbery, but no Arab connection was mentioned."

"No point in advertising the theory."

One of the receptionists came over to me and said, "Boarding time, Mr. Black. We enjoyed having you with us."

"My pleasure." I got up.

"Let me know your plans."

I nodded and went over to the luggage rack. The receptionist smiled at me and I smiled back. Then I went down to the boarding area and took the American flight to La Guardia.

Airborne, I toyed with my second scotch and reflected that neither Sybil or Marcy was going to like my sudden trip to Europe.

And I expected to like it even less.

SEVEN

Jay Black (V)

Copenhagen's Kastrup airport is always efficient, sterile, and impersonal as a bus. I took one to the air terminal a few blocks from Tivoli Gardens, then caught a taxi to the Hotel d'Angleterre on Kongens Nytorv by the Royal Theatre. It was not yet high season so a room was available, and once in it I unpacked while a maid turned down the bed, and opened the blinds and let in morning sunlight. I thanked her with a ten-kroner note, and asked the hotel operator to put me through to Hillerod. A female voice answered Jerningham's number and I said, "This is Jay Black. Did Mr. Jerningham get my cable?"

"He did, sir, and is expecting you today. Are you at the airport?"

"No, the d'Angleterre."

"A car will be sent for you. Is an hour too soon?"

"An hour will be just right."

That was it. I liked the cool, somewhat husky speaking voice and wondered what the owner looked like.

Dressed in fresh clothing I got a small package from my bag. It was the product of an hour's stroll along upper Fifth Avenue and had cost closer to two thousand dollars than the authorized one.

The limousine was a dignified old Bentley, coal black and gleaming in the sunlight. The chauffeur wore a dark gray whipcord uniform with well-shined puttees. He took off his hat, opened the door and let me into the plush interior. The fittings were silver, including the handle of the recessed umbrella, and as we pulled into traffic I felt as though I were going to a coronation.

Northwest out of Copenhagen the highway paralleled a railroad past a small and then a large lake. Plains, then, with scattered farms and wooded acreage until the chauffeur turned off on a side road that led through thick forest to a fenced clearing. The name *Windover* was carved into a sign. Stopping the limousine, the chauffeur got out and began to open the gate.

Two Alsatians streaked toward him until at a sharp command they halted, turned, and trotted back toward their domain.

We drove through the gate and stopped while the chauffeur locked it, then followed a curving road toward the house.

House? Two-story, faced with Ionian columns, it commanded a low rise. Angle perspective revealed wings leading out from behind to form an open courtyard. If Chequers was a house, so was Jerningham's Danish retreat.

As the limousine braked on the gravel a door behind the columns opened and a woman came out. She walked gracefully down the four broad steps, the chauffeur opened my door and I stepped down.

Holding out her hand she said, "Welcome to Windover, Mr. Black. Will you come in?"

Her voice was hazily accented but it was not her voice that fixed my attention. Her hair and curving eyebrows were jet black, her skin the color of cinnamon-dusted cream. A narrow waist accented the voluptuous curvature of her hips and torso, and her contained smile showed white, even teeth. I said, "Delighted to."

Her glance was direct, almost challenging, and as our eyes met I felt a sense of recognition that held me until she turned and went up the steps. She reached the top before she looked back. "Are you tired from your journey?"

"A little," I managed, still shaken by her audiovisual impact, "but I snoozed a couple of hours."

A footman opened the massive door and I followed her into an immense foyer. It was an atrium, really, columned, with a stained-glass dome that let light down onto the central water garden.

My guide halted abruptly, "I'm so sorry. I'm Reba. Obviously I work for Mr. Jerningham."

"In what capacity?"

"I handle his correspondence, as translator and personal assistant."

"Congratulations," I said and returned the smile.

Turning, she walked to the left and I reflected that she was of Semitic blood, but whether Arab or Hebrew I could not tell. She opened a carved oak door, dark with age, and showed me into an anteroom filled with Empire furniture. There was a double-ended

48

bateau sofa ornamented with gold-washed, chiseled bronze; a tripod table whose legs were of gilded, upright swans; a *gueridon* table against the wall, with matching mahogany chairs. The mirror-backed console was supported by Sphinx figurines, and the long brocade drapes were embroidered with the golden bees of Napoleon the First. The effect was heavy, smothering. I sat on a stool whose arched legs ended in gold paws and looked up at Reba who said, "You'll stay for lunch, won't you?"

"Gladly."

Nodding, she moved away, opened a far door and glanced through. She closed the door and came back to me. "Mr. Jerningham is occupied for the moment. Would you care to visit the garden with me?"

There were topiary shrubs and hedges to separate the varieties of roses and other flowers. Blooms from miniature pear trees gave off a special fragrance, and at the far end of the garden a fountain sprayed silver into the light blue sky. The spray came from the mouth of a bronze porpoise around which danced a quartet of naiads clutching each others' hands.

"It's beautiful, don't you think?" Reba asked.

"Gorgeous," I said, eyeing her. "Mr. Jerningham is fortunate to live amid so much beauty."

"He is English, you know, and so he has a special feeling for gardens."

"And you?"

"I share his feeling."

"I meant, are you English, too?"

She shook her head and a wisp of hair detached itself and curled down outlining her left cheek. "No, I'm not English, Mr. Black."

That seemed to close the subject in a polite way, but I said, "Aside from English what languages do you speak?"

"French, Arabic, and enough German and Danish to make conversation."

"Hebrew?"

"No," she said, almost too quickly. Then, after a nervous laugh, "You're Jewish, Mr. Black, so you should know that Mr. Jerningham is not partial to Jews." She breathed deeply. "Why have you come? Your telegram did not say."

"I have a financial proposal for your employer. I'm acting as go-between."

She looked down. "I see."

Breeze carried the clacking of typewriters into the garden. Reba noticed my listening, and said, "That's the staff working on the next issue."

"It must be fascinating work."

"It is."

"Dealing with all those foreign informants."

Her lips tightened. "I'm not privileged to discuss that area. Perhaps Mr. Jerningham will."

"I hope so," I said as she glanced at her wristwatch and turned back toward the manor.

When we reached the Empire anteroom, she knocked at the door, then entered. Presently she motioned me in and I stepped from the Empire period into the subdued grace of Louis XVI furnishings.

My host was seated in a green velvet chair at a gold-trimmed, walnut escritoire. Reba said, "Mr. Jay Black of New York," and left the room.

"DuVal Jerningham, at your service, sir," he said and rose from his chair.

He wore a brocade lounging robe faced with ermine and dotted with the black tips of ermine tails. As he came toward me I saw that his movement was slow, careful, uncertain. His face was long and narrow, atop it a shock of hair that matched the whiteness of the ermine pelts. His pale skin had a curious translucent quality as though the light of life was trying to show through . . . or was being suppressed beneath it. Only wrinkles at the corners of his eyes and mouth suggested that he bore considerable age which I quickly estimated at seventy-five.

When I shook his pale hand I felt small individual bones as when one presses the paw of a cat. At his throat were white starched ruffles, centering a large pearl stickpin. DuVal P. L. Jerningham, laird of Windover.

"It's good of you to receive me on such short notice," I said and relinquished his fragile hand.

"My pleasure," he said in Oxonian accents and indicated a nearby chair. "Do be seated and tell me the occasion of your visit. I must confess myself both mystified and intrigued."

EIGHT

Al-Karmal (III)

Morning light filtered through the grimed windows of a room in Philadelphia's Hotel Renfrow. A partly-dressed man lay on the narrow bed and stared at the ceiling. After a while he got up, ran water in the wall basin and took shaving gear from his overnight bag. He washed face and hands and applied lather with a brush. It was an ivory-handled brush with worn bristles, and it had belonged to his grandfather. Each time George Tisdale shaved he reflected on the generational continuity the brush embodied, and as he stroked his face he recalled that as far back as he had been able to trace the Tisdales, none had approached the professions more closely than an itinerant preacher who had roamed the Appalachians a hundred years ago. Tisdales had been miners, steel-workers, mechanics, salesmen, and storekeepers. None had achieved wealth, George Tisdale told himself, until now.

None of his discoverable ancestors had known college education, but Tisdale's World War II service broke his line's working-class tradition by taking him through college on the GI Bill. He was proud of his BS in Public Administration, and displayed the framed degree on the walls of each Pentagon office where he had worked for the past nearly thirty years.

Unfortunately, he thought, working for the Department of Defense as a middle-grade civilian administrator had not brought the affluence and amenities he had envisioned when he started at the foot of the promotional ladder as a young man.

Two children were grown and distant. He lived alone, now, in a small efficiency apartment, twenty minutes' bus ride from the Pentagon. His savings were gone, his house mortgaged to the hilt to meet the costs of his wife's hospitalization, for their insurance coverage had ended after a year and that had been two years ago. Tisdale's DOD salary was slightly more than thirty-six thousand dollars a year, and the hospital charged forty-eight. He had tried, through Pentagon friends in the Secretary's office, to have Sally admitted to the National Institutes of Health at Bethesda, but after medical review her case was pronounced insufficiently interesting for study, and they were turned away.

In succeeding months George Tisdale realized with bitterness how false an economy it had been to select the lower-cost low option health and hospitalization policy even though at the time no one could have envisioned Sally's becoming a victim of leukemia.

The last few weekly visits had been almost more than he could bear, seeing her deathly-weak, swollen from steroids, ghastly white, fevered, and in constant pain. So when Dr. Afiz, an Arab on the hospital staff, suggested meeting with a man who might be able to ease his financial burden, George Tisdale seized the opportunity as though it had been heaven sent.

As he put away his shaving gear he tried not to think of the uses to which his information might be put, once it was sold. Instead, he concentrated his thoughts on the Rumanian clinic where, it was rumored, miraculous cures were effected. As soon as the payment was his he could put in retirement papers and fly Sally to Bucharest. Then clinic personnel would take them onward to Mangalia on the Black Sea.

His hands were moist with anticipation. As instructed by Mr. Hossan Kassim he had come to this hotel last night for a morning meeting at nine o'clock, and he had brought the documents with him.

At their one previous meeting George Tisdale had asked for a million dollars in cash as the price of his treason, and Kassim, after brief argument, agreed.

He drew on a fresh shirt and knotted his tie, thinking that if only his government had shown compassion and admitted Sally to NIH then none of this would have been necessary.

Tit for tat, thought George Tisdale, my hands and conscience are clean.

It was a few minutes before nine. Tisdale sat on the bed and glanced around the sparsely-furnished room. Last night, before he retired, he had taken the precaution of concealing the documents, and he did not intend to let Mr. Kassim see them until the money—a million dollars—was in sight. Only then would the exchange be made.

He lighted a cigarette and smoked nervously. His build had always been slight, but now it was gaunt from the worry and sorrow that had replaced appetite three years ago. At noon he never left his desk for a sandwich, and at night he seldom had enough energy to warm a frozen dinner. So it had been.

Insufficiently interesting echoed in his mind. My wife, Sally. Mother of my children. At NIH they didn't care about her life or death. To them she was just another file, another folder. Now. . . .

Soft tapping at the door interrupted his thoughts. He went rigid, made himself relax and wiped palms on his thighs. Then he got up and went to the door. In a low voice he said, "Who is it?"

"Kassim," came the breathy voice. "I am alone, so let me in."

Tisdale unbolted the door, turned the handle, and stepped back. Hossan Kassim came in and locked the door behind him. A smile on his swarthy face he said, "Are you prepared?"

"Yes."

Kassim dropped an attaché case on the bed, then another. He unsnapped them and Tisdale saw tightly-packed hundred-dollar bills, stack after stack of them. Eagerly he plucked one and began to count, but Kassim said, "You will find five thousand banknotes in each case. Now, may I see the papers?"

Reluctantly, Tisdale replaced the currency bundle and walked over to the toilet. Lifting the top of the tank he drew out a plastic pouch and dried it with toilet paper. He handed the pouch to Kassim who cut it open with a penknife and drew out the contents.

In large block printing the TOP SECRET cover sheet read: DEPLOYMENT FACILITIES OF THE NEUTRON WEAPON. Kassim examined several sheets and said, "These are not originals."

"Of course not. I made the copies from the original. It's to no one's interest that the original documents disappear."

Kassim shrugged. "If these are not exact copies you will see me again, Mr. Tisdale."

"There will be no need for that, believe me."

Kassim emptied one of the attaché cases and put the Department of Defense documents inside it. "You have your payment," he said.

"What are you going to do?"

"Take the bus back to Washington. I can be there close to noon so I won't have to use more than half a day's leave."

"Very important," Kassim said. "Be sure to resume your normal living. Do not arouse suspicion."

Tisdale laughed. "Last thing I'd want to do, isn't it?"

"Goodbye, Mr. Tisdale." He unlocked the door and went out. Tisdale threw himself on the bed and tossed bundles against the ceiling. It had actually happened, and now it was all his, a million dollars! Enough for the clinic, and for the rest of their lives, the two of them, Sally and George, husband and wife.

When his euphoria subsided he filled his suitcase with loose currency bundles, closed the attaché case, and carried them from his room to the self-operated elevator. At the desk he paid his bill in cash and took a taxi to the Greyhound station.

As far as Wilmington he had window and aisle seats to himself, but there a man got aboard and occupied the aisle seat at his side. Tisdale noticed only that his companion wore a coat, hat pulled low on his forehead.

Tisdale dozed until the bus reached the outskirts of Baltimore. After a while it plunged down into the Bay Tunnel and Tisdale felt uncomfortable in the semi-light. He felt a sudden sting in his side just below the ribcage, and turned quickly to his companion. He was about to complain when he recognized a familiar face. "Dr. Afiz!" he exclaimed, but the doctor smilingly placed a finger to his lips and murmured, "Sorry, George."

Baffled, Tisdale said, "What are you . . .," but was unable to finish the question. His throat closed off and he felt numbness race from his extremities to the core of his being. He could barely move his eyes. He tried to rise from his seat but pressure held him down. Afiz was leaning across him, apparently staring at tunnel lamps flashing by. The bus began climbing the incline toward sunlight, but Tisdale could not see it when the bus emerged. Dr. Afiz closed the eyelids and let Tisdale's head drop forward as though in sleep. Then, very carefully, he removed Tisdale's billfold from the inner coat pocket and palmed it into his own.

At the Baltimore stop, Dr. Afiz stepped into the aisle and took down Tisdale's bag and attaché case from the overhead luggage rack. He made his way patiently up the aisle as passengers crowded to the exit door, and then he walked through the bus station to the far side where a car was waiting.

The death of a Philadelphia passenger was not noticed until the bus reached Washington, where absence of personal documentation made preliminary identification of the corpse impossible. Accordingly, it was taken to the D.C. Morgue for autopsy, under the name John Doe.

NINE

Jay Black (VI)

From my pocket I took the small box, opened and handed it to DuVal Jerningham. He stared at it, held it toward the light, then withdrew the painted brooch. "Magnificent," he said at last and took a magnifying glass from his desk. He studied the miniature and murmured, "Malbone. Edward Greene Malbone, of course. But who is this lady, his subject?"

"Mrs. Fitzherbert," I told him.

"But of course: Morganatic wife of George Fourth!" He looked up. "Malbone was a Colonial, a New Englander, Mr. Black. Surely he must have painted this from a portrait?"

"Possibly," I said, "but you'll recall Malbone went to London with Washington Allston. Benjamin West urged Malbone to stay, and as a founder of the Royal Academy West had access to royal circles. One may assume that West arranged this commission for Malbone and that he accomplished it from life."

Jerningham gazed admiringly at the miniature's delicate tones and set it aside in its box. "I insist on reimbursing you, sir. Merely pronounce the figure."

I shook my head. "I've intruded on your time," I said, "and you know as well as I that time is a valuable resource. So consider this a small recompense."

"But you are too generous," he exclaimed, "and you place me in your debt. *In serio,* how may I repay you?"

"By hearing the proposal I've been authorized to bring you."

"I shall hear it," he said pleasantly, "no matter how offensive it may be." Leaning forward he tweaked my knee with his left hand. "Pray divest yourself of it."

"Well," I said, "in the first place, I'm acting on the behalf of principals whom I'll not name for the present. My only obligation to those who entrusted this mission to me is to make as fair and persuasive a presentation as possible."

"I understand, sir, and I appreciate your frank preamble. Go on."

I cleared my throat. "You publish a unique and well-regarded journal for a limited number of subscribers, surely fewer than five hundred. Among them are four gentlemen who have decided they would like to recapitalize the *Western Europe Intelligence Review* and publish it on a much broader scale. They would concern themselves with the *Review*'s promotion and dissemination. The contents, as always, would remain your entire responsibility."

One long finger tapped the lid of the gift box. "With no interference?"

"None whatever." I looked past him and saw through the curtained window a dog handler walking one of the leashed Alsatians. Also I noticed magnetic alarm contacts at the window's top and bottom. Among other things, DuVal Jerningham prized personal security.

He said, "An amazing and unanticipated proposal, Mr. Black. May I ask if your principals include Zionists?"

"Not that I know of."

"Well," he said silkily, "as the son of the famed Samuel Schwartz you should know."

I nodded. "If you know that much about me, sir, then you are aware that I head a successful advertising agency. Two of my principals are clients. Should you accede to their proposal, the publicity account for your *Review* would come to my agency. So I stand to gain in a moderate way from your acceptance. However, it's hardly a matter of life or death."

He chuckled. "You've revealed your incentive cleanly and openly. Now tell me what their motive is."

I leaned back and gazed at the opposite wall. On it hung a life-size portrait, waist up, of a stern-visaged, sharp-eyed man. I wondered briefly if it was of Jerningham forty years ago. "Their motive is, I suppose, fundamentally commercial. They see in your *Review* a comparatively unexploited but commercially viable property. They feel that with proper exploitation—your servant, sir—and a large injection of funds, they would stand to gain a substantial return on their investment. No, please hear me out." I paused. "Their tax structure is such that they can easily withstand losses on prudent investments."

"What you call write-offs?"

"Exactly."

He made an arch of his hands and touched the tips of his thumbs. "To what extent would they be willing to capitalize my publication, Mr. Black?"

"Half a million pounds sterling."

His lips pursed. "Not an astonishing figure," he said as though speaking to himself. "And I would continue to maintain control?"

"Well," I said confessionally, "my principals have world-wide interests, you understand. Occasionally, *very* occasionally, they might ask you to include an item of their devising."

His face turned foxlike. "So now the cat's out of the bag, is it?"

"Quid pro quo."

He took what was for him a deep breath, and looked at me sharply. "Well, it's something to consider, is it not? I'm no longer young, and my luxuries sometimes run to exorbitant amounts. Even in Denmark my overhead costs are high. And, of course, I must provide my informants material tokens of my appreciation."

"Of course."

"I have a completely professional staff," he said, "drawn from a number of intelligence services. Several have been with me these last twenty years. Such skills are expensive to monopolize."

"I understand."

"Which is to say," he went on with a sweep of his hand, "that I share minimally in the *Review*'s profits. One of the reasons I removed to Denmark was to avoid the confiscatory taxation of my native British Isles. Had I not done so, the *Review* would long since have ceased to exist. Here, fortunately, free enterprise is favored. Denmark has a central situation and is easily reached by—shall I say—travelers? Moreover, British-style police repression is unknown, and the climate is a considerable improvement over Britain's." He spread his hands. "Quod erat demonstrandum."

An unseen telephone chimed and Jerningham said, "Pardon me," as he plucked the receiver from a cubbyhole in his desk. After listening a moment, he said, "Presently," put aside the phone and turned back to me. "I have a spot of business with the chef," he informed me, "after which I will rest briefly before lunch." He glanced at an ormolu table clock. "That will give you some time to examine my collection of miniatures." He gestured toward several glass-topped tables along the wall. "Now, you will excuse me."

He rose as silently as a wraith and moved toward a flush door in the wall and I noticed gold-embroidered, velvet slippers as he walked. Pressing a mid-wall fixture he opened the door and went through the opening. The door closed silently behind him.

As though on signal the anteroom door opened and Reba came in. She said, "Would you care for a cocktail before lunch? Sherry?"

"Whatever you're having."

She shook her head. "Nothing for me. But don't let that influence you."

"Well," I said, "I'm not a heavy drinker as things go, but a tot of schnapps would go well about now. Or is it akvavit?"

"Akvavit," she said unsmilingly.

"Preferably on ice, thank you."

She went out and closed the door, leaving me in Jerningham's museum. Alone. He had not removed the Fitzherbert miniature from his desk where papers seemed carelessly scattered as though an invitation to inspect. I avoided the temptation, got up, stretched, and sauntered over to the display tables. The glass tops served as magnifiers, so it was easy to examine the artwork and read the identifying legends below each miniature. Hilliard, Clouet, Oliver, and Carriera were some of the painters' names. There were about thirty miniatures in each of the three tables and they were painted on wood, parchment, gold, porcelain, and ivory. The collection could be worth, I estimated, a third of a million dollars.

To rest my eyes I stood back from the cabinets and noticed again the oil portrait. A small brass plate on the lower frame was engraved with a name: Oswald Mosley, Bart.

I looked up at the unforgiving eyes.

Sir Oswald Mosley, defunct leader of the Union of British Fascists, was apparently Jerningham's household god. No wonder my host had asked if Zionists were among his would-be backers: Mosley was legendary as a rabble-rousing, virulent Jew-hater.

The door opened and I turned to see Reba enter. She was carrying a small silver tray with two glasses. She put them down on a coffee table and sat in a chair. I picked up my glass, distinguishable by the ice chips, and she lifted hers. "Apple juice," she said and sipped. "Do I disappoint you?"

"No." I tasted the clear, cold fire of akvavit and managed not to cough. Almost at once the fog and fatigue of travel began clearing from my brain. "Do you live here at Windover?"

She nodded. "It is very comfortable."

"Are you wedded to your work?"

"Yes, and only to my work. Is there anything I can tell you about Windover?"

"Well, if you will. How long has DuVal been here?"

"A dozen years, I believe. Before Mr. Jerningham restored it, this place was an old royal hunting lodge fallen to ruin."

"He's done magnificently," I said. "And are you as hostile to Jews as he?"

Her cheeks colored slightly. "Why do you ask?"

"Because I'm Jewish."

"Is it important?" She twirled the small glass in her fingers. "You don't seem very Jewish, Mr. Black."

"Because I don't have a hooked nose and a pedlar's pack? You're too intelligent to deal in stereotypes. By the way, what's your family name?"

"Mizraki," she said and spelled it for me.

"Then you're Jewish."

"I'm not anything," she said, "I'm not Arab or Jewish or Berber or Danish or anything at all. Yes, I have Jewish blood, but I was raised in a refugee camp; I lived on UN food. There was no possibility of studying either Torah or Al-Koran." She put down her glass slowly. "Since you seem determined to personalize this conversation I will tell you that while my mother was Arab my father was said to be Jewish. I don't know. I never saw him."

"Well," I said, "I only wanted to know whether you disliked the Jewish people."

She shook her head. "I asked you if it was important."

"Only when I'm fond of someone."

Her eyes darted quickly to my face. "Either my personality is overwhelming or you're dangerously impressionable."

"Could be both," I said equally, "and how is it your anti-Semitic employer tolerates you?"

"Because of my languages."

"Your English is fantastic. Where did you acquire it?"

"In New York, partly. I left Barnard to attend a specialized school for UN interpreters. I was in New York several years."

"And after that?"

"Oh, Beirut for a time. Cairo, Damascus, even Jerusalem. Being personal secretary to wealthy men is a comfortable way to live."

Evidently she had a yearning for comfort.

I said, "I expect to be in Denmark a day or so. Would you consider dining with me tonight?"

"I don't think so," she said, "but it was polite of you to invite me. I'm sure you'll be able to find an agreeable companion, perhaps at the d'Angleterre bar."

I was about to reply when the anteroom door opened. A white-coated houseman came in and spoke in Danish to Reba. Rising she said, "Luncheon is served. Shall we go?"

I left my akvavit to offer her my arm. She declined it and as we followed the houseman from the room she said, "I must tell you that Mrs. Jerningham will be lunching with us."

"He's married?"

She laughed briefly. "Don't look surprised. No, it's the senior Mrs. Jerningham, his mother. She's very old, ancient, really, and since her stroke she hasn't been able to speak. Mr. Jerningham takes excellent care of her."

"A devoted son," I said, "in this day and age. He sounds almost Jewish."

She looked at me reprovingly, then we went out onto a glassed-in porch that overlooked the garden. At the far end a loose Alsatian urinated on one of the bronze naiads. Well, I thought, it could only enhance the patina; Romans did it all the time.

Jerningham was helping seat his mother. She was a small wren of a woman with sunken, liver-spotted cheeks and scanty white hair held back by a jeweled tortoise-shell comb. I went over to her and Jerningham introduced me in a loud voice. She looked up, nodded briefly and managed a slight smile. I murmured the usual formula and was going to seat Reba but a footman was already there. So I sat at the far end of the table, opposite Jerningham, the ladies across from each other. Reba ate lightly and composedly, apparently paying no attention to her employer who was expatiating on the proximity of Windover to two national monuments: Frederiksborg and Fredensborg Castles, the latter a royal summer residence.

His mother, I decided, remarkably resembled Ouspenskaya in her later years, and I remembered having been presented to the great actress by my father when I was a child. Mrs. Jerningham seemed to lack vitality, for she ate less than a canary and all but ignored her small glass of wine. Poached salmon turned out to be the entrée, and it was exquisitely prepared.

As luncheon proceeded, between small talk and the host's continuing lecture, I sensed a theatricality about the scene. Nothing could have been more theatrical than DuVal Jerningham, from his glistening white hair and brocade robe to the tips of his embroidered slippers. And the restored hunting lodge, a monument to conspicuous indulgence. Then the ancient, feeble chatelaine, a dowager exemplifying old money and aristocratic blood; ambulant cadavers, she and her son. And lastly, the Mesopotamian waif of mixed blood, admirable accomplishments, and unrevealed proclivities. We were all of us, I decided, characters in a stage tableau.

Against a background of attack dogs and alarm systems.

By unspoken agreement, neither Jerningham nor I mentioned my business proposal during lunch. But when it was over the ladies left the table, Mrs. Jerningham shifting into a wheel chair that was propelled into the house by a footman, and Jerningham said, "If you'd care to smoke, I don't mind as long as we're out here. I can't bear tobacco smoke in the tapestries."

"Nor can I." I let the servant refill my cup with rather strong coffee, and waited for Jerningham to bring my visit to a close.

When the servant withdrew, Jerningham said, "Would you care to see the mechanical side of my publication?"

"Not really," I said to maintain my incurious pose. "I don't know anything about the intelligence business, and I've seen magazines put together before, so it would be largely meaningless. I'd rather utilize the time to spell out any answers to questions you may have, perhaps get an indication of your receptiveness before I return."

He smiled. "Many would be eager for a tour of my restricted premises, but I agree that for you it could be a prodigal use of limited time. So, to the heart of the matter, sir. What projections have your principals worked out? How would their proposal benefit me?"

"The guarantee to you for the first year would be fifty thousand pounds, double that the second year. After that you would receive a fixed percentage of profits, giving you incentive to maintain standards."

Jerningham's face showed disappointment. "Already, dear sir, I am gaining more than a hundred thousand pounds per annum. Tell me, why should I accept partners to my financial loss?"

"You shouldn't," I told him and his face relaxed. "My principals obviously underestimated your current revenue. They may want to escalate their offer accordingly." I sipped from my cup. "If you're interested, I'll send a cable to New York."

"Why not?" he said musingly.

"Of course," I said, "there would have to be an examination of your books by a solicitor to be mutually agreed upon. And proof that your foreign informants actually exist."

"They do, of course," he replied and I noticed his fingers twitch, "but I could never permit strangers to examine my records. Not until after the agreement was in effect."

"I doubt," I said, "that they'll agree to that. All I can do is put the stipulation in my cable."

"Then do so," he said. "How long are you prepared to stay in Denmark?"

"Through tomorrow."

"Very little time, sir."

"I should have the reply sometime tomorrow."

"I would not agree to your proposal for less than a hundred and fifty thousand pounds the initial year of the association. Two hundred thousand the second, and thereafter a fixed percentage of the profits."

"I'll tell my principals," I said and got up, "but I should tell you in fairness that I think your demand is exorbitant. Particularly when you leave us in doubt concerning the authenticity of your sources and informants."

"You question my honesty, sir?"

"Let's put it this way: My principals are attracted to the *Review*; in it they see a potentially profitable investment. Having made you an offer, they should be entitled to further information—a lifting of the veil, as it were—before seriously considering your counter proposal. That's how business is normally transacted. No one should be asked to buy a pig in a poke."

"You mistake the situation, sir. I have asked no one to buy my ... pig, as you put it."

"But you're not uninterested."

"Money is always of interest."

Jerningham rose slowly. "My car will return you to Copenhagen. Thank you for the Malbone of Madame Fitzherbert. It will be paired with one of George Fourth in my display. To the advantage of each."

He was not going to accompany me to the door, so I said, "By the way, did you know Sir Oswald?"

"Mosley? Indeed. And well. Very well. A man grossly misunderstood and despicably hounded by men he towered above." His voice rose shrilly but now it lowered and he was in control again. "Mosley was right, you know. The Jews *are* responsible for the triumphs of Russia, the decline of the West. As a Jew, though, you cannot admit the truth. Sir Oswald saw it all so clearly."

"As did William Joyce," I remarked and left the protected porch.

I passed through the lower floor and atrium without seeing Reba again. Outside the chauffeur was waiting. I got into the Bentley and we drove away.

As the chauffeur relocked the gate behind the car I considered Jerningham. Under the effete exterior he was just another crude Jew hater, and that clarified one point for me: Jerningham had never served with MI-6 or even MI-5. The British Intelligence Service often sheltered communists, but it was gospel that no known fascist had ever joined their ranks.

Which made DuVal P. L. Jerningham an even greater *poseur* than I had thought.

Still, how had he been able to predict the assassination of Prince Ahmad? Someone had to have told him.

I wondered if it was Reba.

Because she had been tilting with me, taunting me. Implicitly flaunting sexual promise, then primly withdrawing at my first discreet response. In years no woman had attracted me so violently, and I knew that I had to see her again.

Whether she wanted to or not.

From the central telegraph office I placed a call to Parlay Trade Consultants in Manhattan, using my international charge card. I recognized the redhead's voice and after about forty seconds Wellbeck spoke. "You're in Cope?"

"Just returned from lunching with Precious. An old dear, ain't he?"

Wellbeck chuckled. "How'd you get along?"

"I avoided *lese-majesté* but it wasn't easy. He's got quite a spread and it's fairly well protected, though hardly invulnerable. By that I mean dogs and an alarm system. Apparently all work is done on the premises. His personal assistant is a multilingual lass who said her name is Reba Mizraki. Background obscure, but she could have been Miss Universe a year or so ago. Anyway, he's considering the proposal but says he's already making more than the initial offer. I think we're gazing into a dry hole.".

"Duster, eh?"

"Exactly."

"Meaning you tried to date Reba and failed."

"Well," I said uncomfortably, "that's true. But DuVal won't permit inspection of his books until after the contract's signed. I could tell him we won't agree to that and bow out, no hard feelings."

"So it shouldn't be a total loss why don't you dangle him another day or so? Be hard-nosed about money and book inspection but leave him a glimmer of hope. Ah, how did he like your peace offering?"

"It pleased him but he has ninety better. He lives with his mother, incidentally. She must be close to a hundred. She's mute and. . . ."

A boisterous laugh then. Wellbeck was saying, ". . . *really* his mother? Jay, she's an old relic he picked up from Wolverhampton Repertory, a superannuated bit player. *Mother?*" He laughed crudely again. "She's part of the supporting cast he trots out to enhance his fanciful lineage."

I swallowed, irritated over my gullibility, and said, "You could have told me."

"There were more important things to convey. Besides, I sort of hoped you'd see through the charade on your own."

"Well, he puts on a class act, believe me, and poverty is far from his door. And he's an admirer and onetime associate of Oz Mosley. Did you know?"

"Vaguely."

"He checked up on me, found out my father's name among other things."

"He's got lots of contacts," Wellbeck conceded, "but that doesn't tell us how he knew Prince Ahmad was going to be wiped."

"I told him we'd need a list of his informants before we finalized the deal. He disdained that too."

"Part of the mystique. Look, he's a venal old fabricator, I told you that. And the only informant I want identified is the one next to Al-Karmal. Uh, not calling from your room, are you?"

"Central telegraph Office, and I'll bill you. So, what do you want me to do?"

"Mouse around some more without being obvious. If I turn up anything interesting on Mamzelle Reba I'll give you a call."

"I'm at the d'Angleterre," I told him. "Room three seven three."

We rang off at the same time and I stepped out of the booth.

Midafternoon in Copenhagen. As I walked outside toward the taxi rank I felt played out; jet lag had caught up with me. There was nothing I really wanted to see or do, aside from Reba, so I took a cab back to the hotel, pulled down the window shades, and got into bed.

Hours later the phone rang. As I groped for the receiver I realized it was dark outside. Wellbeck again, I thought as I answered.

But it was Reba.

TEN

Mossad (I)

Soon after reaching New York, Major Eli Pomerantz placed Hossein Bakhari's midtown safehouse under close technical and physical surveillance. Through the Jewish owner of the apartment building, he had acquired occupancy of the unit directly above Bakhari's. During the Al-Karmal leader's frequent absences, probe mikes had been installed in the floors of the upper apartment without piercing the ceilings below. Of metal-tipped plastic, they resembled long knitting needles, and fine-gauge wires connected them to each of the six sound-activated tape recorders that operated in total silence.

He had tapped into Bakhari's unlisted telephone by means of the conduit that ran vertically through their twin utility rooms, and all phone conversations to and from Bakhari's apartment were automatically recorded in Eli's listening post.

Across the street another apartment had been rented from its owners. It was located a floor above Bakhari's, providing visual surveillance of the target windows. Through a high-powered camera lens, the Israeli watchers could see and photograph with fine resolution the faces of Bakhari's visitors.

The street team, on standby around the corner, could be alerted by radio signal from either of the Israeli-occupied apartments. Team orders were to engage in loose, semi-distant surveillance, and to break off when detection seemed imminent.

At first light, Bakhari had been seen to leave the building carrying duplicate attaché cases. There had been no sonic warning of his departure, so the external team had been alerted by the window watchers who noticed him emerge from the street doorway.

In their borrowed taxi, the two surveillants had followed Bakhari to Penn Station and onto the Washington-bound Amtrak coach. At Philadelphia they trailed him to the Hotel Renfrow and waited until he left with a single attaché case, then back to the station where all boarded the Metroliner for New York.

During their absence the window watchers telephoned Eli Pomerantz to tell him that Bakhari's mistress was preparing to leave the apartment. She called herself Sapphire King, but Mossad knew her as Zafira Cohn, a Sephardic Jewess.

Sapphire, or Zafira, they learned, was an occasional cabaret entertainer, age twenty-six. Through an expensive escort service that provided attractive prostitutes, Bakhari had met her a year before, and by money and intimidation secured her exclusive services.

He thought, Pomerantz reflected wryly as he replaced the receiver. So great was Sapphire's love of money that during Bakhari's absences she plied her trade in Madison and Lexington Avenue bars, accompanying clients to their hotels or apartments, but never taking them to the one she shared with Hossein Bakhari whom she knew only as Mr. Salah Dinn, an Iraqui UN diplomat.

To the man who shared his shift, Eli Pomerantz said, "Sholom, I think this is the time to move in."

A night-school law student at NYU, Sholom Zunser said, "Whatever you say, Eli. I better shave."

Pomerantz nodded. "You should look your best."

Sholom shaved rapidly and got into a new leisure suit specially bought for the operation. Pomerantz handed him an envelope of five-by-eight glossy prints and three hundred dollars in twenties.

The telephone rang, and it was one of the surveillors. "Eli," he said, "we're back at Penn Station. Our man's making some pay phone calls. He seems in a good frame of mind."

"That's too bad," Pomerantz replied. "Any indication of his next destination?"

"Not yet, but we're getting the taxi out of the parking lot."

"Don't lose him," Pomerantz warned, "and I don't want him arriving here without notice.

"I understand." The caller rang off.

"*Scheiss!*" Major Pomerantz snapped. "If Bakhari gets here before she leaves we'll have to postpone again."

They heard the telephone ring in the apartment below. One of the tape recorders began to turn. Pomerantz and Zunser trotted to the utility room, turned up the amplifier volume enough to hear Sapphire saying, ". . . I was planning on shopping anyway. Will you be here for dinner?"

"Yes, my dear. We will go out to dine. I should be with you by six." Bakhari's voice.

"Miss you, honey," she said and hung up. But a probe mike relayed her angry phrase, "You *shmuk*!"

Pomerantz and Zunser smiled at each other. "Up to you," Pomerantz said and Sholom Zunser nodded.

Twenty minutes later Sapphire got into a taxi and rode away. Sholom's taxi followed to Fifth Avenue where Sapphire got out at a lingerie shop. With Sholom tailing unobtrusively, she bought a pair of Italian shoes and with her purchases walked across Central Park South to Rumplemayer's where she took a sidewalk table and ordered a drink. Strolling by, Sholom seemed to notice her for the first time. "Well, hel-lo!" he said enthusiastically and leaned over the lattice divider. "Sapphire!"

She eyed him in alarm and then her features relaxed. "Hi," she said. "You look familiar. Do I. . . ? I mean, have we met?"

"Have me *met*?" Sholom chuckled. "Mind if I join you?"

"I guess it's okay. Sure."

Seated across from her he said, "You're a real put down, y'know? Do we *know* each other? Two hundred bucks' worth. That's how well we know each other. And not two weeks ago!"

Her cheeks colored as she stirred her Gibson. "Well, I wasn't sure. Gotta be careful, y'know. Uh, where did we go?"

"Americana," he said promptly, "and, baby, you were worth every buck of my dough." He leaned forward. "Uh, by coincidence, I was feelin' kinda horny. If you got a little time. . . ."

She sipped her drink and considered. Not a bad idea, really. She'd just spent over a hundred dollars, and turning this trick would replace it, and more. "Same deal?"

"Why not?"

They went to a theatrical hotel off Times Square, Sholom paying in advance as was house custom. When they were in the room he counted out two hundred dollars and placed them on the scarred bureau.

Sapphire undressed carefully and went into the bathroom while Sholom took off his clothes. When she came back her skin glowed damply and she said, "Let's get into bed, honey. Brrrr, I'm *freezin*'."

She snuggled quickly against him but Sholom, unsurprised, had noticed teeth marks on her breasts and shoulders, strawberry hickeys on neck and belly, weals across her buttocks and lower back. The probe mikes had carried the sounds of her frequent and often violent couplings with her keeper. Even bruised as it was, Sholom had to admit that the bitch had one hell of a bod.

Tentatively, he licked the side of her neck, felt passion rise. Sapphire murmured, "I kinda forgot your name, honey, it bein' so long and all."

"Mike," he said hoarsely, "just call me Mike."

Warmed, feeling proof of his desire, Sapphire turned and parted her thighs.

As they were dressing, Sholom took the photographs from his jacket and dropped them on the bed beside her. Sapphire stopped fitting on her new shoes and, curious, picked up the top photo.

She screamed, then covered her mouth chokingly, scarcely able to believe what she saw: Salah and her on the sofa. Screwing.

She felt faint. The next photo showed her blowing Mike, the john she'd just finished with. She stared up at him in fear.

"Great artwork," he said as he adjusted his tie. "And baby, you're featured in every one. Think Mr. Dinn'd like to see them?"

"You bastard!" she choked. "You fucked me!"

"Paid for the pleasure," he said calmly, "and like the fellows say, you're a first-class lay. You dive like a Stuka."

Her flesh was cold. Tightly she said, "Whattaya want from me?"

"Very little," he said, "but as one Jew to another let's talk about the man who calls himself Salah Dinn. It's not his name, Sapphire. He's a murdering Arab terrorist named Hossein Bakhari who's killed more than a hundred Jews. And he plans to kill a lot more."

"I don't believe you!"

"That's immaterial," he told her. "You figure because he's cunt-struck he can't be a killer? That's the worst sort of logic." He pulled on his jacket. "Or maybe you don't care?"

"All I know is, he takes good care of me."

"When he's in town. The rest of the time. . . ." He gestured at the scattered photographs. "If you want to test him, *and* me, I'll arrange he gets these photos by messenger at the UN. Then we'll see what happens to you." Under his gaze the voluptuous body contracted visibly. Sapphire looked down at the open shoe box. "Enough, already. Like I said, whattya want from me?"

"That's more like it." Bending over he kissed her damp forehead.

"I want you should phone me from time to time, honey," he said and wrote a number on a sheet of wrapping tissue. Tearing it off, he said, "Just ask for Mike, huh? Every time he tells you he's leaving town for a while. Got it?"

"That's all?" She looked up hopefully.

"That's it."

"No freebie balling?"

He shook his head. "If you do what you're supposed to you'll never see me again . . . and Bakhari will never see these photos. Take them along if you want, I've got the negatives."

Closing her eyes she shook her head.

He gathered the prints together and returned them to his pocket. "So thanks for a pleasant hour, Sapphire . . . I mean Zafira. You sho' know how to treat a fellow well. A real pro," he said admiringly.

"Up yours, buddy."

He laughed. "Take it easy, babe. I don't care if you ball the entire Upper East Side, just give me a call now and then so I don't lose confidence in you. If it happens I lose track of Bakhari for even twelve hours it's your ass. I mean it."

"He's going to Europe," she blurted.

"When?"

"He didn't say. Soon."

"I'll need details," he told her and dropped a pair of twenties on her lap. "I need to know where, when, and how. Whether he'll wear sheets or a suit. Details like that. What about his phony passports, where does he keep them?"

"There's a safe in the bedroom wall. In there, I guess."

"Well, don't go messing with it. Just keep your ears open when he talks."

"Crap," she said, staring at the ceiling, "what a mess you got me into."

"Bakhari, not me. But so far, who's the loser? You haven't lost a thing. There's five hundred in it for you if you can tell me his destination and flight number before he leaves."

"*Five. . . ?*" For the first time her mouth relaxed.

"A business deal," he said, brushing off his lapels. "No big thing, Sapphire. You're selling, I'm buying. Let's forget the photos and keep it at that, okay?"

She swallowed. "Okay." Then, "Y'know, I could really get to like you, Mike."

"I'm flattered," he said as she stood to smooth her skirt. "But then I've already complimented you."

She continued dressing.

"Call me tomorrow," he said and went out of the room.

Behind him she locked the door and went to the bathroom mirror to fix her ravaged makeup. As she outlined her eyebrows she remembered that she had been too scared to ask him who he worked for. CIA? No, the FBI.

But she sort of hoped it was the CIA. They got their kicks in all kinds of weird ways.

ELEVEN

Jay Black (VII)

THE d'Angleterre Bar was as I remembered it from a previous visit: high-gloss bar and tables, thick carpeting, and lighting as subdued as the patrons' conversation. Overall, something of the ambiance of a good London club. As I glimpsed Reba at a small table I recalled the noisy atmosphere of the Sherry-Netherland when I'd last met Marcy there.

But thinking of Marcy would lead inevitably to Sybil and remembrance of my conjugal status, so I pushed them toward the back of my mind and made my way to the table.

Reba had been sipping what appeared to be carbonated water through a colored straw, and when she looked up she smiled.

Tonight her hair was different, parted at the middle of her head and drawn back on each side, then caught in a decorative clasp. Her eyebrows were darker, giving depth to already-dark eyes, and the salmon lipstick made her teeth seem super-white. Around her shoulders an expensive fur throw—stone marten, I thought—and her dress was light, metallic gray. I pulled back the chair and said, "Sorry to keep you waiting, but I needed a shave."

Her lips maintained the smile, but there was a hint of caution in her eyes. "Quite understandable. After all, you weren't expecting me."

"But I'm glad you reconsidered. Mind telling me why?"

One long, enameled fingernail tapped the table. Twice. "That's just it, isn't it? I reconsidered." Her tone was formal.

"And you were confident enough to come in to town tonight on . . . speculation?"

"So it seems." She opened her evening bag and withdrew a cigarette, handing me her lighter in the same movement. To me it seemed an intimate gesture. Cigarette lighted, and lighter returned, I said, "For the world I wouldn't question Providence . . . and I don't mean the capital of Rhode Island. Tell me, did you check the bar before calling my room?"

Her head moved slowly, negatively. "I felt fairly confident you would not act on my suggestion. Did you sleep through the afternoon?"

"The hotel could have fallen down around me."

"And you feel rested now?"

"Completely." To the waiter I said, "Scotch on the rocks. Reba?"

"Nothing now."

"Black Label," I instructed the waiter. "A little Evian on the side."

He went away and I sat back to gaze at her. She seemed well aware of my admiration and I could easily believe that wherever she was, Reba Mizraki drew the longing attention of every adult male. But I liked the way she handled it: with aloofness and unconcern.

She said, "As you might surmise, life at Windover has its limitations. The editorial associates are, well, dullards, and you've seen the Jerninghams. So. . . ."

"I've seen DuVal Jerningham," I said, "and the aged pensioner who poses as his mother. So that makes only one Jerningham, if that's even his name."

If I'd expected a tight reaction I was disappointed. With a contained smile she said, "Did you come by that perception unassisted?"

"Not entirely."

Exhaling cigarette smoke, she said, "It really doesn't matter, does it?"

"What matters is that you reconsidered my invitation. Does DuVal mind such excursions?"

"There are very few," she said, "so they're really nothing to concern him. Besides, he's apparently excited by your business proposal. Did you cable your principals?"

"I phoned them."

"And?"

"I should hear tomorrow."

She nodded thoughtfully. "You could have telephoned from Windover, one of us should have suggested it."

My scotch arrived and I savored it with pleasure. "DuVal was tiring, accelerating my departure."

She sipped through her straw and I drank more Black Label. Presently she said, "In New York I knew a few people—very few—who were in advertising, and you're . . . I suppose I might say you're not typical."

"Please say it."

Again the caution returned to her eyes. She hesitated, then went on. "Are you *very* successful?"

"Sufficiently to satisfy a demanding father."

"And married, I suppose?"

"With two children, boy and girl. Ages ten and seven. Their mother's name is Sybil and we've been married eleven years."

"Happily?"

"For the most part. Tolerably, for the rest."

She tipped ash from her cigarette into a ceramic tray. "Do you have—in a manner of speaking—an outside interest?"

"In a manner of speaking."

"Serious?"

I glanced over at the bar, aware that I was getting a pretty thorough grilling. I said, "Not really."

"Does she think so?"

"I don't know what she thinks," I said, "but we're good medicine for each other. She's recovering from a bad marriage, and mine's on the down slope."

"But you stay married because of the children."

"That's the conventional thing to say. But don't infer that I'm the average Yankee on the prowl for female companionship. I'm not a guy who thinks a night alone in bed is outrageous deprivation."

"Had I thought so I would not have come." She put out her cigarette and held me with her eyes. "Even now I'm not sure it was a good idea. You made me feel quite uncomfortable today." Her voice was cool, even scolding.

"Sorry."

"Anyone but the Jerninghams would have noticed how aware of me you were."

"I'm that ovbvious?"

"After you left I thought about it at length."

"I thought about it, too, Reba. And I made up my mind to see you. I was considering forcing myself on you."

"I wouldn't have liked that," she said severely. "Not at all. And you mustn't misinterpret my coming here, but perhaps you already have?"

"How would you have me interpret it?"

"Surely not as raging desire to go to bed with you." Her face turned slightly. "You have a mistress as well as a wife."

"That I haven't concealed."

"True. But even in Europe—Denmark—an adult couple can share a pleasant evening without physical intimacy. Is it not still possible in New York?"

"Rarely," I said, "but we could give it a try."

She nodded thoughtfully. "Let me tell you, Jay, that I would never want a brief encounter. Do you understand? A casual affair would be impossible for me."

I covered her hands with mine, pressed their vital warmth as it flashed through my mind that they made the ultimate contrast to the desiccative chill of Windover's ancients. "Let's see where the evening leads."

Preliminaries out of the way, relative positions established, we began to enjoy each other's company in a relaxed, low-pressure way. Even so, I retained a certain amount of hope.

At her suggestion we dined at Au Coq d'Or where I bought a corsage of fresh gardenias from the flower girl. Their scent reminded me of long-ago Exeter and college dances, except that I'd never had so completely gorgeous a date. When I told her so she smiled and changed the subject, saying, "One thing that impressed me about you, Jay . . . pride in your Jewishness. I envy you," she went on, "always feeling I ought to conceal that part of me, especially from DuVal. He can be quite difficult, you know."

"I saw the portrait of his idol."

"An unspeakable man."

"Mosley or Jerningham?"

"Both, really. If earlier I made my life there seem dreamlike it was to avoid discussion. You were transient. Why should I discuss my hang-ups—is that the word?—with a near stranger? DuVal can be totally vicious, even to his *soi' distante mère*. And the poor old thing has no other place to go. In return for her silence and acceptance of his abuse, she lives in comparative luxury. I suppose there could be worse things for her."

"Much worse."

After a long silence she said, "As for me."

We shared a fine broiled lobster and a bottle of white German wine, Reba remarking that she did so as a concession to me. "I don't like to see a man drinking alone. His bottle—beer or wine—makes him seem all the lonelier."

"Never thought of it that way, but of course you're right. Reba, I wish I could stay longer with you."

"I wish you could, Jay. Perhaps you'll come again."

"I'll try," I told her. "You have no idea how hard I'll try."

She looked down at the table surface. "Then we'll leave it that way."

That evening progressed from restaurant to cabaret; a stroll beside the park ended at a café for Viennese coffee, and then we took a fiacre ride, clop-clopping over ancient cobbled streets. I took Reba in my arms, drew her close, and kissed her gently, then asked her to share a nightcap with me in my room.

At first she shook her head, murmured, "No," but after a while I asked again. In response, she kissed my lips lightly and nodded, saying, "Only for a little while."

Between sips of champagne we kissed. Kisses grew longer, deeper, our bodies pressed together. In wordless consent we parted and I turned off all lights except a small bulb in the partly-open closet. In a little while, from the bed, I saw her standing naked, gilded by the dim lighting, and I knew that I had never seen a lovelier, more desirable woman in my life.

We came together with an eagerness of lifetimes, and when our bodies joined she uttered a single cry I ended with my mouth.

Sated finally, we lay hand in hand, listening to night sounds from the square below until she whispered. "I feel so close to you."

"Words from my mind," I said and kissed her.

I brought her a cigarette, lighted and placed it between her lips. I could never become too familiar with those lips.

As I stood looking down at her relaxed body I saw that it was as sleekly outlined as a swimmer's. She was utterly feminine and utterly desirable. I waited impatiently until her cigarette glowed out and then we made love again.

In the darkest, stillest hour of the night she spoke to me of Windover and its strange owner. "He doesn't trust you, Jay."

"Why not?"

"Because you declined to visit his editorial rooms. He's offered that opportunity to only a few visitors, and only one declined—you."

I thought it over. "I should have accepted," I agreed, "but the whole atmosphere was overpowering in a strange, off-key way. Besides, I couldn't stop thinking of you. Wanting you, to be frank."

She squeezed my hand tightly. "Will you be frank with me now?"

"Of course."

"Did you come to spy on him?"

"I don't know how to answer," I said, but her fingers closed my lips. "Jay, can you trust me?"

I kissed her cheek. "Why shouldn't I?"

"Then let me help you. What is it you need to know?"

Easing off the bed I went to the Moët bottle and filled my glass with champagne. "Through the *Review*, Jerningham predicted the assassination of Oman's Prince Ahmad. How was he able to do it, Reba?" I carried my glass to the bedside and sat down. "That's become a test for Jerningham with my principals. If he could satisfy us he actually has the resources to produce the kind of advance information, it would pretty much convince my backers they ought to invest and get behind him. But he's not willing to budge, and I doubt my friends will."

For a long time the room was silent. She ended it, saying, "I'm not being melodramatic when I tell you that Jerningham could arrange to kill me if he finds out I told you. So be careful if you care for me."

"I will, and I do. Very much."

Sitting up, she took a sip of champagne as though to steady herself before she said, "The information came by mail, Jay. In an envelope from Paris. It was Arabic, so I translated it for DuVal. Things come that way from time to time, but usually he ignores them. Almost all his so-called 'intelligence' information comes from twenty newspapers around the world, but he has the ability to synthesize their contents and add shrewd guesses. Perhaps you knew that?"

"It was surmised. Why did Jerningham decide to publish this anonymous snippet?"

"Because I suggested he do so." She sipped again from the glass and looked into my eyes. "As part Arab I'm more sensitive, aware, of Arab trends and doings than DuVal whose 'expertise,'" she made a mouë, "is mostly European."

"Go on."

She breathed deeply and her incomparable breasts rose and fell. "I told you I'd worked here and there in the Mid-East, you remember?"

"Yes."

"Well, it was not always exclusively for sheiks and emirs and wealthy businessmen. There was a time when I cooperated with Weisenthal, helping locate Nazis who'd burrowed into the Mid-East after the war." She shrugged. "After the Russians were expelled from Egypt I offered my services there to military intelligence. I had freedom to travel in the countries of Egypt's enemies, you see, though I never worked against Israel, believe me."

"Not if you helped Weisenthal."

"Then I saw this employment offer in a Beirut newspaper. It came at a good moment—my employer was making repulsive efforts to become my lover—and so I applied to Jerningham and was employed. That's really all there is."

"It's quite a lot. How long before Ahmad was killed did the message arrive?"

"Nearly a month."

"And did you, or he, ever learn who sent him the information?"

"Yes," she said calmly, "I learned."

With Jerningham's leave she had gone to Paris, Reba told me, and looked up friends in the Arab milieu: Sorbonne and Paris University students, shopkeepers, Algerian militants, until she heard a mocking reference to Ahmad's assassination, Arabs boasting to Arabs, a hint that the speaker had been in on the affair, and the person had been a Palestinian girl named Atiqa who was known as a lover to Hossein Bakhari. She was a student of journalism at the University of Paris and contributed to militant Arab journals in Europe. It was she, Reba determined, who had written the message to Jerningham.

"Did you do anything about it?"

"No."

"You told Jerningham, of course?"

"When I left Paris I intended to. But on the return flight to Copenhagen I realized that his sharing my knowledge might endanger me. If he named Atiqa in the *Review*, for instance, or boasted to visitors what he knew. So I lied to DuVal, said he'd set me an impossible task, that I had failed and was sorry."

"How did he react?"

"He was furious over the expense, but afterward he never mentioned it again." Her finger touched the tip of my chin. "There was a double element of disloyalty involved, Jay. You see, I knew Atiqa. There was a time when we were together in the same refugee camp, made little dolls of straw and rags." Beside me, her body seemed to draw together. I said, "And until Paris you didn't know what became of her?"

Her breathing was deep, exhaling almost a sigh. "I'd heard of her from other refugees, knew she had survived and found another life. Twice I came across her by chance, in Beirut and Damascus. But by then she'd taken a different path, come under the spell of Fatah, and finally Bakhari. Even so, I couldn't betray her to Jerningham." Her head turned on the pillow and her voice was low. "We were like sisters."

"I won't betray your confidence." I kissed the lobe of her ear. "Have other visitors to Windover been interested in the same thing?"

"Several. From the embassies of Oman, Egypt, and Israel. A Frenchman from the DST tried to interview Jerningham." She gazed at me. "Curiously, no Americans."

"Until now."

"Yes. If you were an agent of the CIA I don't suppose you could tell me. Could you?"

"Probably not. I don't know the regulations."

"It seems possible to me that you may have a ... relationship ... with Mossad."

"I know such people," I admitted. "I worked on a kibbutz for a year."

She stroked my hand. "I won't pry. But now that I've told you what you wanted to find out, does that mean you won't visit Windover again?"

"If you're there I'll go," I said, "because I have to see you again.

82

Before I go back to New York. Since you know of Al-Karmal, what do you think of it?"

"Horrible. Modern brown shirts. I loathe them and all other terrorists."

"The Cairo orphans," I said. "Destroyed by Bakhari and his gang of murderers."

I thought that, having gone this far, I might as well go farther. "Bakhari robbed an armored car in New York," I told her, "to the tune of nearly ten million dollars. I've been told it's to finance some unknown undertaking of his, something unthinkably desperate, unpredictable, and cataclysmic. Atiqa might be involved. She could be a lead in preventing whatever that mad man is planning."

"I know where she lives," Reba told me. "I'll write it down for you." Lights sparkled in her lustrous eyes. "But not now." She drew me down beside her. "Are you strong again?"

"Samson was a weakling."

"Words, words," she whispered. "Convert the idle boast."

Afterward, I went to the bathroom, closed the door, and turned on the shower. But just before I stepped in I thought of something and opened the door. Reba was putting down the bedside phone. The sudden light showed her eyes wide in surprise. Quickly her features relaxed and she said, "I asked the doorman to wake the chauffeur, alert him."

"Leaving so soon?"

"I must. What. . . ?"

"I thought iced champagne would go well after a hot shower." I went to the bedside and filled my glass. "Now I'll find out." I bent over to kiss the top of her head. Reba said, "Jay, you don't think I. . . ?"

"Phoning the doorman? What's to think?"

But as I got into the shower . . . I wondered.

In the morning I spun another tale to Jerningham and glimpsed Reba from time to time when she crossed the room or consulted her employer. Except for one conventional greeting and an occasional covert glance she ignored me, and I had to admire her skilled dissembling. No outsider could have guessed that only hours before this chill and formal woman had lain naked in my arms. As I watched her leave the room with posture erect, precise, efficient stride, no backward glance, I found myself wondering for a moment if she really had, and then I brushed away the fantasy.

On the way to Kastrup airport I stopped at Georg Jensen's Ostergade store long enough to order something sent to Reba: a heavy gold Star of David on a long gold chain.

Wear it for me, I wrote on the vellum notepaper. *Let it guard my place while we're apart.*

Then I boarded the SAS 747 wondering if I could ever return to see her. And I prayed that I would.

Far out over the Atlantic the realization gripped me that I didn't care if Reba worked for Israel, Egypt, or even the PLO. I cared for her, wanted her, had to have her for more than just a night.

But I couldn't tell Bryan or Rosenthal.

II

"... we live in troublous times and desperate situations."
Friedrich der Grosse   1762

TWELVE

THE chief security officer of the Department of Defense, retired Major General Bruce Pickwood, chaired the meeting in a windowless room down the corridor from the Secretary's office. In attendance were representatives of the Washington Metropolitan Police Department, the FBI, the Joint Chiefs of Staff (NATO Section), and CIA.

The general's skull was shaven, and he wore a black patch over his left eye in the manner of Moshe Dayan. He rapped the table sharply and said, "In convening this meeting I specified that only *one* representative of each involved agency or department was to attend. I notice, however, that the FBI has sent *two* special agents. One of you must withdraw."

After whispered consultation, the junior agent from the Washington Field Office got up and went out.

Pickwood said, "I purposely excluded your aides, and none of you is to take any notes or later record on tape or otherwise the discussions that will now take place in this room."

The JCS colonel pushed aside his note pad and pen.

General Pickwood said, "The subject of this meeting is, of course, the death of a former DOD employee, George F. Tisdale. Corrclative is an assessment of the damage he may have caused. Chief Brody, your update, please."

Brody was a pink-faced, middle-aged, professional Irishman with a trim, white mustache and a dazzling set of crowns, who regarded the other four men at the table as amateurs. Clearing his throat, he began to speak in a well-modulated baritone: "Because a small puncture wound was detected below Tisdale's right ribcage, death by narcotics OD became a possibility. Toxicology analysis disclosed no traces of

87

conventional narcotics. However, there were modified proteins and a haemolysin, which is a poison principle."

"The point, Chief," General Pickwood snapped.

"The bottom line, sir, is the forensic conclusion that the victim was killed by hypodermic injectin of a snake-like poison related to the colubrine species."

"In short?" Pickwood growled.

"Venom from a cobra, krait, coral snake, or habu, but in greater concentration than appears in nature. In short, a poison artificially concentrated so as to produce very rapid paralysis of the central nervous system."

"Thank you," Pickwood said drily. "Subject cadaver was injected, in life, with snake poison that someone tinkered with."

Pickwood sipped from his water glass. "Once we knew Tisdale was dead, his supervisor was notified, coworkers were reinterviewed, and two of them recalled seeing Tisdale at the copy machine, near closing time, on the two days prior to his authorized leave. A search was made among the classified trash removed from Tisdale's office area, trash that had not yet been shredded and incinerated. Two crumpled sheets were discovered, each a flawed reproduction of a page in the Top Secret Kronos document entitled: DEPLOYMENT FACILITIES OF THE NEUTRON WEAPON."

The JCS colonel gasped. General Pickwood held up one hand to forestall questions. "As you are all aware, it is a grave security violation to replicate classified documents, particularly any of such high sensitivity. None of the civilian or military workers in Tisdale's vicinity admitted having made the imperfect copies, and polygraph testing supports their statements. Accordingly, we are left to face the high probability that Tisdale copied the Kronos document. No such copy was found in his safe, in the Secretary's file, or in Tisdale's apartment. Which brings us to the likelihood that Tisdale made off with a copy of the Kronos document and disposed of it prior to his death."

The FBI agent said, "We're in a full-court press to determine where Tisdale stayed in Philadelphia. So far, no positive results."

Chief Brody coughed. "I should have mentioned that the stub of a Washington–Philadelphia bus ticket was found in Tisdale's coat pocket. According to the bus company, it had been issued and used the day before his death. The ticket's serial number indicates that

Tisdale rode to Philadelphia on a bus that left Washington a few minutes after seven o'clock on the evening before his death."

The agent said, "Either he stayed with a friend or at a hotel of some sort. Of course, if he was there clandestinely, it's unlikely he would have registered in his true name. However, photographs of him are being shown to desk clerks around Philadelphia. We may come up with a positive make, but I don't think we can count on it."

The CIA representative said, "General, I've never seen the Kronos document you mentioned. What's its significance?"

General Pickwood turned his head in the direction of the JCS colonel who said, "We've long regarded the enhanced radiation weapon, popularly called the 'neutron bomb,' as ideally suited to the defense of NATO countries. Early it was discarded for political reasons, but after the impetus of the Iran and Afghanistan crises, work on it proceeded in great secrecy. Over the past year, neutron-tipped artillery shells and aircraft bombs were deployed to stockpile sites in NATO countries where secure facilities for storage had been prepared. Those stockpiles are increased as deliveries occur. The location and construction details of the facilities are highly classified." Pausing, he glanced at the head of the table where General Pickwood was listening intently. "The Kronos document in question gives full details on how many neutron weapons are in each facility, where such storage facilities are located, and the construction features of each."

Heavy silence permeated the room until General Pickwood said, "Chief Brody, thank you for your summation. You stand excused."

Brody put his files into a large letter-carrier, shoved back his chair, and left the room. When the door closed behind him, Pickwood said, "So there we have it, gentlemen. Apparently this little prick Tisdale delivered a Kronos document copy to someone and got killed for his pains. That's the operative theory we have to work on, and what we must determine, with the help of all of you, is to whom he gave or sold it."

The CIA officer said, "The bomb would be a weapon much to terrorist liking, General. My understanding is that it kills populations by radiation while leaving buildings undamaged."

Pickwood nodded. "For your private information, gentlemen, the Secretary is going to cover the situation in detail with the President who will have to decide whether to make a public announcement concerning our manufacture and deployment of neutron weapons, or whether to remain silent and hope the unknown adversary refrains." He cleared his throat again. "That is a political decision, of course, but the President may feel his hand has been forced and decide to preempt hostile revelation."

A beeper sounded. The FBI man straightened and, with some embarrassment, shut it off. He left the table, went to a telephone at the far corner, and began to dial.

The CIA officer said, "As of now, we've heard nothing from our sources concerning the Kronos document. If information comes in we'll relay it."

The agent returned to his chair and said, "Philadelphia office located the hotel where Tisdale stayed overnight. Tisdale registered about ten o'clock as Graham Townley, had a visitor next morning around nine o'clock, and checked out shortly afterward, paying cash. We have a not-very-useful description of his visitor. The desk clerk described him as swarthy, medium build, possibly in his middle thirties. The clerk speculated he was Jewish or Arab."

"Arab!" The CIA officer exclaimed.

The JCS colonel said, "Frankly, I'd rather the Israelis had the document than the Arabs, but I think the Israelis would simply have paid for it as a business transaction and not killed Tisdale. But the fact that he *was* killed, and by a special kind of poison, suggests to me that his killer was Arab rather than Israeli."

General Pickwood shook his head. "I agree with your thinking, Colonel. Anyone disagree?"

There was no response.

"So," Pickwood said heavily, "unless we can somehow isolate the document, it seems we have no option but waiting for the next shoe to fall."

Mossad (II)

Two days after her romp with Sholom Zunser, Sapphire dialed the number he had given her and asked for Mike. When he came to the phone she said, "Still got those photos?"

"Uh huh. What's happening?"

"Slow down. You said five hundred, right?"

"Right. Five big ones." He gestured excitedly at Eli Pomerantz who moved in to listen.

"Promise?"

"Sure, I promise. *If* you've got the information."

"Well I have. He's going away tonight."

"Where?"

"Europe somewhere. He bought new clothes today, and a black raincoat. Then he was foolin' with that stuff he keeps in the wall safe I told you about."

"You mean passports?"

"Prolly. And money. Listen, I don't know what airline, but it leaves JFK at 11:14."

"Okay, I can check. That's good work, lady."

"Like, I don't work for free. *You* know that."

"I understand. And if he's on that flight, you get your dough, okay?"

"How? Where?"

"I'll tuck it under your door."

He replaced the receiver and Pomerantz said, "Someone has to take the trip with him."

"I'd volunteer only I've got exams coming up. How about cousin Mordy? He hasn't been used in a while, he's cool."

"Send him."

Jay Black (VIII)

From behind the antique reproduction desk Wellbeck said, "So you've heard nothing from Rosenthal since you got back?"

"No."

"Or Pomerantz?"

"They've left me blissfully alone."

"That's not good."

"It's okay by me."

He grunted. "I don't know what the hell they're up to, and I don't like it."

I said nothing.

Wellbeck said, "Ever since you got back from Denmark you've been semi-incommunicado, Jay. Just a sketchy report and, well, frankly I expected more."

I moved my chair aside to avoid the afternoon sun that was moving down into the window behind him. "I did my best," I said. "That's what I was supposed to do."

He shook his head. "*Was* it your best, though? That's what's bugging me. Your attitude's different, as though on the trip you suffered a sea change."

"Air travel," I said. "To and from."

He got up and drew the blinds across the window. Then he came around the side of the desk and leaned against it.

He was right, of course. I'd changed. Since coming back I hadn't slept with Marcy *or* my wife. Because I couldn't get Reba from my mind. Her musky fragrance seemed always present. I couldn't think of anything but Reba.

"You're being difficult," he said, "holding out on me and I don't like it. Pair of roguish eyes steal your heart and seal your lips?" he sneered. "Don't answer. I don't want your bullshit."

I shrugged, remembered something and said, "I don't think I mentioned the cocaine."

"*Whose* cocaine?"

"Jerningham. He snorts it."

Grimacing, he drew a deep breath. "There's a big dust up at Defense. Seems one of their civilian employees Xeroxed a highly sensitive study and delivered it to someone. Apparently that unknown someone then killed the rat who in life was named George Tisdale. No, there's nothing about it in the papers, and won't be."

"Perhaps Tisdale was answering the urgings of a Higher Morality."

"Don't bait me," he warned. "The reason I'm telling you at all is because the working consensus is that Tisdale sold the document to Arab interests."

"How important is the document?"

Turning, he went around his desk and seated himself. "Very damn important. It's Top Secret Kronos and it reveals the inventory and locations of our neutron weapons abroad."

"Abroad? I didn't think we even had them at home."

"What our government is now struggling with," he went on, "is whether to acknowledge in public the development and foreign deployment of our neutron weapons—to forestall announcement by whoever has the Kronos copy—or to stay silent while trying to get it back."

"Quite a dilemma."

"It worsens," he said, "because any paramilitary group with the knowledge contained in the copy could assault one of the stockpiles and probably take away some of the weapons. The storage sites aren't particularly well guarded, unfortunately. Today's Army privates don't care for guard duty: interferes with their studies," he finished sourly. "And the *poilus* and *soldaten* aren't much better."

"You said 'Arab interests,' meaning what?"

He shrugged. "Of the PalLib kidney, but that's not much more than a guess. Mossad might well get a lead before we do."

"Wouldn't Mossad inform you?"

"I'm not sure they would. I can see them picking up a lead, following it and taking possession of our neutron weapons and never saying a word to anybody. But they trust you."

"Not all the way," I said. "Don't forget Teitelbaum."

"Well, you're someone they can turn to and feel comfortable with." He turned in his chair and gazed at the Modigliani reproduction on the wall. "So, with Jerningham you left things ambiguous."

"Standoff. He didn't like the money offer, and he won't open up his subscription books or reveal his sources. He never would, of course, because he can't."

"This Reba—Mizraki, was it?—told you that?"

"Indirectly."

"Do you think an entry job at Windover would be worthwhile?"

"Not unless you know more about Jerningham's affairs than I do. What's to learn, really? I think his information on Prince Ahmad came across the counter, Jerningham took a chance, and printed the prediction. He had nothing to lose. If you think he's in bed with the Arabs you can't prove it by me. I didn't spot a raghead or a scimitar on either visit. Did your files turn up anything on Reba Mizraki?"

"Nothing significant. She was at Barnard for a while but dropped out. Later she was a stewardess on Alitalia and that's about the sum of it. No record of her as a UN simultaneous interpreter or translator. You're interested in her, aren't you?"

"Casually," I lied. "She's a beauty."

He smiled. "Harem Nights and all that? Did you try to recruit her?"

"You didn't authorize it. Besides, she's not the type."

"She's enough the type to work for a fabricator."

I cleared my throat. "What do you want from me, Bryan? You had me survey the territory and I did."

"But you wouldn't mind a return trip, would you? Say, to interview Reba again?"

93

At the PanAm building Wellbeck boarded a helicopter for LaGuardia where an Agency executive jet flew him to Washington National Airport.

In the morning he drove from his Cleveland Park home to a hotel on DuPont Circle and knocked on the door of a fourth-floor suite.

Lev Rosenthal admitted him. They shook hands and the Mossad delegate said, "I went ahead and ordered breakfast."

"Fine." Wellbeck pulled off his topcoat and saw a table set for three. "You don't mind my including Colonel Fuad?"

"Not at all. We work for separate masters toward what I hope is the same goal." He poured coffee for them, answered the door, and admitted the Egyptian officer. Fuad was of medium height and athletic build unlike his Israeli counterpart. He wore a handsomely tailored, dark, business suit and regimental tie. He shook hands with Wellbeck rather formally and said, "Coffee, please."

Serving him Rosenthal said, "You're looking most dapper, Suley. Bond Street?"

The Egyptian smiled. "Almost, Lev, al-most. From Alexandria, actually; the tailor was British trained. One of the meager blessings of our colonial past."

Rosenthal chuckled. "In Israel we have any number of fine tailors. You should visit Tel-Aviv."

They seated themselves and ate shirred eggs and English muffins. Finally Wellbeck said, "I wouldn't have imposed on your time were the matter not so serious. You know about Tisdale's murder. The document he stole concerns weapons technology, and collateral information suggests that the compromise and murder were masterminded by an Arab group."

Fuad frowned. "Because the hotel visitor was swarthy?"

Wellbeck said, "That's only one factor. It's not up to the standards of a Soviet operation. They wouldn't have liquidated Tisdale so sloppily, left a ticket stub in his pocket, allowed the body to be found so soon. No, in reviewing possible sponsors it's not unrealistic to think in terms of Syria, Libya, Iraq, or one of the terrorist organizations."

"Such as Al-Karmal?" Rosenthal inquired softly.

"Why not?"

Fuad refilled his cup. "I don't suppose you Israelis had a hand in this, Lev? No, you would not need to. The Americans give you whatever you ask for." He smiled bitterly. "We, your only Arab allies, must beg and bow and scrape for mere crumbs." He added three teaspoons of sugar to his coffee and let it settle.

Wellbeck shrugged. "I'm telling you what I know, and it's little enough. Since hostile exploitation of the information could affect our countries I'm advising you of the situation and asking you to exchange anything your services pick up that could have a bearing on the theft."

Rosenthal heaved his bulk from the chair and sank onto a settee. "It's of common interest if not concern that Hossein Bakhari has left these shores."

"That *vermin*!" Fuad spat, but Wellbeck leaned forward. "When did he go, Lev? Where?"

The Israeli had been cleaning his teeth with his tongue. Pausing, he spoke. "Last night he flew from New York, ticketed to London. However, at Shannon airport he got off apparently to stretch his legs and did not reboard. I had a man with him on the flight, by the way. Bakhari strolled through the pub, looked over offerings at the duty-free shop, and walked outside where a car was waiting. He got in beside the driver and they drove off." Levanthal looked with satisfaction at his receptive listeners. "My man was unable to determine his destination, but the car is registered to a person who goes under the name of Fergus O'Flaherty."

"Never heard of him," Wellbeck said.

Rosenthal looked directly at Colonel Fuad. "You may remember him under a different name, Suley, his true name: Stoss. Dieter Stoss."

Fuad winced.

"Yes," Rosenthal said easily, "*Hauptmann* Stoss of the SS special operations group commanded by *Oberst* Otto Skorzeny. You will recall, Stoss turned up in Egypt after the war and found useful employment training the Death Commando squads."

"I did not know him," Fuad said primly, "I knew only *of* him."

"But it is a curious thing, is it not?" said Rosenthal, "that Bakhari has run to him. Why? one wonders. What have they in common other than a desire to kill more Jews? Then one recalls that Al-Karmal may have robbed some ten million dollars of Israeli money from the Bank Hapoalim not long ago. Now a missing document having to do with advanced weaponry, and I become intensely interested. Why? Because with such a document, and utilizing the money and manpower of Al-Karmal, Stoss could be quite capable of putting together some deadly project whose target is Israel."

THIRTEEN

Al-Karmal (IV)

THE chateau was three kilometers north of the town of Avesnes-sur-Helpe in northeastern France. A few more kilometers to the east lay the Belgian border and beyond it the village of Chimay where a NATO support base was administered and protected by the Belgian Army.

Because of this proximity, and because both a railroad and a main highway converged at Avesnes, the chateau had been selected by Dieter Stoss and rented by Al-Karmal intermediaries. Long ago the villagers had become accustomed to monied Arabs acquiring villas, arable land, and vineyards, so the presence of a dozen at the rundown old chateau caused little speculation. Interest in them centered on the size of the purchases they were likely to make, the amount of gold they were likely to transfer into the local economy. So far their known purchases were limited to fuel, food, and bedding.

Stoss and Hossein Bakhari were standing at a long oak table in the chateau's great hall. Light from the wood fire showed maps and papers arranged neatly along the length of the table. One of the Kronos document diagrams had been enlarged by hand, and the men were studying it under a fluorescent lamp.

"It is one thing," Stoss said, "to assault a strongpoint blindly. But when one knows its layout and vulnerabilities the matter reduces to a series of simplicities. Here," he pointed, "we know even the thickness of the steel access door. Thus I can easily compute the size of the necessary plastic charges."

"You must be careful not to damage the contents of the bunker," Bakhari told him. "That would endanger the project."

Stiffly Stoss said, "You need not concern yourself about the contents. I take personal responsibility for their integrity. What progress have your men made on the other side of the border?"

"They are on schedule," Bakhari said. "They buy drinks for the imbecile Belgian soldiers in the taverns of Chimay and listen to their talk. Three disaffected ones have been selected, and intimate, persuasive discussions are being held."

"They can provide the uniforms and armored weapons carrier?"

"Otherwise they would not have been selected."

"*Gut.*" Stoss went to the next item on his list. "Arms?"

"A case of NATO rifles is being diverted from the Herstal factory." Bakhari shrugged. "It would have been simpler to take them by force."

"You must learn," Stoss said tutorially, "to let money work for you. By purchasing the weapons, at whatever price, you avoid the publicity of an isolated armed attack, and there is to be only one attack." He gazed fixedly at the Arab. "Is that not so, Hossein?"

Grudgingly, Bakhari said, "Yes, *Hauptmann.*"

"I no longer care for the military title. Try to remember that." One finger moved down the list. "Plastic explosive?"

"En route from Algiers," Bakhari said. "The ship puts in at Marseille for unloading. Our crate will come by train to our little village here."

"When?"

"The ship reaches Marseille in two to three days."

Next item. "Communications equipment?"

"It will be flown from Damascus to Paris as diplomatic cargo. Carried here by truck."

"How soon?"

"Who knows?" He spread his hands. "Soon."

Turning, Stoss gazed at the fireplace flames; age had brought the need for warmth. Especially so in this ice-chill castle. Among the flames he seemed to see a face. It was a younger face, his own; clean shaven, unscarred by battles of long ago. Now, here perhaps, his renaissance would come.

"Are you all right, Dieter?"

"Of course." With an effort Stoss turned back to the work at hand. When his thoughts reformed he said, "The training of the Gaza party is crucial. How is it progressing?"

"It is to be completed in a week. As I told you, each man has already had electronics or radio experience, and all have been in battle, some of them with me. So it is merely a case of familiarizing them with the new, specialized equipment, and training them again in seaborne landing under fire, and holding a perimeter."

With a sardonic smile Stoss said, "If you plan correctly, their landing will be unopposed, Hossein."

"I expect it to be unopposed, Herr Stoss, but one plans also for the unpredictable."

Stoss gave a short laugh that was more of a bark. "How unlike the average Arab you are, *mein freund*. The simple *fellahin* I trained were unknown to give thought for the morrow."

"And that is perhaps the difference between them and me," said Bakhari with a touch of arrogance. "The difference between follower and leader."

Stoss' finger moved down the list, then he looked up. "Had there been men like you, the Arab world would not have been so passive in the great war."

Bakhari nodded agreement. "Still, because of that war there are men like me who will not remain passive before injustice."

Stoss grunted. "That is not something in which I am interested. This is about taking from those who have ... and settling old scores in the process."

Blandly, Bakhari murmured, "As you say."

Stoss was examining the list again. "The landing craft?"

"Already secured and waiting in Lebanon."

"Be sure it is still available when it is needed."

Bakhari nodded.

Stoss stretched his powerful shoulders and removed his lenses. "One matter that has been troubling me, Hossein. It is your penchant for publicity. That degenerate in Denmark published your boast: Ahmad could have been warned."

"But he was not," Bakhari said smoothly. "The effect was to show Al-Karmal invincible."

"This time," said Stoss, "there is to be no advance warning. Not by a minute, not by a second. I have studied the Israelis with care and they are able to react instantaneously. What you proclaim during and after the action is up to you, but I forbid prior boastfulness. It would endanger us needlessly."

"Forbid? A strong word, Herr Stoss."

"It is precisely what I mean. I do not intend to involve myself in foolishness."

Bakhari's face darkened. "You have been paid your fee, *Hauptmann*, a million."

"That can be returned."

Bakhari's thumb moved against his index finger as he considered. Finally he said, "You are right, Dieter."

"You agree?"

"I agree."

"Then instruct your propaganda chief accordingly."

Bakhari nodded. "As soon as Atiqa arrives."

Jay Black (IX)

The afternoon was cool. I walked over to Fifth Avenue wishing I'd worn a raincoat, and when I got back to my office I sat in my chair chafing my hands and debating—while knowing the answer in advance—whether I should phone Reba again.

For two days after my return I'd refrained from calling Reba, but since then I'd phoned Windover daily, giving different names each time. The cool response from Denmark was the same: Mademoiselle Reba was not there. No further information.

Was she avoiding me, or had she left Jerningham's employ?

My secretary brought in the afternoon mail, envelopes slit with one exception: the envelope was marked *Personal* and it bore the imprint of Stockholm's Grant Hotel. I ripped it open and unfolded the letter. Written in flowing script it said:

> My Dear—DuVal forbade me to wear your Star of David so I resigned and moved away. I am here only long enough to collect my thoughts and make some plans for the future. I love you and will always cherish our wonderful night together—but it can never be more than that, so complex are our lives. Having known pain I could never inflict suffering on your wife and children. Please do not try to find me.

I stared at the letter and life seemed to drain from my veins. Then I forced myself to reread it, and noticed that Reba had written it four days ago. Where was she now?

The hotel telephone number was on the stationery, so I dialed it and asked for Reba Mizraki. Waiting, I saw my hands clench and unclench; finally the operator spoke: "Madame Mizraki is no longer here."

"When did she check out?"

"Yesterday, sir."

"Where did she go? Did she leave a forwarding address?"

"One moment, sir."

Hum of the overseas circuit. Finally, "Sir, there is no forwarding address."

"Thank you," I managed and replaced the receiver.

So she was gone. Utterly, irrevocably vanished.

For a quarter of an hour I sat without moving, staring at her handwriting, trying to find some solace in it, some hope. But there was none.

An intercom buzz interrupted barren thoughts. My secretary said the yacht broker was on the phone. I told her to say I'd phone him back.

The transaction in Ft. Lauderdale seemed long ago. I could not recall my former enthusiasm for the yawl. Sailing meant Southern seas and family. I wanted Reba.

The next call was from my father's office, confirming tomorrow's luncheon at his club. After that the bookkeeper came in with salary and other checks to be signed, and when she left I got up and mixed a drink at the cellarette. I was staring out of the window unseeingly when my private line rang. Like an automaton I picked up the receiver and answered.

My caller was Eli Pomerantz.

"We've been out of touch," he said, "and because I moved out of the Claxton I had no way of knowing if you'd been trying to reach me."

"I hadn't," I said.

"I telephoned a few times and learned only that you were out of the city."

"Yes," I said, "I was."

There was a brief pause before Pomerantz spoke again. "You sound preoccupied, detached. Did I call inopportunely?"

"Not really," I sighed. "It hasn't been a good day."

"Lev suggested we meet briefly. Do you mind?"

"Glad to," I lied. "When?"

"Five-thirty? St. Moritz bar?"

"I'll be there," I told him and replaced the receiver.

Half an hour with Eli and I could still meet Marcy in the Sherry-Netherland at six. A few drinks in public might do me good, curtail my brooding. Anything would be better than sitting here watching the ghosts of love swirl through the room.

Pomerantz was at a banquette when I arrived. I ordered a double scotch and he said, "Thanks for coming, this shouldn't take long."

He told me Bakhari had gone to Ireland, joined a one-time SS captain named Dieter Stoss and departed with him. A Bakhari lieutenant in Algiers was seen talking to a shipping company, and the information made Pomerantz apprehensive.

"Bakhari is imaginative," he said, "where Stoss is cold and efficient. And he knows a good deal more about mounting military operations than Bakhari." He sipped the colorless liquid in his glass. "Stoss knows logistics, communications, weaponry, demolitions, assault tactics: a complete German officer who happened to be also a specialist in commando-type raids." He rotated his glass with thumb and forefinger as though it were a chessman. "We must locate those two wherever they are. Any suggestions?"

"What can I tell you? I'm not a detective, not even much of an investigator." Marcy was waiting for me at the S-N bar. Where was Reba? Was she waiting for someone, too?

On the corner of a paper napkin Pomerantz wrote a telephone number and passed it to me. "I'll be here a bit longer in case Bakhari comes back. If not, my mission here is over."

I put the paper scrap in my billfold.

"If you get to Israel, look me up," Pomerantz said, "I'll be glad to show you Tel Aviv."

We shook hands and I left. Walking east toward Fifth Avenue I told myself that I had been right to withhold Atiqa's name and involvement. Reba had asked me to be careful to whom I gave the information. *If you care for me.*

And I was uncomfortably aware that with the information Pomerantz could probably locate Atiqa in the haunts where Reba had found her, and have her surveilled until she led him to Hossein Bakhari. But was any of that worth the slightest risk to Reba?

I went into the crowded bar, stopped at the entrance, and looked around. At first I couldn't see Marcy because a man's head was in the way, and then I realized why: he was kissing her. Marcy's hand curled around his neck, pressing his face close. They were devouring each other.

I swallowed and looked away, thinking this was as good a time as any to bring it to a close.

But for a while I walked the streets.

In an unmarked car two special agents of the FBI tailed Dr. Ghosan Afiz from the hospital to his apartment building in Falls Church. They waited in the outside parking area for a few minutes and then they went inside and took an elevator to the fifth floor.

As they walked down the corridor, one said, "Hope this doesn't take long. We'll be into overtime if it does, and I'll be in trouble with my wife."

"So what else is new?" Jeff pressed the doorbell.

Inside, soft, approaching footsteps. Through the closed door came the muffled question, "Who is it?"

"FBI." Jeff held his ID card to the eyehole. "Like to ask a few questions, Doctor. May we come in?"

"What kind of questions?"

"About a Mr. Tisdale."

A pause. Then, "I'll unlock the door."

But they heard soft footsteps going away.

Jeff rang the doorbell again, but the footsteps did not return.

"What do we do now?"

Jeff shrugged. "Starve him out, I guess. There's no warrant." He looked sourly at his partner.

"Yeah, but, Holy Christ, whoda thought we'd need one? The idea was to talk to him here rather than embarrass him at the hospital." He grunted. "What you get trying to do a subject a favor."

"Well, I'll go get a warrant. Dammit, traffic's murder right now. It's going to take a while."

"Maybe I oughta cover the rear exit?"

"No, stay put."

Suddenly they both smelled smoke.

Exchanging glances, they saw gray wisps curling upward from below the door.

"Clear and present danger," Jeff said. "Let's go, boy!"

Drawing back, they hurled themselves against the door. The lock splintered out of the wood and the door swung inward, Smoke filled the room. It came from a pile of papers burning on the carpet.

"Doctor! Where are you?" Jeff shouted while the other agent tried swatting out the fire with a large cushion. Wiping tears from his eyes, Jeff made his way through the apartment until he came to a bedroom door. It was locked so he kicked it in.

Dr. Afiz was lying on the bed. His left shirtsleeve was rolled up and his face was tranquil. The dark eyes held a fixed stare, and there was no carotid pulse.

The other agent came into the room coughing and wiping his sooty face. Abruptly he halted, stared down at the body.

An empty hypodermic was lying between the doctor's fingertips and his right thigh.

"Whataya know," the agent gasped. "Meet George Tisdale's killer!"

FOURTEEN

Jay Black (X)

My father said, "You seem somewhat glum today, as well as a trifle haggard."

I stirred my iced tea. "Comes from a shortage of sleep."

"Which in turn derives from mental unrest?"

"Sure does." I sipped from the glass. The tea made my throat less dry. "I stayed at the Athletic Club last night."

"May I ask why?"

"To avoid Sybil's questioning. Right now I can't handle it."

"Marcy? Is she the cause?"

I shook my head. "No more Marcy." Well, I thought, I might as well tell him. I had to tell someone. "Have we time for confession, padre?"

My father smiled. "There's always been time. Get it off your chest."

So I told him about Reba Mizraki, and every word felt as though it were wrenched from my soul. When I finished I was drained, but the unburdening improved my morale.

Samuel Schwartz toyed with a teaspoon, nodded at an acquaintance lunching at a distant table. Finally he said, "Sounds like a first class case of infatuation."

"So, what do I do?"

"What any sensible male does: see it through to its predestined outcome."

"Yeah, but I don't even know how to find her."

"That complicates things, doesn't it?"

"Lightning struck," I said, "then vanished. Doesn't seem fair."

"Don't rail at the Fates, Jay. Either you'll see her again or you won't. Meanwhile you ought to try not to suffer. I think you're rather enjoying it."

I had to chuckle. "Such sweet misery."

"We've all gone through it," he said calmly. "Yes, even I. It's not as though you sought out this Reba and invited entrapment; chance brought you together. Chance is all you have to look forward to for a resolution. I don't know of anything you can do except wait it out. If you were to try to trail her through Europe and the Middle East it could take weeks or months, and your business might fail. Even then there's not the least guarantee your quest would be successful."

I took a deep breath. "I guess work's the best therapy."

"Infallibly. Go out and get some new accounts, take courses at the New School or Columbia, do things with Sybil and the children. Take possession of your new boat and get to know it. Invite balance back into your life."

I nodded. "Good advice."

"I'll send tickets for the new Pinter play, tomorrow night. Sybil might like it."

"It'll be a change," I said, "for both of us."

He glanced at his watch on his vest chain and I was briefly reminded of Bryan Wellbeck. I hadn't thought of him lately.

I said, "So, thanks for hearing me out. Will you be in town for a while?"

"I'm taking Barbara to Bermuda for a week. Weather should be nice there now."

"Should be." April was ending. May was always a good month in Bermuda.

"Then I may go on to Israel for the anniversary." He began signing the luncheon check.

"What anniversary?"

"The Jewish State: May fourteenth. I'd like to see old friends again, perhaps for the last time."

"Nonsense."

"Well," he smiled, "like everyone else I'm getting old. And whatever you do, Jay, don't waste your youth. When old age finally comes, let it arrive without regret for things undone."

"Practically a license for profligate behavior."

"Within reasonable limits." He got up and we left the dining room. At the coatroom he embraced me briefly. "Whatever happens, you have my blessing."

I watched him walk away—a warm, proud, intelligent, and tolerant man, handsomely dressed in his gray, lightweight topcoat and Homburg—reflecting with a lump in my throat how fortunate I was to have him as my father, and how terribly I would miss him when he was gone. He punched the elevator button with the tip of his polished cane, turned, and waved goodbye.

I went to a nearby pay phone, got out the number Pomerantz had given me and dialed.

We met at the plaza in front of the UN building, found a bench, and sat down. Gulls hovered over the wake of a barge churning down the East River. All they had to do was wait; something would turn up.

I said, "Because of source sensitivity I had to think things over before deciding to tell you."

"What things?"

"I'll get to them. But first, will there be a big celebration in Israel on the Anniversary?"

"May fourteenth? Yes, it is traditional. Everyone comes."

"Parades, goverment figures, the whole schmier?"

He nodded. "Planning to attend?"

"My father is, and that's what gave me the thought."

"About what?"

"Al-Karmal's target. Some terrible act of destruction during the celebration."

His face seemed to pale. "You have a clue?"

I shook my head. "Not that, Eli, just a hunch."

"I should have thought of it," he said quickly. "It would be an ideal moment for a major act of terrorism. Yes, surely that's it." One fist struck the other palm. A woman stared at the sudden sharp sound.

"This hunch of yours came from your 'sensitive source'?"

"Indirectly." I hesitated, reassuring myself that with Reba gone from Windover, there was no way she could be harmed by the information. "My source told me that the driver of the getaway car in Prince Ahmad's assassination was an Arab woman named Atiqa. Through her you may be able to locate Bakhari."

"Yes," he said excitedly, "where is she?"

From my billfold I took out the address Reba had given me. "She's a journalism student at the University of Paris, and her apartment is over by the Gare de Lyon."

He almost snatched the paper from me.

After reading the address he said, "I wish you had told me before."

"It wasn't possible before. My informant's life could have been threatened."

He stared at me. "Is that so important when compared to the possible deaths of perhaps hundreds of Jews?"

"I can't answer that. You have the information now."

"But not the name of your source."

"You have the information. I hope it's of use."

"All right. I'm glad Rosenthal put us in touch. I appreciate this meeting. The focus has shifted from New York." He stood up.

"To where?"

"Paris now." He tucked the paper into his pocket. "I'll see where it leads."

"Mazel tov," I said, but he was already walking away.

That afternoon I decided to go after a public service account with a TV spinoff, and a hi-fi manufacturer whose product sales were falling behind Sony. I assigned research and presentation responsibilities, then phoned the advertising VPs of both corporations and arranged presentation time in three weeks.

My next call was to the Merrill-Stevens broker. He confirmed the yawl was ready for owner transfer and I told him I'd take possession in the next couple of days.

I phoned Sib, apologized for staying away, pleaded business responsibilities and told her to plan on seeing the Pinter play the following night.

"Courtesy of Samuel Schwartz?"

"Uh-huh. We lunched today."

"He sees you more often than I do," she needled, "but he keeps the family together, doesn't he?"

"Someone has to," I said blandly. "Let's take the children over to Mystic on Saturday, show them the seafaring museum."

"Well, I'd planned on visiting Mom and Dad. The children haven't been to Islip in a long time."

"True, but they've never been to Mystic."

"Mom'll be disappointed, but I'll defer to my lord and master."

"That's the kind of talk I like," I told her. "Wanta eat in or out tonight?"

"If I have a choice, let's go out."

"The Bruxelles? I'll make a reservation at eight."

"Jay, how very nice!" After a brief silence she said, "I bet you're feeling guilty about something."

"Everyone's guilty of something," I said, "but not everyone bothers to compensate. Right?"

She laughed. "You *are* a rat, you know."

"Have the cheese tray out by seven."

After I hung up I glanced around the office and realized my burst of activity had helped a lot. As always, Dad's advice was good.

But toward the end of the working day I found myself thinking about Atiqa, wondering whether Mossad's picking up on her could threaten Reba in any way. No, I told myself, by dropping out of sight Reba had insulated herself from terrorist reprisal. And not even Mossad knew her as my source.

FIFTEEN

At General Pickwood's morning meeting of the Kronos group the FBI representative was speaking: "Residue in the hypodermic syringe used by Dr. Afiz to kill himself is compatible with the poison traces found in the body of Tisdale."

Pickwood grunted. "Too damn bad your agents didn't grab Afiz before it was too late."

"There was no indication of criminal involvement, General. Afiz thought the agents came to arrest him, and did away with himself."

"And most of his papers," Pickwood said sourly.

"The agents saved some terrorist pamphlets in Arabic. Also the telephone number of a New York apartment rented by an Iraqi UN diplomat named Dinn. Mr. Dinn is no longer there, and the Iraqi UN delegation had no information about him."

Pickwood adjusted the elastic band of his eye patch. "Getting us no closer to the Kronos copy."

"Not at the moment, sir," the FBI representative said crisply.

Chief Brody said, "Tisdale's body was released to his son and daughter for burial."

"The crowning irony," said Pickwood, "is that VA funds will be used to bury the little bastard. And his widow's going to get his Pentagon annuity and GI insurance. Not a damn thing to be done about it."

The CIA officer said, "Dinn is an alias used by Hossein Bakhari. He's the leader of a terrorist group calling itself Al-Karmal."

"What does that mean?" Pickwood demanded.

"Haven't the faintest idea. But the Afiz-Bakhari link, however tenuous, is bad news."

Pickwood said, "I didn't think it could get any worse."

The CIA officer sipped water and continued. "From a liaison service we've learned that Bakhari is in contact with a one-time SS commando officer named Dieter Stoss. After the German surrender Stoss took the Odessa escape route to Egypt and settled down training anti-British, anti-Jewish commandos."

"That where this Bakhari knew him?"

"Stoss had a big reputation in militant Arab circles which is probably how Bakhari heard of him." He coughed. "Mossad thinks the Al-Karmal group is planning something very sinister and very big. At the Agency we think the plan is related to the copied Kronos document."

"My God," groaned the JCS colonel.

Pickwood sat forward and his good eye twitched. "You CIA guys been putting all this together and not letting me know?"

"General, these things don't fall neatly in place like a child's toy. Information fragments arrive disparately and at different times, often in connection with unrelated matters. We don't even like to *think* about the possibility I mentioned."

"But you *are* thinking about it," Pickwood said savagely, "so *I* have to be thinking about it, too. My God, Arab terrorists using *our* neutron bombs against Israel! Absolutely devastating to our foreign posture."

"Which is why the Secretaries of State and Defense have been informed."

"Oh? Just who informed them?" he said belligerently.

"My Director. On instructions of the President."

Pickwood worried his eye patch. "Who's got operational responsibility?"

"The Agency."

"You'll report progress here, of course?"

The CIA officer shook his head. "My instructions are to withdraw from further participation in these meetings, General, their purpose having been served. Any follow-up action will be taken by my Agency." He pushed back his chair, and said, "Excuse me, gentlemen."

"You . . . sit . . . *down!*" Pickwood roared, but with a brief backward glance the CIA officer left the room. Chief Brody allowed himself a brief smile, while the FBI agent stared fixedly at the wall.

Pickwood snorted, "Ever see anything like it? CIA bastards take,

take, take. Well, you can be damn sure I'll let the Secretary know the situation."

The JCS colonel mumbled sympathetically.

"Meeting adjourned," Pickwood snapped, "and keep all this very, very quiet. Like the President wants."

Mossad (III)

When Eli Pomerantz reached Paris, the Mossad delegate at the Israeli embassy was expecting him. Coverage of the Arab milieu was good, he informed Pomerantz, and placed a surveillance team at his disposal, having been instructed by Tel-Aviv to lend the major his full assistance and facilities. Pomerantz took an unmarked car and drove around the Twelfth Arrondissement, locating the Rue Lepeu building where Atiqa lived. It was a dead-end street whose buildings were old and badly maintained. A narrow alley ran behind the apartment building, and Pomerantz noted that it lacked fire escapes.

So, he thought, she'll have to enter and leave by the front door. Makes things easier.

Using alias documentation he rented a room at a cheap hotel a few blocks away and slept until nightfall. At a *brasserie* outside the Gare de Lyon he was joined for dinner by the leader of the surveillance team.

"Her place is on the second floor and she lives alone. By tomorrow we'll be able to move into the building next door. We'll set up a radio there to communicate with the car and the men on the street. From the university it's reported she doesn't have classes every day, so we'll try to establish her normal in-out pattern, where she goes, what she does when she's not in class."

Pomerantz bit into a roll. "There may not be a great deal of time, Zvi. If Bakhari's in France he'll either visit her or else she'll go to him. That's the assumption we'll work on. So her travel is important. Does she have a car?"

"I don't know. We'll find out."

"Could Bakhari be at her place now?"

"I knocked at the door, no one answered."

"Inconclusive." He sawed at a tough veal cutlet. "I'd say go in and search the place while she's away, but if she's the tough, smart, little bitch I think she is, she could have traps all over the place to alert her.

113

So we'll stay out for now. But there's got to be some motion soon. It's the last day of April."

Zvi said, "Is that significant?"

"Never mind." He chewed his food, barely tasting it. In Paris only the rich ate well, he reflected, and said, "We'll watch her for four days. If she doesn't make a move, or Bakhari doesn't join her in that time, we'll interrogate her."

"But that will tip Bakhari."

"Not if she doesn't survive. Be practical, Zvi."

"Yes, Major."

"She probably keeps a weapon or two nearby," he mused. "Keep it in mind."

"I always do." He ate a forkful of *haricots-verts*, then said, "I haven't seen Israel in nearly four years. How is it now?"

Pomerantz smiled. "The good time of year, Zvi. Everything blooming, the desert transformed." His smile vanished. "We must keep it that way."

Zvi nodded reflectively. "Do you ever get to see Minister Weizman?"

"Ezer? Less than a month ago."

"I met him once. He decorated me, shook my hand. That was after the Yom Kippur War." His face glowed in remembered pride.

"I'll remind him," Pomerantz said, got up and laid some francs on the table. "Have someone bring me a transceiver tomorrow. And I'll see you here at the same time."

"Good night, Major."

"Shalom."

Walking down the street to his borrowed car, Pomerantz found his mind focusing on Bakhari again. Atiqa was the only lead he had, although it was possible that with luck and bribes the destination of the Algiers shipment could be determined. Rosenthal had hinted at the possible use of an atomic weapon of some kind, but no more than a hint; even so it was an awesome possibility.

Before starting the engine he stretched back against the seat, easing tired muscles while he thought. Although the Russians had provided many weapons to the terrorists, no atomic weapon had ever been entrusted to them. Why not? Because they were undisciplined, petulant, and unreliable as the Russians well knew. Therefore, it was unlikely that the Algerian shipment contained anything of an atomic nature. His mind ruled it out, but the frightful vision of a mushroom cloud over Israel remained.

Where would Bakhari, or any Arab group, obtain an atomic weapon? The Israeli stockpile at Dimona was a closely guarded secret. Was it conceivable some insane attempt would be made to overrun it? Turn our weapons against us?

His throat tightened. Surely not, he told himself; their chances of success would be nil.

Unless they came by air.

Palms wet, he clenched the wheel.

It was close to midnight when Bryan Wellbeck entered the Israeli Embassy on 22d Street. Lev Rosenthal shook his hand and led him directly to his office. Door closed, Rosenthal said, "In my circles the suggestion has been made that Al-Karmal is planning to strike on May fourteenth."

Wellbeck sat forward. "You've heard something then?"

"No. But that is Israel's founding anniversary—leaving King Solomon aside—a time when government and people celebrate in Tel-Aviv. A time Al-Karmal might find an optimum occasion for a deadly blow: one that could not fail to focus world attention on the perpetrators." His hands spread. "I give you that, no charge, to add to the already boiling pot."

Wellbeck laughed bitterly. "So what do I do with it? It's no secret from you the Agency's only a ghost of what it used to be. I told you about the neutron weapons in the hope your people will be able to do something before something cataclysmic happens. Only don't, for God's sake, quote me by name."

"Ha Mossad knows how to protect its sources."

SIXTEEN

Al-Karmal (V)

As Dieter Stoss woke he sensed the body warmth of the Arab boy beside him, reached out and stroked absently. With a murmur Yusüf moved away.

Lying on his back, Stoss became aware of gray dawn—*morgen-grauen*—streaking the ceiling of the chill room.

For a moment he was in barracks again: Hitler Jugend, Wehrmacht, the SS, good *kameraden* around him; dead now, most of them. Frozen on the steppes; corpses strafed and bombed; swaying pendulums on gallows' ropes; carbonized in flaming tanks ... dead in a thousand ways, betrayed by the lunatic dream of an eternal Reich.

But he reminded himself, as always, that Dieter Stoss had survived; he had escaped Vitebsk and the frozen marshes, come through the Abruzzi rescue, the Ardennes finale, and survived a hundred other skirmishes and battles. . . .

And for what?

To show these witless bedouins the way to kill a thousand or ten thousand Jews?

Such an epitaph, he mused, is not devoutly to be sought. Still, the money is good and will provide me with a regal life in Argentina: a palace on the pampas, young boys and girls to tempt me, good food and wine; a splendid, tranquil life. So, what I am doing now is quite worth my reward.

He thought of the Jews who would be killed and found he was not entirely indifferent to their fate. For a lifetime he had been taught to revile, hate, and destroy all Jews, but that, like other hatreds burned out as he grew older. For the same money he would be as willing to destroy an Arab city had the Jews approached him, but they had not.

And so, he thought, I find myself in this strange, medieval place with dark-skinned Semites all around, preparing them to gain a triumph they do not deserve . . . and could not achieve without my skills and aid.

His thoughts drifted to the hairless boy beside him; Yusuf, whose almond eyes, dark lashes, and liquid movements had melted him last night. And who, now, as the graying lightened, he found repulsive as a just-raped elderly whore.

Presently, Stoss rose, went to the bathroom, and turned on the single bulb. Carefully, with scissors, he trimmed the white beard bristles that camouflaged old shrapnel pits, stood back and examined his reflection in the mirror.

At sixty-three, Stoss maintained a remarkable physique. Shoulders and neck thick and muscular; thorax and abdomen flat, the flesh discolored here and there by wound scars. His pectorals seemed turned from marble, and between them ran a downward-spreading furrow of thick, white hair.

Satisfied with what he saw, Stoss rinsed his face with cold water, got into a warm-up suit, and fitted running shoes to his feet. Then he went silently down the stone-stepped staircases and out to the dew-wet wagon road that led down through the fields.

Breathing regularly, he ran over the pebbled dirt, past overgrown pastures and abandoned orchards. Here a trellised arbor had been borne to earth by the weight of heavy vines. There a well remained, half-hidden by the long, wild branches of an unclipped rosebush. Land gone to waste; hard fought-for through the ages but fallow now.

A rim of sun began to gild the east. He saw it green the lindens and the elms, give life and color to the furze that clung beneath the bracken by the road.

The air was moist and clean; its freshness seemed to carry life into his lungs and pounding heart. He ran heavily, not sparing his body, welcoming the rhythmic shocks that toned his muscles.

Rusted harrows in the field, a top-fallen, gaunt-raftered barn beyond. He was reminded of makeshift crosses on a battlefield, but then the image faded and he pounded on.

When Stoss regained his room, his face was red, veins standing out like cords. Yusuf was gone, he noticed, but did not care. He stood under a drenching shower that chilled skin and quickened breathing, and then he dried and dressed and went down to the dining hall, warmed somewhat by a morning fire.

Yusuf was serving three men at the mess table: Bakhari was one, the others, strangers.

Stoss strode to the table and addressed Bakhari. "Who are they?" he demanded.

"Cuban comrades. Herr Stoss, may I present. . . ."

"*Comrades?*" Stoss snarled. "Whose comrades? Not mine, Hossein. I know nothing of these men. Do I need them? No. Your comrades? Get rid of them!"

Bakhari rose from his bench, face dark. "I am in command here. *I* say who comes and goes."

"Ah," sneered Stoss, "then it is *you* who will direct the operation. *You* do the planning then, Hossein; *you* bring the elements together. For you no longer need my services." Wheeling, he strode away.

He had reached the foot of the staircase when Bakhari called, "*Dieter!*" and the German paused.

Walking to him Bakhari said, "You are too hasty, my friend. Yes, I will send them away, but you should know that they are comrades who have helped me in the past, and. . . ."

"Dismiss them, then."

Bakhari spread his hands, shrugged, tried a placatory smile.

Loudly, Stoss said, "I have nothing to do with Marxist swine. Such fine soldiers! Machine-gunning blacks who carried only spears, napalming their thatched huts. *Mein Gott*, how I detest them!" He spat on the stone floor.

Bakhari recoiled, then his hands opened and closed.

Stoss said, "I'm going to my room. When I come down there are to be no Cuban bastards here. Then you and I will breakfast." He ascended the staircase without looking back. In his bathroom he urinated, flushed the noisy toilet, and when the sound died away he heard knocking at his door.

It was Yusuf, saying that the visitors had gone.

Smiling, Stoss rinsed and dried his hands, walked down the staircase. As he neared the table he knew he would have to question Bakhari now. Learn how much the Cubans knew. Find out whether already the operation was endangered. As he took his place, Bakhari said sullenly, "The explosives will reach Marseille today."

"And when will they arrive here?"

"Perhaps tomorrow. A day or so in any case."

Stoss bit into a hard roll, chewed, and said, "We have a schedule to maintain. A certain day in May, is it not so?"

Bakhari nodded.

"The radio equipment?" He swallowed a mouthful of syrupy coffee.

"Atiqa will inform me when she comes."

"Ah," said Stoss unpleasantly. "Your propaganda chief, so necessary to us all, so essential to success."

"Atiqa is an Al-Karmal fighter," Bakhari said stonily. "She is devoted to our cause, dependable."

"Very good, very good. Now I am reassured." He allowed Yusuf to slide a piece of fried meat onto his plate. "Those great fighters, Russian partisan women. . . . Let me tell you, they raped as easily as housewives."

"She is also my woman, Herr Stoss."

"Then see to her, Hossein. Trust her with *your* life. I will be sure not to trust her with mine." He slashed into the meat with his knife. "Today I am going to diagram the attack so everyone involved will understand. Are there watches for each man?"

"Yes, Dieter. Expensive ones."

"The old barn in the pasture, we will use it to simulate the attack. Tonight I will drill the Gaza landing party."

"I will inform them."

The meat tasted like horseflesh, rank and disagreeable. It reminded him of the long westward retreat through the snow. He put down knife and fork and stared at Bakhari. "I want to know about your Cuban comrades, Hossein. How much did you tell them? How much do they know?"

Mossad (IV)

Her Israeli watchers saw Atiqa leave the building shortly after dawn, too early for her to be going to the University. So she was followed to the Diderot Métro station, where she rode the underground as far as the Gare du Nord.

In the concourse she carried her small suitcase in the direction of the ticket windows, seemed to change her mind, and walked instead into the women's restroom.

From benches the surveillors bracketed the restroom door that was both entrance and exit, carefully eyeing each departing female. When, after an hour, they did not see Atiqa leave, one of them described Atiqa to a cleaning woman and tipped her to go in and see if she was there. In a few minutes she returned carrying Atiqa's suitcase. "This was in the trash receptacle. Could it be hers?" She opened it and it was empty.

Eli Pomerantz cursed his caller. "Oldest trick in the book. She took her costume in with her, changed into it and came out. You were looking for the suitcase, not the woman." He swore again. "Nothing was more important than to trail her to Bakhari. Oh, yes, that's where she's gone. Otherwise she wouldn't have troubled with disguise. Now she's on her way to meet him." He pounded his fist against the wall. "All we can do is search her apartment for any sort of clue. Are you capable of entering her place and searching it without being caught?"

"Yes, Major."

At four o'clock a three-man team opened the apartment door and went in. The apartment had a small kitchen, a dinette, and a bedroom. Methodically they searched the premises, finding at first only bundles of propaganda pamphlets, some textbooks, a copy of Meinhof's book *Bambule*, and a year-old photograph of Hossein Bakhari holding an AK-47 and giving the clenched-fist salute.

In the next hour they expanded the search and found a Vzor 7.65 mm automatic pistol stuffed inside refrigerator insulation. Encouraged, they tore apart mattress and sofa, but it was behind a sliding panel in the wainscoting that they finally came across the radio transmitter with its frequency crystal in place.

They could locate no diaries, maps, address-books, or written papers. Either she had destroyed everything telltale before leaving, or else she carried essentials in her head.

On receiving the search report, Czech pistol, and radio, Eli Pomerantz ordered Zvi to send in a fresh team to wait for Atiqa.

Two days later when she returned to the apartment, they were waiting for her.

SEVENTEEN

Jay Black (XI)

Aₓₜₑᵣ a pleasant family day at Mystic I flew down to Ft. Lauderdale, paid the balance on the yawl, and got it insured. The broker's sons volunteered to crew for me, so we sailed across the Stream to Bimini, had a good meal at the Red Lion and cruised back, reaching the dock just after dark.

I was sunburned and tired, but a message at the dockmaster's office turned me instantly alert. From a pay phone I called my answering service in New York. "When did Miss Mizraki call?"

"Just after ten this morning, sir."

"Go on."

"Just a moment. Yes, she telephoned from JFK, the Air Maroc office. She left a number where she can be reached."

"Hold on." I left the phone long enough to borrow pencil and paper from the dockmaster, and hurried back. When I had copied the number I said, "Anything else?"

"Miss Mizraki said she could be reached until nine tonight."

"Thanks." I hung up and dialed the message number. Heart pounding I heard a woman's voice say, "Flight Attendants' Lounge."

"Reba Mizraki, please."

"What airline?"

"Air Maroc, I think."

"Just a moment."

I gripped the receiver even tighter until the woman said, "Yes, she's coming to the phone."

The next voice was Reba's.

"Jay? Where are you?"

"In Florida."

"Oh, I was hoping I could see you before leaving."

"Where are you going? When?"

"Ten o'clock flight to Paris. I'm, as you may have guessed, I have a new job. With Air Maroc."

"Darling, I have to see you. But there's no way I can get to New York tonight, not before ten. Could you skip the flight and. . . ?"

"I wish I could. I need to see you, too. But, well, there'll be other times. I'll be flying to New York again. I'll try to let you know in advance, but as a new flight attendant I fill in where they need me."

"How long will you be in Paris?"

"Two days. Then I. . . ."

"Where will you stay?"

"George Cinq."

"I'll be there tomorrow. God, I've missed you. I can't tell you how bad it's been."

"You got my letter?"

"Yes. Reba, it didn't help. Just made things worse. I tried tracing you, but. . . ."

"I know, I shouldn't have just dropped from sight. But I saw this advertisement, talked with the Stockholm office, and flew down to Rabat. I . . . I was planning to write you again."

"Well, I should hope so!"

"Forgive me?"

"Only if you love me."

"Yes, I'm afraid I do. And you? Do you feel the same way?"

"It's been hell without you. So it must be love."

"It hasn't been easy for me, either. Darling, someone wants the phone, so I'll say goodbye." She paused. "Will I really see you tomorrow?"

"I'll be there. *Au 'voir.*"

"*Toute à l'heure.*" The line clicked off and I closed my eyes while the echo of her voice sounded through my mind.

Moving slowly from the phone I began thinking of what had to be done: New York for passport and clothes, flight reservation to Paris, some kind of credible story for Sibyl and the office. . . . Well, it would all fall into place.

The boys were coiling lines and sheets, covering furled sails and making themselves useful. I gave ten dollars to each and asked them to finish securing the boat. Then I grabbed my bag and taxied to the airport.

Mossad (V)

As Atiqa came into the dark room a head blow dropped her to the floor and knocked aside her long, blond wig.

Noah locked the door while Yehuda and Avram knelt and quickly gagged and blindfolded the stunned woman. Noah turned on a dim light so his teammates could put handcuffs on her wrists and ankles. He picked up her fallen purse, opened it, and emptied its contents on a table.

Yehuda got out a pocket knife and began cutting off her clothing. Atiqa bucked and fought, moaning incoherently as she tried to kick her captors. Roughly, Yehuda pulled off her shoes, and now she was naked before them.

Without the wig her dark hair was short, cropped like a boy's. Atiqa kept trying to kick them with her bare feet until Avram rapped her ankles with the cosh. Then she lay back, breathing in strangled gasps.

Noah stared admiringly at her full breasts and small, dark pubic triangle. What a woman! he thought, as he turned and began examining the contents of her purse.

Avram sat on her chest while Yehuda prepared a hypodermic syringe. Atiqa's body tensed as the needle entered her upper arm, and Yehuda snarled, "Easy, bitch, or you'll break it off." Presently he nodded and Avram stood up.

The three Israelis gathered around the table. On it lay a small amount of French currency and change, lipstick and eyebrow pencil, a ticket stub imprinted with the letters S.N.C.F. A railway ticket, third-class from its color.

"Well," said Avram, the team leader, "that might be useful. We'll ask about her travels."

Noah pointed at a thin gray disk he had separated from the other items. "For a letter bomb," he said. "Wonder what else we'll find?"

"Keep looking."

They shredded her purse, cut apart her shoes, examined every inch of her clothing, but found nothing else that was either lethal or informative.

There was no telephone in the apartment. Avram went to the window and extended his walkie-talkie antenna outside. He transmitted a code word, listened, transmitted again, and heard a scratchy acknowledgment. With a slight smile he depressed the transmit button and said in French, "The mouse is trapped."

"*Bon*! Proceed according to plan."

Avram telescoped the antenna and replaced the transmitter in his jacket. To his teammates he said, "Time to go."

Yehuda checked over the restored apartment for the seventh time: mattress and sofa resewn, pistol returned to the refrigerator wall, radio replaced in its cache. He doubted that even the woman on the floor could have detected evidence of their search.

They rolled her unresisting body in the carpet from under the dinette table. Noah and Yehuda hoisted the roll on their shoulders and Avram let them out of the door. As they went quietly down the stairs he gathered her wig and destroyed clothing and shoved them into a paper bag. He submerged the explosive disk in the toilet where it would dissolve, and put the rest of her purse contents into a plastic bag. Then he turned out the lamp and left the apartment, closing the door behind him.

The sedan was at the curb. He got into the rear seat and arranged his feet comfortably atop the carpet roll.

They carried their burden down into the basement entrance of a large home on the far side of Neuilly. Isolated by a large, walled garden, it was used as a summer residence by the Israeli Minister, but now was vacant except for the four who entered it.

Laying down the carpet roll, they cleared out a tool closet off the furnace room and placed plastic sheeting on the concrete floor. Then they unrolled the carpet and carried the unconscious woman into the dark closet, removing the gag so she could breathe more easily . . . and talk. They closed the locked the door.

The three Israelis went into the basement game room where a tape recorder and a large transceiver unit had been positioned on the billiard table. Avram activated the transceiver and made contact with his chief. In slangy French he reported their arrival and said the mouse was still asleep.

"How much longer?" came the question.

"Perhaps an hour."

That was the extent of the exchange, kept brief to avoid interception by French monitors who searched the wavebands continuously in search of just such illegal transmitting.

A car came through the gate into the grounds. There were six men, a small amount of personal gear in the trunk, and a crop-eared Doberman attack dog.

Eli Pomerantz got out and held the door for Dr. Hadani Shein, a white-bearded man of sixty who carried his medical bag. The dog handler got out, and with him the Doberman. Freed, the dog bounded over the grounds, returning promptly to the signal of a supersonic whistle.

The driver stayed in the car. The fifth man was a guard. The sixth, also a driver, got into the surveillance car and drove away.

Pomerantz gave instructions to the guard and dog handler, and with Dr. Shein carried their bags into the house.

Dr. Shein was a survivor of Buchenwald. One ear was deaf, and full dentures replaced smashed and rotted teeth. He lacked two fingers of his left hand. His sister's son, Nathan, had been killed in the terrorist rocket attack on the Avivim school bus for which credit was claimed by the Popular Front for the Liberation of Palestine.

As an internist Dr. Shein had an active metropolitan practice. He lectured weekly at the Ecole de Mèdecine and served as visiting professor at Tel Aviv University Medical School. But, above all, he honored the summons of Ha Mossad.

He said, "How old is the patient?"

"Twenty-five or so," Pomerantz replied.

"Weight?"

"Fifty kilograms. Perhaps a bit more."

They were walking down the corridor as they talked. Pomerantz opened the basement door and turned on the stair lighting.

The stairs gave out into the game room where the surveillance team was waiting. They got up respectfully and waited for Major Pomerantz to speak.

"Dr. Shein will be in charge," he said. "There is one guard on the first floor, another with the dog patrols outside. Your car has been taken away. Until the woman cracks or dies you will eat and sleep here while guarding her. Take turns preparing meals. Use the radio as little as possible. Dr. Shein's instructions are to be carried out without hesitation. Any questions?"

"No, Major," Avram said.

Pomerantz drew over a chair for Dr. Shein, who set his medical bag on the billiard table away from the electronic equipment.

Shein lighted a cigar and puffed until the end glowed satisfactorily. "None of you has worked with me before. Therefore, I am going to explain the technique in advance." He stopped and glanced around. "Can she overhear us?"

"No, Doctor."

"That is very important, silence. Much of what I hope to accomplish is the result of prolonged sensory deprivation: darkness, silence, lack of speech and communication. This is all preliminary, it seldom works unaided." He drew in on the cigar and exhaled a quantity of smoke. "When I deem the time propitious I will call upon certain chemical aids. One or two will be administered in her drinking water, others in her food and by injection. The overall effect is to daze and disorient the patient, render her incapable of exerting any willpower whatever. Eventually, as time progresses, she should develop a pseudo-affection for her captors. She will crave to talk and tell all she knows in order to ingratiate herself." He paused and looked at his listeners. "Should the patient withstand such comparatively gentle measures, there remains only one other option."

Avram said, "I think she's a hard case, Doctor."

Shein shrugged. "I am only called upon to treat hard cases, so don't interrupt. Eli, is there sulfuric acid?"

"Yes, Doctor."

"And electrodes?"

Noah held up a pair of insulated electric wires. The ends were bared.

"And there are, of course, bathtubs above." Shein flicked ash from the cigar and bit into it again. "Is the patient conscious?"

Yehuda quickly left the room. Presently he came back and said, "She's stirring."

"In restraint?"

"Yes, Doctor."

"Then I will examine the patient." He got up. "Have her vagina and rectum been searched?"

"Not yet, Doctor."

"A possibly fatal omission," he said severely. "Eli, make it standard procedure to search the private parts of all terrorist women who come into your hands." He opened his medical bag, took out a speculum and drew surgical gloves over his hands. Two rubber fingers flapped emptily against his left palm.

Avram led him into the dark furnace room, handed Dr. Shein a flashlight and unlocked the closet door.

Her position was slightly changed from the way she had been left. Narcotized sleep had relaxed her bladder sphincter and she lay in a pool of urine. Shein inserted the speculum into her unresisting vagina and with the flashlight peered inside. Then he repeated the procedure in her rectum. Standing, he flicked off the flashlight. "No poison, weapons, explosive, or message tubes. Let her lie in her excretions until I indicate otherwise. No lights in this furnace room. The only light she will see will be a flashlight trained at her eyes, and then only once a day when she is fed. Lock the door."

When they were back in the game room, Shein pulled off the surgical gloves and tossed them into a wastebasket. "Tomorrow she can have a quarter-liter of soup if she wants it. Be sure the feeding straw is plastic, not glass. I don't want to have to stitch her mouth and tongue." He picked up his cigar and drew on it. "Naked as she is she will begin feeling cold when she wakens. Doubtless she will scream. Let her. If you weary of her screaming you may gag her, but do not talk to her or talk with each other in her presence. Alone in a chill, lightless void she may begin to hallucinate spontaneously." He smiled grimly. "Better for her if she does."

Pomerantz said, "We're working against time, Doctor."

"I see." He looked down at his finger stumps. "Is it important whether she survives?"

"No."

"How long can you give my method?"

Pomerantz said sharply, "Doctor, every moment counts."

"You want results, don't you? Authentic information?" Ash flicked from his cigar. "Doubtless you can beat and twist tactical battlefield information from an Arab soldier, Major, but this subject is literate, intelligent, and experienced. She will have prepared advance defenses against questioning. If you go at her now with physical torture you'll get only first-level responses, and by the time you've checked them out she'll be ready with others. The case will be interminable. Two days spent on her at this time to elicit deep—and truthful—responses is far more profitable than the course I sense you favor." He touched Eli's arm. "This is my business and I've had to become skilled at it. Don't regard my program as needless delay. I want her information as much as you." When Pomerantz nodded slowly, Dr. Shein said, "Will one of you show me to my room?"

Late at night the Mossad radio monitoring team, tired from travel, met with Pomerantz in a soundproof embassy room. "We've come across an agent radio transmitter," Pomerantz explained, and displayed a Polaroid photo of the set's crystal. The frequency markings were clearly visible. A lieutenant looked up from the photo. "You don't have the transmitter."

"We returned it to its hiding place. Our hope is that the agent's cell will notice her absence and retrieve the set. If the set were not there the terrorists would immediately switch to other, unknown frequencies. As it is they have no reason to change."

The lieutenant said, "What else do we have to work on, Major? You're talking one needle in a thousand haystacks."

"Unfortunately so."

"No transmission times?"

Tiredly, Pomerantz shook his head. "You can set up in that artist's studio you used before. In Montmartre, up by Sacré-Coeur. I'll have you driven there. But I say frankly that I don't think you'll find what we're seeking in Paris. We're trying to determine where the agent went before we seized her. She rode a train somewhere, and returned within three days. So there's no time-distance indication. However, I'm having her probable train route retraced, and the agent will be undergoing interrogation." He looked at his hand and it was trembling from fatigue. "Because she may be involved in a plot against Israel, I want you to inform your Center of the frequency characteristics of this crystal, and I want that range monitored as soon as possible and for as long as may be required. All intercepts so acquired are to be flashed me immediately."

The lieutenant nodded. "I'll need to use the embassy radio room."

"Use it." Pomerantz forced himself upright. "The driver will wait for you. Oh, and don't use the telephone. If you need me, there's the special radio circuit."

"I understand. Thank you, Major."

As the men pushed back to stretch, the Lieutenant followed Pomerantz down the corridor and up the stairs to the third floor code room. Through a slit in the steel-faced door Pomerantz identified himself and vouched for the lieutenant. The radioman opened the door and Pomerantz went away.

I should return to the Minister's house, he told himself, stay with Shein and the others, but I don't think I'd make it. I'm too far gone.

He opened a small office on the second floor and sat heavily on a metal cot. With an effort he pulled off his shoes, lay back and closed his eyes.

We have Atiqa, he told himself, and none of her gang knows. Perhaps when they miss her they'll begin transmitting and we'll pick it up.

Or would the intercept, *if* there was one, come from closer to home? From Eretz Israel?

EIGHTEEN

Al-Karmal (VI)

NEAR midnight they began moving toward the Belgian border in three cars: Stoss, Bakhari, and six fighting men. Clouds occluded the moon, an occasional star showed through. With satisfaction Stoss thought that conditions were ideal for surprise attack. They reminded him of the night they glided onto the mountain top to rescue Il Duce on the Fuehrer's orders.

But his experience of Egyptian guerrillas did not encourage him to think that everything would go well across the frontier. It was one thing to hide behind a dune and snipe at Jewish water carriers; quite another to assault a bunker guarded by armed soldiers.

Despite their revolutionary fervor and training the Arabs were *untermenschen*. So, he thought, we'll see how it goes.

In the lead car he rode comfortably over the country road, Walther pistol holstered at his hip, visualizing how the storage bunker would appear in the dark. According to the Kronos inventory it contained ten 500-pound neutron aircraft bombs and forty 105 mm neutron artillery shells weighing approximately 25 kilos each.

The irony, he thought, is that the Belgians don't even know they're there.

Soon the three-car convoy turned off into thick forest, penetrating as deeply as possible before leaving the cars and continuing on foot.

Stoss' field compass gave direction to the march; small hand lamps helped them avoid obstacles as they walked through undergrowth, jumped across small streams. His pedometer told Stoss when they had crossed the unmarked frontier and were in Belgium.

He checked his wristwatch. On time. He gave Bakhari a thumbs up gesture and the Arab solemnly nodded.

Two kilometers of forest buffer zone and Stoss held up his right arm. The column halted and Stoss made his way carefully ahead.

Voices drifted through the still night air. Once again he glimpsed the sudden spurt of a lighter flame, and as clouds uncovered the moon he saw the long angular outline of the armored weapons carrier. Two men sat on a mudguard, the third perched on an open hatch.

Stoss beckoned Bakhari forward, pointed out the tank-like vehicle and said, "Go alone; I don't want them to take fright."

Bakhari pushed forward, called a name, and walked to the vehicle. The soldiers slid down the sloping sides and shook Bakhari's hand. Presently he turned and waved. Stoss and the others filed up to him.

One of the soldiers climbed up and began tossing down uniforms, eight in all. Then eight Wehrmacht-like steel helmets. The seven Arabs changed into Belgian uniforms, and when the stolen NATO rifles were in their hands again, Stoss got into uniform and buckled on the last helmet. It gave him a sensation of eagerness to be uniformed again, have his skull encased in good, bullet-warding steel. He stepped foward and said, "Which one of you can drive this?"

A soldier with a thin, silky beard said, "Me."

Without warning Bakhari shot the other two with a silenced revolver. The soldier-driver dropped to his knees and began to pray.

"Get up," Stoss snapped. "Act like a soldier. Take the controls." He had only contempt for Belgians. They had grown accustomed to defeat. It was their national policy.

Under Bakhari's direction men carried the two corpses into the forest. When they returned, the raiding party climbed up and into the weapons carrier, leaving the hatches open.

Stoss sat next to the white-faced driver. "Drive," he ordered. "Take us to the base. When guards challenge you, give the right countersign." He jabbed the Walther against the soldier's ribs. "*Verstehen?*"

"*Ja, ja,*" the soldier babbled.

"*Vorwärts!*"

The diesel motor hummed powerfully. Eight bullet-proof wheels turned and the big vehicle climbed off the shoulder and followed the country road.

Stoss watched the handling of the drive controls until he was satisfied he could take over. Not so different from a Tiger tank.

Half an hour later, an arrow-shaped roadside sign. *Chimay* it read. 8 *Kilomètres*.

Wind against his face, Dieter Stoss looked upward at slow-moving, bulbous clouds. The whiff of diesel fumes made him feel young again. Battle ready.

Mossad (VI)

From the closet where Atiqa was confined came a faint, high-pitched cry.

Avram put down his poker hand and said, "Have a look, Yehuda."

The Israeli laid his cards face down and got up. "No peeking," he said, took the flashlight and went into the furnace room.

Her cries were louder.

He unlocked the closet door and shined the flashlight inside. Atiqa was balancing unsteadily on her feet. She lunged forward but Yehuda shoved her back and she fell onto the wet plastic. "Pig!" she shouted. "Jewish pig! Get me clothing. Bring water!" She kicked at his ankles.

Smiling, Yehuda closed and locked the door. She was still yelling orders when he reached the game room. He resumed his seat and picked up his cards.

"Well?" Avram said.

"She's up and around," Yehuda said, fingering his stack of red chips. "That's one tough Arab whore."

Al-Karmal (VII)

The gate in the heavy chain-link fencing was surmounted by a tall, white sign. The black letters read O.T.A.N., and below it in much smaller letters: *Chimay*.

At each side of the gate stood a striped sentry box. From one stepped a guard armed with a rifle. Stoss nudged the driver who raised his head through the hatch. "*Babiole*," he called, Stoss tense beside him, ready to shoot their way in.

But the guard acknowledged the password. The other guard helped the first one open the gate. The driver hesitated until he felt the pistol barrel prod. Then he manipulated the levers and the armored vehicle moved ahead.

So far, so good, thought Stoss. "Storage bunker F-6."

135

When the driver said nothing, Stoss said sharply, "F-6."

Teeth chattering, the soldier managed to nod.

"In case you've forgotten," Stoss said, "it's at the end of the fourth street."

Outside the gate he had checked the time; only three minutes behind schedule. He had to steady the driver now, stay alert to any false move. Beyond the driver's profile he could see barracks, a motor pool, the base ciné, darkened for the night. A dozen lingering drinkers in the enlisted men's bar. Then the communications center, radio room topped by a tall antenna mast.

"Slow," he said to the driver, turned and gestured at Bakhari. One of the uniformed Arabs fitted bound sticks of gelignite into his pocket, rolled over the slating side and hit the ground on his feet. He ran toward the single-story building as the weapons carrier speeded ahead.

Stoss glanced at his watch: the explosive was set for a five-minute delay. If the Arab did it wrong, he'd kill him when he reached the bunker.

"Turn here," Stoss said, and the vehicle veered onto the intersecting road.

At the far end was the bunker.

"Approach slowly," Stoss ordered, and saw that the concrete bunker was ringed with newly-installed chain-link fencing. *Verdamnt!* Unexpected. He checked his watch: three minutes until the radio room blew.

The vehicle lumbered on.

Now Stoss could make out another unexpected addition: Set into the earth behind the fencing, and two or three meters in front of the bunker's access door was a low concrete pillbox.

Stoss swore again, and the driver gave him a nervous glance.

As the angle changed, Stoss could see the snout of a machine gun—.50 caliber, probably—sticking out of the pillbox slit. *Scheiss!* Was the slit too narrow for a grenade?

To the driver he said, "Another five meters and stop. Get out and go to the fence. Hail the pillbox and ask for a cigarette."

The soldier's face went bone white. He seemed frozen in the control seat. Stoss jabbed him viciously. *"Now!"*

Slowly the driver climbed out of the hatch, let himself down on the metal rungs. Stoss had his pistol out and cocked.

The soldier strolled to the fence, called something Stoss could not hear over the idling motor. He crawled over into the control seat and stared through the hatch. The soldier was urging the guard to come to him. He rapped on the metal fence.

One and a half minutes.

Gott in Himmel! His left hand clutched the steering control, and it felt like frozen bone. Would the driver bolt? Or. . . ?

A figure emerged from the pillbox rear, looked around, eyed the weapons carrier, and walked toward the fence.

With a shock, Stoss recognized the American uniform.

Another surprise. How long had *Americans* been guarding the weapons?

But there seemed to be only one, although it was possible a comrade manned the machine gun.

The American took a package of cigarettes from his pocket and passed it through the fence.

Thirty seconds.

The American wore no helmet, not even a cap. There was a .45 holstered around his hips. Personal weapon.

Fifteen seconds.

Stoss leaned back and sighted along the Walther barrel. Too distant for a certain head shot, have to settle for the chest, hope for the spine. To Bakhari he rasped, "Get ready."

The first shock wave of the explosion slammed into his ears a fractional second before the booming sound. Stoss squeezed the trigger and the pistol jumped in his hand. The American went down. Stoss saw the moon-pale face of the driver as it turned toward Stoss who got his chest in the sights and fired. With a choked scream the soldier staggered sideways. Stoss slammed the gear stick, hit the speed control and spun the weapons carrier ninety degrees into the fencing.

The heavy wheels passed over both bodies. The vehicle shuddered as it struck the fencing, then rolled on. The fencing collapsed, flattened, and the right front tire hit the pillbox roof. Stoss braked.

Climbing out of the hatch, seeing a blur of uniforms rush toward the bunker, he realized all lights on the base had gone out. Flames soared skyward from the rubble of the radio room.

Reaching down he grasped the demolition bag and dragged it with him to the ground. Bakhari was shouting orders in Arabic, sending the guerrillas to their assigned positions. One, Stoss was glad to see, went into the pillbox.

Lugging his demolition charges, Stoss strode down the sloping ramp that ended at the bunker's thick steel door.

Mossad (VII)

In a small conference room in the Knesset building Prime Minister Begin was closeted with two advisors: Defense Minister Ezer Weizman and Haim Ben-yomin, chief of the organization whose full name was Ha Mossad L'Tafkidim Meyubadim.

The hour was late. Begin spoke in a hoarse whisper. "Unlike your revered uncle, Ezer, I am not a scientist. What can you tell me of the neutron bomb?"

The defense Minister, hulking, imposing, leaned forward, his face drawn with fatigue. "The head physicist at Nahal Soreq spoke in theoretical terms. The neutron weapon—bomb, if you like—requires a concussive force for detonation. Unlike the nuclear bomb its danger lies not in explosive force and heat waves but in radiation. The nuclear components differ from atomic and hydrogen bombs. They produce waves of radiation that, though they have little effect on structures, cause exposed human beings to sicken and rapidly die. To our knowledge none has yet been used. The Americans developed and adapted the enhanced radiation device for aircraft bombs or artillery, to use against troop concentrations and heavy tanks." He paused. "Russian tanks."

Begin shook his head slowly. "Haim, how certain is it that these terrorists are acquiring such weapons?"

"Not certain, Prime Minister. We have . . . indications," Ben-yomin said. "But we have long thought it only a matter of time before terrorists acquired a nuclear device. Gaddafi has openly boasted that Libya will soon produce atomic bombs for the destruction of Israel."

Begin breathed deeply, coughed and wiped his mouth. "Used against Eretz Israel, then, the radiation weapon would have the effect of a sudden plague. Our population would die in the streets, in the fields, in their homes. But," he went on with a thin smile, "our buildings, installations, would remain standing."

After a moment Ben-yomin nodded. "That is correct, Prime Minister."

Fiercely, Weizman said, "Allowing the Arabs to occupy our dwellings, laboratories, and land without a shot being fired! Menachem, this could be the worst menace ever faced!"

138

Ben-yomin said, "Washington speculates that the neutron weapon may be used against us on our anniversary."

"All these things," Prime Minister Begin said tiredly, "sound chimerical, unreal. What you must prevent is nothing less than the death of Eretz Israel. If there is such a plan it must not be permitted to take effect."

Al-Karmal (VIII)

As he wired the plastic charges, Dieter Stoss could hear fire engines screaming, cars accelerating around the NATO base. He had pre-shaped the conical charges, embedded their detonators.

Four gray plastic cones covered the door hinges, a fifth the center lock. He backed up the ramp, unreeling wire, and led it around the side of the bunker where he knelt. Bakhari placed a heavy battery beside him. Stoss connected one end of the wire to a terminal, holding the other wire in his hand. "Tell them to take cover," he said. "All but the man in the pillbox. He will be safe there, able to give us protection."

From the side of the bunker Bakhari barked commands. The perimeter defenders got up and raced around the bunker to take up protective positions at its rear.

All clear. Stoss looked at his wristwatch. Then he touched the bare wire to the other terminal.

The ground seemed to rise under his feet. The concrete wall quivered to a tremendous blast as flame shot up the ramp and heavy metal fell clanking to the concrete.

The Arabs cheered wildly, thrusting their weapons skyward. Stoss walked around the bunker followed by Bakhari.

Smoke and dust veiled the ramp. As the guerrillas reformed around the bunker Stoss used his hand lamp to step over the twisted doors and enter the bunker.

There were aircraft bombs on sledges, crates of artillery shells. Stoss played the light over them, saw them painted yellow, the swirling nuclear symbol on each. Below, the stenciled initials: ERW. Stoss smiled. Enhanced radiation weapons. He felt Bakhari pounding his shoulder. But now, he thought, might come the night's most difficult moment. "Two shells," he said. "We will take only two of them."

"But, there are many here. I want them *all*."

Long ago Stoss had decided that the world did not need an

unlimited supply of neutron weapons in the hands of lunatic terrorists. "No," he said firmly. "Two. One to use, one for standby."

The Walther was in his hand before Bakhari could draw.

"Traitor!" the Arab yelled. "German swine!"

Stoss pushed the barrel against Bakhari's neck. "I have done what I agreed to do. It is you who want to exceed the agreement. I am going to kill you now unless you agree to a limit of two shells." His hand light showed Bakhari's wildly moving eyes.

"Quick," Stoss snapped. "Make up your mind. One shell will destroy Tel Aviv. What more do you want?"

"I . . . agree," wrenched from Bakhari's throat.

Stoss plucked the revolver from the Arab's belt. "I will protect you while you carry out the shells."

Two crated shells loaded in the weapons carrier, the assault party reboarded and Stoss backed the vehicle to the road, turned toward the main gate. They were halfway there before machine-gun-mounted jeeps raced toward them. Stoss braced for a fire fight, but the jeeps shot past without challenge.

Emergency lamps lighted the gate. It was shut, barred by two combat-dressed soldiers holding weapons. Ten meters from them Stoss accelerated the vehicle and crashed through the gate, the soldiers scrambling aside, firing shots that pinged off the armor flanks.

The moon lighted the road so that Stoss did not need to use headlights. He drove at maximum speed, wanting to leave the Chimay zone before communications could be restored and road-blocks established. Would Arabs have thought of destroying the base radio? he wondered. Hardly. They would have gone directly to the bunker wildly flinging grenades, shooting off their weapons, focusing defensive attention on them, and probably not getting out alive.

Five kilometers from Chimay he braked and turned off the diesel motor. Angrily, Bakhari said, "What's the matter?"

Stoss held up his hand for silence.

Off in the distance came the beating, thrashing sound of helicopter blades. A search party airborne, but so distant that Stoss could not see its down-pointing searchlight. I wonder where they think we're going? He turned on the motor and sped toward the French frontier.

Reaching the place where they had received the weapons carrier, Stoss steered it into the forest as far as the vehicle would go. Somewhere nearby lay the two Belgian soldiers, Stoss remembered, and thought it would be a long time before their corpses were found.

He turned off the motor, and in the sudden silence the night seemed preternaturally still.

In the weapons carrier nothing moved.

The raid had been successful. Two neutron weapons were in Bakhari's hands and none of his men was even scratched. My last assault, thought Stoss, and it was perfect.

Drained, he sat in the control seat, hearing murmured Arabic behind him as a shell crate grated on the floor.

The men would take turns carrying the shells through the forest, across the frontier, and to the hidden cars. From there to the chateau, and they could make it easily before dawn. After a day of rest, abandon Avesnes for the next hiding place, closer to Israel, where the Gaza group would rendezvous.

Tiredly he pulled himself through the hatch, climbed down the rungs to the ground. A little more travel, he thought, and then the final trip . . . to Argentina.

He looked up at the high, spreading branches, lifted his arms to stretch, and glimpsed Hossein Bakhari behind him.

"Don't move, Hauptmann."

Stoss felt a pistol muzzle pressing his spine. The sharp detonation seemed to obliterate his senses, his body. Paralyzed legs gave way and Stoss' body fell to the ground. He tried to move his arms, reach for his pistol, but he was powerless.

"German dog," Bakhari snarled. "With what you kept me from taking I could have ruled the world."

Stoss could not open his mouth, move his tongue. There was no pain but he knew that he was dying.

Dimly he saw his slayer turn away, motion the guerrillas into the forest, four men struggling with the heavy crates.

How will they position them? he found himself wondering. Then with satisfaction he told himself that without him they would be unable to detonate the weapon at its target. So, in destroying him they had lost their only means of triumph.

Cold, frightful, unbelievable cold enveloped his body; worse than the worst of frozen Russian winters.

III

"The fight against terrorism is primarily and fundamentally *our* fight. The business of liquidating the terror *our* business."

—Pinchas Lubianiker

NINETEEN

Jay Black (XII)

$\mathcal{P}$ARIS.

Mid-afternoon in Reba's room. While she was showering I sipped a drink and nibbled room-service snacks, decided to scan the complimentary newspaper that arrived with the tray.

Halfway down the front page: ATTACK ON NATO BASE.

BRUSSELS—(AFP)—NATO authorities today acknowledged that an assault on the Chimay support base was launched by a group of from eight to ten unidentified men wearing stolen Belgian Army uniforms. At least five military personnel are known to have been killed in fighting which witnesses say lasted less than ten minutes.

Under cover of darkness a stolen weapons carrier holding concealed assailants entered the base. Destruction of the base communications centre coincided with an attack on the apparent main target, a bunker used to store aircraft bombs and artillery shells.

The attacking group was then said to have driven rapidly off the base. The extent of their casualties is unknown.

One Belgian and one American soldier were slain resisting the attackers. Three Belgian Army radio technicians were killed in the explosion of the communications centre.

According to uncomfirmed reports the stolen weapons carrier was located this morning in a forested area near the French border. Three bodies in Belgian uniforms were said to have been found in the vicinity. Two of the victims have been identified but their names are being witheld pending notification to next of kin. Military sources would provide no information concerning the third victim, although it is believed he was not of Belgian nationality.

Destruction of the base radio transmitter hampered military efforts to organize a prompt search for the raiders. Base authorities denied that any munitions had been taken from the target bunker, but the area has been sealed off by armed guards and correspondents have been refused normal access to the Chimay base for an indefinite period.

One NATO officer who asked that his name be witheld could supply no motive for the murderous assault. However, Belgium's Minister of Interior speculated that the commando-like raid was carried out by antisocial elements protesting Belgian membership in NATO.

It is understood that investigations by civil and military authorities are continuing. No further details are available because of security restrictions curtailing official comment on the surprise attack.

I hardly heard Reba emerge. Turning I saw she had a towel wrapped around her body; with another she was drying her hair. It hadn't been easy to get a standby seat to Paris, but I was glad I had. The rewards were overwhelming.

"Interesting story," I said and laid down the paper so she could see it.

"Cigarette, please." As she smoked she read the story then looked at me.

"Arab style, don't you think? Hit-and-run."

"Arab? Guerrillas are everywhere. Urban and otherwise." The body towel dropped away and I caught my breath. With a smile she scooped it up and rewound it just over her breasts.

I said, "I suppose I have a sensitivity about Arab violence. Could be Al-Karmal."

"Or any of a dozen other groups. And the Interior Minister thinks it's home grown, not imported."

"C'mon," I said. "When the attack vehicle and three more bodies were found by the French frontier? My guess is the attack began in France and the attackers came back here, whoever they are. Terrorists show a fondness for France. Al-Karmal gunned down Prince Ahmad of Oman only a couple of miles from here. So, if I were in NATO I'd be scouring France for the guerrillas despite what the Belgians say." Lifting my glass I drank, speared a bacon-wrapped canapé. "The press account leaves too many unanswered questions. Raiders wouldn't have hit Chimay just for night-firing practice. There had to be something there they badly wanted. Either to destroy in the bunker, or carry away. It sounds as though there wasn't much organized resistance, so the guerrillas probably had time to do anything they wanted."

She was pouring thick, black coffee into a demitasse, then dripping honey into the cup.

"Anyway," I went on, "there's that mysterious third body. If it's not a Belgian corpse, they have to know its real nationality. So, why not specify?"

She resumed toweling her hair. "Security considerations, according to the story."

"To cover up incompetence, or to keep useful facts from the guerrillas? And the storage bunker, why *that* one? Had to be something significant in it or the press wouldn't be barred."

It was cool in the room. I drew the robe's terry-cloth collar around my throat. "Wonder if the full story will ever be known?"

"Does it matter?"

I lowered my bare legs from the chair. "I'm uncomfortable about my father's visit to Israel. He plans to be on hand for the big anniversary celebration the fourteenth. That would be a perfect time for some terrorist group—say, Al-Karmal—to hit Tel Aviv or Jerusalem."

She smiled. "Jay, you're becoming obsessed. Besides, the Israelis are capable of protecting the capital; they always have."

"And Ahmad's bodyguards were always able to protect him until the fatal day." Upending my glass I drained the rest of the scotch.

Towel across her lap, Reba began running fingers through her hair, separating long, damp strands before she applied the dryer.

"Atiqa," I said suddenly. "She drove the getaway car. Maybe she was one of the Chimay guerrillas."

Reba touched the side of my face. "Must we talk about it? We have so little time. I much prefer pleasanter subjects."

"Truth is, so do I."

"And should you worry about your father's trip to Israel?"

"I guess his welfare wouldn't be so much on my mind but for a curious incident not long ago. A man walking near us was gunned down by someone in a car. Ever since then. . . ."

"I'm glad *you* weren't hurt."

"There was never an explanation."

"Some day I would like to meet your father."

"He'll ask how well you make chicken soup."

She drew away. "Where I first grew up, Jay, there weren't many chickens . . . or anything else to eat."

I touched her hand. "Sorry, I was only trying to be light."

She rose. "And I was being morose. But, no more of that. Shall we go up to Montmartre and enjoy the view of Paris?"

"By all means . . . and then?"

"A restaurant of your choice. No, I think it might be safer if we dined in . . . here. Would you mind?"

"It's my preference. I don't want to share you, Reba. But . . . safer?"

"The Arab colony. Paris is where I found Atiqa, remember. And Air Maroc is Arab, so. . . ."

". . . you shouldn't be seen dining with a Jew."

As I looked up at her the towel fell away and the Star of David glowed between her naked breasts.

Al-Karmal (IX)

Seated on a crate in a small room on the top floor of the chateau, Buenaventura had been operating the radio transmitter while Hossein Bakhari paced impatiently. Finally the Cuban flicked off the transmitter and got up. "Waste of time, comrade. She's not responding."

"Then something has happened to her, I feel it."

Buenaventura shrugged. "She is a woman. Women often forget."

"She is an Arab woman, an Al-Karmal fighter. She would not forget. Atiqa was to have signaled her safe return, and she did not. So, something must have happened."

"We have other things—important things—to deal with, comrade: weapons and supplies to load, cars readied. . . ."

"See to them," Bakhari said irritably. "You and Marco. I will monitor the receiver until we leave."

"We should not delay," the Cuban warned. "Your weapons carrier was discovered prematurely," he said with tact, "so tracing you across the border will be the next step." He glanced down from the window at the open, barren fields. "They could come any time."

Bakhari seemed not to hear him. He turned on the receiver and sat down on the crate. The Cuban went out, closing the door and

Bakhari looked at his wristwatch. Yes, we should leave as soon as darkness comes; by daylight a three-car convoy would be too noticeable for even the imbecile French to ignore. He tapped his fingers on the receiver case. Suddenly he heard the key begin rapid clicking.

With an exclamation, Bakhari flicked on the transmitter, listened to the incoming call sign, then tapped out acknowledgment. Atiqa was coming on the air. She was safe!

But as he copied down the coded message his face formed a deep frown: Amir was transmitting, apartment empty, no trace of Atiqa. Instructions?

For a few moments he considered, then transmitted orders to Amir: leave the transmitter in its cache and abandon the apartment. Do not return to it. Make careful inquiries about Atiqa. You will be contacted.

As the acknowledgment came over the receiver Bakhari rose, then turned it off, glad that Buenaventura had not received the message. Atiqa's absence would distress him, perhaps make him and Marco withhold their help. She was safe somewhere, he was sure, but for the present it was better that the Cuban comrades did not know she was missing.

So, there was much to do. The schedule Stoss had drawn up must be adhered to. Even though, he thought, the German pederast is not among us to challenge me and interfere.

As he went down the stairs he regretted the half-million dollars he had been forced to give to Stoss. The money was somewhere in Switzerland, forever lost, unlike the money he had briefly given Tisdale, which could be used again. And again.

Men were moving through the chateau, collecting things to be taken, burning or destroying the rest. Bakhari sent two men to carry down the radio equipment and dismantle the roof antenna. Then he went out on the steps and watched the loading of the cars.

Eleven days remained.

Mossad (VIII)

As Amir left Atiqa's flat he was seized by two men who sapped him and carried his body back inside. There they bound and gagged him, fitted a cloth bag over his head and radioed Major Pomerantz for instructions.

"Take him to the destined place," Pomerantz ordered, "but only when you can do so securely."

Then from the Butte de Montmartre studio the intercept team reported having copied transmissions on the Al-Karmal frequency.

"Good!" Pomerantz slammed the desk noisily. "Coded?"

"Yes, Major, but I think it will yield fairly easily. It shows characteristics of a Fatah code we've already broken."

"Bring me the messages," Pomerantz said, "and I think I can save you some trouble."

"May I ask how, Major?"

"We've picked up the man who transmitted from the place we've been watching. Now, can you tell me where he was transmitting *to*?"

"Somewhere to the northeast. It came in so weakly we'd never have found it without knowing the frequency. The other set is distant, that's about all I can tell you."

"Well," Pomerantz said, "we'll see if the Arab wants to tell us."

For once, he thought as he left the desk, things are beginning to happen, coming into place. Either Atiqa or her cell member was going to have to talk. And soon.

TWENTY

WITH the President in his Oval Office were the Secretaries of State and Defense, the Chairman of the Nuclear Regulatory Commission, the Director of the CIA and the Chairman of the Joint Chiefs of Staff.

The President said, "The guard was killed, the bunker violated, and two neutron-tipped shells stolen, that's the bottom line. What's being done to recover them? What do the Belgians know?"

"Very little," said the Secretary of State, "and because the Belgians are unconcerned they're making no special effort to trace the guerrillas."

The President tapped his tea saucer. "Shouldn't we tell the Belgians?"

"That would be judgmental, sir," said the Secretary of State. "Within the NATO interface word would spread like wildfire. Soon every NATO government would be clamoring for a strict accounting from us." He glanced around the crescent of chairs. "For the record I was completely opposed to deploying those radiation weapons abroad. I felt then, as now, that the Soviet government would interpret the move as a very heavy provocation."

The Secretary of Defense said, "The plan, Mr. Secretary, was to carry out deployment in such secrecy that the Soviets would *not* become aware of it."

The President turned to the Director of Central Intelligence who said, "That depends upon the links, if any, between the terrorist group in possession and the Soviet Union. At the present we have no firm indications of such a link, so our assumption is that Al-Karmal perpetrated the theft for its own narrow purposes."

"How narrow?" the President asked.

The Director dabbed moisture from his upper lip. "An attack on the Jewish state."

"*Not* involving NATO or the Soviets?"

"Apparently not, Mr. President."

For the first time during the meeting the President seemed to relax.

The Secretary of State cleared his throat. "Mr. President, if only Israel's involved perhaps our best policy under the circumstances would be to do nothing."

The Secretary of Defense nodded. "The Israelis have atomic bombs. If they're subjected to Arab attack by neutron weapons wouldn't they take out Baghdad and Tripoli in reprisal? The Soviets would then promptly destroy Israel. And the United States would be involved."

"*That* decision," said the President coldly, "would be up to me, sir."

Pleased, the Secretary of State turned to the Defense Secretary. "Even supposing some Arab gang has the weapons, is it conceivable they have the technological expertise to detonate them?"

The Chairman of the Joint Chiefs responded. "Each crate of ERW shells contains an instruction manual so simply written that any NATO battery commander would have no difficulty using the warheads properly."

The President said, "What do the Israelis know?"

The CIA Director said, "Their service—Mossad—was informed on a strictly confidential basis that the Kronos document had been compromised, and a copy is undoubtedly in Arab hands. The Mossad representative was also told in general terms that this government had secretly sent neutron weapons abroad."

"But not the significance of the Chimay raid?"

"I'd say they've figured it out for themselves."

A lengthy silence permeated the President's office. Finally he said, "Well, you better tell them. We owe them that much. And with our warning it's possible they can work things out for themselves." He drank cold tea from his cup and grimaced. "None of you told me the stockpiles were so vulnerable they could be overrun by a few determined men."

The Chairman of the Nuclear Regulatory Commission felt his face flush. "Mr. President, our own studies, plus periodic assessments by Rand, have indicated just that. In fact the last Rand study came close to predicting theft of nuclear materials at any time."

"Why wasn't I told?"

"Sir, I personally delivered the study to you not six weeks ago."

"I haven't time to read all the shit you people bring me. Something that important, use the scrambler phone, that's what it's for. Now," said the President, "can anyone tell me what effect the explosion of a radiation shell would have on a city? Say, Jerusalem?"

The NRC Chairman glanced around and saw that neither the Secretary of Defense nor the Joint Chiefs Chairman was going to reply. Reluctantly he said, "If a one-kiloton neutron warhead exploded above Jerusalem at an altitude of three-thousand feet, exposed people in a thousand-foot radius would be paralyzed within five minutes and dead in two days. Anyone in a two-thousand-foot radius would die in six days."

Mossad (IX)

Dr. Shein returned to the game room, removed the stethoscope from around his neck and replaced it in his bag. After a sip of mineral water he said, "The subject is getting weak from dehydration. Either she is going to have to be force-fed fluids or coma will supervene and we will have lost her." He looked at Eli Pomerantz. "What is your decision?"

Pomerantz rubbed the side of his face. "We've acquired another subject for interrogation, a man, and we'll work on him for a while. I suspect he's much less knowledgeable than the woman, and I hope his willpower is considerably less. If so, then I have the luxury of waiting for the woman to break."

He heard a car coming over the gravel drive, gestured with one hand and a guard went up the stairs.

"What we must be careful of," said Shein, "is that she is not weakened to the point of incoherence. With all respect, Major, I suggest that she be fed at least a quarter-liter of fluid within the next few hours, in the process of which one of the hypnotics will be absorbed into her system."

Pomerantz nodded. "If that is your recommendation, Doctor. And if the arrival is cooperative I may be able to give you more time to break the woman without force."

"Which," said Shein, "I would much prefer, having seen far too much brutality in my earlier years."

Pomerantz went upstairs. One of the men who captured Amir was talking to the guard. Pomerantz went directly to him. "Good work."

"Thank you, Major."

"Take him upstairs," Pomerantz said, "and give him a bath. I don't want to waste time on this one. Has anyone searched his clothing?"

"No, Major."

"Do so. Then let me know when you're ready. I have a few questions."

The Carte d'Identité gave his full name as Amir ibn-Dakhil and he cursed in Hejaz dialect. According to an enrollment card he took courses in dialectics at the university, and a work permit showed him employed as a waiter in a bar on the rue Gay Lussac. In his wallet, taped to the back of a photograph, was written the name Atiqa and a radio frequency. A cheaply printed Al-Karmal propaganda leaflet was in the pocket of his shirt.

"Enough to hang him," Pomerantz muttered, and went into the bathroom.

Naked, the Arab lay immersed in a tub of cold water. Only his gagged, blindfolded head was above the surface. His hands were drawn behind him and manacled to the faucet handles. His feet were bound at the ankles. There was water on the bathroom floor from Amir's splashing.

"Listen, Arab," Pomerantz said harshly, "you are an enemy of Israel in Israeli hands. I would like to kill you and every other piece of Arab shit in Al-Karmal, and perhaps I will. But I will not kill you quickly. It will be slow and painful. Agonizingly slow and exquisitely painful. This I promise you." He blew cigarette smoke at the exposed nostrils; choking sounds came from the throat.

"Today," Pomerantz said harshly, "you grew worried about Atiqa, hadn't seen her in a while. Where was she? So, as a loyal cellmate you went to her flat. You found nothing, little Amir, and so you decided to use her radio." His voice became taunting, "A loyal little rabbit, Amir, so useful on occasion to Bakhari, but today you betrayed him." He paused. "Think of it. You betrayed Al-Karmal!"

The Arab's thin, ribbed body wriggled in the water. Some of it entered his nostrils and Pomerantz laughed. "You're wondering about Atiqa, aren't you? Wondering where she is, how she could

154

have let this happen." The timbre of his voice changed, became thoughtful, musing. "Atiqa is alive, Arab rabbit, and with us. Perhaps I will let you speak to her, that depends. First, we will determine if you care to save your life. Another of my alternatives is to return you to the *quartier* lacking penis and testicles; no longer the virile rabbit you perhaps were until today. An additional possibility is to free you and let your fellow Arabs learn of your cooperation. Ah, what revenge they would take on you!"

Amir's body shivered, rippling the surface of the bath. Pomerantz said, "Were you not Arab I could almost feel sorry for you. But listen closely: you transmitted to Hossein Bakhari, communicated by radio with him and he with you. First, you will tell me where Bakhari is. Then you will tell me where he plans to go. Later, *inshallah*, if I let you live, you will talk of other things. Many more things, Arab."

A guard wearing long, heavy rubber gloves lowered the bared ends of two wires near the bathwater.

"A sample," said Pomerantz, and the electrodes immersed.

As Amir's body bowed upward a gagged scream tore from his throat. His thin chest expanded as though from abrupt inflation. Water sloshed over the tub sides.

The electrodes left the water and the Arab's body collapsed. Pomerantz felt the racing carotid pulse. "Still with us," he murmured, then more loudly, "Arab, that is only a sample. We have acid for your hands, face, and eyes; a knife for your jewels." He loosened the gag and Amir's stentorian breathing echoed in the small tiled room.

"Where is Bakhari?"

Amir shook his head.

Pomerantz shoved it underwater. Bubbles began breaking the surface.

He removed his hand and Amir's head bobbed up, mouth gasping for air. Pomerantz let him recover and then he said, "Listen, Arab, a Jew is talking to you. Yes, a *sabra* who has seen much Arab butchery. There is no pity in me, no human compassion. Arab beasts raped my mother and sister, tortured my father, and burned them alive. Of my family I alone escaped, and that is why I am here: to deal with Arab animals. It is my life, my chosen profession. Where is Bakhari?"

Amir said nothing. Pomerantz gestured, and gloved hands pried

Amir's jaws apart. Pomerantz removed the gag, pulled out the tongue and nicked its tip. The Arab screeched, began spitting blood.

"Next," said Pomerantz as he rose, "the eyes, Arab."

To the guards he said, "Tell me when he is ready to talk."

Pomerantz went down to the billiard room to confer with Dr. Shein.

Using funnel and esophageal tube they dribbled liquid into Atiqa's stomach. Tube withdrawn, she tried to vomit up the fluid, but her retching was too feeble. Pomerantz shrugged; Amir would soon talk, and with his information they could check Atiqa's . . . when she was ready. From three floors above he could hear the Arab screaming, and the sounds of agony made him feel unclean.

Half an hour later he was summoned to the upstairs bathroom.

The tub water was dark pink, the submerged body barely visible. Blood dribbled from the Arab's mouth.

One of the guards turned on a small tape recorder.

Pomerantz said, "One question, Arab, and if you do not answer I will cut out your eyes. Where is Bakhari?"

Through the Arab's exhausted gasping, Pomerantz made out the name: Avesnes. He had Amir spell it. "Where in Avesnes?"

"A . . . a castle . . . an old chateau."

"How many men?"

"I don't know . . . a dozen."

Pomerantz went down the hall, woke Zvi and repeated Amir's information. "If you move quickly you may be able to seize them all. Take as many men as you need. This must be quick and thorough. If Bakhari gets away it may be our last chance at him."

Zvi swung his legs over the bed. "I understand. You are coming, Major?"

"I'd like to," Pomerantz said, "but I have things here I must attend." He pulled the team leader to his feet. "Go."

"Shalom, Major."

"Shalom."

As he walked away Major Pomerantz wondered how long Atiqa could hold out.

Jay Black (XIII)

From our table just off the Place du Tertre we could see the whole of Paris spread out below. Like a gilded serpent the Seine wound through the city; atop the Eiffel Tower aircraft warning lights flashed on and off. Beyond rose the somber outline of the Church of the Dome, surmounted by its barely visible cross. Eastward, the twin-towered façade of Notre-Dame.

We were drinking from small glasses of iced sweet vermouth, holding hands, watching tourists exploring the sights of Montmartre before climbing the steps to the austere white cathedral of Sacré-Coeur. Along the sidewalks Vietnamese and Algerian artists displayed their paintings, bargaining with shoppers. Music from a three-piece band drifted across the square. I looked over the railing and saw haze coming over Paris from the south.

With a sigh Reba said, "It's been such a perfect day I don't want it to end. And I don't want to leave Paris tomorrow."

"Don't."

"I wish it were so simple." She looked away, smiled at the antics of an organ-grinder's monkey, then her face sobered. "Jay, please don't be angry, but I haven't been fully truthful with you."

"Well," I said, "I've been waiting to hear you admit to two husbands and four children. Never mind, I'll bribe the spouses and adopt the children. Is there anything else?"

"Yes, if you'll be serious." Her hand covered mine. "When I wrote you from Stockholm there was something I couldn't tell you. And when I phoned you from New York it was, well, not the time or place."

I felt my stomach tightening. "This is?"

She nodded. "Since I leave tomorrow. Jay, it has nothing to do with the way I feel for you, believe me."

"That's a relief, a big one. So, tell me."

She breathed deeply and the gold chain around her neck glinted in the fading sunlight. "I left Windover for the reason I wrote you, and because I could no longer stand Jerningham. And I went to Stockholm. There I thought of you—more than you'll ever know—and I remembered your dedication to a cause, the cause of Israel. I thought of my life, my past, and decided that perhaps there was some way I could be of use. And so in Stockholm I went to the Israeli Embassy, mentioned my work for Weisenthal, and asked to be put in touch with Mossad."

"Mossad," I said. "Well, well."

"They had been looking for someone to fill the flight attendant position advertised by Air Maroc and asked me to apply. The rest is as I told you. I withheld only my working for Mossad."

"Hardly a crime," I said with relief. "From time to time I've cooperated with Ha Mossad. I passed them Atiqa's name and location, but I didn't mention you. No further confessions?"

Leaning forward she brushed my cheek with her lips. "My only concern is us. How am I to fit into your life, if at all?"

"You've become more of my life than I ever intended. So, whatever you do, please be careful. And stay away from Israel until after the danger's over."

"You mean the Anniversary."

"Yes."

She laughed liltingly. "Air Maroc does *not* fly into Israel. In fact my employers believe me Arab, otherwise I would not have been hired."

"Don't let them see our star." Reaching over, I fingered the gold suspension chain.

"I'm *very* careful. Besides, considering Arab modesty no one has an opportunity to see it."

"Can you tell me what you've been asked to do?"

"For the present, notice who flies here and there. And I carry messages."

"Well hidden, I hope?"

"Don't be concerned about that. I. . . ."

"What I'm concerned about is a gang of Arab terrorists taking over an Air Maroc plane; they don't care much for the kingdom. If you were on that plane. . . ."

She squeezed my hand. "I'd follow orders docilely, no heroics. You see, I have reason to fear Arab brutality. I was not quite eleven when I saw my mother raped. Then they turned on me."

Her face seemed suddenly to harden, and I realized for the first time that her beauty camouflaged a toughness I'd been unaware of. And it came to me how much of her background and origins was still unknown. In time, though, I would know everything about her. And I wanted to, needed to know. "Don't," I said. "Don't think about it, Reba. Where are you flying tomorrow?"

"Amman, I think, by way of Madrid, Cairo, and Tripoli, but I won't know the assignment until I check in."

"And from Jordan?"

"Probably a layover in Rabat."

"When will I see you again?"

"I wish I knew."

The green-jacketed monkey bounced over and I dropped some francs into his cup. The monkey bowed low, tail sweeping up in a seesaw motion. Both of us laughed and the organ grinder moved on.

In the center of the square the violin, bass, and piano were playing *Under the Bridges of Paris*. Blue haze lay over the city. The moment seemed so theatrically sentimental that I kissed the woman I had come to love. No one paid any attention.

Reba whispered, "I wish I didn't have to, but I must meet someone tonight. It won't be long. Then I'll hurry back."

"What time?"

"Eleven, near the Louvre."

"I'll go with you."

"No." She looked at me tenderly. "I must go alone."

Mossad (X)

In his Headquarters office Haim Ben-yomin studied the radio message from Eli Pomerantz. The major had not requested authorization to strike against the Al-Karmal redoubt; he had simply ordered it. Ben-yomin shrugged. That was the trouble with paramilitary types; their tendency to move precipitately and without consultation. Still, Pomerantz had proved himself at Entebbe and elsewhere, so his receiving authorization would only be a bureaucratic formality.

Let us hope, Ben-yomin thought, that the death of Bakhari will be an object lesson to other aspiring fanatics.

An aide knocked at the door before entering. "You are wanted at the Ministry of Defense. The Minister has received our report concerning the Chimay incident and wants to discuss it with you."

Ben-yomin nodded. Another missed dinner at home. Well, he might have tea or coffee and a sandwich with Ezer. The Minister understood these things.

A specially armored car took him over Derech Aza boulevard with its lighted shops and cafes, then circuitously through darker streets to Israel's Ministry of Defense.

Ben-yomin had to wait a few moments in the reception room before a uniformed colonel invited him in.

Usually courteous, Ezer Weizman dispensed with greetings and indicated a chair for the Mossad chief. Weizman paced back and forth, reminding Ben-yomin of an irritated bear. The Defense Minister was so large that Ben-yomin often wondered how he was able to fit himself into Spitfire cockpits when he flew against the Luftwaffe.

"So they got their weapons, eh?" Weizman said explosively. "And to use against Israel. Where, Haim? When is it to be?"

"Minister," said the Mossad chief soothingly, "by dawn the threat may vanish."

Weisman halted abruptly. Running one hand through his short hair he said, "Good news, then? Tell me, Haim."

Ben-yomin summarized how the Al-Karmal location had been discovered and where it was. "Even now," he said, "our men are closing in. Unless the Arabs have been warned, they will be unsuspecting. Then—*Paf!* They vanish."

The Defense Minister filled his lungs and exhaled. "Haim," he said in a controlled voice, "I have heard many predictions from you in our years together. Once, or just possibly twice, they have not come true."

"Unless the Arabs have been warned," Ben-yomin repeated, "our men will destroy them."

"You are not joking? You are serious?" A wave of one hand dismissed the thought. "No, you would not joke on so serious a matter." His tense body seemed to relax. "It's true?"

"It is as I have told you, Minister." He glanced at his wristwatch. "In a few hours we will know."

"Well, then," said Weizman, "there is nothing left to discuss, is there? Haim, my worries have vanished as the Arabs will." He put one arm over Ben-yomin's shoulders and hugged. "If Eli brings this off I will promote him; on your recommendation, of course."

"Minister," said the Mossad chief, "if Pomerantz succeeds I will forward that recommendation without delay."

Weizman's arm dropped away. "Should I tell Begin, do you think?"

Ben-yomin coughed a trifle nervously. "With all respect, it may be premature to inform the Prime Minister of a tactical plan that has not yet been carried out."

Weizman's thick eyebrows lifted. "Of course you will let me know immediately of any news?"

"Immediately, Minister."

"Thank you for coming, Haim. Now, go home, enjoy a good meal with your family. Shalom."

"Shalom, Minister."

Ben-yomin rode in silence nearly to his door. To the driver he said, "Return to the office and tell the duty officer to awaken me at any hour should there be news from France."

Then he went up the stairway to his flat, and as he was fitting key into lock he could already smell the delicious scent of the supper Leah faithfully prepared.

TWENTY ONE

Mossad (XI)

An hour before midnight Zvi's seven-man team located the chateau. While he moved closer to reconnoiter, taking advantage of bushes and a hedgerow for concealment, the other six men deployed in a spaced formation to cover the entire circumference as they approached. Zvi had said that no one must slip through and escape. The Israelis were armed with lightweight Uzi submachine guns, grenades, and dynamite. Two men carried flare pistols for illumination or signaling, and each man had a walkie-talkie radio.

Kneeling at the bole of a large elm Zvi scanned the chateau through night glasses. In the entire building only one dim light was to be seen, and the team leader found it discordant. His next discovery was the absence of vehicles; there was no transport of any kind.

Odd, he thought, that a combat group should hole up without the means to leave or escape. Could the Arab have lied?

It seemed unlikely. Major Pomerantz had been so positive, and Pomerantz had conducted the Arab's interrogation. So, what was the answer?

Two conclusions: either the Al-Karmalites (as he had come to call them) were awaiting an expected attack or they had abandoned the chateau.

Had they been warned?

If so, who warned them? Why? And how? Perhaps the prolonged absence of the Arab woman alerted them, or a message radioed to Bakhari by Pomerantz's latest captive. Whatever the reason, Zvi thought, it begins to look as if we came too late.

Using the radio he told his next-in-command that he was going in alone. While he did so they were to close within fifty meters and remain concealed. At any shooting they were to rush the chateau.

Zvi approached warily, keeping to the tree-lined side of a rutted road, and presently he noticed the fallen walls and timbers of an old barn. The structure could have weathered down, he reflected, but for the jagged ends of beams poking starkly at the sky. So it had been blown up, and not long ago from the whiteness of the splintered wood.

At least this was the place.

He lay in tall grass ten meters from the southeast corner of the building, chose a door at random, and sprinted to it, keeping low.

The door opened with a diminuendo creak and Zvi fingered the trigger of the cocked Uzi. Should he fire a burst inside to provoke return fire? Or should he go in stealthily and look around?

For a while he waited, heart pounding, and then he stepped in quickly onto a packed-earth floor.

Briefly he shined a light around. Old furniture, bales of hay, a rusted harrow. When he moved, rats scurried around. But no Arabs. He proceeded to the adjacent room, then decided to go up to the next level.

The steps were of smooth stone. The door opened into what once had been the manor kitchen. Strewn in a corner was a litter of empty cans, crumpled paper, and garbage. Zvi touched a tomato slice and found it still moist. The deep sink was awash with coffee grounds, so there was evidence of recent consumption.

He was aware that, if the main party had moved out, one or two terrorists could have been left behind to ambush pursuers. And any Arab refuge held the danger of booby traps.

So he went about his inspection with alertness and care.

The fireplace in the great hall held a bed of black ash where papers had been burned, the charred framing of what could have been a crate. On the long table were crumbs and food traces; mice skittered away, plunging headlong onto benches, the floor.

Zvi decided to have others explore the upper reaches of the chateau, then remembered the light that had been visible outside.

He played his flash on the staircase, saw no trip wires and went up quietly, holding onto the stone railing.

Slipping past closed doors he reached the room whose partly open door emitted a long finger of light.

Before pushing the door inward he hesitated. This would be the obvious place for a booby trap. On his knees, he extended the Uzi barrel to widen the opening. The door moved with a protesting creak and Zvi peered around. No bed frame or chairs in the room. No furniture at all. It was empty.

Almost.

In a dirty waiter's jacket, stained shorts, and bare legs, a body slumped against the wall.

At first Zvi thought the boy was alive, then he realized the strained smile was a death rictus. The open eyes, staring, were dull, lifeless. A spill of blood around the once-white collar drew Zvi's gaze to the throat. It was deeply cut, windpipe completely severed, slashed back to the spine. The edges were darkly crusted.

Zvi expelled breath he had been holding.

Still on his knees, to remain below window level, he reached the corpse and examined it from all sides. Taped to the small of the back were three grenades. A fine wire was wound around one safety pin, its other end fixed to a heavy nail driven into the floor. Lifting the corpse would have dislodged the pin and detonated the grenades.

The macabre find was, he thought as he wiped his moist forehead, final evidence the terrorists had gone. And with their strange turn of mind they had left behind an unwanted member to serve them even in death. Carefully he snipped the wire with cutters, then summoned the team for a thorough search of every room. Ashes were sifted, leavings examined, empty cans and rice bags counted to estimate the size of the departed group.

Finally Zvi ordered an end to it. As his team drove back through Avesnes, Zvi stopped at a telephone kiosk and called Eli Pomerantz to report failure.

Jay Black (XIV)

I was sitting in the George V lobby waiting for Reba to come back from her Mossad meeting when there was a sudden bustle at at the entrance. The *commissionaire* hurried in to hold open the door for an arriving couple. From the train of following baggage including four yellow scuba tanks I should have realized it was Ben Thatcher and his new bride, but it wasn't until he strode over to the registration desk that I saw his profile. I half rose to greet him then thought of complications and subsided into the chair. The movement caught his eye and he boomed: "By God, everyone *does* come to the Joe Schenck! Jay! What the hell are *you* doin' in a first-class hostelry?" He advanced on me and I got up. Ben gave me a bear hug and I waved weakly at Trudy who was dealing out passports to the *concierge*.

"What a coincidence," I said to my Houston friend. "Thought you were in the South Seas."

"Well, not for*ever*, buddy. Say, where's Sib?"

"Home. Baking cookies, putting up preserves, busy with macramé. You know Sybil, real homebody."

He chuckled. "Business trip, eh? Well, we've got some partying to do, unless you're averse."

"Wish I could, Ben, but I'm going back tomorrow."

"Hell, buddy, Paris is an all-night town. I'll pour you on the plane." He dragged me over to Trudy. "Baby, look what the bull just gored."

I kissed her dutifully and she made polite noises. "Why, Jay, how nice to see you. First friendly face we've seen in *days*. Isn't that so, Ben?"

"Aside from moochers, absolutely right. Jay, I suppose we can get room service here? Damn plane came in four hours late and we're in bad need of bed and bottle."

"'Round the clock," I assured him. "You'll have no problem."

"Air Chance," he muttered. "They can stuff it you-know-where."

"Now, now," Trudy said. "Honey, we're all registered and the porters are waiting for us."

Ben nodded. "Listen, Jay, how about brunch with us? 'Bout ten o'clock?"

"Sorry, but I'll be halfway to New York," I said, and saw Reba coming through the entrance. "Well, it was good to see you folks, and thanks for the great time in River Oaks."

Reba was walking toward me. Well, I thought, now's as good a time as any. So I made introductions and caught the obvious curiosity in Trudy's eyes. Ben made a low whistle of approval, and gave me an exaggerated wink. "Miss Mizraki," he said, "just *any* time you're down Houston way, we'd be proud to have you with us."

"Why, thank you." She smiled coolly, and Trudy said, "Of course, it would be delightful. Any friend of Jay's is a friend of ours." But her tone was chill with disapproval. To me she said, "Sybil's well?"

"Splendid."

"Remind her not to forget our class reunion, won't you? I'm counting on her in June."

"Depend upon it," I said.

"Well, 'nite, then." Trudy took her husband's arm and led him off.

When I looked at Reba she was smiling. "Unlucky you," she said. "Caught with The Other Woman."

"So it seems." I managed a smile. "Classical situation."

"Ummm. How are you going to explain me?"

"Given time I'll think of something. I know, you're my night-club guide, hired for the evening."

"An old Paris habitué like you? Try again." Reba was enjoying my discomfiture.

"How about . . . you're my tax consultant?"

"Better, but not fully credible. Still, it's not my problem, is it?" She took my arm, and her lips brushed my cheek.

Later in bed I said, "Where did you go tonight?"

"I told you. Why, Jay?"

"You told me you were meeting a contact by the Louvre. Reba, a few minutes after you left here I took a taxi to the Louvre. I stayed across the rue, in the arcade shadows, and looked for you. But you weren't there."

Her fingers closed my lips. "That's sweet of you, but you shouldn't have worried. My contact arrived by car. I got in and we drove through the Bois. So, that's why you didn't see me." She kissed the side of my neck. "I was elsewhere and quite safe. I'm sorry you were worried, Jay. But you mustn't ever do that again."

"I'm not crazy about your working for Mossad, but I can't order you not to. Mossad is a very tough organization, and its enemies are fanatical and vicious." I took her hand.

"Why shouldn't I work for what I believe in?"

"Because of the danger."

"I grew up with danger around me: danger from Stern and Irgun, the British, the Jordanians, the Palestinians. We never knew when a bomb or shell or grenade would explode in the refugee camp . . . and all too often one did. I've seen men, women, and children torn apart. . . ." She moved away from me.

"All the more reason you shouldn't discount the dangers. Let the Arabs have their kooky heroines; don't be a dead heroine for Israel."

"You exaggerate the risks, but I love you for caring so much." She raised on one elbow to peer at her travel clock on the night-stand. "Three hours, darling, and I must leave. So. . . ."

"Yes," I said, "let's make love while we can." But my mind was partly on her Louvre explanation—that seemed both plausible and contrived.

Mossad (XII)

After receiving Zvi's report from Avesnes, Eli Pomerantz drove to the Neuilly estate and woke Dr. Shein.

As the Doctor fumbled for his eyeglasses, Pomerantz said, "Time is slipping through my fingers like grains of sand. Bakhari's group is gone but if the woman can be made to talk there may still be time to interdict them before they can harm Israel."

Shein pulled on a worn bathrobe, stepped into slippers and said, "Let's go ahead."

In the game room Pomerantz itemized the instruments of coercion: pliers for finger and toenails, scalpel for the eyes, acid for hands and face, an electric curling-iron for anus and vagina. Shein regarded the instruments with distaste, opened his medical bag and took out a hypodermic syringe. As he filled it from a vial he said, "This may encourage the patient to reveal her secrets."

"Yes," said Pomerantz impatiently, "let us hope so. But with or without it she is going to talk."

A guard preceded them into the furnace room, and his flashlight showed an area of wetness below the closet door. "Quickly," Shein said and the guard unlocked the door.

As he opened it a foul outhouse smell spread outward.

The flashlight beam showed the naked Arab woman lying on one side in a pool of blood. Her mouth and chin were covered with blood.

With an exclamation Dr. Shein knelt and pressed the carotid artery, then shook his head. He took the flashlight and shined it at the mouth where the tongue extruded, then got up. "Her tongue is bitten through," he said, "so she could bleed to death and defeat you." He returned the flashlight to the guard. "It took great resolve, Major. One can only admire her courage."

The stench of excrement and death was nauseating Pomerantz.

He turned away and strode to the billiard room. When Shein joined him he said, "My fault, Doctor, not yours."

Shein voided the syringe and replaced it in his bag. "True, Major. Since you have no further need of me I will leave in the morning."

"Yes, thank you for your assistance." He looked up. "Can you help dispose of the body?"

Shein shrugged. "The medical school can always use cadavers for dissection. Call my office in the afternoon and I will tell you where to deliver it." He closed his medical bag. "Only one cadaver? What about your other subject?"

"I can't free him," Pomerantz said, "and I don't feel like killing him, not after this. To hold him here will tie up men who could be useful elsewhere. So, perhaps I'll have him taken to Israel. But not until he's told us all he knows about Al-Karmal's hiding places, the names of others in his cell." He took a deep breath. "Anyway, for now there's only the one body."

"You were counting on her, weren't you, Major?"

"Too much."

"What will you do now?"

"I don't know."

As the Doctor began walking up the stairs Pomerantz told himself that Atiqa had indeed defeated her captors. Her suicide left him with nothing to go on. There were no leads now to the destination of Bakhari and his terrorist gang, no indication of where they were going to strike. Or how.

And if I can't learn that, he thought, then all of this and everything else will have been useless.

Wearily he gave clean-up instructions to the guards, and walked outside. He stood in the clear, cool night and gazed up at the stars as though to find in them an answer to his urgent question.

Where had Bakhari gone?

Pomerantz was still outside when an embassy car drove up and a man from the Mossad office got out.

"Major," the officer said, "I'm to take over from you now. The car's. . . ."

Pomerantz stared at him. "Why?"

"You're wanted back in Israel, sir. There's a seat for you on the morning flight."

"Am I to return to Paris?"

"Apparently not, sir. My chief told me to plan on staying here. You're to take the car."

"I see." He looked down at the driveway pebbles, wondering if Weizman and Ben-yomin were somehow omniscient.

"Major," the replacement said less stiffly, "how are things going inside?"

"See for yourself," Pomerantz said, got behind the wheel, and drove through the gateway with a feeling of utter failure.

TWENTY TWO

Al-Karmal (X)

From Marseille a clandestine charter flight had carried them across the Mediterranean to Benghazi where they boarded a coastal freighter that landed them by night to the south of Tyre. There, on the eastern shore of the Mediterranean, close to the Israeli border and less than fifty miles from Haifa, Hossein Bakhari, two Cuban comrades, and a dozen followers took over a bombed-out Fatah settlement and prepared for the work ahead.

A day later they were joined by six men who had made the run in a Lebanese motor torpedo boat, and toward nightfall a helicopter came in. The Kamov helicopter bore no Russian insignia on its camouflage paint, having been used until recently by Cuban forces operating in the Ogaden against refractory desert tribes.

"So, Hossein," said Felipe Buenaventura, "it all comes together, does it not? As I told you, the Nazi Stoss is surplus to our needs."

Bakhari nodded agreement as they strolled the sands. Offshore, camouflaged with tarpaulins, was anchored the Lebanese MTB. The helicopter, rotor blades folded back, was hidden in the shell of a gutted store.

"I still think," said Marco, "that Jerusalem should be the target. Why not, comrade Bakhari?"

"Because it is a holy place for many sects and I do not want to be regarded as a complete barbarian. The act would alienate many nations whose friendship in time I will need." He smiled at the Cuban. "A pragmatic reason, comrade, and not because I have any lingering passion for Islam." He shrugged. "No more than you feel for the Roman Catholic Church."

Marco spat. "*Hijo de la gran puta!* That is what I think of priests and nuns. Oppressors, bloodsuckers."

"It is so," said Buenaventura, "despite the credulity of our mothers. But I understand your reasoning, Hossein. To strike against Jerusalem would shock the world because of worshippers at the so-called holy places. But Tel Aviv is even more appropriate: there we will slaughter only Jews without destroying Greeks, Muslims, and others with whom we have no present quarrel. Moreover, from Tel Aviv the Jews spread their capitalist tentacles around the world; the city is the giant brain of Zionism. Tel Aviv is thus the obvious target."

Bakhari sat down on the slanting side of a low dune and stared moodily at the sea. The two Cubans arranged themselves nearby.

After a while Buenaventura said, "I suspect, comrade, that you are thinking of the vanished Atiqa."

"It is true." He tossed a small pebble toward the shore. "With each passing day of silence my concern deepens. In my heart I feel that she has been taken, perhaps already dead."

Buenaventura patted his back in a comradely way. "Cheer up, you will return to Paris in glory and be reunited. I am confident of it."

"It is my feeling, too." Marco slapped his thorax. "In here."

Bakhari sighed, seemed to gather his wandering thoughts, and said, "Felipe, I think it is time for you to begin preparing our package for Israel. Marco, the torpedo boat is your responsibility. Be very sure the helicopter can be carried securely to our destination."

Marco nodded. "The crew brought sufficient barrels of extra fuel for the journey. Only tell me, comrade Bakhari, why you selected Gaza as our destination?"

Rising, Bakhari brushed sand from his trousers. "The area is unstable," he said, "and a large part of the populace is Palestinian. Even if the Jews do not yield Gaza to Arab rule, the Gaza people will be sympathetic to our cause, should we need local assistance. And we will locate our base only 64 kilometers from Tel Aviv. An hour's drive by car. By helicopter a twenty-minute flight. Those are my reasons, comrade Marco."

The Cuban nodded. "I admire your foresight," he said, and thought: or that of Nazi Stoss.

As they walked back to the clump of buildings that once had been a village, Buenaventura said, "I will do some work tonight, and more tomorrow. How far is the run to Gaza?"

"Seventy-five kilometers to the south—were we to head directly there by sea—but we will run west-southwest for twenty kilometers to avoid shore radar at Haifa and Tel Aviv, then turn toward land, running east by south to Gaza. A trip of more than a hundred kilometers. Three hours by our Lebanese boat." He gestured over his shoulder at the MTB offshore. "The moon is in its first quarter, giving us the gift of near invisibility, and Radio Beirut predicts good weather for our voyage." He looked at the Cuban. "Any further questions, Marco?"

"None, comrade."

A few paces on, Buenaventura said, "I will not fully arm the weapon until we are at Gaza. Then only just before the operation." He made a Latin gesture. "Some amateur radio operator could transmit on the detonator's frequency, and . . . expressively his arms outlined a mushroom cloud . . . "I prefer Israelis die rather than ourselves."

Lying on a straw mattress, Hossein Bakhari turned on the radio receiver and set it on Atiqa's transmitting frequency. The only light in the dirt-walled, earth-floored hut came from the glowing dials. He thought of Atiqa, of her face and hair, her breasts, her inexhaustible loins, her draining mouth, and told himself that if he did not love her—for love between revolutionary comrades was counter-revolutionary—then he desired her, wanted her with him to calm his spirit, discuss with her what he would do after unleashing the cataclysm on unsuspecting Israel.

From a pouch he took a wad of *khif* and began chewing it as though it were tobacco. The drug desensitized his tongue and mouth and soon a sense of well-being flooded his body. Languorous now, Bakhari thought of Sapphire and realized how seldom he recalled her to his mind, the little Jewish whore. Still, she had catered to his special pleasures, and when he returned to New York Sapphire would be there, waiting in his bed.

His mind conjured up fantasies of the many things they would do.

His eyes wandered to the radio receiver, its glowing dials, and he realized how useless it was to drain the batteries waiting for a signal from Paris that could never carry this far unless by some trick of the atmosphere. And he told himself that Atiqa was gone forever.

His hand brushed the toggle switch and the dials went dark.

Rolling on his back Bakhari stared through shattered roof timbers and saw the unwinking desert stars.

Those Jews who survive, he thought, will spend cold nights like this. And in the end I will annihilate them, too.

Jay Black (XV)

Sybil was lunching with me at the Pierre, toying with a large shrimp salad, while I ate a lamb chop and some cottage cheese. Neither of us had much appetite. She said, "Any more plans for foreign travel?"

"None I know of."

She sipped her bloody mary and put down the glass, extracted the celery sprig and chewed on it for a while. Then she said, "Two trips to Europe in less than a month. What's it all about, Jay?"

"I'm developing a foreign connection."

"Want to tell me about it?"

"When everything's in place."

Her laugh was short and thin, more like a bark. "Trudy Thatcher called this morning from Madrid. Said she'd seen you in Paris at the George V the night she and Ben checked in."

"I forgot to mention it to you." I gulped down more cottage cheese.

"Trudy also mentioned the young woman you introduced. Arab, she thought."

"Quite right."

"Is *she* the foreign connection?"

I nodded. "She and her husband, displaced Lebanese who managed to get their money out. They've bought a French cosmetics house and are looking for an agency to introduce the line over here."

"Trudy said nothing about a husband."

"He was outside in the limousine; Trudy and Ben hurried off to bed. Their flight was hours late and both were dog tired." I chewed a small bit of lamb. "The lady was collecting me."

"And did you get the account?"

"Still have to make a presentation, the usual."

"My, my. I understand the lady is *ravissante*. Have you thought of having her model the line?"

"There's been talk of it," I said, "but Arab husbands—especially wealthy ones—don't like their possessions on display." I choked down the last of the cottage cheese, swallowed iced tea to help it along.

"Speaking of foreign travel, your father phoned from Bermuda and was sorry to miss you. He and Barbara are on their way to Israel."

Momentarily my hand tightened around the cold glass. "He said he might go there for the Anniversary celebration." I sipped more tea. "Any details?"

"There was a cold snap in Bermuda, so they were leaving earlier than planned. It's probably a good deal warmer in Israel this time of year."

"Probably."

"I'd love to see it: Jerusalem, the Via Dolorosa, the Dome of the Rock."

"It's impressive. Of course the Wailing Wall means more to me than it would to you, might even turn you off."

"Oh? Why?"

"All the bearded Jews in funny hats."

"Well, I liked *Fiddler On The Roof.*"

"So you did."

In that moment she gave me a funny glance. It was lightning fast but it told me I hadn't succeeded in disguising the Paris encounter, and the subject of my foreign connection was likely to recur, thanks to Trudy Thatcher.

From my office I phoned my father's secretary and asked for his itinerary.

"Your father had the airline do his booking, Mr. Black, and all he said to me was he could be reached at the Hilton in Jerusalem or the Ramada in Tel Aviv. He also placed several calls to Israel and mentioned he might be staying at a government guest house in connection with the Anniversary celebration. He seemed very eager to be there."

"Yes," I said, "he is. And if you hear from him, try to find out where he'll be staying and when."

"Of course, sir. Two tickets to the new Albee play came for your father. Would you like to use them?"

"Yes," I said, "the reviews are good."

"I'll send them over."

I dialed Wellbeck's private number but his phone rang unanswered.

Two account executives came in to discuss demographics and ad distribution among radio, print media, and television. I went with them to the art shop and examined progress on the presentations being prepared for the stereo and institutional accounts I hoped to bring in. The graphics were moving along on schedule.

Back at my desk I went through the mail; no letter from Reba. Well, it would take a while for one to reach me from Rabat, if that was where her trip ended. She'd described her cooperation with Mossad as essentially low level, and that made sense. There were plenty of well-trained *sabra* women available for operations requiring higher skills.

A bulky envelope from Merrill-Stevens yielded registration papers and the yawl's insurance policy. Also a bill for dockage fees. Initially my plans had been to sail the boat down to the Virgins sometime in July, but now I had no plans at all. I was hoping Reba would come into Kennedy again but neither of us had any idea when that might be.

I was staring out of the window when my private line rang. I answered, and it was Bryan Wellbeck.

I said, "I've got a couple of things to ask you. First, would you run another file check on Reba Mizraki?"

Mossad (XIII)

"Lamentable indeed," said Prime Minister Menachem Begin, "that the Arab terrorists were able to escape from France, Haim." He peered through thick lenses at the Mossad chief and awaited a reply.

"Deeply lamentable, Prime Minister. I assure you our men moved immediately the hideout was known. But we know one of the radio frequencies utilized by Al-Karmal. The monitoring team we sent to Paris, which successfully picked up an Al-Karmal clandestine transmission, has been repositioned at our border to augment the intercept stations already at work. So, that is another potentially productive situation."

Defense Minister Weizman sat up, seemingly pulling himself

from introspection, and planted his elbows on the conference table. "Prime Minister," he said, "the Air Force has increased photographic overflights of suspect areas. Our borders are patrolled and guarded as though we were on the verge of war. The Navy is patrolling our coast, and we have doubled radar coverage of our frontiers. Once we locate this terrorist band I am prepared to strike quickly, regardless of territorial niceties."

Begin turned to his Minister of Interior, Arieh Winograd. "In a week Jerusalem and Tel Aviv will be swollen with visitors from every point in Eretz Israel: families, tens of thousands from kibbutzim, labor organizations, elements of our defense forces, and well-wishers from abroad by the thousands. I don't know, Arieh, if we should cancel our national celebration or whether plans should be allowed to proceed." He stared at the far wall. "There may be a Talmudic answer, but I am reluctant to expose my concerns to our religious leaders."

Respectfully, Winograd said, "Even so, it might be well to take a few into your confidence. Or is it that you lack trust?"

"Even among themselves they are seldom able to agree. I can't have the matter debated, sides chosen. Their concerns are different than mine. So I am calling on you for a number of things: a contingency plan to cancel the national celebration, with a reason given for the cancellation that does not mention a threat of Arab violence; increased internal vigilance to determine whether the neutron weapon has been brought to Eretz Israel, and last, in the event we are attacked, a plan to provide ambulances, doctors, hospital beds, medical facilities, food, water, and all other forms of aid to victims who may number in the hundreds of thousands. Police, defense, and fire units must assert control as soon as the attack is launched." He took off his glasses and polished them. "I assume current plans for casualty treatment and crowd control in the wake of conventional Arab air attack can be modified for this situation." He paused. "*If* we do not cancel the celebration."

Winograd said, "Prime Minister, forgive me, but I do not see cancellation of the festivities keeping the terrorists from attacking."

Begin replaced his glasses. "The thought is rather to minimize casualties, save as many of our people as possible from this new form of Holocaust should, God forbid, the terrorists unleash it on Eretz Israel." He turned to Ben-yomin. "Do anything and everything to ward it off, Haim, and let me know immediately of any

177

change in the situation, better or worse. Ezer, stay for a few minutes; the others may go."

Winograd and Ben-yomin left the room. When the door closed, Begin said, "What is the name of our reprisal plan?"

"*Trumpet*, Prime Minister. It directs atomic strikes against Damascus, Baghdad, Tripoli, and Amman. Your direct authorization is required."

Begin nodded. "Were I to do so, how long would it be before retaliation were underway?"

"About two hours, Menachem." The bombs would have to come from Dimona and other storage places, lorried to the hidden revetments for arming.

Begin shook his head. "Too long, Ezer, and I might not survive to give the order. So I will issue it now. But the bomb transfer must take place in total secrecy."

Weizman nodded. "It is also my desire to keep an effective number of those aircraft airborne from May thirteenth through the fifteenth. It will be hard on the pilots, but they can fly in relays, refueling aloft. This activity will be detected by American satellites, so I propose to tell their air attaché that it is merely a training exercise. We don't need American questions right now, nor the risk of American intervention as happened at Suez." His face darkened. "This is their fault, anyway: sending neutron warheads abroad and failing to guard them properly. So if the American weapon is used against us I don't want the paradox of Americans trying to keep us from retaliation."

"That brings me to my final point. We don't know who is going to survive the attack. It is my duty to appear in public during the celebration, but not yours. I want you to stay in a command bomb shelter so that you will be able to activate *Trumpet* if an attack should occur."

"Prime Minister, the Armed Forces will expect to see me in the reviewing stand!"

"That may be, but your higher obligation is operational, not ceremonial. In the postattack confusion someone—yourself— will have to activate the plan. And you must do so automatically. Before the echo of the terrorist bomb dies away."

Rising slowly he walked toward his desk, poured a small glass of water and swallowed an anticoagulant pill. Then he turned to the

Minister of Defense and said huskily, "Let Eretz Israel strike back even from the grave!"

Jay Black (XVI)

Wellbeck said, "I'll have the files checked on her again, go into liaison info. What else do you want to know about?"

"The situation in Israel."

He gave a short laugh. "You and a hundred others."

"My father's attending the Anniversary celebration on the fourteenth. Is it safe for him—or anyone—to be there?"

The long silence surprised me. When he spoke, his voice held an odd inflection. "Strange you should ask."

"I'm concerned for my father's safety in case of a terrorist attack."

"They take place all the time," he said in an effort at casualness.

"Like that NATO base in Belgium."

"What's the connection?"

"Look," I said, "I was in the Army. The story I read stank of coverup. Those hit-and-run artists went there for something and they got it. What was it, Bryan? CS? Nerve gas?"

"You've got some questions, and I want to ask something of you, so why don't we get together? There's no peace to be found here so I'd welcome a trip to New York. How about it?"

"Tomorrow?"

"I was thinking of tonight."

My desk clock showed a few minutes after four. "What time?"

"How's eight sound?"

"A little rushed," I said, "but I'll have dinner with my family and expect a call from you. Is it likely to be a long night?"

"Not especially. By the way, heard from Lev lately?"

"No, I think he's in Israel."

"Your publisher friend in Denmark's tried reaching you at Parlay. The old dear sounded distraught."

"Want me to phone him?"

"Not until we've talked. Anything new on Reba I'll bring with me."

He didn't phone until eight-thirty, so I had time for dinner *en famille*, some story-book reading with Susan and Michael, and a prebedtime romp. Wellbeck had a room at the Westbury where I joined him a little before nine.

Vest unbuttoned, tie loose, collar open, Wellbeck looked untypically disheveled. He took one of the sitting-room chairs and said, "You reach a point where business is no longer either gratifying or fun, and I've been on that edge for just about a month. Frankly, I'm worn out, Jay. I'd leave if I could find someone to take over from me, but from my level down the talent runs pretty thin. Anyone with experience or ability is overseas and overworked; what's left around Washington are typists and trainees fresh out of The Farm, and far from ready for decision making."

"That why I'm here? So you can unload on me?"

He sighed. "Want a drink? Coffee?"

"No thanks."

He went into the bedroom and returned with a travel-size bottle of J&B. He poured liquor into a small glass, added ice and water.

I said, "What about Jerningham's call?"

"How about me talking and you listening?" He sipped watered scotch, grimaced, and wiped his lips. "What do you know about the Chimay incident?"

"What I read in Paris the day after it happened."

"That's what I was afraid of. What I'm going to tell you I've passed to Mossad in strict confidence, and I expect you to continue to preserve secrecy. Okay?"

"Okay."

He made himself comfortable in the chair, drank more scotch, and told me Bakhari's group, Al-Karmal, had attacked the Chimay base and taken two neutron warheads. They were probably in Arab territory for the moment, he thought, but one intelligence estimate had Bakhari and the weapons heading toward Israel. Wellback said the Israelis had the best chance to stop them. He drank again before going on.

"We know from past experience that the Israelis do what they judge to be in the best interest of Israel even if it conflicts with U.S. policy. I recall to you the unprovoked Israeli attack on our communications intelligence ship *Liberty* at the onset of the Six Day War, an episode shamefully covered up by the Johnson Administration. Present thinking is that, should some Arab group—even if disowned by Arab governments—launch an atomic attack on Israel there will be immediate atomic retaliation by the Israelis, and the entire Mid-East—if not the world—will face nuclear war. That, of course, is totally against our country's policy and desires, but we have very little leverage on the Israelis. So we're reduced to a sideline position of cheering Israeli efforts to locate and destroy Al-Karmal before the terrorists can assault Israel."

"Swell," I said, "usual U.S. impotence. Aside from my father being in Israel why lay all this high-level stuff on me?"

"Jerningham. Better than anyone you know how understated he can be. Well, he sounded gleeful, as though he couldn't wait to divulge information he plans to publish, and which he implied concerns a large-scale attack on Israel."

"Why would he want me to know?"

"Because, presumably, this will persuade your 'principals' to come up with the big money he's been asking as soon as events prove him right, as he was in predicting Prince Ahmad's murder."

"But that source is . . . ," I said quickly, thought better of it and broke off. I'd never told him what I told Eli Pomerantz, and this was not the time.

"You were saying?"

"The source is unknown."

"Is it? When you came back from Denmark I felt you were holding out on me, now I'm convinced of it. How did Jerningham know Ahmad was going to be assassinated?"

"All right," I said, "no big deal. The prediction came in a letter."

"A letter from whom?"

"Al-Karmal."

"So he just went ahead and published it?"

"What did he have to lose? He's a fabricator. The letter offered him a fifty-percent chance of lucking out. As it happened, he did."

"And he confided all this to you?" Wellbeck said drily. "Or was it his helpful female assistant, Reba Mizraki?"

"It was Reba," I acknowledged. "Anyway, she quit Jerningham."

"What reason did she give?"

"Couldn't stand his anti-Semitism any longer."

"How convenient," Wellbeck said, then, "Would it crush you to know you've been had?"

"By whom?"

"By the lady herself. You gave me her name and I ran it through our files. Nothing adverse turned up, remember?"

"So. . . ."

"A computer can't answer what it hasn't been asked." He sat forward. "Did you know she'd worked for Egyptian Military Intelligence?"

"She told me. And before that she'd worked for Simon Weisenthal." I was about to tell him Reba was now a Mossad agent, but decided not to; her life was too precious to me.

"Listen to me: Mizraki is one of several names she uses. Among the Egyptians she was known as Nouri Farraj, that being her husband's name."

"*Husband*?"

"Oh, she's a widow now, has been since he was killed in the Beirut fighting. She's a highly intelligent, highly capable agent, this Nouri—or Reba, if you prefer—and her life is devoted to the Arab cause. Perhaps she worked for Weisenthal, but she definitely worked for various organizations within the Palestine Liberation Organization. Including al-Fatah."

"That can't be," I said, but a feeling of desolation had taken root; Wellbeck would not lie.

He grunted. "So that's how it is: you love her. Doesn't the incongruity shock you?"

"If she were an Arab agent."

"Jay, Jay, would she tell *you*? Mid-East loyalties are fluid. Would she prejudice her ideals, risk her life being frank with you? Does she know you have dealings with Mossad?"

"She probably does, because. . . ."

"She made a play for you. Look at it logically. You arrived at Windover and became a target of opportunity. Get your brains out of your scrotum. Did you confess your relationship to my organization?"

"No." I felt almost sick over what Wellbeck had been telling me. But it had to be the truth. The indications had been there; clues, nuances that I'd avoided adding up. Wellbeck had given me the bottom line.

He said, "Where is she now, Jay?"

I shook my head. If anyone was going to track her down it was going to be me.

"Obviously you know. So I'm going to say this: she's an enemy of Israel, and I'm warning you to stay away from her. I think too much of you to have you become another victim of Nouri Farraj a/k/a/ Reba Mizraki. And I need you to conclude business with Jerningham."

"Send someone else."

"Who? Even if I could find someone else there isn't time to establish him as you're already established in Jerningham's mind. The old fraud is trying to reach you, Jay. Why? Because he visualizes an ensuing flow of gold. My God, the situation's perfect to squeeze him."

"Squeeze him for what?"

"For what we were discussing before Reba/Nouri unsettled you: the substance of what he may know about a planned attack on Israel. Obviously he's not going to divulge it over transatlantic radio telephone, every major government monitors such conversations. He wants you there, Jay. We need details, not a general statement, because we already assume an attack is planned. Have a few sherrys with him, pick his brain. It's the only lead we have."

"*Possible* lead."

"All right. Compared to this, everything else you've helped with is insignificant. You're resentful over what I've told you about Reba, but drop the hostility and see Jerningham."

He went over to his coat. From an inside pocket he took out a ticket folder and a sealed envelope. "You can fly over and back in twenty-four hours. Is that asking so much?"

Wordlessly I took the folder and envelope.

"There's enough cash there to take you to Israel in case you decide you ought to get your father out."

"Thoughtful of you."

"Incentive. And while you're en route to Copenhagen try to revise your view of Reba. If she gets the idea you know what she really is, you're dead."

TWENTY-THREE

Al-Karmal (XI)

BETWEEN midnight and three o'clock Bakhari and Felipe Buenaventura drilled the Gaza landing group in disembarking from the MTB, getting ashore with arms and equipment, and setting up the radio transmitter within a manned perimeter. Secured atop the MTB, the Kamov helicopter resembled a mantis crouched and feeding on a larger prey.

By four o'clock the camp was asleep, except for guards in their positions.

Small-arms fire woke Bakhari, who rolled off his mattress, grabbed his Kalashnikov, and came up in a crouch. Peering around the mud wall he heard four more rapid shots, then silence. Heart pounding, he glanced at his wristwatch: 05:11. The shots had come from landward, in the dunes. Who had fired? Guards or infiltrators?

He was considering whether to go out or wait for the Cuban comrades to check the guard posts when he recognized Saidu's voice calling, "Come quickly, we have killed two Israelis!"

On the street, jogging toward the dunes, Bakhari was joined by Buenaventura, who said, "If the Israelis are dead, why are we hurrying?"

"There may be more," Bakhari retorted, angry at the Cuban's logic. But when they had struggled over the sand Saidu's flashlight showed two bodies in Israeli caps and uniforms sprawled in death a few meters apart.

"Turn off the light," Bakhari snapped. "Rashid, take four men and patrol the dunes. If you encounter a large force withdraw. If you find stragglers, kill all but one and bring him in for questioning."

Five armed men moved silently across the sands.

Kneeling, Bakhari played the flashlight beam on the nearest body, ripped open the jacket, stared at Arabic tattooed across the bloodied chest and cursed. Buenaventura said, "What does it mean?"

"It means these two were Arab fighters wearing Israeli disguise." Another exclamation and he turned off the light and rose. "Still, it makes no difference. We would have had to kill them since they are not of Al-Karmal."

Buenaventura nodded. "Let them be brought in and hidden in one of the houses. The uniforms will be useful. And until we depart, comrade Bakhari, I suggest our vigilance be increased."

"Yes, there must be a nightly patrol." Turning he began walking back to camp, the Cuban at his side. "As an Arab I must regret the untimely death of any Arab soldier, even those whose loyalty is to Habash or Arafat. Had these two lived through May fourteenth, their loyalty would have flowed to me."

"Undoubtedly," Buenaventura said. "Our stroke will be two-fold: desolating Tel Aviv and uniting Arab military might under one leader, you. When that is accomplished, governments will bow to you."

For a while Bakhari said nothing. Then as they moved onto a littered street he said, "A year ago the concept was only a vision. Now it is so close at hand I feel as though the power were already mine. I long to see the Western world dying, dead, as it will be when we destroy every Arab oilfield, eliminating everything but the trickle necessary to supply our Arab needs. Then the Christians will learn to exist as Arabia for so long existed. Like this." His hand swept an arc around the ruined, mud-brick village. "Christians will be the new scavengers, beggars existing from Arab charity."

Buenaventura said, "Once, comrade, I may have doubted your vision but I never questioned your resolve."

To the east the sky was beginning to lighten. Bakhari reached the entrance of his three-sided hovel and unslung his weapon. Four men carrying the two corpses came down the street. He watched them pass and called out a reminder to rinse blood from the uniforms. He was about to gain his mattress when Buenaventura said, "Since we are alone, a word, comrade?"

Bakhari nodded.

The Cuban said, "I want to make sure that it is your intention to destroy the helicopter when the weapon detonates?"

"Yes."

"I thought you might want to fly in it over a dead Tel Aviv."

"No."

"Very well." He shrugged. "That is your affair, comrade."

"Entirely," Bakhari said. "Now let us get some sleep."

When the camp was quiet, Bakhari turned on the radio transmitter and keyed the call word four times: A-S-I-F-A. Storm.

For a while he listened, hoping Atiqa would acknowledge, but realized it was futile. He turned off the set and lay back to sleep.

Israeli monitoring stations at Ma'alot, Nazareth, and Tubas recorded the transmission, but it was too brief for direction triangulation.

In less than an hour Mossad headquarters was informed of the radio intercept. As Haim Ben-yonim remarked later to Major Eli Pomerantz it was frustrating not to be able to locate the Al-Karmal transmitter, but at least the frequency was still in use. Perhaps over the few remaining days it would be used again.

Jay Black (XVII)

At Kastrup airport I was met by the same uniformed chauffeur driving the same black Bentley limousine. It took me through late afternoon traffic up the peninsula, through the outskirts of Copenhagen and onto the highway that led to Hillerod.

The trip took three-quarters of an hour, and when we reached the entrance to Windover I was surprised to find the gate open and no attack dogs visible as we wound up the mansion.

This time, no Reba to greet me as I walked up the steps, but a footman met me under the portico and ushered me in to the atrium where the fountain glistened under the varied lights of the stained-glass dome.

Du Val P. L. Jerningham rose as I entered his study and said, "Welcome again to Windover. It's so good of you to come." He was wearing a green velvet jacket with embroidered lapels, Cambridge-gray flannels, and slippers matching the jacket. The rise of a turtleneck sweater hid the loose flesh of his throat.

I said, "I could hardly refuse the opportunity," and took his thin hand.

"Something to slake the dust of the road?"

"A little iced akvavit should do it."

"Light sherry for myself." He gestured at the footman and indicated a chair for me. "Your bag is being taken to your room, Mr. Black. I thought we might have a preliminary conversation now, after which a nap might be mutually beneficial. Dinner will be at eight-thirty. Then, in civilized fashion we will repair here for a final exchange of views."

"And information."

"Of course." He seated himself again and it seemed to me that he appeared unusually frail, close to exhaustion. With a thin smile he said, "The charming Reba will not grace our table this evening for she is no longer in my employ."

I raised my eyebrows in polite interest.

"Come, come, Mr. Black, it was quite apparent that you were much attracted to her."

"I was?"

He nodded. "Alas, her loyalties were not to me alone. She was— how shall I say it?—working for one of the Arab intelligence organizations."

"A penetration?"

"Exactly. A penetration agent. To what end I know not, but once I was sure of her duplicity I bade her depart forthwith." His hands spread fanlike. "Although Windover now lacks her grace, the security of my operation is now hermetic."

"Well," I said, "that ought to relieve you a good deal . . . fewer worries."

The servant returned with our drinks. The akvavit must have been kept sub-zero in the freezer, I thought as it chilled my teeth.

After sipping his pale sherry Jerningham said, "You will of course recall my intelligence coup in predicting the assassination of the Omani prince by the Arab group calling itself Al-Karmal."

"I remember."

"In consequence of that and other situation appreciations the *Western Europe Intelligence Review* gained a gratifyingly enhanced reputation for accuracy. This new credibility has been reflected in subscription list additions that you may find substantial." He sipped more sherry and I drank as much akvavit as I thought wise. "To continue, Mr. Black, I am in possession of information of so sensational a nature that, once published and authenticated by subsequent events, it cannot fail to persuade your principals that their participation in my project will be worth every dollar I ask."

188

"Quite a claim."

"Indeed. And I would not have sought your return to Windover were I not fully able to satisfy you of its legitimacy."

"You indicated it concerns some sort of attack on Israel." I shrugged. "Israel is attacked every day, sir. Its borders are porous. Settlements are raided, bombs explode in marketplaces, terrorists commander aircraft, school buses are machine gunned, roads mined. Surely your claim is not based on such repetitive happenings."

"Far from it." He paused, savoring the moment. "Suppose that I alone of all the savants, were accurately to predict an atomic attack upon the State of Israel?"

I widened my eyes. "*Atomic* attack?"

"Precisely that, sir."

I swallowed. "Then I would want to know the date of the attack and the name of the attacking nation."

"And so you shall, sir, in general terms, of course. But I find myself tiring, and at my age one can only surrender to fatigue. So let us suspend our conversation for now. Your room is awaiting you, and then we will dine, refreshed."

I finished my drink and stood up.

Jerningham rose slowly. "You return to New York tomorrow?"

"My plane leaves at noon."

"And you will be aboard it, sir, with substantial proof of everything I have said and will say."

A servant led me up a winding staircase and showed me to a large guest room. It was too frilly for my tastes, but I saw that my clothing had been hung up and a dark suit laid out.

Setting my travel alarm for eight I turned out the lights and got into bed. An hour and a half's sleep was only a small part of what I needed.

Backfires.

Repeated backfiring. Some crazy hotrod kid teasing the starting line was the way my mind interpreted the flat, irregular explosions. Some far away, others just outside the mansion.

As my mind quickly revived I realized I had heard it all before in 'Nam and fear gripped me. I wasn't in 'Nam, had no weapon of any kind. Yet there was shooting.

Hastily I pulled on clothing and went to the window. Through a gap by the shade I could see the white-red flash of weapons, abruptly heard the main door slam open, another fast burst of automatic-weapons fire. Something fell heavily to the floor.

Windover was under attack.

My first thought was to lock my bedroom door, but the thought was so ridiculous I almost laughed aloud.

Instead, I threw my laid-out clothing into the closet, arranged a comforter over the bed and stepped into the closet, closing the door except for an inch through which I could scan the dark room.

Footsteps pounded along the corridor. Doors burst open as the intruder neared mine.

Looking for me?

A kick slammed my door inward and I saw the snout of a weapon moving back and forth to cover the dark interior. Abruptly the weapon vanished as the man moved on. He was short, and dressed in baggy clothing. A scarf covered his face to the eyes. He had black hair.

The door of the adjoining room was kicked open. No shots.

Two more doors, a third.

From the open doorway filtered Jerningham's high-pitched voice protesting. Whatever he was trying to say ended in a long burst of fire.

From footsteps I judged that others were joining Jerningham's killer, and for no particular reason I remembered the Alsatian attack dogs that were supposed to guard Windover. Had they been silenced beforehand as a convenience to the attacking party? How many men were there? Why had they come? What did they have against DuVal Jerningham?

I thought these things standing close to the wall, frozen, motionless.

Heavy footsteps returning along the corridor. Guttural voices muttering unintelligibly in a language that sounded like Hebrew.

Mossad? What reason would Mossad have for raiding Windover? Surely Jerningham's anti-Jewish bias wasn't reason enough for killing him. *What in hell was going on?*

As footsteps descended the staircase I left the closet and eased the room door halfway shut, positioning myself by the hinge side in case a clean-up squad looked in. Never again, I swore, would I travel unarmed; the feeling of helplessness was sickening.

From below an explosion shook the house, then another. Grenades, I thought, and heard the sharp crackling of fire taking hold.

Stunned, I stood behind the partly-open door, heard heavy footsteps clumping toward me.

Just then my bedside alarm went off.

Its shrill peal rasped my eardrums.

The footsteps stopped. Suddenly a gun barrel thrust inward.

Without even thinking I grabbed the barrel and jerked. A man came with it and he was off balance. I tripped him and he crashed down still gripping the weapon whose muzzle was pointing at the ceiling. My foot smashed his hand from the trigger guard to keep him from firing. I kicked his head until his arms fell away.

Holding the Kalashnikov I dragged him into the bedroom and pulled down his face-scarf. Never seen him before. Just a swarthy, mustached man.

As I knelt I began to question the wisdom of my reaction. Would others come looking for him? My alarm, unwound, had stopped ringing.

Outside, half a dozen shots came from the general area of the explosions, and it occurred to me that the attackers were picking off whoever was fleeing the fire.

Using his scarf, I gagged the fallen warrior, undid his belt, and bound his hands behind his back. The sheath of a long, curving knife was inserted between trousers and spine. I removed it and thrust it into my belt. I put a fresh clip in the Kalashnikov and laid it on the bed while I dragged the man into the closet that had been my refuge. I tore down my suit coat and got it on. Then I went to the doorway and cautiously peered out. No sign of life.

From outside, distant, indistinct voices.

I went quickly to Jerningham's bedroom and saw his body lying half off the bed, a line of bloody punctures across his chest. Just to be sure, I felt his neck artery and found it still. He had died quickly, and as I got up I wondered why he had to die this way. Some Byzantine reason, no doubt; killed by persons who viewed their reasons sufficient.

Well, I thought, as I turned away, whatever information he planned on giving me was going to be buried with him.

The scent of smoke drifted down the corridor. It wasn't visible yet, just the presentiment. I stared at the only escape route I knew—the staircase—and wondered who was waiting below.

And then I remembered Jerningham's mother, the elderly lady who passed as his mother. Had she, too, been killed?

Quietly I moved down the corridor, peering into each open door, and at the far end I found her.

She was sitting alone in a dark room, back upright against the bedstead, tears coursing down her withered cheeks. When she saw me she uttered a short cry. I put a finger to my lips and went in.

Softly I said, "I'll get you out of here. They've set the place on fire. Can you walk?"

Dumbly, she gestured at the nearby wheelchair.

I shook my head, went to her window and looked out. Scarfed attackers were gathered around a car I hadn't heard arrive, but then, I'd been asleep.

Now I was wide awake, every nerve aware. The group outside was surveying its work. They'd left the old lady to smother and burn, but they hadn't known about me. Flames showed them clearly. Mrs. Jerningham began to cough.

I went into a bathroom, soaked two towels and told her to hold one to her face and breathe through it. The smoke was getting bad. If I didn't move soon, retreat would be cut off. I thought about the killer in my closet but it was no more than a passing remembrance. He'd gotten himself into this; if he was very lucky he might get out.

I said, "Is there a back stairway? One of the servants use?"

Still coughing she managed to nod, gestured with one hand.

"I'm going to carry you," I said. "All you have to do is relax."

Bending down I got her over my left shoulder, and as I raised up I was surprised at her lightness; not even a hundred pounds. Closer to eighty.

With my right hand I wrapped the wet towel over my face and trudged from the bedroom. Where she had pointed there was a service door but when I opened it smoke billowed up, and I shut it quickly, blinking tears from my eyes. I felt her body stiffen, tried to speak soothingly and retraced my steps toward the head of the staircase.

A downward glance showed no guerrillas in the knee-high smoke, so with the Kalashnikov in the crook of my right arm, the old lady over my left shoulder, I gripped the banister and started down.

The question now was whether I would be seen by the lingering watchers. The open entrance door helped feed the encroaching flames. I saw two bodies dimly through the smoke, servants both.

I kept going down, trying to stay clear of the watchers' line of sight, and then the manic thought occurred to me that I should be calling the fire department. Built-up tension made me laugh inwardly with an overlay of hysteria. I could feel my shoulders shake, and so could my passenger who stiffened again. Even if I knew what number to dial, what would I say? In what language? And how foolish the urge was: everyone in the house dead, the place a roaring pyre.

Although for the moment, Mrs. Jerningham and I were alive.

As we entered the atrium, flames reflected from the pool, giving it the tint of blood. Why didn't the watchers go?

I swore: they were waiting for their companion, the man in the closet.

Well, I thought, they'll have quite a wait.

As I looked around I saw the anteroom door, remembered Jerningham's collection of miniatures to which I'd modestly contributed.

The explosions, I now realized, had occurred in what Reba told me was the working wing. It was out of business now: files destroyed, personnel who'd waited overlong to leave were dead. The fire would consume everything.

I felt sudden rage at the destruction, the killing of unarmed humans. The killers deserved to die. A flash of bravado nearly overcame me: I would free myself of this ancient burden, kneel at the open door and rake the killers with bullets. In another country, a decade ago, I had performed the same act frequently enough to make it unheroic and routine. Now, though, instead of killing others I had a chance to save a life however fragile and foreshortened it might be.

So I resisted the avenging impulse and found an exit doorway that led into a smoke-filled corridor. Holding my breath between unavoidable coughs I staggered in the end, opened another door and found myself on the glassed-in porch where luncheon had been served me on a more tranquil day.

The fire burning through the near wing made a rushing, booming sound. Sparks shot a hundred feet into the air. The fountain naiads seemed to be dancing, an illusion caused by the surge and fall of flames. I opened the glass door and felt heat rush against my cheek. Again Mrs. Jerningham stiffened. "We're safe," I said. "I'll find a place to leave you and then I'll come back."

"Don't . . . don't leave me," she sobbed. It was the first time I had ever heard her speak.

"Only for a few minutes." I carried her down the patio steps and laid her in the shadows of a hedge away from the flames. She tried to cling to me but I detached her hand and said, "Trust me."

Keeping to the dark side of the unburnt wing I moved quickly toward the front of the mansion, knelt, and peered around. By their gestures the group seemed to be arguing whether to look for the missing man or drive away. Suddenly flames licked outward from the entrance door, and the portico began to burn, paint catching fire, curling off in strips. The attackers stared at it and almost simultaneously turned away and began getting into their car.

Their face scarves hung around their necks now, and as they fitted themselves inside the sedan I glimpsed one face in partial profile, and then it was gone, swallowed up in the interior. Recognition slammed me with the force of a rifle butt. It was incredible, a trick of the flames, I tried to reason, but excuses failed.

I felt scooped out, hollow, and yet my mind was telling me how logical it was that Reba should be their leader.

Shaken, mouth dry, I watched her car gather speed as it went down the drive into darkness. Sudden hatred pierced the barrier of love and I shouted, *Damn you!* into the night.

She was more than a seductive dissembler, much more. A skilled and dedicated terrorist, a killer without pity, and yet. . . .

Wherever she went I would follow, even if it took me to Arafat's front door. She owed me an accounting, and I owed her far more than that.

I went back to Mrs. Jerningham.

Her sobbing had ceased. Her cheeks were still wet but the worst was over. Kneeling beside her, I said, "Are you able to walk?"

"A little, but the arthritis is so painful."

"Then I'll carry you," I said, and gathered her up again.

The guerrillas had found the Bentley, but it was only shot up, not destroyed. I arranged Mrs. Jerningham in the back seat and got behind the wheel. The keys were in the ignition, and why not? Who would steal it from Windover?

The remaining wing was beginning to burn as I steered down the drive. The door windows were shattered by gunfire, but the windshield was only spidered, so I had reasonably good vision as I followed the dark road. I hadn't turned on headlights in case the guerrilla car was waiting ahead, then it occurred to me that they would want to get away from the scene before firemen and police arrived.

As I neared the open gate I slowed to look back.

Flames from the main section and the two wings had joined. They swept upward gracefully a hundred, two hundred feet in the sky. As the mind sometimes does in moments of stress, I thought of something remote and trivial: the destruction of Manderley Hall in *Rebecca*. Only this was no movie conflagration, it was real. And real bodies were being consumed.

I drove on through the gate.

Where the road branched, I took the one to Hillerod, and when the town was in sight I turned on headlights and braked the limousine.

To my passenger I said, "You can help me now. I don't want to be detained and questioned by the police. I was asleep when the shooting started. Before I found you that's all that happened."

"Yes, yes, I'll help you. Anything."

"Then tell the authorities as little as you can. Leave me out entirely. You can say someone carried you down to the car and drove you to Hillerod—you don't know who—a servant or one of the attackers. But don't speculate on who the attackers were. Can I count on you?"

"Yes."

I parked the Bentley two blocks from the police station and asked an hour's grace before she talked to the police. "If walking's too much," I said, "just keep honking the horn and someone will come."

I was going to close the door, then saw her uplifted hand, so I bent over and kissed the wrinkled flesh. Patting it I said, "Goodbye. God keep you."

At the train station I went into the lavatory and washed my sooty-red-eyed face. My trousers didn't match the coat, and I was wearing no socks, but the coat held my wallet and passport. And I was alive.

The next train for Copenhagen arrived ten minutes later, and by the time it reached the city's central station I was breathing regularly and my hands had stopped trembling.

From the SAS terminal I rode a bus to Kastrup airport and went from counter to counter asking for a flight to Tel Aviv. There was an El Al plane leaving in an hour and a half so I used a credit card for a first class ticket, then went to the men's shop and selected a shirt, tie, and stockings. The salesman let me change in the fitting booth. Next I went to the pharmacy, bought shaving gear and travel bag, and by then my flight was being called for boarding.

With a double vodka martini warming my vitals I sat back feeling the plane moving ponderously to the flight line. Closing my eyes, I visualized the guerrillas getting into their car, and however my mind recreated the scene, the profile fixed in focus was Reba's.

I told myself that she was no mere murderess, but a partisan fighting for a cause. That was how she viewed herself, how she rationalized her dreadful deeds. Well, with difficulty I could give her that, but between us an imbalance needed evening, demanded settling our scores.

If it cost me my life.

TWENTY FOUR

Mossad (XIII)

At the Ministry of Defense, Haim Ben-yomin found Major Eli Pomerantz in the minister's office. The three men shook hands, and Ben-yomin said, "The 'new development' I mentioned may turn out to be nothing at all. Still, my instructions are to report anything out of the ordinary."

"Yes," said Ezer Weizman impatiently, "get to it, Haim."

The Mossad Chief seated himself. "It concerns the disappearance of a motor torpedo boat belonging to the Lebanese navy."

"What do you mean disappearance?" Weizman snapped.

"Just that, Minister. From the naval base at Sidon. One day it was there, nested with other MTBs, next day it was gone. Our sources indicate fairly strongly that Lebanese naval authorities are mystified."

Pomerantz sighed. "Even under normal circumstances their mystification wouldn't be unusual, but now with most of the country occupied by Syrian forces. . . ." He shrugged expressively. "Who's in charge of the Sidon base, Lebanese or Syrians?"

"The Lebanese navy," Ben-yomin said, "as far as we can tell."

Weizman said, "How did you make this discovery?"

"Through overflight photography and photointerpretation. Then we signaled agents to make inquiries."

Weizman nodded vigorously. "I'd like to know if the MTB was lent, bought, or stolen: whether money changed hands." He glanced at Pomerantz. "Not a bad means of fast-landing terrorist commandos."

Pomerantz nodded agreement and Weizman said, "I suppose the MTB could bring thirty or forty raiders to our coast but they could never get far enough inland to detonate their neutron weapons effectively." He shrugged. "Besides, the boat theft may have no relationship to Al-Karmal. Any terrorist group could have acquired it . . . or none. Still, I welcome any leads that might indicate how Al-Karmal is going to attack us. Anything else, Haim?"

"Unfortunately, Minister, nothing positive. Known Al-Karmal adherents are doing what they normally do. There's no evidence Bakhari or anyone else has contacted them for support. We'd been counting on that, you know."

Pomerantz said, "I think we have to view the attack group as a self-contained unit. They operated independently in Paris, and in the Chimay raid, and I think they're able to continue without external aid. If I were Bakhari I would want it that way."

"Logical," Weizman said gloomily. "Any more intercepts, Haim?"

"Nothing, Minister. Just the brief call transmission we know about."

"Asifa," Pomerantz muttered. "The storm. How like Bakhari to choose a call word signifying the radiation storm he intends to unleash on us."

After a moment Weizman said, "I think I must tell you the orders I received from the prime minister. During the celebration period I am to remain in the underground command post ready to activate *Trumpet* in the event we are attacked. The retaliation squadron has been armed with nuclear bombs and dispersed to secure positions. *Trumpet* will automatically go into effect. I have authorization and precise orders to send out the command without reference to the prime minister."

After a moment's silence Ben-yomin said, "Welcome to Holocaust Two."

"That is the policy of this government," Weizman said. "Do you oppose it?"

"I'm not in the political arena," the Mossad Chief said. "Ha Mossad serves the government and its policies. All of them."

Pomerantz had risen and was gripping the back of his chair. "Startling news, Minister. Frightening."

"Well," said Weizman tersely, "that's how it is. And since you know the consequences of an Al-Karmal attack, you also know how crucial to Eretz Israel is the prevention of such an attack."

"I never thought otherwise," Pomerantz said slowly. "But I don't know how much more we can do to locate the terrorists and neutralize them."

"Find a way," Weizman said. "Find it quickly."

Pomerantz and Ben-yomin glanced at each other. Wordlessly Weizman got up and left the room.

Lord of Hosts, he thought, help us now.

Jay Black (XVIII)

I slept through the Athens stop and when I finally woke the plane had already landed at Ben-Gurion airport. With only a handbag I eased quickly through Customs and found a pleasant Tourism Administration aide who agreed to help locate my father while I had coffee in the airport café, bagels and locally made orange marmalade. When I went back to the desk the aide informed me that Samuel Schwartz was registered at the Ramada Continental in Tel Aviv. "It's on the waterfront," she told me. "Why not take the El Al bus to El Al House and taxi to the hotel from there? It will be much less expensive."

"Good point," I said. "Besides I can kill a little time that way. It's barely dawn and my father is a late sleeper. Thanks for your help."

"You are very welcome. Shalom."

"Shalom," I said, realizing I would have to adapt again to the Israeli custom of leave-taking and greeting, so many years had passed since my year at the Kibbutz when *Shalom* was automatic.

At the Foreign Currency Center I bought forty dollars worth of Israeli shekels, strolled to the barber shop and found it, as expected, closed. So I boarded the El Al bus and rode the nearly deserted highway that led northwest into Tel Aviv, feeling the physical and mental thrill of being once again in the land of my father's people . . . *my* people, I corrected hastily.

The morning air was dry and cool, but by noon, I knew, it would be as warm and damp as, say, Miami Beach. As we entered the outskirts there were more cars and wagons on Derekh Ha-Shalom, and by the time we passed Mann Auditorium the street was getting crowded.

From El Al headquarters on Shalom Aleichem I taxied up Ha-Yaroon to the Ramada Continental, paid the driver, and got out. Inside I found the barber shop just opening, and relaxed in the chair for a shave, haircut, steam facial, massage, and manicure.

For the first time since leaving Windover I began questioning the wisdom of having left Denmark so quickly. Through the embassy I might have been able to contact Bryan Wellbeck. Had Jerningham lived to tell me details of his astounding information I would have relayed it to Wellbeck. Instead, I'd found myself in the middle of an Arab terrorist attack where American interests were not directly involved, and Israel's were.

At eight-thirty I called Dad's room and heard him answer sleepily. "It's Jay," I said. "Can I come up?"

"Yes, yes, of course. But, you're in Israel?"

"Flew in a little while ago. Would Barbara mind if we had breakfast together?"

"Not at all. I won't wake her. You know my room number, so come right up."

He was wearing a navy blue robe over white silk pajamas. We embraced each other, then moved into the sitting room. Barbara would be in an adjacent suite to preserve proprieties and, for my purposes, out of earshot.

My father said, "I can't say you look particularly well. Where did you fly from?"

"Copenhagen."

His eyes narrowed. "Because of your lady?"

"Yes, but not in any way you could conceivably think." I swallowed. "I have to talk with someone in Mossad."

"What else?"

"I want you to get out of Israel before the Celebration."

He stared at me as though I had lost my mind.

The disks of Jaffa oranges were unbelievably large and juicy, the Nablus muskmelon sweet as honey. My father served our plates, scrambled eggs and lox, and poured orange-scented tea. As I resumed eating he eyed me thoughtfully. "Were you not my son—a son I admire, respect, and wholly trust—I would find everything you've said incredible."

My mouth was too full to answer.

He said, "Cynical as I may be I still find it hard to credit the American government with such duplicity toward our Allies, not to mention our own people." He shook his head. "As you see it, having let neutron warheads fall into terrorist hands, America is entirely willing to let Israel fend off attack alone."

"That's how I see it."

He muttered something that I took for an exclamation of dissatisfaction if not disgust.

I said, "I want you to leave here tomorrow."

"And go where?"

"Rome, Athens. . . ," I spread my hands. "Tour the Greek Islands."

"I have . . . several times."

"There's one or two you may have missed."

"No doubt. And don't be arch." He ate for a few moments, sipped tea and looked at me. "I thank God you escaped that place with your life."

"Sometimes a nap pays off."

"Almost invariably." He looked at his watch. "How long since I phoned Arieh Winograd?"

"Half an hour."

"So, the minister will phone back when arrangements have been made."

"I'm sure of it," I said, "but the arrangements I want to hear about have to do with your departure."

My father looked at me and shook his head slowly. "My son, it may be hard for you to think of me as having been involved in any violent way with the birth of Eretz Israel, but it happens that I am familiar with the instruments of war. And I used them against Arabs and British. I never avoided combat or shrank from duty. Tell me, what would old friends think of me if I were to flee this sacred land without a word, finding safety elsewhere? What would Begin think of me? Eshkol? Dayan?"

"They won't think anything," I said, "because if those neutron warheads are exploded anywhere near Tel Aviv, they won't survive."

"I see. And you want me to . . . survive?"

"That's why I came."

The telephone rang. He picked it up, nodded at me, said, "Yes," and began to write on a scratch pad. Presently he said, "Thank you," and replaced the receiver. He handed me the slip of paper; on it was an address.

I said, "Where is Montefiore Street?"

"Over by the Observatory: Shalom Meyer tower."

"That doesn't help me."

"About twenty minutes away. You're expected at the house in half an hour."

"Who do I ask for?"

"Judah." He sipped more tea. "On the way back you might stop off on Rehov Dizengoff for some clothing."

"I won't be here long enough to need it," I said, finished my eggs and drank the rest of my tea. As I left the table I said, "Shalom."

My father smiled. "*Lehitraot*," he said. "If you've forgotten, that means 'See you around.' "

It was an unobtrusive, two-story house, white with pastel window arches and doorway. Good-sized date palms grew on either side of the walk. The sparse grass was well trimmed.

A voice answered my ring, asking who I wanted to see.

"Judah."

Sound of sliding bolts. The door opened and I saw Eli Pomerantz. "Come in, Jay," he said and shook my hand. "You didn't come as a tourist."

"Not this time."

He bolted the door in three places and led me into a quiet, thickly carpeted room whose shades were down. By the single lamp I could see a man seated behind a small table. He wore a short-sleeved shirt, collar open, linen slacks, and sandals. Half glasses across the bridge of his nose gave him the look of an intellectual. He seemed to be on the short side of forty, and unathletic.

Pomerantz said, "Judah, this is Jay Black."

I shook his soft hand as he half rose, then seated himself again. "Welcome to Israel," he said in a somewhat thick accent that suggested Mittel Europe. "Do you mind if we tape record? It would allow me to listen to you without interrupting. Eli's English is far superior to mine."

"Good idea," I said. "You're Mossad?"

He nodded slightly. "*Of* Ha Mossad. Aside from Eli we have Lev Rosenthal as a mutual friend."

Pomerantz said, "Your father is very well connected here."

"Too well," I said. "I don't want him here during the Anniversary days; he feels it would be cowardly to leave."

"Then," said Judah, "you told him of the danger we face?"

"Definitely. I definitely told him."

"Anyone else?" Pomerantz asked.

"No one. Now, before I get into my story, Major, how about checking a Jewish-Arab girl named Reba Mizraki who may also go by the name of Nouri Farraj."

"Why?"

"Because she told me where Atiqa could be found. That's how I was able to tell you." I took a deep breath. "Did you locate Atiqa?"

"Oh, yes," Pomerantz said, "we found her. Reba Mizraki you say? I'll make a call." He left the room and Judah eyed me patiently. After a while Pomerantz returned, seated himself near me and said, "Let's get started, Jay. The . . . Judah has a whole series of appointments this morning."

I began with my first visit to Windover, described Reba and her hypnotic effect on me, repeated her claim of working for Weisenthal, and suppressed the impulse to denounce her. Instead I admitted having fallen in love with her.

Pomerantz interrupted. "And now?"

"I . . . well, I'd better go back to why I returned to Windover." I swallowed hard before telling them the background, described Jerningham's exaltation over his intelligence scoop, our postponing details until after dinner, a dinner that never came. And I described how I had been wakened, the ensuing attack, the killings and the destroying fire. Then came the hardest part: "Reba was one of them."

For the first time Judah spoke. "If she betrayed Atiqa, how could she be of Al-Karmal?"

Pomerantz answered for me. "She could belong to another terrorist organization under the PLO umbrella, an established organization opposed to the upstart Bakhari. Why not al-Fatah?"

My throat was tight.

In a back part of the house a telephone rang. Pomerantz went to answer it.

Judah touched the side of his face. "The fact that Israel may be attacked by neutron devices is something only a few of us know. I can understand your wanting to spare your father any hazard, however unlikely, but I must insist that you speak of it to no one else. No one," he repeated.

"Agreed. You think the risk is 'unlikely'?"

"That is not what I said, Mr. Black. Indeed, I hope there is not the slightest threat. But to avoid the possibility of panic, of lending credence to Arab capabilities, we are working very quietly and quite secretly to nullify that potential threat."

"Do you know where Bakhari is?" I wanted to keep talking, needed to think of something other than the truth Pomerantz would return with.

From Judah's face I saw that he was going to be evasive; then his expression changed slightly and he said, "No, we have not been able to locate him since he left France. Now a Lebanese torpedo boat is suddenly missing, and we fear it may be in his hands."

"But you don't know?"

"We don't know."

Peripheral motion. Pomerantz.

From his expression I knew what he was going to say.

He came behind my chair, placed one hand on my shoulder. "Reba Mizraki is not working for or with Mossad. She never was. Her name is Nouri Farraj. She is an enemy of Israel."

Mossad (XIV)

After Jay Black left the safehouse Eli Pomerantz said, "Why do you suppose Jerningham and his publication were destroyed?"

Haim Ben-yomin got up from behind the desk. "To keep him from heralding an event that would give Bakhari preeminence in the Arab world. An episode of mass destruction that is all too likely to take place. Is that your conclusion?"

"Yes."

"What do you want to do with Black?"

"Involve him. Keep him busy. It's been a hard blow. He needs to recover from it."

"I agree," the Mossad Chief said. "Keep him in Israel until after the Anniversary, Eli. He knows far too much. And I do not know him well enough to predict what he might do if left unguided."

From a concealed tape recorder, Pomerantz extracted a cassette and pocketed it. "He has a good deal of combat experience and a good mind. I'll see he has something to do."

They left the safehouse by a back exit and got into Ben-yomin's armored vehicle. "I think," said Ben-yomin, "that we might now take advantage of the Windover affair."

"How?"

"Circulate the rumor that Bakhari was slain there and his burned corpse identified. It might provoke him into revealing himself. After all, credit for attacking Israel would be of no benefit to a dead man. And Bakhari knows that he is very much alive. So . . . let him prove it."

TWENTY FIVE

Jay Black (XIX)

Taxiing back to the Ramada I spotted a post office by the modern Habima Theater, and got out. I used my credit card to call Parlay Consultants in New York, and after hearing the recorded invitation to leave a message, I said, "Bryan, this is your Black friend in Tel Aviv. I'm staying at the Ramada because ragheads torched the old manse." That was all. In Manhattan it was close to dawn; Wellbeck would receive the relayed message in two or three hours.

As the taxi passed Meir Park I wished bitterly that Reba had never come to the d'Angleterre for cocktails and love-making. Her loss was a physical ache. I needed decompression, reprogramming. I needed it now.

From the hotel lobby I called my father. He said Barbara was off shopping and I should come up.

He was wearing lightweight flannels and an open-collar sport shirt. A copy of *The New York Times* was on the sofa. "Everything okay?" he asked.

"I saw Judah, whoever he is, so now I'll help you pack."

"Hardly necessary, since I'm not leaving. And on the assumption you're staying I took the liberty of getting you a room down the hall." He picked up a key and handed it to me. "You need rest. Get some sleep and we'll have dinner together."

"Apparently nothing I said impressed you."

"Oh, I believe your story. But I'm a fatalist, Jay. If something is to happen, it will happen. As for my life, well, it's been a long one and a good one. My affairs are in order." He smiled. "If I had a choice, I think I'd like to expire on the Seventh Tee after a three-hundred yard drive. But . . . choice is seldom given us. So, I'm going to continue with my plans. But I'm going to ask *you* to leave Israel, go somewhere you'll be safe in the event of attack."

"That's absurd. I. . . ."

He shook his head. "You have a wife, two fine children. They need you. As for me, well, I fought for Israel; I don't think I'd mind dying here among my people, should it come to that."

"Don't be a fatalist. You're too valuable to just accept whatever comes supinely. That's a bad Jewish trait."

He sighed. "Analysis from my son? You're a psychiatrist now?"

"Who's being arch? At the meeting I've come from I heard nothing from the Israelis that encourages me to think they can ward off the attack."

He shrugged. "So, we're a pessimistic people."

"The facts don't support optimism. Please leave. At least get out of Tel Aviv."

"And you? Will you leave?"

"All right," I said wearily, "I'm scared, frightened as hell, I admit it. If you hadn't been here I'd never have come. Every instinct tells me to get out while I'm still alive."

"Then follow your instincts. I'm old enough you shouldn't worry about me. So get some sleep and we'll talk later." He patted my shoulder. "Go on."

I went out, looked at the number on my room key and walked down the hall.

I was barely in bed when there was an insistent knock at my door. Thinking it was my father I got up and opened it.

But my visitor was Eli Pomerantz.

He said, "I've come at a bad time?"

I got back in bed. "It's been a while since I slept," I said, "Night fighting drains the hell out of me."

He sat on a nearby chair. "Are you staying around to see things through?"

I propped myself up on an elbow. "The only reason I'm still here is my father who declines to leave."

"He's living up to his reputation."

"He's out-machoing me," I said, "because my strong inclination is to get the hell out of here before we're all burned to a crisp." I lay back and stared at the dark ceiling. "This isn't my bag, Eli. I don't know where I got the idea I could dip in and out of intrigue like a kid testing water with his toe. But wherever the idea came from, it was wild. Mossad doesn't need me. The Americans don't need me. That was all fantasy: Jay Black, Jewish-American Spy."

"You haven't enjoyed it?"

"Oh," I said wearily, "there were highs, but not enough to compensate for last night in Denmark. That took a lot out of me."

"As did your disillusionment with Miss Mizraki."

"That's possibly the worst of it. In all candor it's like being kicked in the nuts." I turned away from him. "On the plus side is this: I know who needs me. My wife needs me, my children need me, and my business needs me. If I'm lucky enough to survive Bakhari's planned cataclysm I'll go back to New York and pick up the pieces of a disorderly life."

"You sound petulant."

"Look," I said turning to face him, "I didn't ask you to come here and pick at me. With you and Judah I was simply trying to perform a public service in private. Why do I rate all this close attention?"

"We appreciate what you've done, Jay. I thought of making your stay more interesting."

"How?"

"I could show you some of the things we're doing to get at Al-Karmal."

"Look," I said, "I was in a real, honest-to-god war. Real bombs, real bullets, flamethrowers, gunships: people getting killed all around me. It went on for years, not for two days, six days, the way you and the Arabs battle each other. What can you show me, Eli? Burned-out tanks at the roadside? Miles of hot sand, barbed-wire, concrete bunkers? Where's the novelty in that?"

He grunted. "You lose your wars, we win ours."

I took a deep breath, let it out. "Weizman said that when he got pissed off at a U.S. diplomat."

Pomerantz smiled slightly. "The minister declined to be instructed by an amateur. Why don't you get some sleep and I'll be back in midafternoon with a chopper to take us around."

"Seems there's no way I can avoid it."

At two-thirty Pomerantz phoned from the lobby and I went down to join him. We got into a military car that drove us up to the coastal road past bathing beaches and over the canal until we were in the wasteland west of Ramat Aviv. Another couple of kilometers and we entered the fenced perimeter of a military base. I followed Pomerantz into a low structure where he had me change into lightweight camouflage uniform, then gave me a webbed belt with

207

a .45 pistol and a full canteen. Jump boots and a fatigue cap completed my outfitting. I slid out the pistol's magazine, cleared the chamber and slammed the full magazine back into the grip.

Pomerantz said, "The uniform is to make you inconspicuous."

"I was afraid you were going to take me on border patrol."

He laughed. "Would you go?"

"Spirit's willing, but my leg is weak."

We left the building by the rear exit and I noticed a large antenna field covering at least ten acres of sand.

"Thanks to you," Pomerantz said, "we discovered the Al-Karmal transmitting frequency. Lately it hasn't been active, but we're monitoring it from here and several other places."

"You got that from Atiqa?"

"Ah, indirectly." He led me into a sandbagged building whose air-conditioned interior contained massive banks of radio equipment. A dozen uniformed technicians with headsets listened in silence, some slowly turned dials. Pomerantz went over to a Telex unit and examined what was being printed. With a frown he came back to me. "The PFLP is planning to take over the Rembrandt Museum in The Hague, kidnap Dutch officials, and threaten to blow up everything unless Holland releases nine Arab terrorists from prison."

"What are you going to do?"

He sighed. "Israel is the only nation with a policy of not negotiating with terrorists. Holland will negotiate if only to save the Rembrandts, and we don't want those jailed killers released."

"So?"

"Merely agreeing to negotiate signals willingness to surrender. I wish other nations would understand that simple axiom. So, we now have to quash the plan before anything happens."

"By notifying Dutch authorities?"

He laughed bitterly. "No, I'll have to send a team to Holland to dispose of the terrorists. Excuse me." Pomerantz walked to the far side of the room and through a guarded doorway. I went over to a water cooler and drank from a paper cone. As I looked around the communications room I wondered if Mossad agent traffic was handled here. Probably not; I didn't see any transmitter keys or techs working them. I thought of Lev Rosenthal and wondered if he was in Israel. Who was the Judah I had met earlier? Obviously a high Mossad official. How high?

After a while Pomerantz came back. "Let's take a ride," he said, and guided me outside where heat struck me like a shockwave. Under camouflage netting rested a medium-sized Hughes helicopter. The pilot got off his cot, stood up, stretched, and saluted. Pomerantz returned the salute and spoke with him in Hebrew. We got into the chopper and four soldiers peeled back the netting. I buckled my seat belt and the rotor began to turn. Sand picked up in swirls, then flattened under the rotor blast. Slowly we lifted off, turned west into the sun, gaining altitude until at a thousand feet we crossed the coast. Half a mile offshore the pilot turned north and Pomerantz handed me a headset with a small throat microphone. When I had it on he pointed out the resort town of Netanya and said he occasionally took his wife and children there. I had never thought of Pomerantz as a family man, rather as a dedicated loner, but that was the only side of him I'd seen. Then he told me he had taken archeology courses and dug at some of the sites along the coast. It was a hobby he greatly enjoyed.

From the west, out of the sun, appeared two fighter jets trailing streams of dark smoke. They weren't Mirage or F-5 fighters and I asked him what they were.

"F-18s," he told me with a smile as they slammed overhead, rocking the chopper under their wakes. "Your government doesn't have them in full production so we're sort of testing them to get out the bugs."

"Battle testing?"

Pomerantz nodded. "Officially we don't have them at all. I understand these are recorded as being in Arizona."

Ahead I could see the port of Haifa and the hook of Haifa bay. Pomerantz said, "We think Al-Karmal may have got hold of a Lebanese Navy torpedo boat. If it's to be used in the attack it will have to come south along this coast."

"Wouldn't your radar detect it?"

"Not if it has a wooden hull, and it does. This one was Soviet-built, P-6 class, so at least we know what to look for. As for radar detection, there would be scope blips from the metal super structure if the boat came close enough, but even a very good operator would have an impossible task distinguishing it from an Israeli fishing boat, of which there are many."

"It's faster than a fishing boat."

He shrugged. "And if for deception it travels slowly?"

"I see the problem."

The Haifa docks were active; marine cranes moved ponderously, trucks loaded and unloaded at shipside; other cargo ships lay off in the bay waiting for dock space.

"Border's about twenty miles ahead," Pomerantz told me, "but let's not get too close. Lebanon's not in any shape to send up fighters, but the Syrians might—North Korean pilots, of course." He tapped the pilot's shoulder and we turned east gaining altitude until ahead lay the Sea of Galilee like an endless spill of silver. The air was cooler and I took off my cap to let perspiration evaporate. Overhead, two specks in the sky orbited lazily. I pointed them out to Pomerantz who spoke with the pilot, then said, "Jordanian fighters; they're looking over the F-18s."

"I hope they're impressed by the competition."

"Realistically they have to be."

For the next half hour we followed the west banks of the Jordan River, and when the Dead Sea came into sight, Pomerantz gestured to the east, "Amman is over there . . . about twenty-five miles if you're interested."

"Should we buzz the little king?"

Pomerantz chuckled. "Not home today. He's taken his family water skiing. We could probably spot them on the water, but why stir things up? The time may come when he'll be needed."

"In a Mid-East settlement?"

"Exactly."

The helicopter turned west, into the sun again, and presently I saw the distant domes and minarets of Jerusalem. To Pomerantz I said, "Do you really know where the King of Jordan is today or are you guessing?"

"We know," he said, "because we need to know. Ever since he cleared out the PLO camps he's been a target of terrorists, no matter how often he and Arafat kiss in public. If he's assassinated we'll have trouble on our eastern border. So far he's led a charmed life, and when he dies I hope it will be of old age."

We skirted Jerusalem to the north, heading due west to avoid the traffic pattern at Ben-Gurion airport. Off Yafo, the port of Tel Aviv, we turned north and Pomerantz pointed out my hotel as we flashed by. Offshore were naval patrol boats, and a cluster of small trawlers scooping up the riches of the Mediterranean. I thought of the motor torpedo boat that could be in Bakhari's hands and wondered how it fitted into his plans for assaulting Israel. Thirty or forty terrorists could be landed under cover of darkness, but what then? For full effect an atomic warhead had to be exploded above its target, not at ground level, particularly a neutron-tipped artillery shell which was a short-range weapon. How could a bunch of Al-Karmal ragheads get their weapons into the air? Standing on each other's shoulders like Chinese acrobats?

I considered practicalities. A big balloon? No, the Israelis would shoot it down on first sighting. Besides, wind directions shifted at the coast; even a first class meteorologist couldn't predict where a balloon launched offshore would carry. Kite? Hang glider? Same problem.

The air warmed as we descended toward our departure point. Tents and buildings stood baking under the searing sun, and as I looked down I was gripped by a sense of timeless history. Joshua in the *midbar* before the hosts of Amalek; God answering Joshua at Gilgal in defense of Israel. And I thought: Where is the modern Joshua to invoke the Most High to protect Israel from its enemies?

The chopper settled smoothly and dustily. I coughed as billows entered the doorless cabin, removed my headset and put on my fatigue cap. The pilot flicked off the engine and as I sat there a verse of Isaiah came to my mind: *Behold, the day cometh, it burneth as a furnace; and all the proud and all that work wickedness shall be stubble; and the day that cometh shall set them ablaze. . . .*

Pomerantz shook me out of my brief reverie, and we went to the small, clean mess hall for iced tea. I drank close to a quart, realizing how thirsty the desert dryness made me. Pomerantz contented himself with a single chilled glass, and said, "Where you fought, Jay, there was no lack of moisture."

"Couldn't escape it," I agreed. "The dessert seems healthier."

"Only if you have enough water to survive."

"And oil."

He glanced out of the doorway at the spreading sand. "So Rommel learned. But, we're talking historical absolutes. Today's problem is different. Is there anything you've, ah, forgotten to tell me?"

"About what?"

"Leads to Bakhari, Al-Karmal? You held back Atiqa's name far too long."

"I know," I said uncomfortably, "and you know why."

"Not much of a reason when you consider it now, was it?"

I shook my head. "No, I haven't held anything back, Eli." I was tired from the flight, the wind battering at me, the strain of the sun in my eyes. "I appreciate the tour of Samaria; never thought I'd see Israel from the air." I swallowed the last of my tea, crunched ice fragments luxuriously. "Where do we go from here?"

"It's up to you."

"I thought there might be more revelations."

His eyes narrowed and I said, "It seems to me you have to assume Bakhari can reach Israeli territory."

"We're not willing to make that assumption. I haven't shown or told you everything we're doing to prevent that."

"I hope there's much more I haven't seen and don't know about. Otherwise, the attack would be a piece of cake."

He was angry now. "Don't tell me my business, Jay."

I got up from the folding chair. "I thought you might want an outside opinion. How much did you get from Atiqa?"

"Very little."

"Strange. I thought. . . ."

"She killed herself," he said coldly and stood up. "I'll have you driven back to the hotel. How long will you be in Tel Aviv?"

"I'm not sure. I want my father to leave. When he goes I'll go."

"Otherwise, you'll stay."

"I'll stay."

I changed from the borrowed uniform and he walked outside with me. I got into the waiting car and before he closed the door he said, "I'm hoping for a development that might be helpful. Otherwise. . . ." He closed the door and spoke to the driver. The car backed around and we drove out through the guarded gate.

At the hotel, I walked down the corridor to my room. A man was sitting on one of the wall benches reading the Jerusalem *Post*. I got out my key and the man stood up and came toward me. "Mr. Black? Have you got a few minutes?"

I faced him. A sandy-haired, light-skinned, young man with dark glasses and an air of politeness. "Who are you?"

"My name's Duff." His voice lowered. "Wellbeck sent me."

I'd forgotten my call to Bryan. "Sure," I said, "Come in."

Inside my room I said loudly, "Coincidence running into you over here, Fred. In Vegas I promised to look you up but never did. Still got your card, though." Then I turned up the radio, and in a barely audible voice my visitor said, "Actually my name is Tom, not that it matters."

I pulled over facing chairs and we sat down. Tom Duff said, "I don't know what this is all about, Mr. Black. I'm mainly here to listen."

"Then we'll start with my reaching Copenhagen on Wellbeck's orders. Go ahead, take notes."

He took out a pocket notebook and a ballpoint pen. Slowly enough that he could keep up with me I related the events at Hillerod. It was hard to tell the notebook I'd recognized Reba Mizraki—I spelled the name—as one of the guerrilla attackers, but I did. Then, mouth dry, I stopped talking, got up and went over to the window. There were bathers on the beach, frisbees and a big inflated beach ball that the wind took and pushed across the sand, splashing into the gentle surf. I said, "That's it, Tom. Any questions?"

He joined me at the window. "My cable instructions are to tell you that the subject—I mean Reba Mizraki also-known-as Nouri Farraj—is in Cairo at the Semiramis."

My hands tightened on the railing. "Why would Wellbeck want me to know?"

"I don't know what the implication is. Perhaps he thought you would."

"It's a little too cryptic," I said and turned back from the window.

"Do you want to query Mr. Wellbeck?"

"Not really."

Al-Karmal (XII)

They had moved the MTB and its cargo into a nearby cove, stretching camouflage nets over its narrow width for concealment from the air.

In one of the half-destroyed mud-brick hovels lay Aboud, fevered, in pain and delirious. Marco, who had had some first-aid training, drew Hossein Bakhari aside. "This is not dysentery, comrade, but a problem of the appendix. Either it is ruptured or on the point of rupture."

"What can be done?"

He shrugged. "The sulfa has had little effect. Clearly the comrade cannot go with us."

"Well," said Bakhari, "he cannot be left behind." In a low voice he said, "Do you have something to bring an end to his suffering?"

Marco nodded.

"Then I may leave the matter in your hands?"

"With confidence."

Bakhari patted Marco's shoulder and left the hut.

After a while Marco opened his medical kit and carefully took from it a small glass vial packed in cotton. Kneeling beside Aboud he held his breath, broke off the tip of the vial and drained its contents into Aboud's open mouth. Quickly Marco got up and moved to the open doorway. Aboud's eyes opened wide, he retched and struggled briefly, then lay back. A light scent of almonds drifted through the heated air. Marco ground the glass vial into the sand and walked away.

Bakhari found Felipe Buenaventura squatting beside the radio receiver. The Cuban looked up. "They say you are dead, comrade."

"Dead?"

"Radio Beirut reports it. As do Radio Amman and the Fascist Cairo radio stations." He reached up to touch Bakhari. "Even so, you live."

Bakhari nodded. "Interesting, eh? The Jews, of course."

"Assuredly."

Bakhari thought: How clever to liquidate the Englishman before he could tell the world Israel is to be destroyed by me. But he was far from certain Jews had done it. Nouri must have found out what was planned and moved against the Englishman with her Habash group. She was capable of it . . . and she hated him. Yes, Nouri.

His hands opened and closed. All because of Atiqa. Atiqa would know how to turn those lies against the Jews, make them bear responsibility. If only she were here. Had she been captured? Destroyed? Ten times ten thousand Zionists would pay with their putrid lives.

To the Cuban he said, "Take men and bury Aboud."

"Aboud? I thought. . . ?"

"He died of his illness," Bakhari said. "Let him be wrapped in a shroud and I will say some words over his grave."

Buenaventura got up slowly. "I saw him less than an hour ago."

"I will name a street in his memory," Bakhari said. "In Tel Aviv. Aboud was a true revolutionary fighter. As one of my early followers he will not be forgotten." He approached the transmitter and turned it on. Buenaventura said, "What are you going to do, comrade?"

"I am going to transmit a message to the world, revealing Jewish lies, confirming that I, Hossein Bakhari, am alive and will live to strike at Israel."

Grimacing, Buenaventura stared at the transmitter. "I counsel against it, comrade."

"*What?*"

"If you transmit, you play the Jewish game. Reflect, and you will conclude that the false broadcasts are Jewish provocations. They know you are alive. What they do *not* know is where you are. I urge you to reconsider."

"*No.*"

"Do not give us away."

Bakhari's hand moved toward the revolver grip. The Cuban saw it and bit his lip. The Arab fanatic could not be permitted to destroy the assault on Israel. He, Felipe Buenaventura, had his orders, orders of which this megalomaniac knew nothing. If necessary. . . .

They heard the first soft *whish* of the oncoming jet only seconds before it was overhead. Then it thundered over, blasting their eardrums, shaking the ground, dumping foul smoke, and Bakhari started out of the hut, revolver in hand. "*No!*" Buenaventura shouted. "Stay concealed!"

Halting, Bakhari turned as Buenaventura joined him at the doorway. Coughing from the jet's exhausts they saw it whip suddenly upward, rolling into the sky, displaying its blue-and-white insignia, the Star of David.

Hand on Bakhari's arm, Buenaventura said, "An old Mystère on photo reconnaissance. Let us hope none of our men was caught by its cameras."

The jet's sudden appearance, its deafening sound, and the quick danger it symbolized had shaken the Arab leader. Licking his lips he said, "You were right to restrain me, Felipe. I wanted to empty my gun at the warplane but. . . ." He shrugged. "A useless gesture."

"And dangerous."

He looked at his revolver and replaced it. "Always speak your mind, Felipe; I value your counsel." Turning in, he went to the transmitter and shut it off. "Let the Jews play their foolish games," he sneered. "Soon none will be alive to lie and insult me."

Relieved, Buenaventura nodded. "I will see to the burial of Aboud, comrade, and then, if you desire, I will demonstrate to you the firing mechanism of our birthday gift to Israel."

IV

"Don't be eager to give your life for your country; make the other son of a bitch give *his* life for *his* country!"

—Ezer Weizman
Israeli Minister of Defense

TWENTY SIX

At the Pentagon, the Deputy Director of Central Intelligence and Bryan Wellbeck briefed the Secretary of Defense on the following points:

The warheads stolen from Chimay had not been located;

The Israeli Minister of the Interior was revamping disaster plans in a manner suggesting preparation for atomic attack;

The Israeli government would probably not cancel the Anniversary celebration;

If attacked by atomic weapons, the Israeli Air Force would retaliate against Arab cities with atomic bombs.

The Secretary remarked that such an action would probably bring the Soviet Union into the conflict. "To avoid that," he said, "we might have to shoot down Israeli planes," and sat fingering a pencil. "The Air Force Chief of Staff wants me to have the President institute Red Alert for the Anniversary period."

The Deputy Director said, "That would tell the Soviets things we don't really want them to know."

The Secretary nodded. "One carrier—the *Kennedy*—is in the western Med, but the *Nimitz* is down in the Indian Ocean. If it's to be of any use I'd have to order it to change station right now. And of course our Secretary of State wouldn't care for that. Not at all."

For a while no one spoke. Finally the Secretary sighed. "I'm going to ask the President for an emergency meeting of the National Security Council. Before that I'll consult the Joint Chiefs for alternatives." He looked at the Deputy Director. "Tell your boss I'm counting on him to help me lay land mines for State."

"I'm sure he'll vote his conscience."

"Oh, yes," the Secretary said drily, "I'm confident of that. Just remind him this isn't the annual war game. It's for real."

Riding the Agency limousine back across the Potomac, Bryan Wellbeck wondered what the outcome of the NSC meeting would be, and whether in the end U.S. fighters would have to shoot down the Israeli strike force. Then his thoughts turned to Jay Black. By now he should have received the message telling him Nouri Farraj had shown up in Cairo. And Wellbeck wondered whether Jay would try to see her there.

Jay Black (XX)

We came down into Cairo airport in the cool of evening, after the soft blues, pinks, and magenta of the desert sunset over the long purpling reach of the Sinai wasteland; across the sunset-bronzed sliver of the Suez Canal, then Cairo silhouetted against the setting sun.

In the years since I'd been in Cairo the city had changed; parts of it were even shabbier, but here in the city's center, crowded along the banks of the Nile were new hotels and apartment buildings.

I was in a third-floor room of the old Semiramis. Through the open balcony doorway I could see the lights of houseboats in the river. Below, stubby little streetcars jolted along. The balcony was draped with thick vines; until nightfall birds had been chirping and singing there. Now the river-cooled air drifted in carrying the scent of jasmine and bougainvillea.

During my kibbutz year Mossad had sent me into Cairo and I had come by jeep and foot, swimming the canal in the dark of night, boarding a small felucca on a branch of the river and sailing the rest of the passage to the Cairo docks. In the folds of my *galabia* were crystals for an agent radio transmitter. There was no face-to-face contact with the Egyptian agent; I delivered the crystals to a bronze merchant in—where was it?—the part of Cairo called Shubra. Thinking back on the shop I was sure I could never find it again. Before returning to Israel I had visited the pyramids at Gizeh, sipped tea at Mena House, and toured the Egyptian Museum to see the Tutankhamun artifacts. How did I, a Jew, manage all that? By pretending to be mute. Gestures were universal.

And back in Israel I had met Lev Rosenthal for the first time.

Now, I thought, as I turned back from the open doorway, I was in Cairo on a different mission: personal, unauthorized.

My father had protested, begged me not to go, threatened to call Minister Winograd and have me jailed. Then Barbara had come in and Dad stopped talking. To her I said, "He's making a big thing of me going to Jerusalem for a day or so, but I'll be back for the celebration."

Heavily, my father had said, "Is that a promise?"

"Promise," I said, and kissed them both goodbye.

But Dad followed me into the corridor and I said, "Don't you remember telling me this was something that had to be followed to its logical conclusion?"

"Yes," he said reluctantly.

"That's what I'm doing."

He took my arm. "Use your head, Jay."

"I plan to," I told him. "Don't forget, I saw her at Windover with a machine gun, staring at the flames. She was transformed, somebody else."

And even now as I looked up at the slowly rotating fan blades I had no idea how I would react to seeing her again.

The pistol I'd liberated from my afternoon's loaned equipment was between my belt and spine. I took off my coat and wiped perspiration from the .45, jacked a shell into the chamber and set the safety. The knurled grip felt solid in my hand. I gripped it for a moment, then returned the pistol to my belt.

I put on my coat and trod the staircase down to the lobby and out to the terrace. Bakshish to the room clerk brought me the information that Mademoiselle Farraj was expected back during the evening. Breeze fluttered the cloth at my table. I sipped a glass of cool mint tea and waited.

Cairenes strolled past the terrace, some well-dressed, most of them not. Dragomen and street vendors offered guided tours and merchandise to the better dressed. A doorman kept them off the terrace.

Across the river, on the island, was the Gezira Sporting Club. I knew of it because Sybil's father and brothers had told me of pigeon shooting there, the unspoken implication that as *goyim* they were admissible, whereas a Jew such as I could never aspire to its exclusive precincts.

Well, I thought, the hell with all that. While Nasser ruled there had been a good deal of shooting at Gezira, and not at pigeons.

A donkey cart plodded by, the skinny animal prodded listlessly by its turbaned driver. One of the many *fellahin*, I thought, who had yet to savor the fruits of Nasser's social revolution.

Briefly as I had been in Egypt I sensed the contrast between Cairo and Tel Aviv. Cairo was a bedraggled city in suspense, comatose almost. Tel Aviv was new, vibrant, on-moving. Arabia needed what Israel could offer; perhaps my grandchildren would see a great Semitic fusion in their time.

Fusion.

I considered it in the nuclear sense, recalled the neutron warheads in Bakhari's power, and thought of his ally, Reba.

How did the two of them intersect? What had been her role all along? I felt my face tighten.

The waiter came by and I asked for a cold beer. He said there was German beer but not very cold, so he brought me another glass of tea.

The evening coolness was refreshing but the rainy season was ending and soon the *khamsin* would blow hot from the desert, billowing dust through the streets, withering vines, and whipping sand in your nostrils for a legendary fifty days. During which Egypt lay somnolent as the pharaohs in their tombs.

A Rolls Royce purred up to the entrance and a doorman hurried to open its door. Was this how Reba would arrive? No, there were diplomatic license plates on the rolls. From it emerged a man in dinner jacket and Arab headdress, then a woman dressed in Rue St.-Honoré elegance, a translucent veil across her face. She followed him up the steps into the lobby. The Rolls moved away.

I stirred my tea with a sprig of mint.

The terrace was filling for what passed as the cocktail hour in Islamic Cairo, but I could see only one red fez; they were viewed as unwelcome reminders of the ancien régime. If there were as few beggars as fezzes, I thought, the revolution would have accomplished something significant.

Another car at the entrance. This one a well-polished Renault. From it came a man in European clothing, then a woman.

She descended with sure and sinuous grace, a woman beautiful enough to stop my breath. She gave her hand briefly to the man, they spoke a few words, and she turned and came up the steps. My impulse was to leave the table and take her arm, draw her into the shadows, and kiss her full, warm lips, for this was the Reba I knew: composed, lovely, and alluring. Her glance straight ahead, she never noticed me sitting rigidly, staring at the voluptuous curves of thigh and breast, at her total femininity. Despite myself I wanted her, desired her as I had from our first encounter. It was unbelievable that she was everything I knew her to be. Nouri Farraj, an intruder who had nothing to do with either of us. Yet. . . .

Turning slightly, I saw her claim her key at the desk, then walk to the lift. When the door closed, I laid some piasters on the table and called over the waiter. Before I left the table I saw the Renault pull away, her escort in the rear seat. His face was Arabic. Was he one of Windover's attackers, this chauffeured cosmopolite? Would I recognize him with a scarf across his face?

I forced myself to walk slowly through the lobby then waited for the lift to descend. "*Quatrième étage,*" I said to the elderly operator and leaned against the handrail, feeling it force the pistol uncomfortably against my spine.

The fourth floor corridor was empty. I went to room 414 and knocked. In a few moments I heard a voice answer in Arabic. Huskily I called, "*Mademoiselle? S'il vous plaît.*"

"*Oui. Un moment,*" the voice replied and presently I heard soft footsteps approaching. The door opened.

Mossad (XV)

Haim Ben-yomin was walking the corridor to the Prime Minister's office when Major Pomerantz caught up with him. The Mossad Chief said, "Eli, can it wait?"

"It could were I not going on patrol through the night. Forgive me, Haim, but I thought you would want to know: Jay Black has left Israel."

Ben-yomin smote his forehead with open palm. "You were to prevent his leaving."

"He slipped away, boarded the evening flight to Cairo."

"Because he fears the Al-Karmal attack?"

"He did not check out of his room, so he will probably return."

The Mossad Chief shook his head disgustedly and continued walking. "You were right to tell me, Eli. One bitter pill after another."

He passed between two guards, opened the door and entered the conference room where Ministers Weizman and Winograd were seated near Prime Minister Begin.

223

"My apologies, Prime Minister," said Ben-yomin as he sat next to the Minister of Interior.

"I was saying," the Prime Minister said drily, "that we are decided on going ahead with the celebration. Ezer has his final instructions and Arieh has prepared plans to help minimize casualties in the event of atomic attack."

Weizman said, "The American defense attaché has been notified of our fighter refueling exercises."

Begin said, "Also notify the Egyptians, Jordanians, and Lebanese. It will allay their fears and also reach the ears of the Russians whom I do not want unduly concerned about our aircraft."

Weizman nodded and Winograd said, "I have arranged to procure quantities of blood plasma from a variety of countries including West Germany, South Africa, and Spain. They are due here tomorrow on El Al cargo flights. Civil police and the military have established special offices for immediate cooperation in the event of surprise attack. Our emergency supplies of food and water have been augmented and are stored underground where they will not be affected by radiation." He cleared his throat. "The roads leading to Jerusalem and Tel Aviv are already filling with trucks and busloads from *kibbutzim* and outlying towns. Ben-Gurion airport notes the expected increase of tourists from abroad, and the projection is that the total will exceed even last year. There is hardly a hotel room available in Tel Aviv, and the youth hostels are having to pitch tents wherever they can."

Weizman got up and gestured at a wall map. "Those killers are somewhere to the north of our border, I'm convinced of it. Yet, neither radar or photo reconnaissance has picked them up. It's as though they vanished."

"So," Begin said, "we must prepare for the worst, accepting that our fate is in the hands—as always—of the Most High." He stared moodily at his clasped hands, then his head lifted slightly. "Have the Americans helped us?"

Weizman grunted. "Only by confessing the theft of the warheads from their unguarded storage place. Such help we may thank them for from our graves."

In the corridor Ben-yomin halted Defense Minister Weizman, "I need a helicopter tonight, Ezer. To take a man as near Cairo as possible."

Weizman frowned. "Couldn't we go by morning El Al flight?"

"There's no time. And this has to do with Al-Karmal."

With a sigh Weizman said, "Very well. I'll alert the base. One traveler?"

"Only one."

In his office Ben-yomin busied himself until there was a knock on his door and Lev Rosenthal came in. "You're leaving for Cairo, Lev."

"When?"

"Now."

"But the flights. . . ."

"A special flight, brother, just for you. Courtesy of Minister Weizman."

Rosenthal lowered his bulk into a chair. "May I ask the occasion?"

"Our friend Jay Black is suddenly in Cairo. No one seems to know why he went, so I deduce that the Farraj woman may have drawn him there. Lev, he knows far too much of our plans and preparations to fall into terrorist hands. If he is there innocently, well and good. But if Nouri Farraj is also there I want them both."

"I understand."

He moved to a situation map and beckoned Rosenthal over. "The helicopter will get you as close as possible to Cairo, about there. I will alert one of our people to drive out and meet you so you won't have to walk the rest of the way." He eyed Rosenthal's corpulence disapprovingly. "Locate Black. Or locate Nouri Farraj. Or both."

"Cairo is a large city," Rosenthal remarked.

"But familiar to you. My car will deliver you to the helicopter base. Take money, false identification, and a weapon. Shalom."

Rosenthal left the office and went down to the waiting car. He had been in the middle of a televised string recital when summoned by his chief. On the way to the base he stopped at the Mossad transient apartment long enough to pick up the items ordered by Ben-yomin, and then he sat back in the car's rear seat as it drove out into the desert.

Jay Black (XXI)

"Hello, darling," I said. "Surprised?" I pushed in and took her into my arms. For a moment she was rigid as a statue; then her body relaxed and her hands moved around me. The mirror showed her face pale, eyes frightened. I stroked her hair, kissed her lips.

"Jay," she murmured, and I felt the pounding of her heart. Mine was pounding, too, but for a different reason. I noticed an open suitcase on the baggage rack, and wondered how long she planned to stay.

Slowly she began to respond. Her hand pressed the back of my head, then she stood back and brushed hair from her forehead. "How . . . how on earth did you find me?"

"Call it chance," I said, "but isn't it great? There I was sipping mint tea on the terrace, and suddenly you arrive." I kissed her again. "This calls for celebration." I moved to the center of the room and looked back. "Unless you have a date with the fellow who delivered you? Uh, who was he anyway? Air Maroc type? Mossad?"

"Shhhh!" She placed a finger to her lips and looked around. "You mustn't say that, not in Cairo. Surely, you know that."

"Well, I do, and I won't make that mistake again. Do you suppose we could get a little iced champagne sent up?"

"I think it can be arranged." Picking up the telephone she spoke in Arabic, came to me and took my hands.

"Just like Paris," I said, "and I'll bet you have a lot to tell me."

One hand toyed with the folds of her sheer dressing gown. "Why did you come to Cairo?"

"I decided to join my father in Israel for the celebration. His friends are getting on in years and we agreed it was meet them now or never, so I came along with him. I was just starting to enjoy Tel Aviv when some Cairo business came up and he asked me to handle it for him. You'll understand his reluctance to visit an Arab country, given his work as a Jewish Resistance fighter."

She seemed to stiffen at the words.

"So," I went on, "I agreed to come in his place—simple exchange of papers—messenger job, really. I could have come on the morning flight, but I've always heard Cairo at dusk is memorable, and so it is. How long will you be here?"

"Until tomorrow. Then. . . ."

"When will you get to Paris again?"

"I, I don't know." She couldn't take her eyes from my face; it was as though I were a ghost. And but for considerable luck I would have been.

"London, then," I urged. "We could have a ball in London: operas, plays, the gaming clubs." I went behind her and clasped my arms around her thorax, then let my hands lightly caress her breasts. She shivered even though the air was warm.

My nose nuzzled the back of her ear. "Don't you want to make love, sweetheart?"

"I, of course I do, Jay, but, well, I'm still in a state of disbelief. Let's have the champagne, and relax, shall we?"

I nodded. "We'll dine here, too."

"I was just going to change when you knocked. Why don't I go ahead with that while you take care of the champagne?"

"Excellent idea." I released her and she walked away, gown flaring behind. The lump in my throat was the size of a grenade.

I checked the room; she had barely unpacked as though this was only a fast stopover. The closet held shoes, a blouse, and slacks. I wondered where she kept her Arab battle dress.

One eye on the bathroom door I went quickly through her suitcase: lingerie, cosmetics, pantyhose, the sort of things Sybil would pack for an overnight. But the bag's elastic pocket held three passports: Libyan, Jordanian, and Lebanese. Each passport showed a different photo of her. I could read two of the names but the third was in Arabic.

Knocking at the hall door.

I opened it carefully, one hand near my gun, saw a waiter bearing a tray with glasses and a toweled cooler. He placed it on the table and I signed the chit. I tipped him and locked the door.

I removed the towel from the cooler and twirled the dark green bottle. Its neck was developing a nice bead. It wasn't French champagne, but an Alsatian sparkling wine; probably hock. It would be overly sweet to the palate, but my life was turning so sour a little sweetness would be welcome.

The overhead fan was motionless, so I switched it on and opened the balcony doors. Unlike my room, no view of the Nile, just the nearby military barracks.

Sounds of movement from the bathroom. She must be worried as hell, I thought; confused, wondering how to play it. Well, she had nothing on me, for I had no clear idea of what I was going to do. Oh, part of me was still in love with her, but the rest had burned away at Windover.

In my mind I heard automatic weapons fire again, the rush and crackle of flames, saw the gun sticking into my room, her face profiled by the flames.

The door opened and she came toward me wearing an avocado evening gown. I popped the bottle cork and filled our glasses. She took one composedly and touched its rim to mine before we drank. Our eyes met, then she glanced away. "It seems so long since Paris," she murmured.

"A lifetime."

She looked back at me and her eyes were guarded. "It's almost as though we've taken different directions."

"Except for this meeting."

She nodded and sat on the small sofa. "I can't help but wonder if chance is all it was." Her eyes lifted to mine. "I sense something different between us."

"Do you?" I sat next to her. "Maybe I'm depressed about Jerningham."

"*Jerningham?*" Her eyes widened.

"Yes. Windover was assaulted and burned, almost everyone killed."

"*Almost* everyone?"

"I survived."

"You, *you* were there?"

"Yes," I said, "asleep when the attack began, but I lived through it." I placed my glass beside hers. "I saw the attackers leave, all but the one I'd disabled. Strange, the visual tricks flames can play." I eyed her steadily. "I thought I saw you watching with the others. I reasoned it couldn't have been you."

A faint smile appeared on her lips.

"But it was," I said. "It *was* you, Nouri. You shouldn't leave your passports lying around. You took part in the killing. I was going to prolong this through dinner but I'm sick of lies."

"That's too bad," she said softly. But there was a strange, reckless anger in her eyes. "I thought I might be able to deceive you indefinitely. You were a convenience, you see, and at the same time a threat, so it made our love making more exciting."

"Obscene," I said, and drew the pistol from my belt. "Confide in me, Nouri. Tell me the truth behind those many lies."

TWENTY SEVEN

Al-Karmal (XIII)

On the hull they painted a blue-and-white Star of David insignia and prepared an Israeli flag for hoisting to the truck the following night.

To compensate for the helicopter's weight, Marco supervised jettisoning the MTB's twin 21-inch torpedo tubes and their firing mounts, the steel depth-charge tracks and the two smaller searchlights. They discarded two of the four deck machine guns and cut away most of the protective metal railing. Even so Marco doubted that the Russian-built P-6 would be able to run faster than seventy-five percent of its 42-knot rated speed. Except for boarding men, battle gear, and the all-important radio, the boat was ready for sea.

After three hours of generator-charging the radio batteries reached full potency. Felipe Buenaventura turned off the gasoline generator and disconnected the batteries. With Bakhari watching, he armed the radio-controlled bomb trigger, still isolated from the neutron warhead, and turned on the radio transmitter. "Press the key," he instructed, and Bakhari knelt beside the transmitter. For a moment he savored what he was about to do, then closed the key. Immediately a sharp click came from the trigger mechanism.

"What takes place," Buenaventura said, "is that the radio signal is received here in this small receiver. A solenoid activates the relay releasing the trigger bolt." He cocked the spring-loaded trigger and Bakhari closed the transmitter key again. He dry fired five times more in near-orgasmic exaltation, then Buenaventura said, "Enough, comrade, let us not fatigue the spring. The system works."

Reluctantly, Bakhari turned off the transmitter and watched the Cuban carefully place the trigger mechanism in a box. An adjacent case held the detonators and gelignite that would explode the warhead over Tel Aviv.

Mossad (XVI)

At Nablus and Ma'alot, Israeli monitoring stations intercepted the Al-Karmal radio testing and informed their headquarters. Major Eli Pomerantz was notified near Shelomi, in sight of the Lebanese border.

Bakhari and his commandos were somewhere in Fatah land, not Jordan as he had feared, and only some forty hours remained before the Al-Karmal strike.

Jay Black (XXII)

"So melodramatic," Nouri said, eyes lifting from the pistol. "You feel the need to protect yourself . . . from me?"

"A little caution, however late, is preferable to the kind of recklessness I demonstrated in the past." I picked up the wine bottle with my left hand and refilled our glasses. As she took hers I said, "I had this recon patrol up near Lai Binh and a girl stepped out of her hootch. She opened her blouse enough to get my corporal excited and made the money sign with her fingers. The corporal said, 'Lieutenant, I ain't had none so long I believe I forgot what it's like. How's about givin' me a fast ten minutes with Miss Vietnam, here?'" I sipped from my glass. Nouri's face was expressionless. "So I let him go with her while the rest of us sat down and waited. After ten minutes I called him but no answer. We went in and there he was, wire around his neck and very dead. The girl had sneaked out the far side."

"Your corporal deserved to die," she said stonily. "Exploiting, taking advantage of a peasant girl."

"Well," I said, and sipped again, "she was more than just a simple peasant, Nouri. She was Cong and trained to kill. Just as you're PLO and even better trained. So, yes, I need the gun between us."

"What are you going to do with me?"

"That depends. You can come clean here or in some cellar in Tel Aviv. And if anyone tries to break in, believe me, you're dead."

Her eyes regarded me thoughtfully. They seemed to have a soft luster as though transmitting a silent caress. Like a chameleon she was reverting, adopting a persona I was familiar with. She said, "What do you want to know?"

"Who brought you to the hotel?"

"My superior."

"What is his name?"

"Haroun."

"Why are you in Cairo?"

"To join him and others."

"Who did you meet in Paris?"

"Haroun, of course."

"Why is your group gathering here?"

She glanced over at the open balcony doors and I said, "Don't even think about it. Answer the question."

"We are going to destroy Hossein Bakhari and Al-Karmal."

"Fascinating. Where are they?"

"Southern Lebanon."

"Go on. Tell the tale."

She sat back in the sofa. "Our agents learned Al-Karmal left France with the Chimay weapons. From Benghazi they took a freighter to a point off the Lebanese coast where they disembarked and occupied a burned-out village."

"How could your people locate them when the Israelis couldn't?"

"Because we sent out a scouting patrol to find them . . . and our men did not return."

"You want the neutron warheads, of course."

She nodded. "And it is important that Al-Karmal and Bakhari be liquidated."

"Why?"

"Political reasons. The Arab triumph over Israel should not be accomplished by a megalomaniac and his renegade followers. Our victory must be pure, one that will draw together *all* Arabs, not divide them even more."

"You can forget that victory," I said. "The Israelis will wipe out Al-Karmal before your commandos can leave Cairo."

"Perhaps," she said huskily. "But first you will have to return to Israel, will you not?"

"There's a morning flight," I said, "and I'll be on it. Bakhari can do a lot of things, I credit him with that, but can he detonate the warheads? Has he got the technical know-how?"

"He has a pair of Cuban advisors."

"Aah," I said, "no one figured on that. Now tell me about your impoverished childhood, the horror of growing up in Fatah-land. You've alluded to it but I'd like details now. And be sure to include your husband. I suppose he was killed by Israelis?"

"By Christian Phalangists. Jay, would you order dinner? If we're to be here all night. . . ."

I went to the telephone and lifted the receiver. The angle was awkward, but peripherally I could see motion. Her hand lifted from between the cushions and there was a gun in it. While I was thumbing off my safety her arm rose steadily, and as I saw the muzzle she fired.

The bullet hit my chest, spun me around, and I fell backward.

Nouri Farraj (I)

As Jay's body collapsed on the sofa Nouri moved quickly aside to avoid blood on her gown. She replaced the telephone receiver, turned and set the pistol muzzle on his forehead. But blood was spreading rapidly across his shirt front, and she decided not to fire again. If not dead, Jay was dying, and a second shot might bring people to her door.

She put the pistol into her purse, drew out her watch, and saw that she could still reach the assembly point before the commandos left. Changing into a street dress she cleared out the closet and bathroom, jamming everything into her suitcase, and as she lifted it from the rack she looked at the bloodied man on the sofa and thought of checking his pulse to make sure. Briefly she remembered the warmth of his body and thought: I could have loved him had he been Arab and not an enemy. She went to the door, turned off the light, and took the back stairs down to the service alley.

In the taxi, moving through dim streets, she thought of Jay's sneering challenge: "Tell me of your impoverished childhood, the horrors of growing up in Fatah-land." How could he, a well-born Jew, comprehend what she had suffered and survived? How could she have told him what it was like when the men came in the night, not bedouins as she had suggested to him, but five Jewish outcasts from the Gaza Strip, entering the tent with knives and drawn guns. Fierce, unshaven animals whose leader bore a long, purple birthmark from ear to shoulder, menacing her mother, herself, and her half-sister, tearing off their garments and gagging them, holding a knife to her mother's throat, forcing her thighs apart and taking turns. She remembered their hands on her own small body, the probing fingers, while the violation of her half-sister was underway, childish limbs all but hidden by huge hairy bodies. . . .

All only prelude before they made her mount a supine Jew. She remembered her soundless screams from the agonizing ravishment between her legs, the monstrous torture when their sodomy began. Fainting was a gift from Allah, and when she was conscious she lay like a discarded doll at the edge of the tent where her mother once had hidden a long thin blade. Alone now, the birthmarked pig was rising from her mother when she drove the blade into his back. Stabbing again and again, shrieking madly until he fell aside in death, finally she fled the tent for help from Arab males.

In the morning she had been allowed to cut the genitals from the Jew she had killed, then watched while the living four were buried to their heads in heated sand. All this took place away from UN camp inspectors, and the dying lasted two long days.

At night outside the camp five bodies were buried in a deep-dug grave, her mother mute and childlike in the aftermath. So it came about that she was separated from mother and half-sister, and for her courage taken to Cairo and schooled until she was old enough to enter the American University in Beirut on a scholarship provided by the Arab League.

When she was seventeen men with the rank of *sheik* had brought her to a council place and told her that her bravery, intelligence, and beauty fitted her well to serve the cause of Pan-Arabia if she were willing. And before she left the council place that night she had sworn her oath of dedication to that cause, receiving orders to expand her knowledge of the world and practice the seductions that made fools of men. *For it is written that by artifice the weak may dominate the strong. . . .*

She remembered her hunger for knowledge, the studies that consumed her life, eschewing the frivolous companionship of well-born students whose hatred of Israel was less than hers.

That was before she came to know Hossein the Mad (as he was known in covert circles), before she met again, after long separation, her Arab half-sister, Atiqa.

The taxi stopped in front of the dark warehouse. She paid the driver and when the taxi pulled away, she went to a side door and knocked. Knocked again and gave the password.

Inside were the others, dressed in battle gear, loading pallets for the airlift to Beirut. She put aside her suitcase, discarded her dress, and began to put on her uniform.

Mossad (XVII)

The helicopter carrying Lev Rosenthal flew the Sinai wasteland at near-zero altitude, crossed Great Bitter Lake causing an up-rush of water birds, and landed just east of the Muqattam Hills.

Leaning against the silent helicopter Rosenthal wondered if Egyptian radar had detected the flight and a patrol sent out to investigate.

When he saw car headlights in the distance he walked to the concealment of a dune. The car came on—from the engine, not a military jeep or personnel carrier—and he let himself relax.

Briefly headlights outlined the helicopter, then went out. The lights blinked four times and Rosenthal left his place of concealment. To the pilot he said, "How long can you wait for me?"

"I must be back across the Sinai before dawn. Four o'clock and I leave."

"*Shalom*," Rosenthal said and went to the car. Zaki Awad opened the door, looked out and said, "*Ah-lan wa-sahlan.*"

"*Al-hamdillah.*"

"*As-salaam 'alaikum.* Who is it I have the honor to greet?"

"One with whom you have dealt in the past." They embraced each other and Awad said, "Permit me the honor of presenting my son, Ibn. He is a student of medicine."

"Most honored, sir," said the youth as Rosenthal got into the car.

Half an hour later they were in Awad's house sipping syrupy coffee while Ibn telephoned the major hotels in turn. Rosenthal felt safe with his grizzled host, for it had been Awad who first brought to his attention the treachery of Teitelbaum. Rosenthal said nothing of Teitelbaum's fate and Awad had been a Mossad agent too long to inquire. Ibn entered the room smiling. "Black is at the Semiramis."

"Good. The woman?"

"She, too."

"Then have the operator ring Black's room. I want to know who answers." He drained the cup and stood up. "If you will permit, I would like to have your son accompany me into the hotel."

"Ibn will deem it a privilege."

Ibn returned unsmiling. "Neither room answers," he said. "Not Black's or that of Nouri Farraj."

"Do not forget the room numbers," Rosenthal told him as they left the house.

From the Semiramis lobby Rosenthal rang Black's room, then said, "They may be in her room. If not, we will wait inside."

They approached room 414 quietly and Ibn kept watch along the corridor while Rosenthal placed his ear to the door before working on the lock.

The door opened to an unlighted room.

Drawing his pistol, Rosenthal went in low, followed by Ibn who took the opposite side. Rosenthal reached for the lightswitch and pressed it.

Ibn quickly closed the door.

Sprawled on a sofa, legs thrust forward, was Jay Black. His clothing was bloodied around the chest.

Rosenthal opened the closet and bathroom doors with the muzzle of his pistol. No one, no clothing, baggage, or trace of anyone. He walked to the balcony doors, closed them, and pulled down the blind. Turning he said, "Is he dead?"

Hand on Black's carotid artery, Ibn Awad looked up.

"Comatose," Ibn said. "In shock, but not dead." He lifted the left side of the bloodied jacket to expose the blood-drenched shirt. Kneeling beside him, Rosenthal pulled wallet and passport from the jacket's inside pocket. Both had been pierced by the bullet. He shook his head slowly.

With a pocket knife, Ibn cut away the shirt's left side. He went to the bathroom, ran water and came back with a towel. Carefully he cleared away clotted blood and with an exclamation bent close to the wound. "Look!" he said. "Do you see it?"

"I do," Rosenthal said excitedly. "Yes, I do."

Half hidden by torn flesh was a small, gray-black object.

Ibn soaped and rinsed his knife blade, then with the tip pried out the flattened bullet. With it came shreds of flesh, a bright splinter of bone.

"It was slowed by his money carrier," Ibn said exultantly, "so it only smashed against the rib." Fresh blood began to seep from the wound. Ibn cut compress squares from towels, pressed them against the wound; then they drew their patient upright and removed his coat so Ibn could tie a rough bandage around his chest holding the compresses in place.

Black began to groan.

Ibn pointed to a pistol on the floor. Rosenthal picked it up. For a moment he weighed the heavy .45 in his hand, then gave it to Ibn. "A souvenir," he said. "Use it more wisely than this fool."

With a nod Ibn pocketed the pistol. Rosenthal said, "Can he be moved?"

Ibn shrugged.

"Is hospitalization necessary?"

"The wound should be sterilized and stitched before he travels. One or more ribs may be broken. Tell me your requirements."

Rosenthal sighed and sat on the couch. "If it's not absolutely essential to save his life I don't want him in a Cairo hospital. Can you get disinfectants and bandages, perhaps a painkiller?"

"I have those things in my father's house."

"Then we'll put his jacket on and take him down the back stairs. I'll stay with him while you bring the car." He felt in the jacket pocket, brought out a room key. "I'll ask your father to clean out his room." He looked around. "As this one is."

For the first time since entering he wondered where Nouri Farraj had gone. Black, in his headstrong way, must have backed her into a corner, given her no alternative but shooting her way out.

And Jay had not fired back.

Blinded by love, he thought, and grunted disgustedly.

Still, Black might have learned one or two things of value from this many-faceted Arab agent, so he could not be allowed to dream the night away.

They replaced the jacket and Ibn tried wiping blood from it, but the fabric was deeply soaked. As they lifted his arms to their shoulders, Black groaned again and opened his eyes.

"Stay silent," Rosenthal snapped. "Try to use your feet."

At the doorway they turned out the light, then opened the door and scanned the empty corridor, waiting until a couple entered their room. "Quickly, now," Rosenthal ordered, and they half-carried, half-dragged the wounded man to the service exit.

Down three flights of stairs, seeing only one hotel servant who quickly averted his glance. In the alley they propped Black against the wall, and Ibn ran off for the car.

When Black began babbling, Rosenthal closed his mouth with one hand. "You've caused a great deal of trouble," he hissed, "and nearly lost your life. Want a piece of advice? Don't screw Arab women."

The darkened car came up the alley. Groaning in pain, Black eased into the rear seat. Rosenthal closed the door and got in the other side next to him. The car began to move.

Rosenthal said, "Don't talk now, stay awake and listen. The bullet went through your passport and billfold, slowed by leather, money, and credit cards." Briefly he saw lights glinting along the Nile, then the car moved into thin traffic. "You're not going to die, we'll take care of you, get you back to Israel. You must tell me exactly what happened. Did Reba shoot you?"

TWENTY EIGHT

Jay Black (XXIII)

"Yᴇs," I groaned, "she shot me." Hot pain seemed to flame out above and beyond my heart, my breathing was shallow, in little gasps. I felt as though a baseball bat at full swing had slammed my chest. Each bump of the road's irregular surface made me grit my teeth to keep from crying out. As my mind cleared I realized it was Lev Rosenthal beside me. But where had Lev been? I hadn't seen him in a long time. I remembered I was in Cairo.

Rosenthal said, "You're lucky the lady used a .32 with a lead bullet. If it had been jacketed, or if she'd turned that .45 on you, we wouldn't be talking now. Incidentally, how did you get that pistol?"

"Borrowed it," I managed, and closed my eyes, but Rosenthal slapped my cheek. "I'm not finished yet, you've a lot of talking to do before the night's over. Our driver is Ibn Awad, a medical student, thank the Lord, and son of a trusted friend whom you will shortly meet. We are going to his house for temporary repairs and then we are going to drive into the desert to return to Israel on the helicopter that brought me."

My hands pushed down on the seat to absorb some of the painful jolting, but that was a bad idea. My left arm felt as though it was being wrenched off. My forehead dripped sweat. I said, "She knows where Al-Karmal's located; her gang is going after them. They want the neutron warheads."

"Naturally. And where did your ex-lady say Bakhari is to be found?"

"In Lebanon. Near the coast." Pain slashed my chest.

"Keep talking."

"I . . ." Memory was returning. "She spoke of a bombed-out deserted village, said they were hiding there."

"What makes you think she was speaking the truth?"

"Because she'd decided to kill me." I looked down at my blood-stained jacket.

"Made her feel good to talk about it?"

Silently I nodded. Another jolt, another quick stab of pain. When it subsided I breathed again and said, "She told me Al-Karmal flew from France to Benghazi, took a freighter to the drop-off point. That's how her group knew."

"Now we're getting somewhere," Rosenthal said. "Perhaps our impromptu trips to Cairo may prove worthwhile."

Without turning his head the driver said, "We are almost there."

"*Courage, mon ami,*" Rosenthal said with a sarcastic smile.

"Do you want to hear more?"

"I have a profound interest in hearing as much as possible."

"Bakhari has two Cubans with him; they're the ones who can detonate the bombs."

Rosenthal's face turned away. "Cubans," I heard him mutter. "Why not?"

The car slowed, headlights went off. They helped me out of the car into a dimly lighted house. The pain made me groggy. Then I was lying on a bed staring up at a ceiling light. The driver was stitching my chest. The stab of the needle made me yell.

Rosenthal chuckled. "There is an English phrase: 'just deserts.'"

I couldn't talk through clenched jaws, and I was determined not to satisfy his sadism. The needle piercing my flesh had a gritty feeling.

Ibn dusted powder on my wound, wiped his perspiring face and said to Rosenthal, "He is fit for travel."

They got me upright and fed me a couple of pills with a glass of water. "It s only empirin," Rosenthal told me maliciously, "don't get alarmed."

"You *schmuck!*"

He chuckled again as Ibn's father brought me a cool glass of tea. I started gulping it down but Ibn said, "Slowly, sir."

"See?" Rosenthal said. "They like you. You're a hero to them. Know what you are to me?"

I wiped the back of my free hand across my lips. "Can it wait?"

Rosenthal sighed and stood up. "We have a flight to make."

Ibn brought compresses and bandages, taped my chest, and hung my left arm in a tight sling and strapped it to my middle. Ibn's father, whose name I'd forgotten, draped a loose-fitting Arab blouse around my shoulders and said something in Arabic that I took to mean good luck.

The empirin helped enough to get me over the rougher parts of the drive without yelling aloud. Rosenthal sat stolidly beside me. His mind was elsewhere, figuring our possible counter actions, rejecting, selecting, refining. It was as though I wasn't there.

So I watched the clear heavens, the coldly distant stars, and thought of the eternal land through which I was traveling, the slaves and the pyramids, the millennia of history around me, the predictable flow of the Nile, and. . . .

"There it is," said Ibn, and before he turned off the headlights I glimpsed a helicopter sitting in the darkness, waiting like some huge nocturnal insect.

"Out," said Rosenthal, and it was the first word he had spoken since leaving Cairo.

Standing on the sand I thanked Ibn. We shook hands and Rosenthal shoved me toward the helicopter. The pilot threw away his cigarette and spoke to Rosenthal in Hebrew. I heard the car back away.

Rosenthal helped strap me in. The engine whined, rotor blades began slowly turning, sound blasted from the engine. The only lights came from the instrument panel and the stars.

We lifted off in a furious swirl of sand.

I must have fallen asleep almost immediately, for when I woke we were over the Mediterranean, coastal lights blinking ahead.

I glanced over at Rosenthal. Asleep, his arms were folded over his paunch, his bearded chin rested on his chest.

Jabbing him, I pointed ahead.

He blinked, yawned and nodded. We flew up the coastline for a while, then turned inland north of Tel Aviv.

It was a different base than the one I had flown from with Pomerantz; two or three dozen helicopters glinting in the first light of dawn. Most were heavily armed gunships; others, like ours, not armed at all.

Rosenthal had the pilot take me to the field hospital building and disappeared. Israeli medics got me onto an operating table, gave me a shot of something and cut off Ibn's first-aid bandages. One of the operating-room assistants said, "Hey, you American?"

"Yeah."

"Me, too. From Boston."

"Doctor?"

"Training to be. I'm at the university. Tel Aviv medical school. Right now I'm a paramedic. Gunshot, huh? Who stitched you up?"

"A friend."

"Small caliber, huh? Let's get some x-rays here."

They wheeled over a portable unit, had me turn this way and that until my eyes were half out of my head with pain. Finally it ended and they gave me another shot. It didn't make me sleepy, but magically the pain oozed away.

"This is like Mt. Sinai," I said.

"Better."

After a while Boston came back and said, "Two fractured ribs, nothing serious. If you want, the surgeon will restitch the wound."

"How bad does it look?"

"Cosmetically? So-so. Any allergies? Penicillin?"

"No."

"Well, we'll give you a good jolt to clean you out. Stay off the sauce a few days, paisan." I felt a needle enter my rump, the customary hot discomfort of penicillin flowing in and backing up. Boston massaged it until the pain diminished. "We're going to put on a fresh bandage now, strap your chest pretty tight. Okay?"

"Okay."

The pain returned while they had me upright, working on my chest, pulling and tightening the tape. Boston fitted a loose sling around my neck and eased my arm into it. He said, "All you need now is a fife and drum," and chuckled. An orderly took me down a sloping ramp into a hospital ward. There were thirty beds but I was the only patient. "Hey," I said, "I'm going back to my hotel."

"Not for a while," Lev Rosenthal said behind me. "You brought back dangerous information. Reba's gang would want to finish what she bungled. No, you'll stay here until things are resolved."

"Hell I will."

"Listen, Jay, the last thing I need is you lurching around the landscape, tying up the attention and energies of Israeli officials who have far graver things on their mind." He paused. "I was

242

enjoying a string quartet concert when I was sent to retrieve you. That doesn't sit well with me."

"Go on, you loved it. Bet you felt young again."

He scratched his beard slowly and finally a grin showed through. "I did," he confessed. "Every minute of it. Truce?"

"Truce. But I'm not staying here."

"Is there anything you forgot to tell me?"

"No."

"All right. Pomerantz is away on patrol, but he's coming in to talk with you. I've got some reports to make, and my boss will have to make decisions. You can be most useful by staying quiet, letting your wound start to heal, talking with Eli. He'll have questions and you'll manage better after some rest."

"Can I phone my father?"

"No. I'll have him advised you're back in one piece."

He walked away up the ramp and I lay back on the clean-sheeted bed. Never, except in the 'Nam field hospital, had a mattress felt so good.

There must have been something slipped into one of my injections, because when I closed my eyes I couldn't open them again.

Before sleep surged over me I remembered the carved-stone expression on Reba's face when she pulled the trigger.

And I wondered where she was now, what her fate would be.

Nouri Farraj (II)

The plane landed bumpily at a crude airstrip southeast of Beirut where three trucks were waiting. She helped transfer cargo, working with the others in the cool night air, and when the trucks were loaded she sat beside the woman driver, Safia, leading the convoy southward into the night.

Half dozing, she tried not to think of what she had done in the hotel room. Jay was dead but it might be two days before his body was discovered. By then, another lover from her past would also be dead. Strange, she thought, the sentiment I feel for the Jew, when my loathing for Hossein is so great.

She had first seen Bakhari during *fidayun* training near Alexandria, and felt herself drawn to this fearless spokesman of Arab renaissance. Then he disappeared from camp, and she learned only later and with difficulty that he had gone to the Soviet Union for specialized education and training.

Afterward, hearing that Bakhari was seeking volunteers for a high-risk mission, Nouri offered herself, but her Fatah adviser insisted she refrain, saying her long-range potential was too great to risk. So she performed a covert support role for the Vienna assault on the OPEC Ministers.

Two years older and still above suspicion, she was chosen to smuggle gelignite into Amman for Bakhari's unsuccessful try at assassinating the Jordanian King. Hiding with Bakhari in the aftermath, she became his lover, and the relationship lasted until he brought to bed a militant young recruit from Quwwat an-Ansar, her half-sister, Atiqa. He found her, he said, younger and more exciting.

Personal vendettas were discouraged in her revolutionary milieu. Sullenly, Nouri helped Bakhari destroy the Cairo orphanage. Then, mission completed, she returned to the orthodoxy and discipline of the PLO while Bakhari—and Atiqa—organized Al-Karmal.

With renewed dedication she embraced her studies and took first as lover, then husband, Esmail Farraj, one of her professors, PLO militant and disciple of George Habash, whose dialectics she absorbed as a desert plant drinks rain.

Before being sent to Barnard, Nouri was assigned the task of murdering a wealthy Jerusalem Arab believed to have secret dealings with the Jews. She found it unbelievably easy to attract his attention, coyly decline his gifts and proffers of love until the moment was propitious. Then in his bedchamber she gave him poisoned coffee and watched him writhe and choke his life away.

At Barnard, Nouri began her scheduled transition into a double life. Earnest language student by day, by night Arab orator at gatherings in Village lofts, smoke-filled with hashish resins. And she learned how to switch identities as occasion required.

Mingling necessarily with Jews—Sephardim, Hasidim, Ashkenazim—she learned the culture and history of her father's people, a father she had never known. Angrily she had recognized the intellectual attraction of his race, rejecting it on the injustice of Partition, the hopeless sufferings of Palestinians driven from their homes by the same race that degraded her and the only two humans she had ever loved. Whenever tempted to feel sympathy for a Jew she had only to recall the savage violation of her body and revulsion swept over her with a nausea that left her ill and shaken.

Yet she had been drawn to Jay Black, powerfully attracted—she could not deny it—as he had been to her. What distinguished him from all the others? His New World innocence? His basic decency? The underlying pride in his Jewishness? Nonetheless, he had been prepared to turn her over to Israelis who would have tortured, then killed her. He must have understood that only one of them could live.

Headlights picked up a solitary jackal crossing the road. The eyes glinted then vanished as the animal sped into the blackness of a ravine.

Bakhari will not escape us, she told herself. Of Al-Karmal only the Cubans will survive.

At the Pentagon the senior military aide of the Secretary of Defense entered the Secretary's office and said, "Sir, the *Nimitz* has company."

"Soviet?"

Brigadier General Kirk nodded. "Two helicopter missile cruisers, *Leningrad* and *Moskva,* are following just over the horizon, and two nuke ballistic missile subs are trailing on the surface. One's a 'Y' class, the other a 'C.' The *Voroshilov* is still patrolling way up ahead. There's concern it might challenge the *Nimitz's* entering the Gulf of Suez. The Chief of Naval Operations wants to know if additional instructions should be sent."

"Not until I've talked with the President. Where is he?"

"Returning from Camp David. Touchdown at ten o'clock."

"I'll meet him," the Secretary said. "Get the White House situation room visuals current and tell the Joint Chiefs I want them available. Shit, we may have a war on our hands."

"Yes, sir. The *Kennedy* is scheduled to reach station this evening. So far only the usual Soviet long-range reconnaissance planes are reported. No bombers."

"That's a blessing." He got up and pulled on his suit coat. A desk telephone rang—the inter-Cabinet scrambler—and he heard the Secretary of State say, "The Soviet Ambassador's requested an emergency meeting with me, then an audience with the President. Do you folk know what it might concern?"

"Haven't the faintest idea," the Secretary said and broke the connection. Glaring at his aide he said, "Move your ass, Jack, we haven't a hell of a lot of time."

He left his office thinking that the first battle was about to be fought: to keep the President's backbone stiff against the Secretary of State pleading for a stand down, maybe holding open house aboard the *Nimitz* with vodka cocktails for all hands.

The only thing we've neglected to do, he thought glumly, is inform the Soviets we're preparing to shoot down Israeli aircraft in order to protect the Soviets' Arab clients.

Jay Black (XXIV)

The man shaking me was Eli Pomerantz, sand and sweat streaking the stubble of his beard. I blinked, tried to stretch, felt a jab of pain and lay back. I didn't want to get off the bed, but Pomerantz was telling me I had to. "Need a wheel chair?" he sneered.

"I'll manage." I got my feet over, felt suddenly dizzy but Eli's hand steadied me until I pushed it away. Boston, the paramedic, came over, pulled down my lower eyelids and shined a flash on them. I said, "I'm feeling better."

"With half a liter of good Israeli blood in you, you're perfect. He's yours, Major."

I managed the ramp on my own, not speedily, but steadily, and as I walked my strength slowly returned. The chest ache was constant, but I slipped my arm from the sling and let it hang down, feeling needle prickles as blood surged into finger capillaries.

A staff car whipped us away from the base. Pomerantz said, "Rosenthal gave me your basic information, but if I'm going to take a squadron of assault helicopters into Lebanon I need a precise target. A cross-border attack at this time is going to ruffle a lot of international feathers. The result must be worth the risk."

"I can't tell you what I don't know."

"But you can try. You've been physically shocked by a pistol bullet; your entire body and brain have been reacting to that. Well, the trauma's fading and I want you to put it aside and use your brain. So I'm going to show you aerial photos of the general area your lady was talking about; they'll have place names, identification aids that could help you tell us where Bakhari's holed-up."

"A bombed-out, abandoned village."

"Dozens of them," he said. "Scores. We had planes out all night looking for lights where there shouldn't be any lights. There was a photo recon run at daylight. Nothing out of place."

It was coming to me, developing. Then I had it: "I asked how her group had been able to locate Al-Karmal. She said men had been sent out on a probe. They didn't return."

His tired eyes lighted. "Where were they sent?"

"She didn't say."

"*Damn!*"

We were speeding past buildings now, houses, streetlights. I saw children in a playground. "She was in Cairo last night, her commando was assembling to strike at Bakhari's group and capture the warheads. Does anyone know where she is now? Where she went?"

"Probably to Beirut by air, so they're hours ahead of us. But that's useful information. We might be able to spot them heading toward Bakhari." He stared at the road ahead. "Maybe things are starting to move in our direction for a change. If you hadn't been a damn fool and gone to Cairo you wouldn't be telling us all this. And if Rosenthal hadn't pulled you out, got you patched up enough to talk and brought you back!" He turned and gave me a hard glance. "I don't know whether to deport you or decorate you."

"Winner's choice," I said. "Let's see how it all turns out."

The car slowed, turned into a military compound and we got out, I slowly because my side was stiffening again. Pomerantz led me into an air-conditioned building. Two corridors, a metal door, and we entered a photo interpretation center. A long, broad table held a mosaic of black-and-white terrain photos and goose-neck magnifiers. Around the table were officers in Navy, Army, and Air Force uniforms.

Pomerantz said, "Let's clear a little space, gentlemen. Mr. Black is going to have a try at this. Meanwhile, I want air coverage between our border and Beirut. What we're looking for is an armed group proceeding by land or sea in a southerly direction. Use one of the old Soviet planes or an unmarked C-47; if we locate them I don't want them to realize it."

With a curt nod an Air Force officer left the group.

I sat on a cushioned stool, looked down at the photomosaic and got oriented.

Pomerantz said, "If Al-Karmal went ashore from a freighter, the chances are they didn't travel far into the desert. That means you're looking for an abandoned village fairly close to the coast. And there's that Soviet-built Lebanese navy MTB, also suggesting proximity to water and some place for concealment: among fishing boats, in a narrow cove. We've looked but we haven't located it yet. Conceivably it's standing offshore, but I doubt it. Refueling would be a major problem.

"How big a boat is it?"

"Fifty tons, 28 meters in length. Fast, too, if the engines are in good condition."

I peered down through the magnifying glass, swiveling it slowly along the coast. All of it looked barren to me. The Israelis had done a thorough job of creating an uninhabitable buffer beyond their northern border. There were at least a dozen bombed-out villages all looking pretty much the same. Farther from the border, and inland, there were signs of habitation: goats, donkeys, wells with women drawing water. White ink labeled settlements in Hebrew and Arabic, neither of which I could read. To Pomerantz I said, "I don't even know what I'm looking for."

"Take a rest, have a cup of tea."

I went over to a table that held what looked like a large aluminum coffee urn, beaded with condensation. I filled a plastic cup with cold tea and drank gratefully. Suddenly I was hungry. My last food was a quick sandwich at Ben-Gurion airport before boarding the flight to Cairo. I didn't want to recall details of the bedroom scene in the Semiramis.

There was a rising murmur of voices around Pomerantz. I made my way back to the table, looked inside the rim of lights and saw a finger jabbing at one of the coastal towns on the maps. The officers were gesturing like a bunch of diamond merchants. Finally Pomerantz held up his hands and spoke in rapid, commanding Hebrew. That seemed to resolve matters, for his brother officers listened respectfully. A few questions were asked, then the group dissolved.

Pomerantz glanced at me, eyes deep-set with fatigue, "The consensus—*my* consensus—is that Bakhari's located in this place, Faiqal, on the coast. It's been dead for over three years, but enough buildings are still standing to provide cover for say fifty men. And there are coves where the MTB might be hidden. We're going to concentrate on it just at sundown, take high- and low-level slant-photos while searching north for the group from Cairo. We might just get a vector."

He moved back from the table and stretched arms and shoulders. "The Al-Karmal radio frequency came alive yesterday, so we learned they were somewhere close to Israel. Now we have a better idea just how close."

"What do you think they'll try to do?"

"Try?" He grimaced, drew himself a cup of tea, and came back to the table. At the far end a photo interpreter wrote on the overlay with a colored grease pencil. "I wish I could think of it as only a try, Jay, but all along Bakhari has enjoyed the luck of Satan. I think he plans to take the MTB near Tel Aviv and fire those warheads at the city. Just when the celebration is at its height. Midday. The parades start at ten, Begin and the Cabinet will be in the reviewing stands from eleven o'clock on. So we have to hit Bakhari at dawn, before he can leave Faiqal."

"Air strike?"

"I'm taking thirty men by fast launch and rubber boats. We'll land above and below Faiqal, converge, and find out who's there."

I said, "I'd like to go, Eli."

"Well," he said, "I like your spirit, but even if you weren't wounded you're out of condition and you don't speak Hebrew." He looked away, then back. "Leave this to the experts."

"I've been of help," I said, "I want to be in at the finish."

He grunted. "The finish may come in the sky over Tel Aviv. I'm not going to let you stay at the Ramada tonight because I can't trust your recklessness. Right now I'm going over to command head-quarters to make preparations for the strike. You can stay there tonight. The room will be comfortable, field-grade, and your bandage will need changing. Rosenthal might come by to listen to radio messages; he'll tell you what's going on."

"You're putting me under house arrest."

"Military detention."

"How long?"

"Until morning."

I tried to take a deep breath but the combination of pain and strapping prevented it. "Yesterday you mentioned something going on at The Hague: Rembrandts, terrorists. What happened?"

"It was taken care of."

"Let me go tomorrow, Eli."

"No."

"You suggested making my stay 'more interesting.'"

"You stole an Army weapon. I could have you jailed. So don't argue with me."

"At least let me go in one of the reconnaissance planes; I won't be in anyone's way."

He closed his eyes, massaged them with his fingers. After a while he said, "Maybe. That's not a promise, and it's contingent on developments in the situation."

"What developments?"

He took my right arm and walked me outside. "You'll be told."

TWENTY NINE

For this presidential briefing the SitRoom staff had been augmented and upgraded. The President and Vice President were present, the Secretaries of State and Defense, the Director of Central Intelligence, three of the Joint Chiefs, the Director of NSA and the President's National Security Advisor. In addition, the President had invited the Speaker of the House and the Leaders and Whips of both Houses of Congress.

They had assembled as unobtrusively as possible, yet numbers of them had been noticed by the ever-present White House Press Corps, and overhead the White House Press Officer was fending off media inquiries concerning the nature of the unscheduled high-level gathering. His reiterated "routine consultations" and unwillingness to expand on the phrase failed to satisfy media representatives who sensed a story in the making.

Brigadier General Kirk spoke from one side of a stage that displayed blown-up projections of the Eastern Mediterranean, while a large-screen cathode scanner printed out Order of Battle information covering Soviet air and fleet dispositions that was fed continuously from computers in adjacent rooms. Kirk was accustomed to briefing top brass at the Pentagon and occasionally the President, but as he looked across his audience in the half-darkened room he realized he had never appeared before so august an assemblage. Still, he was not intimidated, and his strong, crisp voice conveyed the harmonics of courage and truth as though he wanted to instill those qualities subliminally in his listeners, however unpleasant his message.

"The carrier *Kennedy*," Kirk said, "will be within air-strike distance of the Israeli coast four hours from now. The carrier *Nimitz* is being followed by Soviet submarine and surface vessels and may be challenged when it attempts to enter the Gulf of Suez after dark

251

tonight. Unless *Nimitz* can proceed into the Gulf, the distance to Israel will exceed the range of its aircraft." He adjusted the lighting rheostat and the ceiling lights went up.

There was silence until the Speaker of the House said, "I find it hard to believe, really *believe*, that we've allowed ourselves to be drawn into what appears to be the makings of a confrontation with the Soviets over the doings of a small gang of Arab terrorists."

"The point is," said the President with a show of irritation, "that it's happened and we have to face whether we are willing to permit Israel to retaliate atomically against the Soviets' Arab allies for an attack by a bunch of renegades for which the Arab powers are not even responsible."

"But the results of which they would applaud," observed the Secretary of Defense.

"Doubtless," said the Secretary of State. "But the scenario is one of attack, retaliation, then large-scale counter-retaliation. I believe the DCI will agree with my prediction that the Soviets' in order to maintain credibility, will totally destroy Israel if even one Arab capital is bombed with atomic weapons."

The DCI nodded. "That's our current estimate."

The Senate Majority Leader said, "I don't believe this Administration could survive politically if we ordered our aircraft to shoot down Israeli aircraft after a neutron attack upon Israel."

The Vice President, in his role as Chairman of the National Security Council, said, "Isn't that better than being forced into atomic confrontation with the Soviets? I mean, I've been a long-time supporter of Israel despite what it's cost us in terms of Arab hostility and oil shortages, but here it seems to me American interests are clear-cut. We're not formally responsible for the defense of Israel against Arab attack, even if atomic-type weapons are used. That's Israel's responsibility. Neither are we responsible for defending Arab cities against Israeli attack. But if we don't prevent such an attack the Soviets are going to hold America responsible since they already view Israel as a U.S. surrogate. So if it comes down to a choice between our shooting down a few Israeli aircraft or war with the Soviet Union, I don't think there's any real choice at all."

After a few moments' thought the President said, "In the event *Nimitz* can't reach striking position, can the *Kennedy*'s aircraft destroy *all* the Israeli bombers before they reach their targets?"

The Chief of Naval Operations said, "We have approximately

seventy-four attack aircraft aboard the *Kennedy*. The Israeli retaliatory squadron is a dozen or so F-15s. I'd say, yes, we can dispose of them. But our fighters will have to be already airborne when the Israeli planes start for their targets."

The Secretary of State shook his head. "If I may, Mr. President, other distinguished gentlemen, I'd like to suggest taking the Soviets into our confidence."

"You mean," said the Secretary of Defense harshly, "*encourage* the Soviets to shoot down Israeli aircraft?"

"If it comes to that. Better they do the dirty work than us."

The President's National Security Advisor said, "It occurs to me that we could simply tell the Israelis *not* to retaliate, regardless of provocation."

The Speaker of the House said, "What I know of the Israelis, and I have many prominent supporters of Israel among my constituents, strongly suggests they'd simply tell us to go to hell. They view their interests in a much narrower way than we in this room do, and it comes down to the survival of Israel as a nation."

The President said, "What orders have been issued to *Nimitz* and *Kennedy*?"

"So far," said the Secretary of Defense, "they're to take station twenty miles off Israel and maintain a high state of readiness to launch aircraft. No targets have been indicated. Attack orders can be issued minutes after you authorize them, sir."

The Senate Minority Leader said, "I can't swallow the idea of telling the Soviets our dilemma. Even if we do the Soviets would tell us to shoot down the Israeli planes ourselves, or suffer the consequences."

"So," said the President, "what do you recommend?"

The Senate Minority Leader grimaced. "*If* Israel is attacked by neutron warheads, and *if* their planes start a retaliatory flight, then I guess we better stop them. But our planes will have to have their insignia obliterated."

The Secretary of Defense snorted. "Each of our carriers has five thousand men aboard. How long do you think that artifice will remain secret from the press? Better we do it boldly, openly, out of conviction—to prevent the spread of nuclear war—than to try to hide the deed. In any case the Soviets won't be fooled." He took a deep breath. "As for the Soviets, they aren't allies, they are our dedicated enemies. *They* are the reason we have an army, a navy and an air force. Isn't it time *we* said, the U.S. assumes responsibility for what goes on in the Mid-East and we will not tolerate Soviet intervention in Israeli or Arab affairs? Put the bastards on notice, Mr. President."

The Secretary of State said, "You want to nullify all the progress we've made in arms control, provoke the Soviets unreasonably, invite a nuclear showdown?"

The Secretary of Defense ignored him. "The leaders of Congress are here. An immediate joint session can be convened for an unprecedented address by you."

The President's eyes scanned the faces of the Congressional leaders, but he said nothing. The Secretary of Defense continued: "A bold Presidential statement would. . . ."

"Bold!" exclaimed the Secretary of State. "Arrogant, you mean. Provocative!"

"Please! I have the floor. Yes, a bold statement by the President would suit the mood of the country as I perceive it, and I believe that once you've stated that policy the Soviets would abide by it, and. . . ."

"Ah," interrupted the Majority Leader, "but would they?"

"Time will tell. Certainly the Israelis should welcome it, and all but the most fanatical Arab leaders would breathe a sigh of relief. When Jack Kennedy challenged Khrushchev over the Cuban missiles the entire country closed ranks behind him. This could be a time of true historic greatness for you."

The President eyed his Secretary of Defense. "It *would* be dramatic, wouldn't it? Now, if the leaders of the Congress agree. . . ."

The Secretary of State's face was a pained mask as the Congressional leaders drew together and whispered. Quietly the Secretary said, "I hope you will permit me to give Ambassador Konstantinov some intimation of what's ahead?"

"In due course," the President said and stood up. The others rose, and the Senate Minority Leader said, "What about shooting down Israeli aircraft?"

"That option," said the President, "remains open. Until Israel comes under attack."

Mossad (XVIII)

In the late afternoon Haim Ben-yomin made his report to nearly the full Cabinet. They were assembled around an elongated oval table, Prime Minister Begin at one end, the Mossad Chief at the other. Defense Minister Weizman was absent from the meeting; the explanation given by the Prime Minister was that he was inspecting troops along the Jordanian border. Ben-yomin knew differently.

The Mossad Chief said, "We have reason to believe that the Al-Karmal group has been hiding in a former Fatah settlement. An amphibious commando unit will close in on the village before dawn."

Scattered murmurs of satisfaction from the Cabinet.

The Minister of Foreign Affairs said, "Just before coming here I was handed an urgent cable from Blum in Washington. It seems that many American government officials are at the White House for some kind of special meeting. Moreover, Soviet Ambassador Konstantinov has been at the Department of State for several hours. He is said to want an emergency meeting with the President, but as yet he has not been received by the Secretary."

Begin said, "Ask Blum to go to the Department and try to find out the reason for all this."

Arieh Winograd said, "Final dispositions of fire and rescue units, crowd control forces, and emergency care stations have been made. The blood plasma has arrived and been distributed. There are sufficient supplies of food and water for all survivors." His voice rose. "Prime Minister, there is still time to cancel the celebration, the parades. . . ."

In a harsh voice the Minister of Labor said, "Menachem, you have acted high-handedly in this throughout, as though these decisions were yours alone to make. If Eretz Israel survives the Arab attack, your conduct is going to be made an issue in the Knesset."

Begin said calmly, "The majority of the Cabinet is with me. If you care to resign on the eve of peril, I will accept your resignation."

Surlily, the Minister of Labor shook his head.

"Then," said Prime Minister Begin, "we have done what we could and all that we could to avert disaster. Our fate, as always, is in the merciful hands of the Most High." He turned to the Minister of Religious Affairs. "Rabbi, we will be grateful for a prayer to the God of Abraham."

Reverently, Haim Ben-yomin bowed his head, hoping the rabbi's words would not echo the Kaddish, the Prayer for the Dead.

Nouri Farraj (III)

They had driven all night and for two hours after sunup until the paralyzing heat forced the convoy to take cover under the rock shelf of a *wadi* that provided some shelter from the sun's rays, from the prying eyes of reconnaissance aircraft. Camouflage nets added to their security while the commando slept under their trucks.

In her dream she had been a scabbed, filthy child again, hungry—always hungry—her scrawny body covered with a sack stitched up by her mother, and the hawk was plummeting toward the sand, striking unseen, then lofting swiftly, a writhing snake in its claws. And she had yearned for its meat, thinking how roasted snake and part of the hawk would fill her belly, savoring the imagined feast until her mouth watered.

Atiqa was laughing at her, understanding a shared fantasy, telling her to come to the tent for her portion of the day's bread.

She remembered playing in the sand with her sister, finding a nearly-round stone to roll as a ball, then, tired of the sun, sitting where the tent cast shadows, and picking lice from each other's hair. She felt lice crawling and woke. Sand was trickling on her leg, cast there by a moving scorpion.

Rigid, she saw its curling sting as the forelegs began to test her flesh. Slowly, she lifted her automatic weapon and with a downward thrust of the butt crushed the scorpion into the sand.

Releasing pent-up breath she drew her legs away and sat up, wiping moisture from her throat.

Her watch told her that it was time to rouse the commandos, break out food and eat. Afterward it would be dusk and cool enough to travel.

She gave orders to the two guards, broke open boxes of canned and dry rations, checked the supply of water. As the tired, dirty men filed past, she doled out food to each, taking her and Safia's share to where they ate together.

Haroun brought over his compass and she checked it with hers, choosing the next hour's course from the map. The man seemed exhausted, she thought; too long the soft life of the cities. She gave him a little extra water from her canteen, thinking there would be water among Bakhari's stores, and they could rest there for a day before returning with the warheads. Perhaps desert travel was easier for her, she thought, because she had been raised in the desert among scorpions, thirst, hunger, snakes, and jackals. Her one lingering fear was of brutish men . . . Jews.

Bakhari would die like any man, either better or worse, and with him would die his dream. It was his irrational genius, she conceded, that had brought about the capture of the neutron warheads, but with them he would have become a menace to all Arabia. His egoism was unappeasable. Hossein the Mad.

To Haroun she said, "Let all weapons be checked again. This will be the last opportunity before the attack."

Nodding, he went away. Nouri and Safia gathered emptied cans and food wrappers and buried them in the sand. Then they got into the cab and Safia started the engine.

Twelve hours to Faiqal.

Al-Karmal (XIV)

Toward sunset they saw the Mystère flying north just off the coast; presently it returned, heading south and inland at a higher altitude. "Let them search," Buenaventura said contemptuously. "They will find nothing. Only villages they themselves destroyed."

Later as they were eating cold field rations they heard a twin-propellor aircraft flying east and out of sight. Marco said, "It sounds like an old Dakota C-47."

"The great Israeli Air Force," Bakhari sneered. He got up to stretch and walked to the doorway of the hut. Far offshore, silhouetted against the dying sun was an Israeli patrol boat. Without question, Israeli vigilance had been increasing, but now on their final evening all the Jews could probe with were two obsolete aircraft and a plodding patrol boat of the type used to prevent smuggling.

Behind him, Buenaventura tuned the short-wave receiver to the Beirut weather broadcast. Nearby, seated on a crate, Marco worked on a board-backed chart of the Eastern Mediterranean with dividers and parallel rules. After a while Buenaventura turned off the receiver. "Light seas," he said. "Wind from the north-northeast at ten knots."

Marco said, "That will help our outward leg, but not our inbound."

Bakhari went over to the chart and bent down to examine it. "In case something should happen to you, I need to know the sailing plan."

"Very well, comrade. From here, the point of departure, we follow a compass heading of two-five-eight degrees." He indicated the course line slanting into the Mediterranean. "We need to follow it for a hundred and forty nautical miles. At that point we turn back toward the coast, here. The course to be followed is one-two-two degrees. It should put us directly on the Gaza beach."

"At what time?"

"Dawn is at 6:12, and we will need a certain amount of light for safe landing. Now, the total distance to be covered is two hundred and forty miles. If the MTB was not burdened with the helicopter and its engines were perfectly tuned, we could calculate on a six-hour voyage. However, to compensate for wind and tide and the condition of the engines I think we must allow seven hours at sea. Accordingly, our departure will be eleven o'clock tonight."

Buenaventura said, "The helicopter is fully fueled, as you know. At most it will take an hour to board our men, supplies, and equipment. The transmitter and warhead components will be put aboard last. I will not connect the circuits until we reach Gaza."

"Why not?" Bakhari demanded.

"To avoid the possibility of premature detonation. Our transmitting frequency is not exclusive. Besides, I will want to test the warhead trigger during the voyage."

"So," said Bakhari, "we will start loading and boarding three hours from now."

Through the doorway they could see the sun's afterglow gilding a narrow strip of the horizon. Above, the sky was already deep blue, nearly cloudless. Tomorrow night, he thought, the sun would set on a dead Tel Aviv.

The Secretary of State rose from his desk to greet Ambassador Konstantinov who shook hands unsmilingly. He was not accustomed to waiting three hours to see the Secretary, and it confirmed his suspicions that something extraordinary was in the making. Tersely declining coffee, he said, "I am under instructions to confer with the President, Mr. Secretary. How soon can it be arranged?"

The Secretary seated himself on a sofa facing his visitor's chair.

"I doubt it can be scheduled today, Mr. Ambassador. The President—"

"This is very urgent. Most urgent. The Chairman. . . ."

"Perhaps you could give me some idea of what you propose to convey. Then," he shrugged, "perhaps we can resolve it between ourselves."

Konstantinov eyed him sharply but the Secretary's placid face was unrewarding. "My Chairman demands an explanation of the extraordinary behavior of your aircraft carriers *Nimitz* and *Kennedy*."

"Extraordinary, Mr. Ambassador? Extraordinary in what way?"

"Both appear to be headed toward the Eastern Mediterranean at a high rate of speed."

"Indeed?" The Secretary frowned. "Forgive me if I am unaware of specific naval movements." He sipped coffee from his cup and set it down carefully. "This is a busy time for the President and I doubt that he would know more of the matter than I do. So, while you are here let me call my colleague at Defense and attempt to answer your inquiry." He went to his desk, picked up a bright yellow phone and pressed a buzzer. In a moment he heard General Kirk answer.

"General," he said, "this is the Secretary of State. Is the Secretary available?"

"Always to you, sir," said Kirk. "One moment." Then, "Yes, Mr. Secretary."

"Sorry to trouble you, but I have the Soviet Ambassador with me. He wants to ask the President something about the activity of two of your carriers. I know nothing of the matter, but thought you might. Can you help out?"

"Which carriers?"

The Secretary of State turned to Konstantinov. "He wants to know which carriers you refer to."

"The *Nimitz* and *Kennedy*," he said with controlled impatience.

After repeating the names the Secretary of State listened a few moments, said, "Thanks so much," and replaced the scrambler phone. Returning to the sofa he said, "Seems to be no mystery whatever. The Secretary says they are conducting speed trials, that they will rendezvous in the Eastern Mediterranean to launch and retrieve aircraft."

Before the Soviet Ambassador could speak, the Secretary said, "In return, my colleague asks whether you could explain the extraordinary attention being paid to the *Nimitz* by Soviet surface vessels and submarines."

"I am not aware of any such attention," Konstantinov said stolidly.

"Further, my colleague at Defense notes the presence of the Soviet warship *Voroshilov* off the mouth of the Gulf of Suez and suggests that it be advised the *Nimitz* is preparing to pass up the Gulf and through the Suez Canal."

"Why is the carrier making such a trip?"

The Secretary spread his hands. "My dear fellow, if it is to rendezvous with the *Kennedy* in the Mediterranean there is hardly any other way, short of shoving it across the sands."

A knock at the door and an aide entered. Without looking at the Soviet Ambassador he handed a half sheet of paper to the Secretary of State who read and returned it. When the door closed he said, "The President is preparing to address a joint session of the Congress tonight. And. . . ."

"But I must *see* him," Konstantinov said. "Those are my orders."

The Secretary of State had begun to enjoy his unusual role in the diplomatic charade. "Really, Mr. Ambassador, I've answered the questions you were instructed to ask, have I not? What possible further reason could there be for intruding on the President's time when he is preparing an important address to the Congress, the nation, and the world."

"The *world*?"

"Indeed. Just as every address of Chairman Brezhnev has a worldwide audience, so has every pronouncement by the American President. You agree?"

The Soviet Ambassador nodded.

"You will be invited to be present with the entire Diplomatic Corps."

"Of course, of course. But what is the subject of this sudden Presidential appearance?"

Smilingly the Secretary of State spread his hands. "Who knows? Perhaps we're repudiating the gold standard. No, seriously, I haven't the slightest idea. But if you'll meet me at the East Entrance of the White House at, say, seven-thirty, I'll see if the President can see you for a moment before he leaves for the Hill."

Konstantinov's face relaxed. "I would be grateful, Mr. Secretary. Most grateful."

The Secretary rose and the Soviet Ambassador shook his hand before being guided to the door. Before opening it the Secretary of State said, "It could ease the way if I were able to tell the President that the *Voroshilov* will stand well clear of our carrier, to avoid misunderstandings, you know. Freedom of the seas, eh?"

Konstantinov stared at the Secretary. Had he been outmaneuvered? "I will see to it at once, Mr. Secretary."

"Good. And I will see you at the East Entrance. Now if you care to telephone me regarding the *Voroshilov*, I plan to be here the balance of the day. Good of you to come; sorry about the delay."

"Quite all right, Mr. Secretary," Konstantinov said as he was ushered through the doorway.

The Secretary beckoned the aide who followed him to his desk. "Start issuing diplomatic invitations to the Joint Session by telephone, but tell the Protocol Office to downplay any hint that something big is up."

"Is something big up?" the aide inquired.

The Secretary of State grinned. "Brother, you have no idea."

Picking up the yellow phone he rang General Kirk and told him the *Voroshilov* would not challenge *Nimitz* at the Gulf of Suez. The Secretary of Defense came on the line and said, "Good work, Mr. Secretary. I'm beginning to enjoy working with you."

"Pure chicanery," the Secretary of State chuckled. "I find I enjoy it myself. See you on the Hill."

He replaced the phone and swung around in his chair. It had been almost beyond memory since he had been able to persuade the Soviets to do anything more than release a few Jewish dissidents, and he thought with pleasure of the shock awaiting Ambassador Konstantinov in the Oval Office.

THIRTY

Mossad (XIX)

AFTER film strips from the day's last photo reconnaissance flights had been processed and examined by photo interpreters, Major Eli Pomerantz was awakened by a sergeant who brought a cup of coffee. Pomerantz drank it sitting on the edge of the military cot. The few hours' sleep had drained off some of his accumulated fatigue. He pulled on his boots, splashed water on his face, and dried it. Then he went down the corridor to the photointerpretation room.

The senior PI officer said, "Major, the sunset run over Faiqal produced nothing tangible." He pushed over a swivel-necked magnifier then pointed to a large photo of a ruined village. "It's close enough to the water, but we can't find any sign of recent habitation. The only possible item of interest is this coastal point here."

Pomerantz said, "I don't see anything."

He slipped another photo under the magnifier. "This photo was taken two years ago when we were also looking for guerrilla encroachment. Now here—this point on the coast—shows a narrow, rock-sided cove. This evening's photo doesn't show that cove at all."

"What happened to it?"

"That's the question. Wave action on the rocks, then a rock slide could have filled it in. Or, it could be camouflaged."

"Can't you tell?"

"If we used infrared film we could, but—" He shrugged. "We used high-speed black-and-white that doesn't reveal latent heat differential."

Pomerantz swore.

The PI officer adjusted his glasses. Hesitantly he said, "We could

263

rephotograph tonight if you want the place lit up with magnesium flares."

"Last thing I want." Pomerantz shook his head and straightened up from the table. "Anything else?"

The officer shoved aside the Faiqal photographs and laid down another film strip. "Southern Lebanon. This village is Qana, about twenty miles northeast of Faiqal. The Dakota slant-photo run produced this interesting shot out in the desert just south of Qana." He placed a large magnification in front of Pomerantz. "Because the sun was low in the west it produced these long shadows. That's what we saw first, so we blew them up. The three darker spots—what caused the shadows—are vehicles. They're moving where vehicles aren't usually found. By following the tracks, then projecting a line ahead, it comes pretty close to intersecting Faiqal."

"What kind of vehicles?"

"Trucks, military trucks. Big tires for sand travel, everything camouflage-painted to resemble desert terrain. We'd never have spotted them from overhead, it was the shadows that revealed them."

Pomerantz said, "I think you found the Popular Front commando."

"I was hoping you'd say that. All right. They're three-axle trucks, four wheels on each of the two rear axles. We identify them as Soviet-built troop carriers, same type the Soviets used in Afghanistan. But they don't carry insignia of any kind."

"Well," said Pomerantz, "we know they aren't ours. The Soviets haven't been generous to Israel for quite a few years."

"The topography is bad for vehicular travel—sand, dunes, wadis—and the area lacks anything resembling permanent roads. That means they're moving slowly. They have to. Out there broken axles can be fatal. So we estimate they were making no more than eight to ten miles an hour during daylight. In darkness they'll have to reduce speed even more. If it's a covert movement they won't use headlights, they'll probably stop until the moon rises enough for visibility."

"I know," Pomerantz said, "I've done that a good many times." He went over to the cooler and came back with a glass of tea. After sipping he said, "Even if you can't find signs of life at Faiqal, somebody thinks there's something there, with enough certainty to make that desert trip." He pointed at the trucks. "Assuming five miles an hour, what time will the convoy reach Faiqal?"

The PI officer used dividers, a map scale, and figured briefly. "About four o'clock tomorrow morning. Of course they might sleep while it's cool and resume driving in the morning."

"But I don't think they will. So, I'm going to get my group there before the trucks arrive."

"Anything further I can do, Major?"

Pomerantz smiled. "Not unless you can tell me how many Arabs are in those trucks and what kinds of weapons they have."

"Sorry."

"Shalom." He went into the unit commander's office and telephoned his second-in-command, alerting him for earlier embarkation. "We'll leave at two. I'll tell you why when I join you."

He went outside and drove a jeep out of the PI center. The air was cool, Pomerantz reflected; it would be even cooler at sea.

From the naval base at Haifa to Faiqal was just twenty-five nautical miles. The *Daya* would take a zig zag evasive course to target, extending the distance; but the French-built PT boat was fast and seaworthy. He expected it to make the run in less than an hour, slowing just enough to wet-launch the six rubber boats offshore.

Then, he thought, we will learn who inhabits Faiqal, and who travels in three camouflaged trucks. I should have reconfirmed the morning photo overflight before leaving just now, but I can do it from Haifa.

It could be a historic photo, he reflected moodily, or it could show nothing more than a lot of bodies in the sand.

Our bodies.

Around him the night air seemed suddenly more chill.

Al-Karmal (XV)

They cut away the camouflage netting, and the outlines of the torpedo boat emerged under the moonlight. The boat rocked gently, the Kamov's rotor blades responding flexibly to the P-6's rise and fall. Wooden platforms fashioned from fallen village timbers spanned the space between the edge of the cove and the decking. While Marco supervised loading weapons and ammunition, Buenaventura and Bakhari ran up the radio batteries a final time and disconnected the generator. Bakhari emptied a handful of sand into the fuel tank, though he would have preferred seeing it burn and explode.

Carefully they closed the radio equipment in two wooden crates to protect it from sea spray. Buenaventura oversaw its loading by four men, then returned to where Bakhari waited beside the lead-lined nuclear weapons crates. Buenaventura said, "These should be stowed in the cabin in line with the keel. I am going to hold the detonating mechanism myself and will ride near the stern."

"Why?"

"The heat may have made the explosives unstable. If I cushion it on my thighs we avoid undesirable risks."

"You are indeed a dedicated comrade."

The Cuban looked at the illuminated dial of his watch. "On schedule," he said. "I want six men to carry each warhead aboard."

Bakhari gave the orders and walked beside the working party until they had the crate aboard and stowed below. Then the second warhead. The smell of diesel fuel permeated the cabin's still air.

The time was 10:55.

Bakhari saw Buenaventura coming aboard, carrying the box with the detonating mechanism. Now 21 men were aboard. Aboud, Bakhari remembered, would have been the twenty-second. *Assalaam 'alaikum*, he murmured and turned his attention to his followers. Zayid, the helicopter pilot, was to ride in the cabin where he could rest more comfortably than the men who lay along the weather decks. Buenaventura had found a spot at the stern.

With a deep burble of power the P-6 thrust out of the cove through shallow waves. The helicopter blades, though folded back, flexed slightly in the increasing airstream. Gradually, Marco pushed forward the throttles, watching the twin tachometer dials, as with the moonlight behind them they gained the open sea.

A mile offshore, Marco pointed at the compass and eased left until the card stopped at two-five-eight degrees. Then he shoved the throttles ahead until the hull was planing and water in a high plume rose above the stern.

"Four and a half hours on this course," he shouted at Bakhari. "Then we turn shoreward for Gaza." He marked the time on a pad: 11:15.

Forty-five minutes until the anniversary of the birth of the Hebrew state.

Except for minor vibration due to the topside weight of the helicopter, the boat ran smoothly over the calm Mediterranean. Bakhari sat on one of the cushioned stools and pinched off a wad of *khif*. He chewed silently, watching the dark horizon, and when they had been an hour at sea he saw a large, garishly lighted ship in the distance. Bakhari drew Marco's attention to it, but the Cuban shrugged. "A cruise ship," he said, "such as come into Havana. Perhaps it is headed for Haifa bringing more Jews to be destroyed."

But the ship was the carrier *John F. Kennedy* taking up station off the coast of Israel.

Its radars picked up a small surface blip, fast-moving to the south-southwest, but its course and distance were nonthreatening and so no chopper was launched to investigate.

In Israel the day of celebration had begun.

Mossad (XX)

Lights at Haifa's Bat Galim naval base were darkened while the *Daya* slipped quietly around the breakwater and into open sea. Then it came on course, accelerated gradually, and the captain spoke by radio to base command. Light flooded the harbor again.

Standing in the pilot house, Eli Pomerantz watched Haifa fading astern. The moon came from behind a cloud and showed the decks of the darkened craft, the cargo of six jet-black rubber boats preloaded with watertight containers of weapons, small arms, ammunition, explosives, recoilless rifles, and communications gear. The thirty men of the assault commando unit were trained to attack from the air, by surface boat or submarine, and all of them were battle proven.

We have, thought Pomerantz, a final chance at Al-Karmal and they must not elude us as they did in Avesnes. Before dawn we are going to destroy that human filth: Israel depends on us to do so.

He looked at his watch: 01:48 in the morning of Israel's Independence Day. Pray God, he thought, that all goes well.

On the far side of the pilot house the radar operator monitored a hooded scope, searching for other vessels ahead, marking the boat's progress by navigation features along the irregular coast. He was to notify the captain as the boat passed the Lebanon border. Then the commando would prepare for launching.

The *Daya* was running radio silent, but a radioman with a

headset was guarding the command frequency that could order mission abort. Pomerantz did not think the commando unit would be recalled.

The captain said, "Major, what do you make of that American carrier's arrival?"

Pomerantz shrugged. "What I've been told. It's come to conduct joint training exercises with another carrier."

"*Another* one?"

"Yes, due before dawn, coming up through the Canal."

The captain frowned. "A courtesy call for our celebration?"

"I don't know what to think, but I don't like it. Normally we'd get a couple weeks' notice. So. . . ."

The radarman called, "We'll be off the border in one minute, Captain."

Pomerantz said, "Considering the seas, what's the maximum speed we can launch at?"

"Just under twenty knots. I'm turning toward shore. Better get ready."

Pomerantz climbed down to the deck and passed the word among his men. Like their commanding officer they wore black, close-fitting elastic suits, black gloves, and a headpiece that covered their faces to the eyes. Weapons belts and shoulder straps were of black nylon as were their rubber-soled boots. Narrow armbands displayed the light blue Star of David, and there were no symbols of rank. Methodically the three starboard crews lowered cargo netting over the side, edged the rubber boats into position. The first three would be launched south of Faiqal, and Pomerantz would see them underway. Then he would launch north with the portside group and develop a pincer movement to penetrate the village.

To each boat crew, Pomerantz said, "If possible I want Bakhari alive, but don't sacrifice your life in sparing his."

The *Daya* slowed, bow meeting water again, and at the captain's signal the boats went over the side, each tethered by a line. Uzi machine pistols across their backs, fifteen men climbed quickly down the netting and into the pitching boats. *Daya* crewmen cast off the lines in sequence, and the rubber boats vanished astern.

Four minutes later the other boats were launched, Pomerantz in the lead craft. Free of the tethering lines the rubber boats slowed and turned toward shore, propelled by silent electric outboards.

The coastline was dark except for the glinting phosphorescence of low surf spilling on the sand. They beached sooner than Pomerantz expected, but then the tide was low. They hauled the boats onto dry sand, unloaded them rapidly and turned the boats' prows back toward the sea. Pomerantz used his walkie-talkie to confirm the landing of the southern group and ordered them to move in toward the village.

As they left the beach they could see Faiqal a few hundred yards down the coast, unlighted, silent, ruined. Five men moved rapidly ahead, scouting for Al-Karmal guards, ready to kill with knives. Soon Pomerantz and the others overtook them. No guards. Rejoined, they cut inland around a deep cove, and Pomerantz wondered if this was what had been shown him on the photograph.

Not even a barking dog in the settlement. As Pomerantz reached the nearest rubbled wall he felt a premonition that the huts would be deserted, the enemy gone.

He radioed his lieutenant, speaking softly, and learned that the other half of the commando unit had encountered no guards. "We'll go in," Pomerantz ordered. "Carefully."

So they slithered along the street, keeping close to the remaining walls, entering each hut—Uzi first—until both halves of the unit joined in the center of Faiqal.

"Gone," Pomerantz said loudly, "or they were never here. Check each place with a light. Go!"

Handlights revealed rough straw mattresses, empty tin cans, spilled ammunition, a slit trench with still-soft excrement, the air-dried bodies of two naked men tattooed in Arabic.

When he saw them Pomerantz decided they were the two sent out by the PFLP group and who did not return.

A sergeant led Pomerantz to a roofed hut and shined his light on a gasoline generator. Pomerantz pulled the starting cord and the engine began running, died out. Light showed fuel in the tank, sand clogging the bottom.

Only one other point to check. Pomerantz took five men back to the cove where lights showed discarded platforms, severed mooring lines, slashed camouflage netting, and on the bottom a litter of metal: punctured fuel drums, machine guns, and torpedo tubes. The lieutenant called his attention to sunken cans of blue and white paint.

Pomerantz shook his head slowly. Too late again. "All right," he said, "we've seen enough to report. All lights out."

Using the field radio, he contacted headquarters and said, "They were here but they've gone, probably left just a few hours ago. By boat over-painted with our colors.

My suggestion is you guard the sea approaches to Tel Aviv as never before."

"Yes, of course," came the reply. "Are you going to stay there a while?"

"Yes," Pomerantz said. "So the night shouldn't be a total loss."

"Very good."

"I'll keep you informed. Over."

Pomerantz looked at his watch. Barely three o'clock. The operation had run like an oiled weasel. Unfortunately, little had been accomplished. The salvation of Israel had slipped from his hands.

Calling the commandos together, Pomerantz told them to take up positions behind the inland walls of the battered settlement. Under the moonlight he saw them find protected locations, set up machine guns and bazookas, open grenade and ammunition sacks, and settle down to wait.

Arms resting on the sill of an open window, Pomerantz stared out at the ridged dunes, the empty blackness beyond. Al-Karmal was on its way, traveling at sea, moving rapidly toward the finale of its frightful plan. But how were they going to bring it off? How to fire neutron warheads from a stripped-down MTB?

The Cubans were professionals. Somehow they had devised a launching platform.

Somehow.

The dejection of failure came over him like the coils of a python. Success had seemed so near, victory over Hossein Bakhari almost reality . . . so much depended on him. The realization of failure was devouring him.

He forced air into his lungs, tried to fight off depression. Phase Two of the mission had yet to be accomplished but now it was incidental, a postscript to failure. His eyes welled over, tears wet his cheeks. Reminding himself that he was still a soldier he wiped them away, blinked, and stared fixedly into the darkness.

At 03:47 when he was half asleep, Major Pomerantz heard a strange sound in the distance. Alert suddenly, he listened, and heard it again: a sound that somehow combined low humming, the steady breaking of gentle surf. Then he knew it for what it was.

Engines.

THIRTY ONE

THE Secretary of State shepherded Ambassador Konstantinov into the Oval Office where the President was reading the final draft of his policy statement.

The two arrivals stood in respectful silence while the President finished a page. He took off his glasses, rubbed the bridge of his nose, looked up and smiled. "So good of you to come, Mr. Ambassador. Thank you for escorting our distinguished visitor, Mr. Secretary. Please stay. I'd offer something by way of refreshment but I must leave shortly for the Hill." From his desk he lifted a legal-length Xerox copy of his address and handed it to the Secretary of State. "For the Soviet Ambassador with my compliments. Gentlemen, make yourselves comfortable."

The visitors seated themselves as the Secretary handed over the stapled copy.

"Mr. President . . ." Konstantinov began, but the President held up one hand. "Permit me to presume on long association, Mr. Ambassador. The Secretary tells me the two of you were able to resolve whatever it was, the warship matter, you were instructed to see me about. So, that no longer being on the agenda, you are here at my invitation so that I can convey to you succinctly, in advance, and to avoid any possible misunderstanding, the thrust of my message this evening." He got up from his high-backed chair and came around the front of his desk. Leaning his haunches against it, he folded his arms and looked down at Konstantinov. "A previous Administration tacitly accepted what has come to be known as the Breshnev Doctrine. As generally understood it arrogates to the Soviet Union full hegemony over the affairs of Communist— excuse me—of the Warsaw Pact countries, those once-free, now communist-governed nations of Central and Eastern Europe. Chairman Brezhnev enunciated this doctrine unilaterally, without reference to the post-war European policies of the United States of America. So be it. My country has no desire to interfere with the realities of Soviet domination."

The Soviet Ambassador smiled in satisfaction.

Clearing his throat, the President glanced at his desk clock. "There is another area of the world in which the Soviet Union has its client states and we have ours. I refer to the Middle East. They are Semitic people, Mr. Ambassador, unrelated in heritage either to Russia or the United States. For more than thirty years the Soviet Union has taken advantage of their ancient religious animosities and pitted Arab against Jew. During that period the United States intervened only twice: in Lebanon and in Iran. The continuing tumult and turmoil in the Middle East has strained the resources of the United States and exhausted our political patience." He gestured at the address in Konstantinov's hands. "A situation has now arisen that bears the gravest implications to the peace of that area and of the world. You may be aware of it. Today, in consultation with my advisers and the elected representatives of the American people, I have concluded that American interests—and those of the entire world, and specifically the Soviet Union—require a new and comprehensive statement of American policy toward the Middle East. Its essence is this: As of this day the United States of America is assuming full responsibility for the maintenance of peace in the Middle East. What Israel does to Jordan is henceforth the exclusive province of the United States. What Libya does to Israel is also the exclusive concern of my country. As best we can we are going to work out peaceful accommodations among adversaries, and we decline to accept the advice, threats, or subversion of the Soviet Union. If war should break out in the Middle East—and I pray God that it does not—then my country will force an end to hostilities.

"We have no designs upon the territorial integrity of the Soviet Union now or in the future. This you must understand clearly and not undertake further aggression cloaked as self-defense, publicized as 'fear of encirclement.' Let me speak even more plainly: Soviet intervention in the Middle East whether tonight, tomorrow, or at any future time will cause a direct confrontation between our two powerful nations. And I want you, your Chairman, and the Central

Presidium to understand that you will face war with the United States of America."

Ambassador Konstantinov's face was rigid. The Secretary of State sat immobile. The President said, "Even now, our direct circuit to the Kremlin—the Hot Line—is transmitting the full text of my address. In the interests of world peace and international understanding, I suggest that you return to your embassy and send an immediate message to Chairman Brezhnev stating that I, the American President, have told you, the Soviet Ambassador, that any response by the Soviet Union to whatever events occur in the Middle East will mean war. I want Chairman Brezhnev further to understand that the United States wants peace, but that the Soviet Union can no longer have peace on its own inflexible terms, if true peace is what your country desires. Do as you will in your captured nations; we will do as we choose in the Middle East. Do you understand, Mr. Ambassador?"

The Soviet Ambassador stared at the President. He opened his mouth to speak, then nodded.

"Very well," said the President. "I appreciate your coming, sir, for I feel that what I have said is of crucial importance to the future of both our countries. May I depend upon you to report to Chairman Brezhnev the full substance and flavor of my words?"

Swallowing, Konstantinov managed, "Yes, Mr. President."

The President strode toward him and shook his hand as the seated men stood up. "Again, I thank you for coming, regret the brevity of this meeting, and look forward to talking with you soon."

Again the Soviet Ambassador nodded.

The door opened and a White House usher said, "Mr. President, your escort is here: the Sergeant-at-Arms of the United States Senate."

"I await his pleasure," the President responded, picked up his speech and left the Oval Office.

For a moment the Secretary of State and the Soviet Ambassador looked at each other. Then Konstantinov glanced down at the document in his left hand. "I," he said, "I hope you will excuse me from attending the Joint Session of Congress, Mr. Secretary."

"Of course." The Secretary took the Ambassador's elbow and guided him toward the still-open door. "As a fellow diplomatist let me urge a parting thought on you: No one can have his way at all times in every part of the world, not even the Soviet Union." He patted Konstantinov's shoulder fraternally. "Don't hesitate to consult me on problems as they arise, Mr. Ambassador. My door is always open to you."

He watched Konstantinov walk away.

In the outer reception room the Secretary was met by the Deputy Secretary of State who said, "The *Nimitz* is in the Mediterranean. That's the only word we've heard from Israel."

"Well," said the Secretary of State with a bleak smile, "let's hope it's all we'll hear."

Outside, under the portico, he got into his waiting limousine and settled back for the five-minute drive to Capitol Hill. As police escorts sped the procession along Pennsylvania Avenue the Secretary reflected, almost in awe, that the President's composure, his choice of words, and his directness had been magnificent. The crisis had transformed him, somehow conferred those qualities of leadership so desperately sought by the nation. The Chief Executive had risen to the requirements of his high office.

But he could not help wondering how much of what the President said to Konstantinov had been five-card Hoosier bluff.

Nouri Farraj (IV)

Her body ached, her eyes were strained from peering ahead where headlights thrust a cone of visibility across the undulating sand. Her hands clenched the steering wheel. Although Safia dozed beside her she felt curiously isolated, alone in a barren expanse that from time to time her dulled senses perceived as endless, unrelieved ocean. Then she would blink and look upward through the dirty windshield at the heavens, striving to ward off sleep.

To stimulate her mind she sought out constellations: Cassiopea, Andromeda, Draco. She recognized the star Algenib and thought how few were known by their Arabic names. The ancient Mesopotamian preoccupation with astronomy had been absorbed by the Greeks, as were other arts developed by her Arab ancestors: mathematics and medicine. So the modern world was ignorant of Arab contributions to humanity, and thought reflexively of camels, oil, and Mecca.

And the bloated sheiks of OPEC who pretended to speak for teeming millions and whose limousines she often craved to bomb. They, too, would be disposed of, with their mercenary guards and troops, their extorted wealth at last distributed among the masses who existed as she once had lived, dispossessed, despised, and homeless.

Though Atiqa defended Bakhari's ambitions as pure and selfless, Nouri had known him first, in action and in hiding, had heard his oaths and imprecations, his unguarded boasts. To unify Arabia under Hossein, she knew, would be to crown another venal, autocratic king.

But that was not to be.

Not if they reached Faiqal undetected and attacked before Al-Karmal could organize itself for battle.

Her eyes felt gritty. The constellations had shifted a few degrees, and she checked the course by compass. Her heading was correct. Behind, the other trucks, darkened, followed blindly through the night.

Lamentable, she thought, gripping the wheel harder, that Arab partisans must fight among themselves to see which vision will prevail, but this assault is as necessary as crushing the head of a krait before it can strike and kill.

She remembered overbalancing a boulder with Atiqa and finding in the cavity a nest of newborn kraits, banded bodies squirming in the warming sunlight. Made bold by fear they stoned and clubbed, shrieking, until the snakes were dead, decapitating and burying the heads beyond another dune lest in darkness they reunite and seek revenge.

But that was long ago and childish superstitions had been purged. If Atiqa was at Faiqal she, too, would die and their lifelong rivalry would end. Her sister's death was as essential as Bakhari's. Their venomous nest must not survive.

Startled by headlights, a jackrabbit bounded to the shelter of a thornbush. The unexpected motion roused her senses and she concentrated on details of the battle plan.

Her flank was to the north as the skirmish line moved westward toward the sea. She touched the grenades on her jacket; they were for emplacements first, then were to be used to flush Al-Karmal from such buildings as remained.

Her watch showed that it was Safia's turn again to drive. She would have let her comrade sleep but she badly needed two more hours of rest.

Touching Safia's wrist, she spoke her name, and the woman reached quickly for the weapon across her thighs. Nouri's hand covered the trigger guard as she said sharply, "Wake, there is no danger."

Safia's eyes were wide. "No . . . danger?"

Slowly she shook her head. "Not for a while."

She turned off headlights to scan the far horizon and saw a star streak earthward through the sky, trailing an arc of cold blue fire.

An omen.

Al-Karmal (XVI)

Running by dead reckoning the P-6 reached the end of its seaward leg and turned shoreward on a course of one-two-two degrees. The port engine was misfiring occasionally, but picked up promptly and regained sync at 3950 r.p.m.s. Marco yielded the helm to Hossein Bakhari and went below to sleep through the final three-and-a-half hour run. Because the inbound course was perpendicular to the shoreline, the MTB presented only its narrow bow profile to coastal radar, and Bakhari expected to slip through without challenge.

He thought: if, somehow, they know of this boat they will be expecting us near Tel Aviv, not forty miles south at Gaza. Even then they know nothing of the helicopter and how it will be deployed. How the blow will come.

Spray had begun to fleck the windscreen. Light wind came toward the port bow and the MTB developed a slight roll. Five or six men were already seasick; stretched prone on the deck they vomited into the scuppers. Now, Bakhari feared, more would become ill, but they would have to endure it until their feet trod Gaza sand. No one died from vomiting, and there were other, more useful, ways to die.

Turning, he glanced astern where Buenaventura dozed upright, the precious box on his outstretched thighs. He noticed the compass card turning, compensated, and brought the boat back on course, wondering how far he might have strayed.

Zayid—good, skilled Zayid—slept below. His task was the heroic one, though how heroic the helicopter pilot did not yet know. Would not know until the ultimate moment over Tel Aviv.

A distant light caught his eye; far off the starboard bow it twinkled. Green. Then a minute red companion. Running lights of some offshore craft. Probably a trawler working through the night.

I have come far for this, Bakhari mused; halfway around the world; survived battles, skirmishes, betrayals, and many unknown dangers, so that I may fulfill my destiny.

Nine hours from now.

Mossad (XXI)

Through the red fields of their night scopes they saw the first truck lumber over the dune and crawl slowly down to where the sand leveled off below. There it halted. A second truck appeared, traversed the dune and stopped beside the first.

Waiting, Eli Pomerantz felt his throat tighten. Where was the third? Broken down in the desert? Would its riders escape the battle about to begin? Was he to be denied the fullness of even this unimportant victory?

Then he saw its tarpaulin emerge above the ridge, nose and body appear. It seemed to steer downward with difficulty, and when it was lined up beside the first two trucks their engines went off.

The sudden silence was eerie. Pomerantz fancied he could hear his own sweat dropping on the sand. In his hand the grip of the signal pistol was slick, and as always before battle he felt half sick with fear and anticipation.

From the rear of the trucks bodies dropped onto the sand. Armed men in dark headcloths, bandoliers across their shoulders, automatic weapons in their arms.

They formed an uneven line in front of the trucks. A leader stepped forward, gesturing at the village, describing an enveloping, twin-flank deployment that Pomerantz thought was, of course, the only way to come in. He estimated forty fighters.

From two hundred yards away they spread out and began advancing through the darkness. Two men carried a heavy machine gun between them, apparently the attackers' largest-bore weapon. He had feared preliminary mortar attack that could have caused Israeli casualties, but he had not been thinking as an Arab:

they wanted the neutron weapons intact; random mortar explosions could have destroyed them.

Ironic, he thought; they expect Al-Karmal to be here just as I did. Instead, their attack will be without real purpose and against Israelis.

Before the flankers could spread beyond the sweep of the commando's machine guns, Pomerantz thrust his pistol through the window, pointed upward and fired.

As if on command the Arabs halted. The parachute flare broke high above them, spraying magnesium sparks, illuminating the desert as brightly as high noon. Reloading quickly, Pomerantz fired again and swiveled his Uzi onto the window sill.

Continuous fire poured outward from village walls. Already a dozen Arabs were down, the others confused, some burrowing forward, others scattering toward the trucks. He heard the heavy roar and whoosh of bazookas; their projectiles slammed into the trucks and exploded. One truck vanished in a huge sheet of flame. Another salvo finished off the other two. Their spurting flames reddened the sands, replacing the fading flares, and now the commandos' firing concentrated on survivors silhouetted fatally against the billowing flames of their vehicles. A gas tank let go in a bulbous burst of flame, and Pomerantz left his sheltered wall and started moving outward, aware that he was visible to the remaining attackers who lay prone, firing wildly at the village walls.

Forming behind him the commandos went forward, crouching and firing. He saw a man drop, and kept going. He hurled a grenade at four prone riflemen, fired the Uzi at an Arab crawling toward the edge of darkness. Pomerantz flung another grenade at rifles sticking outward from a sand rill. They disappeared in an eruption of white flame.

Suddenly he was on his knees and toppling sideways. He felt his face strike sand, as enormous, uncontrollable pain flared outward from his thigh. He managed to twist belly-down, sight the Uzi, and drop an Arab hero who was racing toward them, firing an automatic weapon from his hip.

Weakness overcame him. As he lay prone, he turned his face to clear his nostrils of sand. Hot wetness covered his leg and he reached down to touch the sopping fabric. Great waves of pain drove breath from his lungs, and he remembered his python-coil fantasy before the battle.

Only sporadic firing now. His men would be killing off those

Arabs not yet dead, giving the coup de grâce to maimed terrorists. Ending their suffering.

The third truck gas tank exploded, sending fresh illumination across the desert. Pain receded long enough for his lungs to gulp a fresh supply of air. Steeling himself against the sure onrush of pain, he raised his torso on his elbows and saw only black-suited figures moving between himself and the burning trucks. There was no more firing. The PFLP group was extinct.

Pain clouded his vision. Hazily he made out men running toward him. They seemed to come in long, loping strides as in slow-motion film. It was taking them an eternity to cover the final fifty yards. His strength gave out and he collapsed onto the sand.

They were doing something with his right leg. Miraculously the pain had vanished. Morphine. Of course, morphine. He felt like sobbing in gratitude for its release.

On either side blackness. He was lying on the bottom of a rubber boat, tourniquet around his thigh. The lieutenant said, "Feeling better, Eli?"

"Yes, much better." He tried proping himself up and nearly fainted.

"You've lost blood. We're going to transfuse."

He felt the alcohol swab, the tightness of the ligature, the smooth insertion of the needle. His eyes traced the thin plastic tube upward into a bottle held by a corpsman. The ligature loosened and he felt warm, life-giving plasma flow into his vein.

The lieutenant sat on the edge of the boat, smoking a cigarette, eyes on the major's face. "No survivors," he said. "We killed all 37."

"Our losses?"

"One dead: Landau. And Frumkin took a bullet in his chest. He's, well, he's still alive." The lieutenant tossed his cigarette toward the water. "Ben-josef's ankle is shattered. Others have superficial wounds."

"I'm sorry," Pomerantz said. "I'm always sorry."

"But it was worth it," said the lieutenant. "You know it was."

He thought of Bakhari, Al-Karmal, the Lebanese MTB that even now might have reached Israeli soil. But he could not confide in his lieutenant. The men must never be allowed to think this night had been in vain, learn that its once-high prospects had deteriorated into a desert sideshow that accomplished nothing to preserve their people and their land.

The lieutenant said, "You haven't asked about yourself, Eli."

"I'm alive."

"True, but your thigh. . . ."

The corpsman said, "The bone seems to be broken, Major."

He felt nothing on his right side from the hip down; was the leg already amputated? The sight of bandage and tourniquet reassured him.

After a while he said, "You've made your report?"

"Yes, Major. They'll send choppers at first light."

"Can't they do better than that? Frumkin. . . ."

"I'm afraid we'll lose him anyway. One lung is collapsed, we think there's a bullet fragment in his heart."

"Don't leave him here," Pomerantz said fiercely. "Leave none of us here in this . . . this *Arab* sand."

"We'll all go home," the lieutenant said soothingly. "You know we never leave anyone behind."

Pomerantz breathed deeply. "I know," he said. "I know. You've posted a perimeter detail?"

"Yes, Major." He looked up, inland. "Trucks still burning. They'll burn a long time." Brushing sand from his knees he said, "Two of the dead were women."

"Have all papers and documents been collected?"

"What little there was. Yes. Major, I've done everything you would have done. Don't worry about it. Get some rest."

The corpsman deftly removed the empty plasma bottle, replacing it with a full one without interrupting the flow.

I need to get back to Israel, Pomerantz thought as darkness obscured his vision. I failed. Now I want to die with my people.

Menachem Begin was awakened so that he could watch the President address Congress. Impassively the Prime Minister listened to the Presidential words, and as the television camera scanned the members of Congress rising in a body to applaud he phoned the Minister of Defense at his underground headquarters. "Ezer, you heard the President?"

"Yes, Prime Minister." His voice was tired.

"What does it mean for Israel?"

"Unless we survive the next two days . . . nothing."

"Yes . . . yes. So it is not coincidental, the arrival of the American carriers."

"I agree, and don't particularly like it."

Begin sighed. "Nor do I. Is there news, Ezer? Hopeful news?"

"None, Prime Minister. When our commando got there the Arabs had left Faiqal. We believe them to be at sea, armed and coming toward Tel Aviv."

"Then the situation has actually worsened."

"I am afraid so. You . . . are having second thoughts about *Trumpet*?"

"No. Everything will proceed as planned." He laughed bitterly. "Without warning the Americans have suddenly made themselves masters of our destiny, yet they cannot even guarantee our survival this one day."

"No, Prime Minister."

"Forgive me for disturbing you."

"I was awake. I appreciate your call."

"L'haim."

"Shalom."

As the Israeli Prime Minister replaced the phone he wondered if "Peace" was the last word he would ever hear Weizman speak.

He turned out the light at his bed. There were still a few hours until dawn.

At Command Headquarters Lev Rosenthal had been listening to radio exchanges with Pomerantz's commando. He made only one telephone call: to Haim Ben-yomin, informing the Mossad Chief that the commandos had found Faiqal deserted, and entered unopposed. He relayed information about the MTB's Israeli colors and promised to keep Ben-yomin further informed. Now he was debating whether to wake him a second time with news of the fire fight and its outcome.

Really, he thought, it has nothing to do with Al-Karmal, Hossein Bakhari, the neutron warheads. In that sense the mission was a total failure. As a border skirmish it was successful though the loss of good men was always painful. And Eli was severely wounded. There was a chance he would lose the leg.

He got up from his chair to stretch back and shoulders, drank a glass of water, and gazed at officers silent at their desks. He had been too occupied with the commando unit to watch the Presidential address, but from a radio summary he was not at all convinced the Americans had acted wisely. So, he thought, henceforth Israel is to live under protection of the American nuclear umbrella. But what use were the offshore carriers with their mighty striking power if Hossein Bakhari could devastate Tel Aviv with a single neutron blow?

Suddenly he felt useless. He had not even been able to forewarn his wife and children of the danger threatening Tel Aviv. How long since he had even seen them? Two days? Three?

A voice channel dedicated to the airborne retaliatory squadron became active, and Rosenthal listened to the air-ground conversation. From thirty thousand feet the squadron commander was commenting on what lovely targets the two lighted carriers would make as they slowly cruised below. Knowing the Americans were monitoring the conversation, the ground commander told the pilot curtly to shut up and fly a different, distant sector.

We're all tense, Rosenthal mused; like prisoners waiting for the axe to fall, those of us who know the implications. And inevitably the number had increased as more and more radio and radar men were assigned to special duties. Another week, he thought, and the whole country will share the secret. But a week from now the secret will no alonger exist.

He thought of Jay Black, né Jacob Schwartz, asleep in another part of the building, and decided that if Jay wanted to rejoin his father in the morning that would be fine. If Jay wanted to ride the helicopters with him to Faiqal, that was equally fine. He deserves something, Rosenthal reflected; Jay gave us our final chance at Al-Karmal.

Returning to his chair he stared at doodles he had made on a paper pad, then heard a radio message from the commando: Frumkin was dead, please notify his family.

The military commander swore.

Rosenthal wadded his doodle sheet and hurled it at the wall. It struck the face of the twenty-four clock whose hands had moved significantly since last he looked.

5:15.

One hour to dawn.

He decided to go and waken Jay.

For better or for worse it was going to be a memorable day in Tel Aviv.

With other guests at a Georgetown dinner party, Bryan Wellbeck and wife had watched the Presidential address, and its bold implications became the sole topic of dinner conversation. Wellbeck's inner reaction was one of immense relief; finally the line had been drawn. The Director's morning meeting would reveal something of the future.

He sipped Bordeaux as his wife said, "You're unusually quiet, Bryan."

"I'm thinking," he told her, and put aside the wine.

As he did, he wondered if Jay Black had gone to Cairo and found the Arab terrorist-trollop. If so, Mossad might have gained information to pass along. But perhaps Jay was back in New York again, tending the store. Tomorrow he might call, find out what had happened to him since the burning of Windover.

Probably not much.

Al-Karmal (XVII)

Through the salt-stained windscreen Marco made out a narrow strip of gray on the far horizon. That would be the first indication of dawn, he realized, so at least we're heading East.

During Bakhari's hour at the helm the boat had been allowed to go off course, whether from inattention or the dulling effects of *khif*, Marco did not know. So in a way it was lucky that the port engine began losing revolutions and causing the boat to veer quite naturally to port. Ignorant of what to do, Bakhari had wakened the Cuban in near panic, and Marco had taken stock of the situation, synchronized the starboard engine with the port, although it somewhat slowed their progress, and brought the P-6 back on course.

Now, with Bakhari sullenly below, Buenaventura was using the radar to try to locate recognizable features on the coast, but they were still below the horizon and the radar ineffective. So the question remained: at what part of the coast were they headed?

One hand on the wheel, Marco consulted the navigational chart and saw that uncorrected torquing could have brought their heading toward Tel Aviv, forty miles north of Gaza City. In between there was very little to help verify position: navigational lights here and there, if the Israelis were still using them. Still, he thought, from fifty miles out a heading error of a degree or two was not much to worry about: wind and tide could have caused that much drift even if he had been at the wheel rather than Bakhari.

The Arab had been indefinite concerning the length of time the port engine's revolutions had dropped even though it was an important factor. Bakhari had become surly and defensive, cursing the Lebanese for maintaining their ships poorly, then gone below to sulk, leaving everything up to Marco to correct.

As usual, the Cuban thought, and hoped that after today he would never have to work with Arabs again. Africans were bad enough, but Arabs were in a class by themselves for ignorance, slovenliness, and indiscipline. Just look at the terrorist soldiers puking their guts out though the sea had been calmer than anyone had any right to expect. Only two or three of them could hold their heads upright.

Buenaventura left the radar scope and came over. "I may have something," he said. "If so, you ought to steer right five or six degrees. I'll be better able to tell when we get closer."

Marco turned the wheel slightly, and above them the helicopter creaked and groaned as the deck canted and wind came from a different angle.

A quarter of an hour later Buenaventura turned off the radar and said, "I found Gaza City, so come left about ten degrees and we'll be where we ought to be."

"What range?"

"Twelve miles."

"Closer than I thought," Marco said with relief. "Better tell our all-knowing Leader."

With a smile, Buenaventura ducked down into the cabin.

Marco eased back the throttles, dropping five knots of speed. The sky was grayer now and he could make out deck features that had been invisible before.

Rubbing his eyes Bakhari emerged, looked around, noticed the light gray distance and said, "Ah, the Promised Land."

"It's time to rouse the men, Hossein. We'll be at the beach in half an hour."

"Listen," Bakhari said, "*I'm* giving the orders. I'll rouse the men when I want to." But he went down the ladder and began kicking the soles of boots, picking up discarded weapons and thrusting them into feeble hands.

Zayid came from the cabin, yawned, and said, "A good trip, comrade. I slept all the way."

"You're the only one who did," Buenaventura said as he came up the ladder. Zayid was gazing up at the helicopter whose nose and plexiglass were coated with salt spray. Never before had he lifted off a moving vessel, but there was a first time for everything. He climbed up on the superstructure and began examining the shackles and runners, the damp underbody. From there he could see land quite clearly, and no Israeli patrol boats in sight. If theirs had been detected during the voyage, the entire Hebrew navy would be converging on them. But . . . nothing.

He patted the side of the Antonov, longed to be at the controls, heading for Tel Aviv, warhead armed and ready.

Thanks to Hossein Bakhari, he was being allowed to carry out the age-old Arab dream.

THIRTY TWO

Jay Black (XXV)

WHEN Lev woke me I tried sitting up, forgetting my wounded ribs, winced, and got sideways out of bed. He said, "How do you feel?"

"Rested."

"Want to travel?"

"Tel Aviv?"

"Let me tell you what's been happening while you slept the night away. Then decide."

I looked at my watch: 5:38. He helped me put on an Army shirt and field jacket. My left arm belonged to me again, but my chest was still in the grip of an unkind giant. So I swallowed a pain pill and set about the challenge of lacing my boots.

Rosenthal took me downstairs to a mess hall where there was coffee, bread, honey, and fresh fruit. I sweetened the thick coffee with honey, poured some on a chunk of fresh bread, and came into the real world as he told me about the Faiqal mission, the offshore carriers, and the President's policy declaration. Only Eli's condition interested me. "How is he?" I asked.

"I thought you might like to go with me and find out. Al-Karmal's headed this way, we're quite certain now, and I find there is little for me to do at this late stage."

I pocketed an apple, got up and said, "Let's go."

Four choppers were warming up when we reached the base. Stretchers, medical supplies, corpsmen, and doctors were loading. Two were hospital craft of the kind that had air-lifted me to Camranh Bay after my leg was shot, one was a troop carrier, and the fourth a big Huey gunship escort.

The base commander greeted Rosenthal and we got into the

troop carrier that was empty except for pilot and crew. There was just enough light in the sky to make out the shoreline as we got airborne, the Huey leading the way.

We flew a few miles inland, north over Israeli territory, dropping altitude as we neared the border. I recognized Haifa harbor, saw a few early lights on cranes and ships below. Rosenthal was either asleep or deep in thought; his closed eyes were puffy with fatigue.

Beyond the border our diamond formation opened up, and in a few minutes I looked down and saw the smouldering remains of trucks inland from the ruined village. Dark figures were scattered across the sand.

I tapped Rosenthal's shoulder and pointed down. There on the narrow beach were the black rubber boats that delivered the commando unit, men grouped nearby. They waved as we came in.

The hospital ships landed first, then we settled down on the sand. The gunship cruised above us like a mother hawk. Lev and I got out and went over to where the wounded were being stretchered and attended to. They had a plasma bottle over Pomerantz; with his headpiece off I could recognize his pale, shocked face. Somehow he saw me, one hand lifted and beckoned. I went over and said, "Hi. Glad you're okay."

He smiled weakly. "Good of you to come." Then Lev was beside us. To the doctor he said, "Load the others, we need a moment to talk, please."

Pomerantz said, "Any news, Lev?"

"None, Eli."

"I should have been here earlier, hours earlier."

"What was it? A hunch, that's all. Don't even think of blaming yourself. There's still time, we haven't given up."

For a few moments Pomerantz was silent. To me he said, "Almost forty dead. Two women. I thought you ought to know."

My throat tightened. "Thanks for telling me." I felt my hands open and close. The commandos had nearly boarded. A detail was deflating the boats, bringing them back, too. For the next mission in the endless war. Pomerantz was looking at me oddly, searchingly. I said, "Anyone I might know?"

"Ask the lieutenant; he has everything we recovered."

So I found the lieutenant counting heads as the black-suited warriors entered the carrier craft. "Documents?" he said. "There hasn't been light enough to look." But he untied a canvas bag from his waist and handed it to me. Just then I saw them lifting Eli's stretcher into the chopper. Rosenthal was walking toward me.

I opened the bag and spilled its contents on the sand, knelt, and began searching. Paper money fluttered in the light onshore breeze, fragments of letters, mementos. Then coins: dull silver, copper, a glint of gold. I drew it from the sand. Not a coin, but a six-pointed star, linked to a scorched gold chain. I didn't need to look for the Georg Jensen imprint, I knew it was there. Looking up at Rosenthal I held out the star.

Quietly he said, "I'm sorry, Jay, truly sorry." He turned and pointed toward the settlement, the sands where bodies lay. "She's somewhere over there. If you want, I'll. . . ."

I couldn't trust myself to speak. So I scooped coins, paper money, and carnets back into the bag. Getting to my feet I handed him the collection bag.

Without speaking again we walked toward the nearest hospital ship and climbed aboard. Two body bags were being hoisted carefully into the other. Two dead Israelis. She could have killed one or both. And she had tried to kill me.

The rotors churned faster and we lifted off. Something was being fitted into my hand. Lev sharing a bottle of medicinal slivovitz. I drank deeply, drank again, coughed, and handed him back the bottle. He drank briefly, wiped his mouth, and said, "You haven't asked me anything."

I pointed at the collection bag. "What happens to it?"

"Mossad keeps the paper, of course, for future operations. The valuables are turned over to ILAN, the foundation for handicapped children."

He drank again and capped the bottle. "That was a toast to Israel, to survival."

I took the bottle from him, and drank again. A toast to the living, a salute to the dead.

Al-Karmal (XVIII)

Still burdened by the Kamov helicopter, the P-6 moved slowly into the shallows off the deserted beach. When the keel scraped bottom, Marco reversed engines quickly, then steadied the boat against the current while Zayid started the helicopter engine. They had neglected to shield it from spray and it took the pilot three tries before it coughed into life. Zayid ran up pressure and engaged the rotor blades. The helicopter shuddered, transmitting its vibrations to the boat. Four men clung to the superstructure ready to open the restraining shackles, and when the whirling blades were invisible Zayid gestured sharply with his free hand and the shackles dropped away. He added power and the Kamov began to lift, tail first, in a sort of stagger. Then it was above the boat and moving toward the beach. The Arabs cheered.

Lighter now, the boat was able to ground closer to the beach. Anchors were heaved and Marco cut the engines for the first time since leaving Faiqal seven hours ago.

Standing on the bow, Bakhari searched the beach for signs of life, then signaled disembarkation.

Rubber boats were unlimbered, shoved over the sides. Armed men dropped into hip-deep water, some floundering from weakness and apprehension. Marco supervised the unloading of weapons, supplies, and radio equipment; everything was hauled ashore in the inflated boats.

The helicopter, rotors drooping, was halfway up the slanting beach and facing the sea. Zayid dragged a packed cargo parachute to the door and shoved it onto the sand. Then he got out and watched the disembarkation.

The crated warheads came in separate boats followed by Buenaventura carrying the detonating mechanism in its protective box. He got out of the boat and went to a place near the helicopter where two men spread a tarpaulin on the sand. Buenaventura lowered the box, turned and waved at Marco who restarted the engines, cut the anchor lines, and turned the boat until it faced the sea. He lashed the wheel, shoved the throttles full ahead and jumped over the side.

The Arab commandos halted their work to watch the P-6 accelerate until it was hidden behind a high crescent of spray. Then Bakhari deployed six men along a ridge of sand, automatic weapons pointing inland.

Dripping wet, Marco staggered onto the beach, turned, and saw a trace of white spray that marked the departing boat. Perhaps the Israelis would sink it and think they had destroyed Al-Karmal.

Without it, there was no escape from Gaza if they were attacked, and he had a feeling of abandonment.

Sitting down he got off his water-soaked boots and saw Buenaventura beginning to assemble the bomb components.

It would take a while to rig the warhead to the cargo chute, then Felipe would want to test the radio detonator circuit before final installation.

Beyond the beach, inland, the sky was the color of a sooty sheet. In another few minutes the rim of the sun would be visible.

Soon the streets of Tel Aviv would begin to fill with Jews.

Jay Black (XXVI)

Pomerantz and the other wounded were choppered to Rokach Hospital, and by the time Lev and I got there through streets already thick with vendors, buses, school children, and parade organizations, he was on the operating table. The commando lieutenant noticed us sitting in the waiting area and came over. "It's going to be a long operation; a soft-nosed bullet shattered the femur and tore up a lot of flesh and tendon. So they're going to try to rebuild with bone from the other leg." He shook his head. "I guess Eli's headed for early retirement."

"There are worse things," Rosenthal observed. "If that occurs Eli will have the time he's always wanted to delve into our archeology."

"And he'll be available to Mossad," I suggested.

Rosenthal smiled and got up. "As long as we're here, perhaps you ought to have that dressing changed."

"Not a chance. I could use some coffee, though."

So we went down to the clean, well-lighted cafeteria, and the rubble and death of Faiqal seemed very far away.

We were drinking coffee and talking very little when the lieutenant came in, looked around and walked to our table. In a low voice he said, "There's been a development and they'd like you at command headquarters. A chopper's on the way."

We finished our coffee and went out to the pad. Presently a helicopter came down from the light-blue sky and took us aboard.

In the command room a white-shirted Naval captain briefed Rosenthal with the aid of a chart overlay. They spoke in Hebrew, so when the captain stopped speaking and put aside his pointer, Rosenthal beckoned me to the chart. "We've sunk a motor torpedo boat at this point, about thirty miles offshore. It bore our flag and insignia but it ignored radio and blinker challenges and so our patrol boat blew it out of the water."

"Well," I said, "that's great . . . isn't it?"

Rosenthal shook his head. "The trouble is that neither air or sea search of the flotsam was able to find any bodies. They dragged a Geiger counter over the area, and there was no radiation. Now I'll grant you the warheads could be on the bottom, intact, but why no bodies? Not even fragments to attract the gulls?" He stared at the chart again. "Another thing. The boat was headed outward, away from shore. There's nothing out there for Al-Karmal, unless Bakhari rather implausibly decided to attack the two American carriers. So what I conclude from all circumstances, is that Al-Karmal got ashore, then sent the empty boat to focus our attention on it, persuade us that sinking it ended Israel's danger."

"How could Bakhari be sure the boat would be sunk?"

"Because our Navy always attacks when challenges are ignored or improperly answered: standard operating procedure."

"Maybe they just wanted to get the boat away from their landing point. In daylight it was bound to attract attention."

"Then they had a double purpose," he said. "We don't know where they landed, and we have to assume they'll act as quickly as they can before being detected. Either they're on the move toward Tel Aviv, or they're holed up and hiding as they did at Faiqal where our best efforts couldn't locate them." He looked at the overlay marking the location of the sinking. "The boat was going fast, less than an hour. Which means the landing took place around dawn."

"So what's the answer?"

"Keep on searching, but I don't think we'll find Al-Karmal in any conventional way. If we locate the terrorists—and I say *if*—my present guess is that it will not be due to Israeli brilliance, but to Arab error."

"It's possible some citizen will spot them and make a report."

"Possible, yes, but suppose they're dressed as Israelis? Suppose they're already in Tel Aviv, mingling with hundreds of thousands of our people. How can they be singled out?"

He intended the question rhetorically but I made a small attempt at humor. "When they whip out their prayer rugs and face Mecca."

"Not funny." He went over to a group of officers.

My wound was throbbing again. I walked up to my overnight

room, swallowed two tablets, and went back to the command center. There were fewer officers than before, and Rosenthal was at the conference table having a snack of black bread and *borscht*.

"Care for some?" he asked. "Might as well die on a full stomach."

"Typical Jewish philosophy."

He wiped his mouth with a paper napkin that seemed too small in his large hand. "Your carriers are displaying a burst of activity: take offs, landings, exchanging planes from one flight deck to the other. And overhead, what do you think? They're doing high altitude air-to-air refueling."

"I think I'd try to take some comfort from it."

He bit off a chunk of bread and swallowed. "It so happens an Israeli Air Force squadron is aloft, has been since yesterday."

"For protective purposes?"

He shoved over a copy of the Jerusalem *Post* and said, "Your President's speech, the new Mid-East policy is getting mixed reviews."

I scanned stories from Washington, Paris, London, Rome, and some of the Arab capitals. My countrymen were solidly behind the President's unexpected declaration; Parisians and Romans viewed it as American expansionism, and Arabs shrilly denounced the policy as opening a new era of American colonialism. The *Post*'s editorial comments criticized the unilateral move and hinted the Israeli Cabinet would decide whether to accept or reject American governance.

Only the British reaction was relaxed; not supportive, just relaxed. I glanced through the paper but saw no reaction from Moscow. Perhaps the Kremlin was still in a state of shock. The idea pleased me.

Rosenthal was sponging up the last drops of soup. The wall clock showed nine o'clock. I wondered if my father and Barbara were having breakfast.

In New York my children should be sleeping. Sybil, too. Events had kept them from my mind for too long. I yearned to be with them, and found myself hoping I would still be alive at day's end.

Rosenthal left his chair and headed toward a radio monitor who was gesturing excitedly. He was getting something through his headset inaudible to the rest of the room. Rosenthal flicked on a speaker and I heard a long, perhaps three-second, sound. It ended in the breathy hum of carrier wave. Again the sustained dash, as though a transmitter key was closed overlong. It broke off, and again there was nothing audible but the carrier hum.

Lev pounded the radioman's shoulders. "Al-Karmal," he shouted exuberantly. "*Al-Karmal!*"

Al-Karmal (XIX)

Restlessly, Hossein Bakhari watched the Cuban testing the isolated trigger mechanism. Finally he went over to the tarpaulin, squatted, and said, "Let *me* test it, Felipe."

Reluctantly the Cuban cocked the spring-loaded trigger, got up and went over to where Marco was stretched out on the sand.

Marco watched the Arab leader work the trigger again. Disgustedly he said, "To him it's magic."

Buenaventura let Bakhari repeat the circuit closing a few more times and then returned to the tarpaulin. "Let's not waste battery power, Hossein." He turned off the radio, ignoring Bakhari's resentful gaze.

Without a word Bakhari strode to where the guards lay prone on the slanting dune. He replaced them with another six men and walked to the helicopter. Beside it was the crated warhead, open now while Buenaventura connected wires among the small receiver unit, the trigger detonator, and the neutron shell. Noticing Bakhari's shadow, the Cuban said, "The bomb is armed. The next time our transmitter key is pressed it will explode." He fitted on the top of the crate, wound it with heavy nylon cord in two directions and tied binding knots. Then he measured off twenty feet of cord, tied one end securely to the bomb crate, the other to the shroud ring of the cargo parachute.

Wiping his face he stood back to survey his work.

From the open helicopter door Zayid stared down thoughtfully. In order to survive the explosion he would have to be a mile from the parachute as it descended on Tel Aviv.

Quietly, Buenaventura said, "Hossein, I think we should send the helicopter now." And before the Arab could object, "Our position here is exposed to any plane that chances overhead, to any boat offshore." He touched the helicopter's skin. "I hope you agree with me."

"No," said Bakhari angrily. "The parades, the celebrations, will not be at their height until noon. I want to destroy as many Jews as possible." His voice rose. "*I* dreamed of this, made it possible. You have helped me, but I can get rid of you as I rid myself of Stoss." His eyes were wild, lids twitching.

Buenaventura had not anticipated the fury of Bakhari's reaction. His stomach tightened as though awaiting a bullet. Finally with a shrug he said, "You are indeed in charge, comrade Bakhari. But let us load the weapon and ready the helicopter should danger threaten."

Bakhari looked down at the bomb assembly. "Proceed."

Throat dry, the Cuban sighed in relief. "Marco," he called, "you are needed here."

With Marco and Bakhari listening, Felipe Buenaventura toed a shackle sewn to the parachute casing. "We will affix this to the ring in the deck of the helicopter, load the bomb inside, and coil the connecting cord. When you shove out the case it will pull the parachute from its casing and both will fall free."

The pilot nodded.

"All right," said Bakhari, "your voice transmitter and this receiver are on the same frequency. You must notify us when you drop the bomb. Thirty seconds later comrade Bakhari will close our transmitter key to detonate the warhead over Tel Aviv."

"I know," said Zayid impatiently, "and then I fly here."

Except, thought Buenaventura, the parachute will not detach. Helicopter and pilot will disintegrate, leaving Israeli aircraft with nothing to follow.

Buenaventura hoisted the cargo chute into the open door. Zayid pulled it to the far side and snapped the shackle to the deck. Two men lifted the heavy crate onto the cabin deck and Zayid coiled the connecting cord.

Ten o'clock. In another hour and a half he would be flying the great American death bomb on its way.

THIRTY THREE

Escorted by Israeli and foreign dignitaries Prime Minister Begin left his office for the Kikar Malkei reviewing stand. Because of rapidly choking streets, he had been advised to start out somewhat earlier than planned.

The air was filled with the echo of marching bands, singing voices, chanting. Colored balloons drifted into the cloudless sky, some carrying ribbons and blue-and-white flags. Houses and buildings were festooned with flags and banners. The national celebration was underway.

Ever since rising, Menachem Begin reflected, he had prayed and hoped for word that the terrorist attack had been forestalled. But the special telephone had not rung.

Now, he thought, as he looked at the exuberant faces of his people lining the streets, there was nothing he could do to save them. He had gambled their lives . . . and lost.

Until the last he had believed in Ha Mossad, trusted the service to come through. But it seemed as though Ben-yomin and his people were impotent, and he hoped they were as resigned to their fate as he was to his.

Mossad (XXI)

Rosenthal was trembling with excitement as he hurried to the communications center, Jay Black at his side.

As direction-finding reports came in from outlying radio-intercept stations a captain plotted them on a plastic overlay, and gradually the lines joined, intersecting on the coast south of Gaza City.

"A reading from seaward," the director said, "would truly fix transmitter location. Convergence error is plus or minus five degrees."

Rosenthal said, "So it's possible the transmission came from *within* Gaza City?"

"Possible."

Rosenthal turned to the officer replacing Eli Pomerantz. "Muki, there's no time for photo recon. What are you going to do?"

"Send the nearest units in. From seaward we'd be seen so it has to be overland." He looked at his watch. "Coming?"

"My friend, too. Jay Black, Captain Muki Telman."

He hurried away, and Rosenthal summarized for Jay what had been going on. "I still can't figure how Bakhari expects to get the warhead to Tel Aviv. No artillery piece in the world can carry forty miles."

Black said, "Maybe it's already there."

"That's a frightful thought, Jay. Any others?"

Black nodded. "Al-Karmal doesn't want to be irradiated by the bomb so Bakhari's staying a safe distance away."

"How could he detonate it?"

"I've been thinking about those transmission sounds—long dashes—and I remembered the radio-controlled robots and trucks I get for my kids. Press a button in the remote-control box and the toys respond. That's only a very low-power radio transmission. The Al-Karmal short-wave signal can carry from Gaza, we've just heard it. Why did we hear it? Because someone was testing the transmitter to make absolutely sure it would work."

Rosenthal shook his head. "Even if you're right I can't think of any way to find the bomb and disarm it in the time remaining."

They went outside to where two helicopters rested in the sunlight. Captain Telman called the pilots together. Using a field map he showed them their destination. "Ground units should get there in another ten or fifteen minutes. I don't want our choppers alerting the enemy, so we'll stay low—invisible, understand?—until the attack's begun. I'll join it, and my guests will stay upstairs out of danger."

Rosenthal snorted. "Yet you are going to expose yourself unnecessarily? That. . . ."

"I missed Faiqal," Telman said curtly. He got into one helicopter and Black and Rosenthal boarded the other. In less than a minute they were airborne.

From a garrison camp eight miles inland a reinforced combat team streaked toward the coast: forty men in troop carriers and jeeps, dust billowing behind them from the sand-earth road.

At that moment Prime Minister Begin was standing to acknowledge the cheers and applause of the crowd. Below the stand, ranks of *kibbutzim* children were marching by, faces upturned. Begin was unable to prevent tears from filling his eyes, rolling down his cheeks. By tonight, he was convinced, they would all be dead.

Half a mile from the coast the combat team's vehicles slowed to diminish dust and sound. Another quarter mile and the unit commander signaled a stop. Soldiers poured out and jogged toward the sea.

Close to the last vegetation, the commander sent scouts forward. They ran in a crouch, crawling the final ten yards to the dune lines on their bellies, weapons on their backs.

From the cover of rocks they peered down at the beach.

Jay Black (XXVII)

Where the empty combat vehicles waited Telman's chopper turned seaward, lifted over the dune ridges and disappeared. The attack was underway. Rosenthal tapped our pilot and gestured.

We rose quickly and saw Telman's chopper land. The captain bailed out fast and began shooting at the soldiers of Al-Karmal. There was another helicopter on the beach. I pointed it out to Rosenthal who frowned. "Not one of ours. Let's go down."

The pilot shrugged and headed for Telman's chopper. Just then the other helicopter's rotors began turning and it lifted off.

As we landed I pulled an Uzi from the rack, and jumped out. Grenades were exploding. Shrapnel whistled and we ducked beside our chopper.

I saw an Arab stand up and rake Telman's helicopter with an automatic weapon. I squeezed the Uzi trigger and cut him down. The jolting pained my side, but adrenalin warmed my blood and I didn't care.

More grenades. I heard Rosenthal grunt and saw the back of his shirt slashed as though by a razor. Blood oozed along the edges. I was deafened by firing, heavy explosions, and when I looked across the sand I saw the Al-Karmal helicopter fleeing seaward: neither of ours was armed to bring it down.

Kneeling beside Rosenthal I glanced at his wound, a shallow gash. I told him to stay down and moved on.

In a crouch I stepped over and around bodies, some still stirring, toward a tarpaulin close to where the Arab helicopter had been.

On it was a radio receiver and transmitter, dials glowing. Atop the transmitter a telegraph key.

Beyond a shell crate something moved. An Arab dragging himself toward the radio, pistol in hand.

Our eyes locked. He squeezed off a shot but I was on my knees and raising the Uzi with my good hand. I saw him reach the canvas edge, claw at the wiring, and then I fired.

The top of his head disintegrated, bullets tore into his throat and chest, and then he was prone, my shots puckering the sand beyond. I fired again, impacts fluttering his robe.

A grenade explosion knocked me down. I rolled over wondering—as in 'Nam—if I was wounded, dying, but the pain was in my chest. On my knees I managed to crawl to the transmitter, breathing hard, eyes gritty, sand lining my mouth.

He'd pulled a battery wire free. I made contact again.

Squinting, I found the helicopter in the distant sky, rotors a silver disk under the sun.

I touched the key.

Pressed hard.

Where the disk had been, a red-orange glow swelled to the size of a tangerine. It was falling into the sea when the blast-wave carried to my ears. The sound of the detonation passed, the fireball vanished.

Suddenly the beach was silent.

Beside me Telman said something in Hebrew and I saw that his eyes were moist. Like mine.

For a while I stared at the empty sky, then stepped over the Arab's body and picked up my Uzi, brushed sand away.

Men were searching bodies as at Faiqal, and when that was done I held a compress to Rosenthal's wound as we flew back to Tel Aviv.

EPILOG

Jay Black

THE body of the Arab near the radio was Bakhari's. With two Cubans and seventeen others on the Gaza sand. All were quietly buried and the incursion officially described as routine. As for the strange explosion two miles at sea, the government had no comment. Not to this day.

After I got back home and made peace with my wife we sailed to the Out Islands, and the children liked it better than skiing at Aspen. Even Sybil conceded it was pretty much okay, so we plan to do a lot more. As a family. And my wife is pregnant again.

I never tried to see Marcy, and it was weeks before I let Wellbeck debrief me. I gave him a selective version of events and after I stopped talking he sat looking at me thoughtfully for quite a while. "Inspiring tale," he said finally. "Inspirational. One last question: Is there any chance the Israelis will give us back that other neutron shell?"

"They still have it?"

"They have it."

"Not a chance," I said. "It might be stolen again."

He gave me a long, searching glance. "Well, that's it, then, isn't it?"

"That's it."

He took a deep breath. "Take care of yourself, Jay."

I haven't seen him since.

Before leaving Israel I saw Eli Pomerantz, though, a big cast on his leg, reasonably comfortable in a hospital bed. He showed me the papers retiring him as a lieutenant colonel and I wished him well. He thanked me, we shook hands, and I went away.

Part of me died there at Faiqal, too.

Lev Rosenthal is still working: Egypt, my father thought. But I haven't tried to find out. A trip back to Cairo, a glance at the Semiramis and it would start all over again: the memories of birds in the vines outside my balcony, the scent of jasmine, the taste of cool mint tea. And the beautiful, lost woman who opened the door of her room for me. . . .

Sometimes in the evening when I'm alone at the office I think of her that first day at Windover, remembering her voice, the way she looked coming down the steps to greet me. And that's all I let myself remember. The rest is gone, drifted away like thinning smoke in a desert breeze; ever more faintly until there's nothing at all. And it's better that way, much better.

For me.